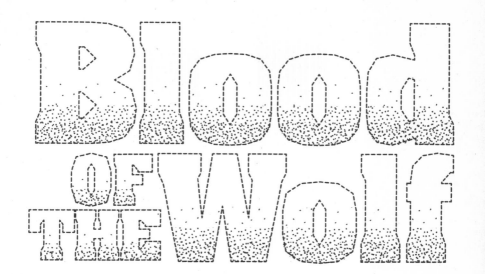

Blood of the Wolf

GW00503087

EOIN STEPHENS

First published by Brown Bull Publishing in 2023.

www.brownbull.ie

ISBN number: 978-1-9169029-1-6

Design and illustrations by the author. For contact details, visit:

www.eoinstories.com

I.

London 1692

This time they were better prepared for cutting off heads. The first attempt, one week before, had been near farcical. Pepys' wood saw, borrowed from Bagwell in the Navy workshop, had been an adequate but brutal tool. The head had come off, certainly, but the ensuing mess had depressed the conspirators. By the time they found themselves wallowing on their knees in the putrid remains of the Viscountess Ranelagh, they had already spent the best part of the night digging, lifting, sawing, and – judge not lest you be judged – drinking. It was not a job for December and it was not a job for gentlemen. But Wren was better organised tonight. Decapitating the brother would be easier.

Sir Christopher had asked that his guest wait in the drawing room. It was not what Samuel Pepys had expected. For one thing, it was used for drawing, not withdrawing. For another, it was in the garden – and well out of sight of the other members of the household. This was where the great architect brought his work home. One wall, facing north, was dominated by enormous glass windows in the Dutch style, and the roof was dotted with two lines of dormer windows through which Pepys could see the moon. In the dim winter twilight, the space seemed uniformly blue and, to Pepys, bitterly cold.

He shuffled from foot to foot while examining a wooden model of the proposed new Saint Paul's cathedral. It was certainly different. Pepys had fond memories of the old church. It was part of the old London – medieval and narrow. Its lines thrust upwards – the only direction the city allowed. To Pepys, that was the natural order. Cities ought to grow like forests, he thought, and buildings, like trees, should compete without the nursemaid hand of man. Then some will thrive while the runts starve, as God decides. Pepys knew this was an old-fashioned outlook but he was nearly sixty and his old-fashioned ideas had served him well. He wasn't going to change now. He marvelled at the piazza-like space Wren had left bare in front of the new cathedral. This was no fire break. This was simply a space where Wren's admirers might stand and appreciate the graceful Roman lines of his masterpiece. The grandeur of the new church was expressed as much by the space it dominated as by the space it occupied. It was, for Pepys, all very Italian.

"Well?" Wren had appeared silently in the gloom. He was, like Pepys, a man of around sixty, though his features were more angular and his frame less run to fat. He also sported an elaborate periwig which offered some insulation and acted as their only signifier of rank since they were otherwise dressed in their shabbiest winter clothes.

"It's a little small," Pepys answered looking down at the model.

Wren was stony-faced, "I wasn't asking your opinion, Pepys. Are you ready to go?"

He was standing at the end of the long line of drawing desks carrying what looked like a short, steel sword that glinted in the moonlight. "This compass saw will serve us well. I borrowed it from my master carpenter on Hampton Court. I told him I'd bought a buck from Richmond Park for Epiphany and I needed it butchered. He said it would sail through bone."

Silence fell between them as Wren's words formed an image.

Pepys spoke, "...and he reposes in the crypt? No digging?"

"No. That was a mistake with Katherine."

Silence again. They had both known Katherine Jones, the Viscountess Lady Ranelagh. Neither was especially close to her but Wren and Katherine's brother, Robert Boyle, were founders of the Royal Society some thirty years earlier and Pepys was a former president. They had all enjoyed the fortune of health and long life and, in their dotage, this small community of pioneering scientists had come to resemble something like a family. Digging up a sister and cutting off her head was hard enough. It was better not to invoke her name.

"Come on," Wren said, "I have a coach waiting."

The pair exited Wren's residence by the garden gate. They were keeping a low profile. Snow fell lightly on their shoulders as they mounted the coach. The white, silent streets, illuminated only by moonlight and their lanterns, offered a perspective on the city which was prettier than usual and certainly happier than the business they undertook.

As they had for Lady Ranelagh, a week earlier, they were carrying out the last private wishes of Viscount Robert Boyle, a fellow of the Royal Society, alchemist, philosopher, physicist, and devout Christian. Boyle's death, a week on the heels of his beloved sister, surprised no one. But its proximity to her Ladyship's passing certainly irked the two men on whom the night's onerous duties fell. Wren and Pepys were silent as their coach trundled through the ghostly London streets. Both men were quietly weighing the cost of a Christmas of cancelled engagements, the excuses half-believed by friends, credit exhausted with family, to say nothing of the ruined clothing and the hazard to their health. They were getting too old for this.

These private complaints provided a welcome distraction from the sublime implications of the business. They were dealing with the paranormal. Ten years earlier, Boyle had written to the President of the Society – a role then occupied by Wren – on a matter of the strictest secrecy. Boyle had been concerned for his health and desired to set in place certain special arrangements for when he died. Wren had expected directions on the posthumous publication of scientific theories. It was not uncommon for Society members to hold back their most dangerous publications till they were out of the reach of the courts. But it was much worse than that; the Boyles desired that their heads be chopped off post-mortem.

Over a series of meetings which first roped in Lady Ranelagh, and then Pepys – as Wren expressed the need for a witness – the Boyles explained that they had reason to believe that their physical bodies might be hosting some diabolical presence. They feared that their deaths might release these monsters from whatever restraints their immortal souls had held them in. The only solution was to separate their heads from their bodies. They had become 'infected' – this was the word they used – in Ireland during the Cromwellian conquest some forty years earlier. They declined to offer further details. "When we are both dead, you can read our full testimony," they had said.

Wren and Pepys had refused to believe a word. The Boyles tried and failed repeatedly to convince their peers of the urgency of their request, to no avail. In the end, they resorted to blackmail. Carry out their wishes or they would arrange for the publication of their story. Robert Boyle was a founding member of the Royal Society. The damage to its reputation would be enormous, so Wren and Pepys relented.

As they approached St. Martin-in-the-Fields, Pepys produced a bottle of Malmsey and offered it to Wren. He took it and drank deeply, passed it back to Pepys, and tapped on the roof of the carriage to call it to a halt.

Wren had confidence in his coachman and his footman. Indeed, the previous week he had been tempted to press them into the job of digging up Lady Ranelagh but the business was so transgressive that he couldn't take a chance on their silence. No, yet again, the two gentlemen would have to do this themselves. Once they'd dismounted and retrieved a tool bag and a lantern, they dismissed the coach for an hour and crossed the street alone to the dark church.

As they approached the door, Pepys slowed down. He was carrying the lantern and the tool bag so Wren could manage the doors. Still, he wasn't weighed down. Wren sensed his hesitation, "What is it?"

In the flickering orange light, Pepys looked nervous. He wanted to say something but was reluctant.

Wren tried to reassure him, anxious to get off the street and out of sight. "Look, it won't be as bad as last time. The arrangements were fixed. He lies in the crypt. It'll be over in minutes."

Pepys spoke, "It's the flowers..."

Wren thought he understood. Pepys had a superstitious streak. This was nothing to worry about, "the flowers we found on Katherine's grave?"

Pepys nodded. There had been plenty of flowers on Lady Ranelagh's grave. She had many friends. But one arrangement had caught their eyes: a handful of dull, creamy, dried flowers tied at the stem with a rolled sheet of paper. On it was written a cryptic message, 'For the healing of monsters. Your wisdom will not be forgotten.' The word 'monsters' had transported them back ten years to Lady Ranelagh's library in Pall Mall, to the earnest faces of the siblings and their outlandish story.

Wren searched for soothing words that would allow them to get a move on but Pepys spoke first, "I discovered their name, the flowers, I mean. I kept one, you know, and sent it to the botanist, John Ray. He wrote me back today. They're rare, a type of orchid, 'dense-flowering' or something. Anyway, he only knows one place in the three kingdoms they might be found – the rocky desert in the West of Ireland called the Burren."

Wren was taken aback: The Burren, the scene of the Boyle's alleged adventure. He searched for a mundane explanation, "So, Robert must have put them there. He was alive last week. He believes in this fantasy. He'd have us believe it. He left them there for us to find. I can't fathom his motivation for this hoax but hoax it is…"

"Yes, but…" Pepys looked to the door of the church. It was plastered with handbills that cast wild shadows from their little lantern as they fluttered in the night air. He seemed afraid of what lay beyond it, "…what if they're also present on his grave?"

"So he'll have had someone else deliver them. We're doing his posthumous bidding, why should we be the only ones?"

They were interrupted by the sound of revellers approaching from the direction of The Strand. Wren was done talking. He produced an enormous iron hoop laden with keys from under his cloak and proceeded to unlock the church door.

St. Martin-in-the-Fields was not one of his churches – the present building had survived the Great Fire to the East – but it was up for renovation and Wren had surveyed it to price his services. He'd retained keys. They entered. The interior was black, save for a few feet beyond their lantern and the faint blue moonlight which lit up the mullioned windows but stopped short of lighting the interior. Wren knew the layout well and walked briskly down the nave with Pepys following close behind him. When they got to the altar, they turned left and Wren dug out his key ring again. The entrance to the crypt stairs was barred by a locked wooden door. Wren unlocked it and they proceeded down the cold stone steps – the light from their lantern dimming as the air thinned out. Two turns of the turret stairs later, they stepped onto the soft earth floor of the crypt.

Pepys carefully rested his lantern on a ledge and used the flame to light another candle from his pocket. As he did, a few rats scuttled under his feet and into the dark. He used the new candle to light up two oil lamps attached to the wall on either side of the stairway. Soon they could see a line of brick vaulted arches stretching before them. The crypt was silent apart from the chattering vermin. They weren't long finding Boyle's tomb. He was lying in a temporary chamber close to the stairs. The crypt-keeper had left any tributes delivered in his name on top of the stone lid. There were some flowers. Wren and Pepys looked at each other before examining these more closely.

There was no sign of the Irish flowers nor of any mysterious note like the one found on Lady Ranelagh's grave.

Pepys seemed surprised, "What does it mean?"

"It means nothing," Wren answered, "like this whole business. Our poor friends lost their senses in their old age. They were always too full of religion. We're on a fool's errand, Pepys. Let's get this over with so we can return to Pall Mall, destroy their papers, and safeguard their reputation."

"...and the Society's," Pepys offered, feeling sure this was what Wren really had in mind.

"Indeed." Wren had cleared the tomb lid of all flowers and was bracing himself against the crypt wall to give it a push, "Take the other side, and help me push."

The two men heaved and the lid moved, revealing Boyle's coffin. With a few more pushes, the lid was clear. As Wren caught his breath, he examined the fastenings on the wooden box to see what tools he'd need to open it. The job looked simple.

Pepys offered him another drink and with a slight hesitation said, "if we find the papers, what then? We don't really need to cut off his head?"

"I don't know."

It wasn't like Wren to express doubt. Pepys let it drop. They finished their drinks and set to work on the coffin. Soon they had it open and the body of Robert Boyle lay before them. The sight of their old colleague's body cost neither a thought. No one lived to sixty without seeing many a friend dead. Indeed, Boyle's taste for elaborate periwigs caused Pepys to smile. His luscious grey curls seemed comical beside a face shrunken in death.

Wren wasted no time searching the body. Soon, he found the note he was looking for. He read it silently and summarised for Pepys, "It's in Pall Mall alright, in a strong box in the back parlour. He includes a key." He showed Pepys the note and the small key tied to it. He lowered his voice and passed it to Pepys, "he asks us to finish the job. Pepys took it and skipped to the end. It read, "...whereas I understand you now have nought to gain from seeing this through, pray keep your bargain and finish the job you started. In this, I beseech you, brothers."

When Pepys looked up, Wren had returned from the tool bag, saw in hand, "Let's finish this, then," he said.

2.

Though it was late when the two Society men reached Lady Ranelagh's house on Pall Mall, the door was answered quickly.

The housekeeper had been expecting them. "Mr. Pepys and Sir Christopher, I presume. Please come in."

She was a woman of around forty, tall and well-bred though possibly Irish to judge by the trace of an accent.

The pair kicked the snow from their boots and entered. The housekeeper attended to them alone which was unusual at that hour but the house was in the process of shutting down now that its two residents had passed on.

She noticed them looking around for other staff, "The kitchen staff are all let go since Sir Robert's passing. But perhaps I can offer you a drink to warm you as you go about your business? I'm Mrs. Feeney." She began to usher them into the front parlour.

"Yes please," Pepys answered, "but we'd really be more comfortable in the back parlour."

"But there's no fire lit there, sir."

"I'm sure it won't take you long to light one. And a brandy will warm us up nicely."

Mrs. Feeney raised an eyebrow but said nothing and led them to the back parlour which she had to unlock to access. She lit a couple of lamps first then busied herself lighting a fire while the two men made themselves comfortable. The room was full of scientific apparatus; books, bottles, and charts. There were two distinct working areas in different corners, one for each sibling, it seemed, and a card table in the middle with two chairs where they must have convened. Pepys and Wren were exhausted and sat at the table. After a few minutes, the housekeeper left them to the sound of damp coal spitting and crackling on the grate. As the flames grew brighter, Wren noticed bloodstains on Pepy's cuffs.

He pointed and said, "hide those. We don't want that servant talking."

"It doesn't look like she has anyone to talk to," Pepys answered. Nevertheless, he pushed the cuffs up under his coat sleeves and checked himself for any other clues to their violent enterprise.

Wren was looking around the room, "Well, what do you think?"

Pepys was still examining his clothes, "Nice! Well preserved, comely face, a most luscious figure. She's lucky we're so tired, being alone in the house with us."

"The strong box, Pepys!" Wren answered with a note of disgust, "I see no sign of it."

There was a soft knock on the door and the housekeeper re-entered carrying a tray with two generously measured brandies and a plate of plum cake. She looked severely at Pepys who guessed she'd been eavesdropping. He broke the silence, "Mrs. Feeney. Your master had a strong box in this room. Can you tell us where?"

"It's over here sir," she crossed the room to a coffer under one of the windows. She lifted the lid to reveal an iron strong box inside. She added, "but I have no key."

"Oh, don't trouble yourself over that, dear. We are executing your late master's Will and he has entrusted the key with us."

"Very good, sir," Mrs. Feeney answered and, with a faint curtsy, she left the room.

"She's a watchful, one," Pepys said when the door closed.

"Probably, she's wondering what legacy her master has left her. She'll be doubly curious now you've told her we're executors of his Will."

"Well, we are, sort of," Pepys had crossed to the coffer and produced the key they'd found on Robert Boyle's body, "Now, let's see what we've got here."

He opened the strong box and searched within for a minute before humming with satisfaction and returning to the card table. He dropped a carefully tied collection of hand-written pages onto the table. Wren read the inscription, "A True Account of an Experience of Werewolves as Witnessed by Robert Boyle and Katherine Jones-Boyle in Ireland in the Year 1651." Underneath were the signatures of the siblings and another note, added later, "Followed by Certain Remedies and Observations upon the True Nature of Werewolves".

Wren untied the bundle and scanned the contents. Most of the pages contained a long narrative in which he noted references to the late Civil War, Ireland, the Boyles themselves, and, as he read on with increasing dismay; pirates, werewolves, witchcraft, and other subjects of a paranormal nature. The second, smaller part of the collection was scientific. There were formulas, recipes, and drawings, including a drawing of a flower just like the one found on lady Ranelagh's grave.

"This is all for the fire, once it takes," Wren said dropping it back on the table.

"Shouldn't we read it first?"

"Wherefore?" replied Wren taking a drink of brandy.

"Wherefore did you cut his head off?"

There was a creak of floorboards outside the room and Wren shushed his colleague. The pair listened till silence was restored. Wren answered quietly, "it was his will."

"Was it not his will that we read these papers?"

"No," he put down the glass, "it was not. We've indulged his superstition. Our duty, now, is to protect his reputation and the Society's."

"Are you not curious?"

Wren didn't answer. He looked to Pepys and then to the papers on the table.

Pepys took a large drink and spoke, "you know, for a man of monkish habits, he kept an excellent cellar. It would be a shame to waste it."

Wren smiled and picked up some plum cake.

Pepys lifted the pile of papers and began to read aloud, "Limerick, November 1651..."

3.

forty years earlier...

Captain Salah of the Meshuda had been sailing for fifteen years and he had seen every complexion of war. It was never pretty but this was just an ordinary day for the Barbary corsair. When he saw the commotion on the docks at Tarbert he ordered his boat to sit sixty feet out till he decided what to do.

The pier was crowded with refugees. These were Irish Catholics fleeing the city of Limerick which had just fallen to the English Parliamentarians. They were clearly desperate. Many were crying, all were exhausted. Salah had sailed up from Dingle where he had already heard stories of the unnatural violence which had presaged the breaking of the siege. Likely, these people sought passage to Connacht where they would not be persecuted. Salah watched an argument break out. A group of refugees was arguing with a man wearing a long, tight-fitting black coat and hat – a priest, Salah thought. These refugees must believe their God has deserted them. Salah knew he risked his ship being swamped if he landed. Still, there was money to be made here.

He heard growling behind him and turned around. The English boy and his dog – another problem he needed to address. The boy, William Manning, was nineteen. He thought himself a man. He was taller than anyone on the boat though he still had the lean build of youth. He'd already spent a year as a soldier in the New Model Army which had just blazed through Ireland and since his discharge he'd made the price of a good horse by hunting wolves. He'd bought his way out of the army and with it the price of his kit. He still wore the distinctive red coat and broad-brimmed felt hat of his former comrades. He'd added a leather necklace lined with wolves' teeth which he embellished with every new kill. He carried a long flintlock carbine which he handled expertly and he was the master of Samson, the wolfhound that sat growling at his feet. It was the dog more than the soldier who intimidated the pirate captain. Captain Salah crossed the forecastle to settle his business with the soldier. The dog growled quietly as he approached.

"You owe me money," Salah said.

"I told you, I have in my possession a small fortune," Manning gestured to two large blood-stained jugs on the deck on either side of the dog.

"And I told you, I want no part in your this infidel witchcraft," Salah looked disgusted by the soldier's cargo, "I want silver."

"There's no witchcraft here. It's just wolf's blood. General Ireton in Limerick will pay fifteen pounds for what I have here."

Salah was distracted by the noise on the pier. He noticed the priest had faced down his foes – at least temporarily. He had an idea, "The English commander has a thirst for wolf's blood," he said, "that is devilish enough. But I understand he also has a taste for Popish blood?"

"He hates papists, naturally."

"And he pays ransom for priests?"

"Yes, live ones," Manning looked to the pier and began to catch Salah's drift, "I'm not a priest-catcher. I prefer a prize I can carry in a jug."

"I'll catch him for you. But you owe me money. Take the priest to Limerick and trade him for something I can use. Return here with silver and you can collect your wolf's blood." He kicked one of the jugs gently, "I'll keep these safe while you're gone." The dog growled once more.

Manning had sailed up from Dingle with Salah. He had been so anxious to cash in his prize, he hadn't allowed money for the fare. That was stupid. The boats that sailed these waters since the war started were mostly pirates, certainly outside the law, and apt to throw debtors overboard without a fuss. He looked to the pier and saw the priest waiting at the front of the line. He was still young, a man of about twenty five but he was small and hungry-looking. "Very well, but take care of my cargo."

"Don't worry, I wouldn't touch it," Salah answered. He shouted to his crew in a language Manning could not understand and they began the process of docking.

On-shore, even at that distance, the priest recognised Manning's livery for New Model Army and he and others who feared the Cromwellians shrank back behind the curtain of the crowd. The boat docked and Manning was among the first to disembark. He was, of course, outnumbered by these enemy Irish but he had confidence in the threat his gun and his dog posed. These people were tired, hungry, and cowed by the misery of a long siege. They had no fight left in them. They let Manning pass. He noticed they were mostly well-dressed, though filthy from the road, and the few words he heard spoken were in English. They were a different breed to the peasants he saw on the land who were shoeless, often breech-less, and Irish-speaking. He spied a few Confederate soldiers among them. They hid behind children and women, staring into the dirt. They wanted nothing more than a passage to Connacht.

A shout went up in English from Salah's first mate, "Galway! Passage to Galway for the first sixty people with the fare, twelve shillings."

Many cried out as they realised the fare was out of reach. The people on the dock began to re-arrange themselves; those who could not pay sinking back, those who could pay pressing forward with renewed vigour, taking with them those too desperate to give up hope of charity.

The city of Galway was the gateway to the province of Connacht. The city was itself under siege but the English were happy to let refugees pour in. The new arrivals put more pressure on the city's dwindling resources. All property-owning Catholics in Ireland had been given the option of migrating to the province to re-settle on near-worthless plots of land to make way for the protestant takeover of their former homes. It was that or death. These wretches in Tarbert had chosen Connacht.

Manning walked on till he was through the crowd. He wanted to find a vantage point where he could observe Salah and make sure the priest was caught. He had no guarantee the pirate would keep to his bargain but the corsair had better things to do than risk dealing directly with the English army in Limerick. Hostages were trouble and Manning did not relish the job of transporting him but the bounty on a priest was good, ten pounds – the same as a wolf bitch.

He was thirsty. He spied a stream that fed into the harbour and climbed down to it. At the bank, Samson drank greedily while Manning filled his horn cup to quench his thirst. When they were satisfied, the pair climbed a dune that overlooked the pier and sat down on the grass. Manning shared some biscuits and cheese with the dog and allowed himself a swig of wine from his flask. The turnaround of the boat was happening quickly. The passengers and cargo were already off and the refugees were boarding. The pirate crew was highly organised and ruthless in the application of their law. Several would-be passengers had already been beaten away for not having the requisite fare. Salah watched this from the quarterdeck. When the priest boarded and paid his twelve shillings, Manning grew nervous. The crew soon drew in the gang-plank and prepared to sail. Salah stood motionless and glanced once at Manning acknowledging his presence. The soldier and his dog stood up and started down the dune towards the pier. The pirate captain stepped down onto his deck and mingled with his passengers. His crew was using sweeps to push the boat away from the pier. Manning looked down at the fuse on his matchlock. It was hot. There was little he could do save get off a shot in anger but, should the pirate betray him, at least that was something.

A commotion on the ship made him look up. Salah's first-mate Ahmad, a short barrel of a man, was arguing with the priest. He was gesturing wildly. The other passengers backed away. The priest seemed confused but quickly matched the pirate for passion once his predicament became desperate. But he was alone and no match for the big corsair. Ahmad grabbed him by his long black coat and lifted him easily over the gunwale. The priest dropped into the harbour and flailed madly in the water. Salah defended his mate's actions with some words for the erudition of the other passengers but he was looking at Manning who nodded and trotted down to the edge of the pier to make sure his hostage didn't drown.

4.

"Do you fear the devil, Mary?"

"Yes, sir. Of course sir."

"Good."

Thomas Worsley was conducting a job interview. The old man was sitting at an ancient oak table surrounded by the tools of his trade. An observer might have thought him an apothecary. He held a carved, jewel-topped walking stick in one hand which he toyed with as he spoke. He was an apothecary, of sorts. Depending on his audience he'd call himself one, or a doctor. To those he trusted, he was an alchemist. There were books, ledgers, and charts as well as every conceivable shape and size of glassware and stoneware, piled high on the table and on the shelves behind him. The room was dark apart from the light from an enormous fireplace and the twilight squeezing through the arrow-slit windows. They were in King John's Castle, Limerick.

The alchemist reached for a drink and avoided a few mysterious-looking vessels before choosing a chalice which he sniffed and then raised to his lips. His unkempt beard soaked up as much as he swallowed so he wiped it with a filthy rag from inside his doublet.

His rheumy eyes dared Mary to judge him. She was impassive. Somewhere, behind the haze of wine, Worsley felt the dim light of passion blink and then fizz out. She was tasty. She was young, tall, and still as a statue. But she thought herself too good.

"He's closer than you think."

"Sir?"

Worsley smiled unsuccessfully, "...the devil. We keep a close eye on him here." He stamped his stick hard on the stone floor. It was a reference to the prison cells on the floor below. Mary wondered, did she hear a voice cry out?

They were in one of the mural towers of the castle, recently occupied by the conquering English.

Limerick was in chaos. Most of the Irish had abandoned the city so the occupiers were running a recruitment drive just to keep basic services going. As she'd passed through the castle bailey, Mary had to weave around countless tents and camp-fires set up by the occupying troops. Those lucky enough to find a home within the castle walls were in a festive mood. Mary had given the drunk soldiers a wide berth. They were celebrating the end of a long siege. The conquest of the whole island was in sight. Galway was the only city still holding out. Also, it was November fourth – the day before Guy Fawkes night, a night sacred to the Parliamentarian cause. They were not short of gunpowder so they would celebrate the taking of Limerick with feasting and fireworks and a commemoration of Protestant victory over Catholic villainy.

The influx of soldiers was a particular strain on the castle. Mary had seen the bill posted on the Thomond Gate for kitchen staff. She had applied along with a dozen other girls. Five had been short-listed for interview and had been told to present them-selves to various parts of the castle. The girl selected for work in the prison tower reacted tearfully to that appointment so Mary volunteered in her place.

It pained them to hire local Irish Catholics but needs must and Worsley needed staff just like everyone else. Mary would do. She feared the devil, if not the pope. She looked strong and her petticoat and apron were clean. She wore her hair in a modest fashion, hidden under a white linen coif.

"We keep sick people here... the unclean. Just one right now. He must be fed. But he has the devil in him," Worsley was rolling his cane from one hand to the other as he spoke, "We keep apart from the rest of the castle so we need our own scullery and kitchen girl. You'll clean and bring up food from the Keep. You'll feed us and the prisoner," he tapped his cane again, "but you mustn't get near him."

Mary nodded.

"Peeter will show you your duties."

Mary was about to respond again when he screamed, "Peeter!"

Footsteps raced up the turret stairs. A boy appeared. He was about fourteen. He was much shorter than Mary but broad and likely to make a strong man. He was pale and his still childish face was framed by a mop of long brown hair and a fringe that stopped just above his brown eyes. His clothes were worn but clean and he went barefoot. He was carrying an armful of what Mary first took for scrolls.

"Peeter, what have you got there?" Worsley barked.

"Fireworks for Fawkes," he said.

"Lock them up. I have a job for you. Mary will be feeding us from now on. Show her around."

Peeter looked her up and down, smiled, and gestured that Mary should follow him. She curtsied for Worsley and followed. As they disappeared down the turret stairs, Worsley shouted after them, "And Peeter, remember; she's Irish!"

Mary understood; "Don't trust her."

5.

The priest sat shivering in the grass. Manning feared he might die. He'd attempted to start a fire in a hollow amongst the dunes but it wouldn't take. It hadn't rained for a couple of days but the West of Ireland held onto the damp. He couldn't find any dry kindle and quickly found he could produce nothing more than smoke from the damp grass and twigs.

They were all alone in the harbour. Salah had sailed away with a heavy load of refugees. Those who could not pay, and in the end, could not fit aboard, had drifted towards the village and out of sight.

He hadn't bound the man. The wretch was so cold, there was no need to secure him. He had said nothing when Manning fished him from the water. Presumably, he understood what was happening; the pirate had cheated him of his fare so the English soldier could collect his bounty. Manning took a break from his attempts at a fire and sat down beside his dog. They still had plenty of daylight left but he needed to make a plan. Salah had told him he'd find a boat to Limerick from here. There were none right now. He looked his captive over. He was short and thin but his face was long, his nose and cheekbones sharp and his eyes pale grey. He had the russet complexion of an islander. Salah and his corsairs were a minority here; most of the ferrymen Manning had sailed with up and down the West coast looked like this priest. In middle age, their cheeks and eyebrows sprouted gardens of wiry grey hair with which they proudly advertised their age. The priest was staring back at Manning.

"My name is Ambrose Skerret," he said, "What's your name, soldier?"

Manning stood up and searched the horizon, "We'll not become friends, priest. My name is my own business."

"Perhaps some food, then, since your fire has failed?"

"Your cursed country never dries out."

"Cursed, yes," Skerret said. He stretched his neck and looked inland towards a cluster of cottages far from shore, "I was just thinking of making my way to France. It's a far kinder climate."

"Too late for that," said Manning.

"There's a house up the road serves travellers. I had some pottage there last night when we came in from Limerick. They had a nice warm fire."

The priest started shivering again.

If a boat didn't come soon they'd be stranded for the night. Manning wasn't completely broke. He didn't have the twenty shillings Salah had demanded for passage from Dingle but he had enough to feed himself and secure passage on a small boat up the estuary to Limerick. It galled him to have to pay the fare for his captive too but he had little choice.

But he had no intention of feeding his captive. He reached into his leather satchel, found a biscuit, and split it between himself and the dog. He wasn't hungry but he wished to make a point.

Skerret watched him quietly for a minute, "I can pay," he said.

Manning threw his crumbs to the dog and walked over to the priest. He pulled out his dagger and commanded, "on your belly."

Skerret was slow to react but looked at the knife, then at the soldier, and obeyed. When he was lying flat, Manning sat on his legs. Skerret heard the soldier undoing his own belt.

Manning barked, "hands, give me your hands."

The man complied and felt his hands being roughly and securely tied with the belt. Then he felt the soldier's hands search him thoroughly – the pockets he could reach, the lining of his black hat, under his collar. When he finished, Manning climbed off and ordered Skerret to roll over. He unbuttoned his coat and searched inside till he found the priest's purse on a string around his neck. He pulled hard and freed it. There were a few coins, half a dozen pennies, a couple of farthings, and five shillings.

"This buys you nothing," Manning said. He stood up and threw the purse down beside his own kit.

"That's not what I meant," Skerret answered. He struggled into a sitting position.

"What then? Is there more?"

"I can pay you with information."

"You know nothing I care to learn."

"I know why he wants wolf's blood."

Manning froze. Then he turned away from Skerret and stroked the dog, trying to look casual, "I don't know what you mean."

"You're not a bounty hunter. You're a wolf-hunter. Your necklace tells me that. And your hound... and your smell."

"So I'm not as freshly washed as you," he answered.

"Don't you want to know what that blood is for? What use are those bible verses you stuff in your hat if you serve the devil with witchcraft?"

"I see. You wish to pay for dinner with a sermon," Manning glanced back at his prisoner, "I don't want to hear your Popery."

"As you wish, forget your soul. But I can tell you what Ireton would pay ten-fold for."

The soldier stood up and faced him, "what do you know?"

"No, not here," Skerret answered, "Food first, and a warm fire. It's worth investing a little in my health."

Manning looked back at the pier. There was no sign of a boat. He bent down and picked up Skerret's purse, showed it to him, and said, "very well, but you'll pay."

6.

As night fell, the solid walls of the prison tower felt like a refuge to Mary. She'd had to cross the bailey a few times to fetch turf from the shed or water from the well and she'd observed the conduct of the soldiers deteriorate. Their bonfires grew bigger, fed as much by the spoils of wanton looting as by firewood. They fired their guns randomly in celebration. Occasionally, Mary heard a heart-stopping cannon blast followed by lacklustre cheering. She'd had to fend off one drunk who'd thrown himself at her. After that, she'd learned to walk through at speed with her eyes down and with a sharp kitchen knife visible in one hand.

The prison tower was grim. The walls which faced the river were slick and cold. There was a smell of human waste only partially masked by the sweet perfume of the turf fire. The layout was labyrinthine: The four floors of the tower were each accessible by two turret stairs which meant occupants could navigate the building without necessarily meeting each other. Two prison cells were on the first floor above a room where Peeter seemed to live and where rusting implements of torture still lined the walls. Above that was the main hall where Worsley had interviewed her. Up top was the solar where the old man slept and ate. Mary herself was allocated a cot in the female servants' quarters in the keep. She could come and go across the battlement. There was a door from the main hall. It was a long walk along the dark stone ledge but at least it was thirty feet above the marauding soldiers in the bailey. While she was awake, she preferred the solitude of the tower.

It was oddly peaceful. It was built to house many but was now occupied by just four; Worsley, Peeter, Mary, and the solitary prisoner. She saw nothing more of Worsley. He seemed to spend most of his time elsewhere in the castle complex. Peeter, on the other hand, she had to keep track of.

That first evening, she was cleaning the solar where Worsley slept and ate when she felt Peeter's presence. She turned quickly but he stayed hidden on the turret steps. She called out casually, "Come in Peeter."

He poked his head into the room. In one hand he was carefully carrying a kerchief he'd folded into a bundle.

"What have you got there?" Mary asked while continuing her work.

"Fish," he answered. He stepped cautiously into the room and walked over to Mary stopping only when she could smell tobacco on his breath.

She stepped around the table she'd been polishing, putting it between them, and said, "Show me."

He placed the bundle on the table and unfolded it. Inside were four small trout.

"Would you like me to cook them for your dinner?" Mary asked.

He nodded, "and for you."

"And for Mr. Worsley?"

He shrugged his shoulders, "...suppose so."

"And for the prisoner?" she asked.

"No! Not for him."

"You can have two, then?"

He smiled.

"Thank you, Peeter."

He nodded but he was out of small talk so he started to leave.

She spoke again to keep him a minute, "I'll finish up here, then I'll cook up the fish over the fire in the main hall. I don't feel like crossing the bailey again tonight. Perhaps, you'd fetch some bread for me. The master has ale and he might have a spot of tobacco for you."

Peeter smiled broadly at this.

"Peeter..." she started to fold up the kerchief around the fish, "how did you come to work for Mr. Worsley?"

"Indentured," he said simply.

"You're a war prisoner?"

He nodded. He was standing at the door. This ordinary conversation was making him shy but he liked the attention.

"You're not Irish, though, you were English Royalist?"

He nodded again and added, "I was a doctor's help for the Royalists at Rathmines. I was taken prisoner there. On account of my age, I was indentured. Worsley was a Roundhead field surgeon. He found me and bought my debt."

"So you're stuck with him for a while?"

"Another five years," he answered with a resigned smile.

"And then what will you do with your freedom?"

He shrugged but then said, "I thought I might get a hound and a musket, do some wolf-hunting. It's good money."

"If there's any wolves left."

Why did every boy think shooting wild animals was the height of glamour, she wondered.

"Aye, five years is a while," Peeter answered.

"Unless you pay your debt faster?"

"I make a few shillings fishing and I do some mending, but the extra money mostly goes on tobacco."

"I don't blame you."

He started to go. Before he got to the solar door, Mary called after him, "Peeter, do you not like the prisoner?"

He shook his head and looked around the room for the right words, "You haven't seen him?" he asked.

She shook her head.

"He's a monster," he said.

***

Mary looked through the solar window and watched for Peeter. Soon a firework exploded and she saw him jogging toward the bakery. She thought about his words. The poor boy, just a child and already a veteran of war. And now a jailer. It was no life for a child.

It was just her and the prisoner left in the tower. She crossed the room quickly and started down the turret stairs. When she got to Worsley's room, she found a wooden bowl, cleaned it, and filled it with soup that had been simmering over the fire. She found the bread she'd hidden earlier on a tray together with a tankard of ale and a candle. She lit the candle with a taper and carried the tray down to the next floor where the prisoner was locked up.

She hadn't met him yet. Peeter's tour had skirted over this part of the building. He'd waved a finger at the solid wooden door of one of the cells as they'd passed and had murmured, "prisoner," then he'd spent twenty minutes showing her his cellar room. At the end of his tour, they'd walked back up the other turret stairs and had passed the other cell. That door had been open. Mary had looked in. The cell was miserable, the floor was lined with rotten straw. At that hour, only a meagre light had penetrated the one tiny window. She'd noticed something odd. Recently, a small window-like aperture, a foot wide and no higher than eight inches, had been cut into the partition wall about a foot above the floor. It was an opening into the cell next door. A set of shackles fixed to the wall was chained to a second set which threaded through from the cell next door.

Mary had asked, "what's that?"

"For feeding the prisoner," Peeter had answered.

***

Now that she was alone, Mary intended to do just that. She carried her tray into the empty cell and knelt beside the hole. The air inside was warm and stale. She heard shuffling on the other side.

"God be with you, sir. I've brought you food,"

There was no answer. She heard the rattle of chains. The prisoner seemed to move closer to the opening.

"God be with you," she repeated.

He tried to speak, "God..." she couldn't hear the rest. A man's voice, hoarse but young, Irish, or Old English, she thought.

She took some bread from the tray and left it on the sill of the little opening. A hand reached though and took it. Long, dirty finger nails like an animal but the movement was delicate.

"I'm Mary," she said.

"Mary," the man repeated.

"What's your name?" she asked.

Silence. She heard him eating, then he started coughing violently.

"Have some ale."

She passed the tankard. He took the drink.

His coughing stopped and he regained his voice, "Thank you."

"I have soup too," Mary said. She put the bowl of soup and a spoon on the sill. Two hands reached through and took the food. The other hand was like the first though she noticed a tan line where a ring had once spent many years.

"What's your name?" she said again.

"Valentine," he answered.

"There's plenty more soup, Valentine. I'm sure you're hungry." She could hear him eating greedily in the dark. "And there's more bread coming. Peeter's getting it."

"The boy?"

"Yes."

"He doesn't like me."

"No. He seems to be afraid of you," she tried to put it lightly.

"He's right. You should keep your distance too."

She had heard enough to place him. He was of city merchant class but not Limerick, she thought... Galway, perhaps. These people were of uncertain allegiance. Their ancestors were English, they spoke English but they were a different breed to the Cromwellians. For one thing they were Catholic.

"It's nice to have someone to talk to," Mary said, "and Peeter's a child."

"He's old enough to admire a woman."

"Yes, but that makes for worse conversation."

Valentine let out a short, clipped laugh. He hadn't spoken to anyone for a long time. He didn't know what to say. He finished his soup and returned the bowl to the flat ledge of the opening. In the dark he misjudged its position and dropped it.

"Let me help you," Mary said. She lifted the candle from the floor and raised it to the opening. She ducked her head to see what she was doing. As she did, she briefly caught sight of the prisoner. His face was young, handsome, and frozen in fear. She looked down and saw the reason why; the candle had thrown light on the stone ledge and now she saw that it was covered in blood.

7

As Manning and Skerret walked up from the pier in Tarbert, they saw an army camp flying the Parliamentary colours. The New Model Army were here. Manning was relieved. It was one thing to step off a boat into a crowd of enemy refugees; quite another to spend a night in territory controlled by Irish Confederates, especially with a prisoner in tow. On the downside, he'd have to pay a courtesy visit, show his credentials and likely face the bitter remarks of former comrades who'd view him as practically a deserter.

Manning had received his commission from General Ireton – Oliver Cromwell's son-in-law, no less. The hunt for wolves and priests was a priority but the common soldier wouldn't see it that way. Manning had experienced run-ins with his former comrades before. He was well paid, they were jealous. He was seen as a privateer and a war profiteer.

"Your friends are here, I see," the priest said, inferring that a man like Manning would not be well-loved by army regulars. His sarcasm masked his disappointment. Skerret knew it would be much harder to escape this bounty hunter where the English army held sway.

"Your food and fire will have to wait. I need to present myself," Manning said.

Skerret still had his wrists tied behind his back. His large black hat hung around his neck and identified him as a priest. Manning wore the clothes of an English musketeer, but his boots were more expensive and the presence of a wolf-hound told sharper observers that he was a bounty hunter. As they marched up the road, they passed some of the refugees who had failed to catch the boat. They stopped and stared. It was not good to feel the pity of such men, Skerret thought.

The camp consisted of no more than thirty men and a single heavy gun which, doubtless, was intended to cover the harbour. They had apparently just arrived since the gun was still hitched and would do little good in its current position a hundred yards from shore. The soldiers had set up camp a short distance from the small cluster of thatched, whitewashed cottages where, the night before, Skerret and his fellow refugees had found shelter and food. The villagers were scarcer now that the English soldiers were present. The soldiers themselves were subdued, more from fatigue than good manners. There was a line of communication open with the villagers and food and drink were being traded peacefully. These soldiers were probably at the vanguard of the English advance so they were treading cautiously.

Manning identified the company's commanding officer and marched over, doffed his cap and said, "William Manning, late of John Pickering's Regiment on a commission from Lord Ireton."

He presented a letter to the commander, a small red-faced man in an orange coat crossed with bright red sash. The captain fetched an eye glass from inside the sash, read it carefully, then returned it, "Bounty-hunter, eh?"

He looked over at Skerret, "You want me to string him up for you? The boys could do with a little fun."

"Thank you, no. I must deliver him to Limerick," Manning answered.

"...and collect your bounty," the officer added coldly.

"Lord Ireton's orders," Manning replied.

"Ireton's word won't be good for much longer."

"But good enough for the moment."

"Oh, aye. You're alright. But you'll have to keep that matchlock away from my powder. I can't keep you here. The village will have you and your... pet," he chuckled.

"No problem," Manning said, "I just wanted to pay my respects. How goes Limerick?"

"No concern of yours now, boy. You're not a soldier anymore," the officer turned and walked away as he spoke. That was that. The regular soldier wanted nothing more to do with Manning.

They stood in silence for a minute till Skerret spoke, "They weren't too fond of you?"

"They wanted to kill you," Manning replied then added, "They're fusiliers. They don't like musketeers. They have a horror of naked flames. They're afraid my matchlock fuse will blow them and their gunpowder to hell. We'll have to find accommodation in the village tonight," he added, "we won't be welcome, but we'll be safer with an English garrison at the door."

You'll be safer, Skerret thought.

✳✳✳

Skerret led Manning and his dog to the public house where he'd been fed the night before. They were greeted unenthusiastically but when Manning produced Skerret's purse and paid in advance for food and drink, they were given a couple of chairs in front of the fire. A family of refugees were evicted from the warm hearth to make room for the paying guests. The two men shifted as close to the fire as possible; Skerret, to warm himself and dry his clothes; Manning, to better observe the room which seethed with hostility. Samson sat between them. It was a long three-window cottage. Through the haze of smoke, Manning could make out about a dozen people in the room, half refugees, half local, everyone an enemy. It was quiet apart from the crackling fire and the sound of the English soldiers outside barking orders as they established their camp.

A woman came over carrying drinks. Manning held out his hand to take one but she held them to her chest and spat some criticism at the soldier in Irish. He was at fault in some way.

"She won't have men tied up in her house, she says," Skerret translated the Irish.

Manning considered forcing the issue but he was hungry and tired so he told Skerret to turn around and untied his hands. The woman was satisfied and handed over the drinks. Skerret smiled and knocked his back.

Manning did the same but spat most of it out immediately, "Oh God, what is that?"

"Clabber," Skerret answered, "– fermented milk." The priest was smiling broadly. He looked up at the woman and said, "íontach."

She threw a dirty look at Manning and left.

Skerret leaned over and asked, "What did that soldier mean, 'Ireton's word won't be good for much longer'?"

Manning didn't like the conversational tone his prisoner was beginning to use with him but in this situation, it was probably wise to strike a friendly pose with the priest. Besides, his question was on point. The man claimed to know Ireton's motives and Manning wanted to know more, "Ireton has the plague," he answered.

"He's a dead man, so."

"Aye."

"No wonder you're in a hurry. His successor might not pay his debts."

"I have no fear on that account," Manning said, "his successor is the man paying the bounties."

"Hewson?"

So, the priest was well informed, "What do you know of it?"

"It is, as I said, the blackest kind of magic. If you fear your God, you'll give up this trade."

"That would suit you, wouldn't it?"

They were interrupted by the arrival of food. There was coarse brown bread and a creamy fish stew. A young woman, a daughter perhaps, brought this over. Manning thanked her and she answered in English. Seeing his chance, he asked her for beer. She nodded and left. They went quiet for a minute to start their food then Manning picked up the conversation, "It was Hewson who told us to deliver wolf's blood. He didn't say wherefore. If you know, tell me."

Skerret chewed his bread slowly, he looked hard at Manning and spoke quietly, "Hewson has a werewolf," he took another mouthful of bread and watched for Manning's reaction. The soldier was uncomprehending. Skerret continued, "...a changeling, a man become wolf, a creature of the devil, as strong as ten men, a body that cannot be killed. He let it loose in Limerick before the city fell. It broke their spirit."

"Ha!" Manning's laugh broke the silence in the gloomy room. Everyone looked over and Samson sat up and licked his master's hand.

Skerret looked hurt, "scoff, if you will. I only tell the truth."

Manning's mirth continued, "Well you earned your crust with a good story, priest. I've not heard that before. But, pray, continue... he has this wolf-man but I don't understand, what does he now need with the wolf's blood and the priests? I'm fascinated."

"He wants to make more of these creatures. There's a potion..."

"...a potion? Of course, there is."

"Believe what you will. You can reckon the cost later with your creator."

"No. Please tell me more,"

Skerret summoned all the gravitas he could muster, "Blood of the wolf, blood of the dead, blood of the youth whom the wolf hath bled."

"A pretty verse. What does it mean? I mean apart from the wolf's blood. I get that."

"These are the ingredients of Hewson's potion. Whosoever drinks that becomes a werewolf. 'Blood of the wolf', you understand, 'blood of the dead', well that's readily available in these evil days. 'Blood of the youth whom the wolf hath bled' – that's the trick."

He trailed off as the young woman returned and deposited two large tankards of black beer in front of the men.

Skerret continued, in a quieter voice, "he needs his werewolf to bite a man unknown to woman."

Manning looked puzzled.

The priest explained, "he needs virgin boys."

"Virgins!" Manning exclaimed. The patrons and the serving girl all looked at Manning again.

Skerret smiled weakly at them, then glared at Manning.

The soldier caught up, "I see. So he thinks, 'priests'."

Skerret continued, "don't misunderstand me. Hewson would have every priest in Ireland strung up just for the crime of living. And he's not short of virgins among the lay community..." he tapped Manning's tankard with his own and winked. The soldier responded with an uncertain smile, "...it just hasn't been working out for him."

"The priests not honouring their vows?" Manning asked.

"That..." Skerret had a large swig of beer, "...and they weren't always priests."

Manning was nodding thoughtfully.

"Also, his werewolf has a habit of finishing his meals."

"So he bites them and they die."

"He hasn't had a man survive yet."

"Then it's all for nought?"

"No. He'll succeed. I told you this is something he'll pay generously for. If the price is right, someone will find a way. He has an alchemist working on a solution right now. The man is dogged," he smiled at his own pun then grew serious, "and you're helping him unleash hell."

Manning sat up, "It is a colourful story, priest. You nearly had me convinced. But it serves you too well. You'd have me free you and every other priest."

"I didn't expect you to believe me. I only bargained for my dinner."

8.

Mary was nervous about returning to Valentine but he needed breakfast so she couldn't put it off. She wasn't afraid. The blood-stains on the opening into his cell had alarmed him more than her. "Leave me!" he'd shouted when her candle had lit up the ledge. She'd tried to calm him down without success. He'd crawled away to the other side of his cell and the few words he'd spoken had been incoherent and not directed at her. She'd left him in peace after a few minutes.

She was nervous about regaining his trust. The weak yellow sun was well over the horizon before she decided how she was going to approach him.

Her duties required her to visit the bakery. She didn't mind leaving the safety of the tower now that it was morning. The soldiers were all asleep, clustered around their smoking bonfires, filling the bailey with the sound of their snores. She collected bread for her charges and filled a bucket at the well. As she returned to the tower, she noticed, for the first time, the odd-looking scaffold leaning against the wall. It was twenty feet tall and about six feet wide. There was a ladder leading to the top where she could see a curtain blocking all light to one of the tower windows. She considered the position of the window and realised it was Valentine's cell. The poor prisoner was being denied every privilege - even light. Back inside, she prepared breakfast for four, ate her own and delivered Worsley's and Peeter's to their quarters. Once she was confident they weren't in a hurry to get up, she prepared breakfast for Valentine. She took his food in one hand and carried the bucket of water in the other. She entered the empty cell and was glad to find a sliver of sunlight had also found its way in. The beam of light was sitting just above the opening to Valentine's cell. It was so sharp and narrow, it seemed to move in real time like a sundial. Rather than rouse him straight away she put the food to one side and set to work. She knelt once more beside the opening to his cell and soaked a rag in her bucket. Then she started to scrub. She couldn't see much but the stains on the rag told her she was making a difference. After a while, she heard Valentine stirring. She said nothing.

He cleared his throat and spoke, "why do you do this?"

She continued working and said, "I have your breakfast here. I'm sure you'd prefer a clean table."

"Aren't you afraid?"

"It's a foolish woman that fears the sight of blood."

That silenced him. She stopped scrubbing and reached for a clean rag.

"Give me your hands," she said.

He obeyed. He reached through the hole till she could see his two dirty hands. She started to wash them.

"I'm sorry I shouted at you," he said.

"You got a shock."

"Yes."

She finished with his hands, pushed them away gently and reached for the tray of food, "Here, your breakfast. You need to build up your strength." She laid the tray on the ledge of the opening and watched as his hands helped himself. The shaft of light from the window had moved down and to the right so the ledge was partially illuminated for him. She had brought him porridge, sweetened with honey, a pear, fresh bread with butter and gooseberry jam and a pot of ale. He started with the ale. She sat there listening and he seemed content to have her company.

He was finished his bowl of porridge when he spoke again, "where are you from, Mary?"

He remembered her name, and the question was acute. He must be feeling better.

"Not far from here," she said.

"And you've had schooling?"

"A little."

He started into his pear and said nothing more.

She thought it best to take over the conversation, "You're from Galway?"

He stopped mid-crunch.

"They told you?"

"No, a guess."

He finished eating the fruit and said, "You're wasted as a servant girl."

"Work is scarce."

"Indeed," he started to arrange the various utensils on her side of the ledge for her to take away, "Mary, you need to leave this place. You've met Worsley. He's not to be trusted, nor the boy. And there's worse..."

"What do you mean?"

He was silent. She didn't want to press him so she started to clear the remains of breakfast from the ledge. As she did, she saw she had done a good job cleaning it; there was only a faint reddish stain left.

Valentine replied, "I mean 'me'. You saw that blood. I did that. There was a man where you're sitting now. I killed him. And before that, they sent me into Limerick as part of a prisoner exchange... and waited. At night, in the moonlight, I changed. I became an animal. There was so much blood, I became... a monster." His voice trailed off.

"A werewolf?"

Valentine leaned forward. She was well-informed. "Yes," he said.

"I heard rumours. Everyone in Limerick has been talking..." She continued. "They say the werewolf cannot die, it's like the sídh or the selkie, caught between worlds..."

"...cursed to wander the earth forever," Valentine said.

"There's some would covet an earthly eternity," Mary said.

"The rich?" Valentine said with a bitter laugh, "Rich fools, perhaps. It's a heavy price to pay for eternal life."

Mary was silent for a minute. Eventually, she said, "I was taught, there's no such thing as monsters, only God's power in the hands of evil men."

Valentine answered her quietly, "Then this castle is not short of evil men."

As he spoke, she noticed the light was now illuminating the shackles which had been fixed so close to the little opening. For the first time, she realised, they too were covered in blood.

"Why do they do it? What do they want?"

"War," he said, "They'll do anything to win."

"No, I mean, this mechanism, the chains, the hole in the wall. What is their purpose?"

"They want to make more of 'me'. More werewolves."

"But they've won. Limerick is fallen."

"Limerick is. But not yet Galway," he said.

"I see." She seemed to ponder this for a minute. "Is that why they chose a Galway man?"

Valentine took a while to answer. "No, there's no connection. I came here by chance. I had to leave to protect my family's name."

"Why Limerick? The city was about to fall. Why did you come here?"

"I had help," he let out a snort as he recounted the story, "from a pirate. My father had me chained up..."

"Chained!" Mary couldn't help but interrupt.

"For my protection and everyone else's. He was right, it turned out. One night this pirate broke in. Flaherty was his name. I knew him from the wine shop. He offered to help me escape. I agreed. I couldn't drag my father down with me. I had to get away. Flaherty brought me here. Promised me passage from Limerick but he betrayed me. Delivered me straight to Hewson."

"What did you mean 'from the wine shop'?"

"My father is Richard D'Arcy. A wine merchant."

She thought for a moment, then said, "What if I could get you out? You'd be free to sail away."

Valentine was taken aback, "They'd hang you."

"Not if we both got away."

"What about your people?"

"I have none here. Nobody knows me in Limerick."

Valentine was suspicious, "Why would you do it?"

"They're using you as a tool of the devil. It must be stopped."

"Yes," he said, "but I've been free before and I know; the pain I suffer here is nothing beside the evil I'm capable of as a free man."

"But what if you could be cured?" she suggested.

"That would be sweet. But I know of no doctor can cure me. No, I won't leave here while I'm a danger to others."

9.

It was cold on the river. The spray over the front of the boat was icy and Manning felt his face burn as he was whipped by the salty water. He was sitting at the front of the little pinnace he'd hired to bring himself and his captive up the Shannon Estuary to Limerick. Samson was beside him, crouched down, his ears twitching nervously with every creak and splash of the oars. He did not like boats. Skerret sat behind them, lost in thought, his hat pulled low on his forehead, its drawstring tight around his chin. Manning and Skerret were the only passengers. They'd watched the little craft pull into Tarbert laden with refugees, its hull dangerously low in the water. The crew of two fishermen were pleasantly surprised to win two fares back to Limerick. Nobody else was going in that direction.

Manning was low on money. Their food and lodging in the public house had used up the money he'd taken from the priest. He was now eating into his own meagre funds.

He had felt better at this hour. Though he'd been relatively abstemious, the black beer had been a mistake and he'd spent much of the night running to the outhouse. The need to keep a close eye on Skerret hadn't helped his night's sleep. When he did drift off, he was plagued with dreams of wolves and blood and death.

He'd seen enough of those in real life to fill out Skerret's werewolf stories with disturbing detail.

Life on the river bank had seemed normal enough at first. The south bank which they kept close to was mostly forested but where it was cleared there were farmers working and livestock grazing. Apart from the ceaseless whispering of the river, they could hear the echo of axes chopping wood. Unlike England, this country was still covered in trees but the Conquest had brought an insatiable demand for wood and the land was being quickly stripped bare. As they sailed closer to Limerick, there was less activity and more signs of war. Pillars of smoke rose up, concentrated in the east. Detritus floated passed them. Gulls swooped into the river, fighting over unidentifiable remains.

Manning found himself doubting his choices. What was he doing in this wasteland? He tried to remember: There hadn't been much of a future for him in England. His family was large, he was a younger son, so there was no land to inherit. England itself had been at war for most of his childhood. The King was dead. Only the army seemed a stable institution. For Manning, that meant the army of Parliament. And the army had promised land, albeit on a foreign shore. So he joined up. Six months later he'd sold the land without ever seeing it – for fifteen cents in the pound. It seemed like madness now but it had been the only choice. Every man he knew had done the same. Indeed, many hadn't fared as well – some had sold the land due to them for ten per cent of its face value. They had to eat, they had expenses. Financial advice was scarce on the battlefield.

And now this dirty trade: Manning didn't like killing wolves. He did it because he was good at it and because it was lucrative. He was patient and he was a good shot. His commanding officer, the same man who'd bought his land allocation, had helped set it up for him. He'd used the cash to buy the commission and equip himself. The biggest expense had been Samson. Financially, it was paying off. But what was he doing? He didn't believe Skerret's story. The priest was going to his death; he'd say anything. Nor did he pity him. He felt more pity for the wolves. But the wolves' blood was being used for something. How could that not be devilish? He decided to find out more. This war had sent many men to hell so far, Manning did not want to be one of them.

***

When they were a few miles from the city they heard cannon fire. Manning was concerned till one of the fishermen told him it was probably just preparations for Guy Fawkes Night. He had forgotten what date it was. The fisherman had spat out the words. Manning was aware of how inflammatory this celebration of anti-Catholic feeling would be in the newly conquered city. The Parliamentarians were becoming sore winners.

By early afternoon the river had narrowed considerably and after a few sharp bends, the walls of Limerick came into sight. It was impressive. Though they'd left the estuary far behind them, the river was the grandest Manning had ever sailed and the city straddled it at a point where it still seemed wide as a lake. The walls were modern and imposing and flush with the bank. At first, it was hard to pick out the castle as it was seamlessly integrated into the city defences. But soon he spotted the three round mural towers that could only be part of a military installation. He smiled and gave Samson a pet. Even the wolfhound seemed to appreciate the significance of the sight. He sat up, licked his master and panted cheerfully. This was their destination. To the left was a defensible bridge and to the right a pier where Manning instructed the fishermen to dock.

Manning had ignored Skerret till then. He turned around to acknowledge the journey's end with the rest of the boat. The fishermen were preoccupied with their own conversation but the priest looked back at Manning. He looked desolate. The smile died on Manning's face.

When they disembarked, Skerret noticed that Manning crouched at Samson's feet and seemed to adjust the dog's collar. When he stood up, he had the fee for the ferry in his hand. He thanked the fishermen and bade them farewell. That's a clever hiding place for loot, Skerret thought.

Manning instructed Skerret to walk ahead of him through the Water Gate. From there, it was a short walk past the cathedral to the castle. He hadn't tied up his prisoner. There was nowhere to run and English soldiers were everywhere. They looked hungover and ill-disciplined. Manning wondered how much plundering they'd been allowed once the city had fallen. They threw dirty looks at Skerret as he passed. They were no friendlier to Manning who experienced the usual hostility the enlisted man reserved for the freelancer. As they walked past the cathedral they saw three bodies hanging in the doorway. One wore a bishop's mitre.

"Come on," Manning said, "sooner we get you to the castle, the safer you'll be."

Skerret just grunted ironically at the statement.

***

At the castle gate, Manning showed his commission papers and asked to see Colonel Hewson. He was told to wait in the bailey. The grounds were thronged with soldiers, mostly idling or cooking, playing card games and music. The more energetic were hauling piles of wood into the centre for a great bonfire. The smell of fresh bread was wafting over from the bakery. Manning decided to buy some. As he passed through the camp, he had second thoughts. The soldiers were mellow from their previous night's drinking but the Catholic priest in their midst was still a provocation. They were a notorious source of anti-English propaganda. Manning found himself pushing Skerret roughly in front of him. The priest scowled back at this sudden display of tribalism. When they got to the bakery, Manning bought himself some bread and threw a lump to Samson.

Skerret spoke, "I'm hungry."

Manning didn't answer. He turned his back and gave the dog a pet.

"Coward," Skerret said.

Manning spun and hit the priest hard in the stomach with the butt of his gun. Skerret collapsed on the ground. Some nearby soldiers cheered and the two men stared at each other. Manning was thinking of something to say when a young woman appeared at the injured man's side to help him. She glared at Manning.

"You're a brave boy with a gun in your hand," Mary said.

She'd been approaching from the prison tower when she saw the incident. It would have been risky talking to an English soldier like this but he wasn't a regular soldier. She'd seen the wolfhound and the other signs that marked him out as a wolf-hunter. She could criticise him without fear of the other soldiers rushing to his aid.

Manning's demeanour changed instantly, "I'm sorry, my lady. He was provoking me but I'm in the wrong."

The onlooking soldiers turned away, disappointed by the turn of events. Manning held his hand out to help Skerret but the priest refused the offer and helped himself up. He thanked Mary. They both ignored the soldier as she asked after his injuries while he brushed the dust from his coat. Manning stood dumb and watched. She was a servant, he guessed, but she looked like a queen. She was tall and strong and very pretty. That voice had been a marvel too. He was forming a second apology in his head so he could detain her longer when the gatekeeper shouted to him that Colonel Hewson would see him now... in the prison tower.

"We've got to go," he said to Mary, "if you don't mind?"

"Not at all," Skerret answered.

The priest and servant shared a smile and Manning could do no more than doff his cap to Mary and led his captive away.

10

"Blood! Blood! I must have more blood!" Colonel Hewson was banging on the table in Worsley's office.

"Yes sir."

"Not my words, Manning. Lord Ireton's, on his deathbed! He wants blood! And you bring the leader of our glorious Protestant army... a priest?! Perhaps you think he desires a Popish sacrament before he meets his maker?"

"No sir," Manning answered.

Worsley was looking on, warming himself by the fire. Colonel Hewson occupied his chair. The colonel was a short, round man in his forties. He wore a red coat like Manning but also a metal breastplate which glistened in the firelight. His hair was long and grey, matching a goatee-style beard. He wore an eye patch but the scarring which extended down his cheek flared like his temper.

"Where's my blood?" he asked.

"I have it sir, or rather, I can get it. I heard there was a bounty for priests so I brought this one here. I'll need the capital to secure the wolf's blood."

"Capital? Ha! Listen to him, Worsley. Free an enlisted man and he becomes a businessman overnight!"

The alchemist forced a laugh, then ventured, "Colonel, the wolf's blood is welcome... but a priest, if he is suitable, might be just what we need for our eh... subject downstairs."

The colonel thought for a minute, "this priest... is he a young fellow?"

"Yes sir."

"Pious?"

Manning had an idea what answer Hewson wanted, "Yes, sir."

"Perhaps he might be of use, after all."

Manning saw his chance, "Might I ask sir: the blood, the bounty on priests, are they related?"

Hewson looked suspicious.

Manning tried to make it sound like he was making a business enquiry, "I only ask because they were priced equally but now it seems that wolf's blood carries a premium? Will the price reflect this?"

"You're a wolf-hunter, Manning. That's what your licence says. Leave the bounty-hunting and the horse-trading to others. Deliver us wolf blood and ask no questions," Hewson looked to Worsley who nodded and said, "I'll give you five pounds for the priest."

The offer disappointed Manning but he couldn't show it. The bounty on a priest should be ten pounds. Hewson was ripping him off. But he had to accept it. If he argued, he might lose his commission altogether. Five pounds was still a lot of money.

"Yes sir."

Hewson stood up, "Worsley, write a promissory note of five pounds for the purchase of a priest from Mr Manning."

"Promissory note?" Manning was worried.

"It's Guy Fawkes night. You won't find the paymaster sober till tomorrow. You'll get your money. We'll mind your prisoner till then."

The alchemist sat down, scribbled a note and sealed it.

Hewson stood before Manning and patted him on the shoulder, "Stay here tonight, boy. Celebrate the fifth with us. Then be off tomorrow. Get me that blood. Our victory depends on it."

Manning pocketed the note and left, taking Samson with him. As he walked down the turret stairs he looked at the money order.

His mind was in turmoil. Five pounds was welcome. But it was half what he'd expected.

Also, he had tried to find out more about this strange trade in wolf's blood but he had left knowing only that 'victory depends on it'.

Then, there was that servant girl. The business with Hewson had been critical but Manning had spent most of the meeting thinking about her.

***

"He might be a spy?"

Worsley was looking through the window at Manning who was walking across the bailey towards the bakery.

Hewson was warming himself by the fire, "He's no spy, he's a greedy upstart. The army's full of them. They've no principle that can't be bought with a hefty principal." He smiled at his own joke.

"And yet there are spies. We know Ormonde already knows some of our plans." Worsley added. He returned to his table and put away his order book and seal. He sat back down on his chair.

"The Irish Confederates are always trying to infiltrate us, as we do them. Yet our plans remain secret," Hewson answered.

"I didn't like his questions."

"No. But there's no need to worry. The army's paying him to kill wolves and collect their blood. It would be a sick mind that didn't wonder why."

Worsley found a cup and seemed to be searching for a drink. Hewson watched him. The alchemist found a small, dark bottle. Before he had time to pour, Hewson spoke, "Not now! We have work to do. Come downstairs. Let's make sure the priest is ready to meet our guest."

Worsley looked disappointed but rose and followed Hewson. They descended to the next floor and stopped outside the second cell. It was securely locked. Skerret had been taken straight to the empty cell when they'd entered the prison tower. There was a shutter in the middle of the door which allowed for observation and for food to be delivered. Hewson opened it, bowed his head and looked in. Inside, Skerret looked up and asked for food. Hewson ignored him. He wanted to make sure Peeter had shackled him correctly. Sure enough, the priest was sitting right beside the little opening to Valentine's cell. His right arm was attached to a chain which disappeared into the neighbouring cell. His left arm was attached to another chain fixed above the hole.

"Perfect," Hewson said, "he'll lose a hand, maybe, but he should live."

He looked at Worsley who nodded. Then he straightened up and closed the shutter. He fixed his gaze on the alchemist and said, "You've done well, Worsley. We'll do it tonight. Remove the curtain from outside D'Arcy's cell and let the moon do her work. The timing is perfect; the sky is clear and the fireworks will drown out the screaming. There'll be no questions asked."

"I said you could rely on me," Worsley said, smiling.

Hewson smiled back, "yes, you've earned your fee," then his expression grew serious, "but for God's sake, stay sober."

Worsley looked chastened and nodded.

II.

When the shutter closed, Skerret whispered into the next cell, "We have to get out of here! You must know a way?"

Silence.

"Please! Don't you want to get out of here?"

There was a clink of chains but no answer.

"If we do nothing, I'll be dead in the morning!"

Skerret bent down and looked into the dark hole. He could see nothing. He looked at the chain which led from his hand into the cell next door. He gave it a tug. There was about a foot of slack. Enough for the monster next door to pull Skerret's hand into his own cell but no more. The alchemist had been clever; he had devised a system that allowed the werewolf to bite the subject but not devour him.

The prisoner spoke, "you might survive."

"I'd be better off dead, Skerret said. "Better I die a whole man than walk the Earth as a creature of the devil."

"Then you understand why I have no desire for freedom."

"Yes, I know what you are... and I'm sorry for it. Have you no pity for me?"

"Aye, I'm sorry for your trouble. But I can do nothing for you."

The light in Skerret's cell had grown dim but he could still see the stains of blood on his shackles.

"You did nothing to help the last man, I see."

"No."

"Then your corruption is complete."

"I do less damage here than I would outside. It's easy for you to sit in judgement. You don't know what I've suffered."

"I know a little."

He heard Valentine move closer to the aperture, "What do you know?"

The priest thought before answering. What was there to gain from talking to this man? Could he hope for his help? Perhaps – with the right motivation. Skerret had nothing to lose but he knew that talking to this monster might put others at risk. If he did nothing, he was a dead man. Surely it was better to take a chance now and face the consequences later than submit to death?

He spoke, "You're Valentine D'Arcy, the youngest son of Alderman Richard D'Arcy of Galway..." he heard a jolt of chains as the other prisoner straightened up.

Valentine interrupted, "...the only son."

"Yes, since the death of your brother, Donal. God rest him."

The two were silent for a moment.

"You're a priest?"

"Yes."

"From Galway?"

"Aye."

"How do you know my family?"

"Everybody in Galway knows your family."

"But no one in Galway knows of my condition."

"No, your father wouldn't let anyone know it and live" He could hear D'Arcy's heavy breathing on the other side of the opening, "there's a closer connection," Skerret braced himself for a fight. "I'm sure you'll remember my mother, Dearbhla..."

There was a mighty tug on the chain and Skerret's hand was pulled next door. D'Arcy twisted his hand and shouted, "Dearbhla Skerret? The witch who put me here!"

D'Arcy was big, but he was weak, and Skerret was indignant. He pulled back, hard enough to bang D'Arcy's head against the adjoining wall. He retrieved his hand and, at least temporarily, secured it under the weight of his body. That would resist a man if not a monster. "You're a fool, like your father, D'Arcy. My mother was no witch..."

"She killed my brother!"

"An English sword killed your brother. No doctor could cure that wound."

"But she put this curse on me!"

"I know nothing of that. I know your father slandered her and had Tadhg Flaherty drive her out of Galway."

"What? You're a lying whore's son, Skerret."

The lock turned on the priest's door. The two prisoners went quiet. Mary entered. She looked wary; she'd obviously heard the arguing. She left the door open and fetched a tray of food she'd perched on the turret stairs.

She spoke to Skerret, "I have food for you. I'm not allowed to approach you, Peeter says," she smiled apologetically, "I'm sorry. Show me how far you can reach in those chains and I'll leave the food there for you.

Skerret nodded. He was starving. He sidled towards her till the chain on his right hand went taut, "that's as far as I can go," he said.

She placed the tray in front of him and came no closer. It smelt heavenly. There was soup, bread, cheese and ale. He looked up and smiled, "Bless you."

She smiled back. Valentine bent down and watched from the dark. He hadn't talked to Mary since he'd warned her to stay away from him yet he desired her company. He made a noise with his chain.

She reacted by calling out to him, "I'll have food for you later, Valentine".

Skerret threw an evil look behind him and spat out a piece of cheese rind. Mary felt she needed to address the tension, "Please, gentlemen, try not to fight. Your situation is bad enough. Don't make fresh cause for grief."

"I won't say another word to him," Skerret answered her loudly, "though he slandered my mother... and she the only doctor in the kingdom who could help his sorry state." The priest was planting the germ of an idea in Valentine's head.

Mary looked at Skerret with fresh interest then addressed Valentine, "Think on that sir. I'll be back to you with dinner."

Her response intrigued Skerret. Perhaps he wasn't the only person scheming here.

She nodded a farewell to Skerret and to the hole in the wall, knowing that Valentine was watching. Then she turned and left. The prisoners said nothing to each other. Valentine withdrew into the dark recess of his cell and Skerret ate his food. He had expected Valentine's anger. The monster believed that Skerret's mother had put this werewolf curse on him.

She certainly had a motive: Dearbhla had been a doctor in Galway. Not a respected doctor, of course; she was a woman, and the medicine she practised was based on Gaelic folklore and frowned upon by the established city doctors. She was a doctor of last resort, and the D'Arcys had brought Donal to her at the eleventh hour. Unfortunately, his wound had been beyond help and he died shortly after the treatment had started. The D'Arcys dealt with their grief by lashing out. She was accused of witchcraft and driven out of Galway. She disappeared before a more violent punishment was conceived.

Skerret knew a little about werewolves. He knew that a werewolf had the strength of ten men. If anyone could break out of this prison, perhaps Valentine could. With his help, they could both escape. His mother's medicine might provide the necessary incentive. And only he knew where to find her.

12.

When he left the prison, Manning settled down at a camp-fire on the edge of the bailey. He ingratiated himself with the soldiers thereby buying them wine and food. He'd be flush tomorrow so he planned to live well tonight. The castle bakery had been taken over for the night and the ovens were given over to roasting meat. The soldiers were butchering half a dozen pigs with a disturbing level of skill. Another group had seized a stash of wine which they were selling cheaply to their comrades. Manning loaded up with supplies for himself and his new hosts but neither he nor they had any desire to grow more sociable.

The castle became very busy as evening set in. The bonfire erected for Guy Fawkes Night was a pyramid twenty feet tall. It told a tale of looting and destruction. Among the twisted timbers making up the structure, Manning could see a child's bed, a good wagon wheel, a butter churn and a front door. The sun, which had been shining for most of the day, finally set at around six. A brilliant orange sunset turned to inky blue then some of the scattered clouds parted and a large creamy moon appeared in the East. The soldiers took the dark as their cue and lit the bonfire with a great hurrah. They threw paper twists of gunpowder into the fire and cheered the resulting bangs. A couple of fiddlers started playing music which together with the dark and the warmth of the fire created a festive atmosphere. Many of the soldiers looked up from their card games and started singing.

Manning's mind was elsewhere. He'd joined this particular group because they'd looked focused on their game and likely to leave him in peace. Also, they were on the route from the prison tower to the well. He'd seen Mary pass by three times already. One time she'd looked over and recognised him. Her expression was unreadable. He had not yet dared to address her.

He saw the door of the prison tower open again and she emerged. He finished the ribs he'd been eating and passed the bones to Samson. As he stood up, he accidentally trod on one of the dog's paws, causing it to howl. Mary looked over. He smiled weakly, waved at her and walked over with the limping dog in tow. She stood waiting. He noticed she was carrying a large kitchen knife. She was glorious, he thought. The firelight danced in her eyes and warmed her cheeks. The hand that rested on the hilt of the knife was long, elegant and showed few signs of toil.

She knelt down, ignored him and spoke to the dog, "You poor darling," she stroked the wolfhound's paw and he licked her hands in return, "he's always hurting someone, isn't he?" She glanced up coldly.

"I beg pardon, my lady. I made a bad impression earlier, and now... it seems I'm clumsy before you."

This boy was the limit. She said nothing.

"Only, I wanted to apologise and explain; I'm not the villain you think."

"Don't be so quick to read my thoughts," she said. She looked at Samson as she spoke. She was unusually comfortable with the giant hound, Manning thought.

"Again, I apologise. I was in a hurry to see you and I stood on his paw. It was an accident."

She stood up and looked at Manning. Samson nuzzled into her skirts for more attention, "You make a habit of making your excuses to me when you hurt another."

She wasn't letting him off the hook for beating the priest, "Perhaps, if you had heard the calumny that priest laid against me? It was a fair beating for such slander."

"I've spoken to him. He seems a gentle soul. Perhaps you could tell me what makes him so vile – or is it just his Popery you despise?"

Manning saw an opening, "Yes, yes, happily. Let me buy you dinner so I can explain more. I'm not a bigot that sees the devil in every priest's frock…"

"You're a bold one. Lucky for you, my master bid me leave for the evening, and I'm hungry, and I enjoy the company of your dog."

Manning smiled back, "Come, there's tables by the bakery where decent folk can sit."

They crossed to the bakery where Manning paid a cover for a table and ordered food and wine. This was the only place in the bailey where any other women were in evidence. None were wearing head coverings and their coarse language and free manor with their male companions mocked Manning's pretensions for the spot.

Mary was unperturbed. She chose a spot with her back to the wall and started into the bread that was offered to her.

Manning was relieved to see her settle.

"What's your name?" he asked.

"Mary."

"I'm William. William Manning," he took some bread, tore it in two and offered half to the dog, "from Gloucestershire."

She chewed her bread but said nothing.

"It's in the West of England. It's a pretty country, good land. Not as wet as here."

She laughed. He wasn't wrong.

He continued, emboldened. "I would be a farmer again if I could. Is that your background? A farm?"

"No." She didn't like to say, but this was revealing little. She'd let him talk.

"It was a good life for my father and mother, tougher now though. The land's being enclosed and there's little for the youngest in any family."

"So you came over here?"

"Soldiering's a job. And there might be land at the end of it. I'm not a born soldier."

She nodded at Samson. "But you're a crack shot. Only the best get a hunting dog and a licence. You're not with Colonel Pickering's men."

She was better informed than he'd expected.

"No... I was. I have a commission for wolf-hunting now. From Lord Ireton himself."

He dropped the commander's name with pride but a celebratory cannon blast drowned him out. Cheers went up around the camp.

He noticed her shudder and realised how intimidating this display must be to an Irish catholic. "We're not all like that," he said softly.

She smiled. He's not completely tone-deaf, she thought.

"Perhaps, when we're finished eating, we could take a stroll away from the fireworks?"

Her smile twisted into ridicule. God loves a trier but this boy needs to learn how to slow down.

"I mean... to escape the noise and the garrison."

She decided to throw him a bone. "Perhaps we will." But it was time to get down to business. She continued chewing, and casually asked, "why are you killing wolves?"

"It's a lucrative business. I've made twenty pounds in six months,"

"No, I mean, what's it for? The wolf killing."

"It's complicated... I suppose it's a land clearance thing... fewer wolves allow more livestock. There's really so much more can be done with this land..." Manning realised he was on very shaky ground so he added a personal detail, "I grew up with a musket in my hand. I learnt young. We had wolves at home too."

She nodded. One of the part-time waiters interrupted with two plates of food and a bottle of wine. He assessed Mary as he delivered the food and smiled at Manning.

Mary started into the meat and spoke as she ate, "when did you start hunting priests?"

Manning was dismayed by the direction of the conversation, "it's really not a big deal. There's a bounty on priests. I have nothing personal against them. I'm no bigot. But this one, trust me, I spent two days with him. If any priest deserves the rope..."

"Where's he from?"

Manning shrugged, "He's just some priest. He's a scoundrel."

"He sounds like a Galway man."

"I don't know. Everybody here sounds the same to me."

She smiled at his shameless ignorance. He took a big drink of wine and wondered how he might take control of the conversation. She hadn't been impressed by his money and hadn't responded to his plans to become a farmer. There was a tearing, whistling noise in the sky followed by the bang of an exploding firework. They were briefly illuminated in purple light.

"He says his mother can cure werewolves."

"Werewolves! Nonsense." So that's where Skerret got his stories from. The soldier took another drink, pretending to be uninterested.

"Why do you collect wolf's blood?" she asked.

Manning spat.

Some neighbours looked over and laughed. Mary remained serious. Manning apologised and wiped the table. Samson made a little sing-song noise at his master's curious behaviour.

"I'm sorry, you surprised me. How do you know... ?" then he answered for himself, "...oh, the priest told you."

Mary didn't correct him.

"I can't really talk about it," Manning was picking at his food as he spoke. He wasn't really hungry; he'd only ordered because he was flush and he wanted to impress her, "I'm sorry, the army has certain secrets... " he looked up and realised he'd lost her attention. She was looking over his shoulder in the direction of the prison.

He turned and looked. Peeter, the boy from the prison was atop the scaffold and had opened the curtains to Valentine's cell. It was an upside-down act for an upside-down world, Manning thought – curtains outside a window, to be opened only at night. He turned around again. Mary looked worried.

He needed to regain her attention, "...anyway, I can't tell you the details but Commander Hewson himself told me that the wolf's blood is very important. He said, 'victory depends on it'. But old Worsley seemed to think the priest was all they need."

She looked surprised. She stood up and said, "I have to go. Thank you for the food." She was about to walk away when she had second thoughts. He had been helpful. She smiled at him, squeezed his hand and said, "Perhaps, we'll go for that walk later."

Before he could respond, she had walked away in the direction of the prison. Manning heard laughter and noticed one of his neighbours grin at him before burying his face into the long curly hair of the woman sitting on his lap.

13.

There's only so much a man can take, Worsley thought, as he opened the bottle. He needed to numb his mind to the coming trial. He drank till he coughed, paused to catch his breath, and then drank till the little green bottle was empty.

It was a mixture of his own concoction; part tincture of opium, part brandy, sweetened with honey. He took a deep, relaxing breath and rested both hands on his desk as the drink warmed his blood. A cannon blast shattered his peace.

"Peeter!" he yelled.

No answer. Outside, the cannon blast was answered by the rat-tat-tat of fireworks.

He half yelled, half coughed, "Peeter!"

A minute passed then he heard footsteps on the stairs. Worsley's head wobbled as he looked to the door. A figure appeared. Not Peeter.

"Beg pardon, sir. Peeter's outside on the scaffold," said Mary, entering the room.

Worsley had seen so many executions of late, his mind first pictured the boy swinging from a gibbet before he remembered the scaffold outside Valentine's cell and the task at hand. But what was she doing here, he thought?

"You can't be.... go Mary. I told you to stay away this evening. Business, not fit..."

"Yes sir, right away sir. Only, Peeter wondered, if... he might have some tobacco for Guy Fawkes. I said I'd ask for him."

She'd caught him in that mellow sweet spot that would last just half an hour before depression and an uneasy sleep took over. He tried a smile and opened his arms in a gesture of generosity before reaching for a key around his neck and unlocking the strong box on his desk. From within he produced a little pouch of tobacco and held it aloft for Mary.

Taking care not to get too close she took the pouch and said, "Thank you, sir. I'll bring it out to him and leave you in peace."

"Peace," he repeated grinning, till another cannon blast made him wince.

Before she left, she noticed he'd left the key in the strong box and the lid open.

***

Mary took the back stairs down to the next level and stopped outside Valentine's door. She had no key for this and, to date, all her communication with him had been through the hole in Skerret's cell. She called his name and knocked. There were sounds inside but no intelligible response. She opened the hatch, crouched and looked in.

The cell was bathed in blue moonlight. Valentine was lurking in a corner, his body quivering, his doublet pulled up over his face, Even in this dim light she could see he was a strong, broad man around her age. His hair was fair and his clothes, though filthy and torn now, were once fine.

"Valentine," she said.

He made a snorting, groaning sound in response.

"Valentine," she repeated, "I'm going to get you out."

With an effort that obviously hurt, he responded, "No, too dangerous... don't... "

She spoke calmly and quietly – she didn't want to draw Skerret's attention, "It has to be now. They're going to succeed. We have to stop them. I'll get you out.

"No," he said louder, his agitation increasing.

The noise reached Skerret who pressed his face to the hole. He called out to Mary, "Please, unchain me. He'll kill me!"

"I have no key for your chains," she called back.

"Then for the love of God, block out that moonlight."

She didn't need to be told twice. She continued down the next flight of stairs to Peeter's cellar. There was a dim light coming from his quarters.

She called out, "Peeter!"

He was sitting on a stool sharpening his knife by candlelight. He stood up as soon as she entered.

"Mr Worsley has changed his mind," she said, "he wants those curtains closed again... quickly. Can you do that please?"

Peeter looked uncomfortable and didn't move.

"It's quite urgent, Peeter," she added.

"You're not allowed here," he said.

"Oh, I'm sorry, Peeter," she turned and left his room but waited on the turret steps.

He spoke again, louder, "I mean, you're not allowed in the prison tonight."

She called back into his room, "Don't worry, Peeter. I spoke to Mr Worsley. He told me to ask you to close the curtains. It has to be now, Peeter."

He was quiet for a minute.

"I'll ask the master," he said. He started towards her.

71

"No, no, don't do that," she said as he reached her, "He doesn't want to be disturbed. He's had his... medicine."

The turret stairs were narrow and dark. Peeter was standing too close and his breath warmed her neck. He was fiddling nervously with the knife. She was in his way.

"I'll ask the master," he repeated and started to squeeze past her.

She let him pass but as she did, she retrieved the tobacco pouch from her apron, showed it to him, and said, "Peeter, would you like some tobacco?"

His face lit up. He nodded.

She held it to her chest and said, "Promise me you won't disturb the master?"

He nodded again.

"And you'll close the curtain?"

"I can't do that," he said.

She gave up on that point. She handed the pouch to him but her grip lingered and their fingers touched while she added, "Go outside Peeter. Watch the fireworks."

He was happy with this lingering contact and nodded. Finally, she let go and he went scurrying up the stairs. She heard the door to the bailey open and shut.

***

She leaned against the wall and exhaled deeply. She looked down at the cellar. There was a heavy door into Peeter's room with a key in it. And it was windowless. Perhaps, if she could move Valentine there? Then she looked up. Strange noises were coming from the cells above. When she heard Skerret scream, she ran. She had the key to his door and opened it quickly.

"Get me out of here," he shouted at her. He had pulled his body as far away as the chain allowed from the hole to Valentine's cell.

For the first time, a little light penetrated the hole and Mary could see Valentine's legs pacing back and forth.

She ignored Skerret for the moment, "Valentine, we'll help you," she called out.

He answered with a roar of pain.

"What about me?" the priest demanded.

"I'll look for the keys," she said to Skerret. She turned and left. She ran up another flight of stairs to Worsley's room but slowed at the top and entered cautiously. The old man was asleep, face down on his desk. He was drooling onto his papers and snoring. The strong box was open on the desk beside him. Inside she saw a large iron hoop loaded with keys. She crossed the room quietly, keeping an eye on the alchemist, and took the keyring. She gathered the keys in her palm to muffle the noise and stepped lightly back to the stairs. She went to the priest first, opened his door with the key she already had and entered. Once inside, she held up the set of keys for him to see.

"You found them. Give here! We haven't much time."

"No," she answered.

His face fell.

"You must help me. If I can get him out of the light, maybe I can get him out of here but I need your help."

"You're mad," Skerret said.

"You said your mother could cure him. Where is she?" she said.

"I can't tell you that," he answered.

She raised the key chain, "Tell me if you want these."

"Galway." Valentine had gone quiet next door. Was he listening? Mary stared at the priest. He had answered too quickly. She started to undo the buttons of her bodice and then the shift beneath. Skerret was confused till she removed a crucifix from around her neck. She held it out to him and said, "Swear it."

"I can't."

"Because you lie."

Skerret's shoulders sank. He took the cross and looked at his chains. Then he spoke quietly, "She's in Inchicronan on the Galway road, there's a cave two miles to the West. You'll find her there."

"Swear it."

He kissed the cross and returned it to her, "I swear it."

She threw the keys to the priest then hunkered down by the hole to speak to Valentine, "We're going to move you somewhere dark. We'll stop the transformation, then we'll get you out," she turned to the priest and asked, "what's your name?"

He was frantically trying all the keys in his shackles. He had one off already. He looked up, "Ambrose," he said.

She smiled as she reconciled the name with the man undoing chains in front of her. Then she addressed Valentine, "Ambrose is going to help us," she looked to Skerret for validation.

"Valentine?" Mary wanted an answer. But he was beyond reason. He let out a groan, oblivious to her question.

Another clink clink and Skerret was free. He stood up, looked at the open door then back to Mary.

"Well?" she said.

"What do you want me to do?" he asked.

She stood up and held out her other keys, "Swap. Here's the key for the front door. Go downstairs and lock it. We can't be interrupted. Give me the other keys and I'll get Valentine out — he'll be safe in the cellar. Then come back upstairs and help me move him."

Skerret nodded and started to leave.

"Thank you," she added.

14.

Manning was worried. He'd been so keen to impress Mary he'd told her too much of his business. He'd spoken too freely and now she'd run off, somehow affected by his news. And he still hadn't impressed her.

He'd had enough of the bakery. The company there was depressing him. He paid up and left the wine unfinished. He offered the food to Samson but even the dog had eaten his fill. He returned to where he'd left his kit closer to the prison tower. He thought of Skerret and his stories of werewolves and conspiracies. It was nonsense; it had to be. But Mary was acting strange. Okay, he barely knew her. Strange for a servant, then. But wasn't that part of her appeal? Everyone in that prison seemed strange, he thought. Or was he being paranoid? It was hard to think straight with the constant explosions from the bonfire and fireworks.

When he got back to the camp-fire he was greeted with indifferent nods from the other soldiers. He sat and faced the prison. He calmed his nerves by attending to his kit. He took a light from the fire and kindled the end of the slow fuse on his musket. It was a nervous habit borne of the bitter experience of war. Be prepared. He still wore the bandoleer which held his musket balls and a dozen measures of powder. He saw Peeter leave the prison. He was another oddball. But perhaps he could enlighten

Manning. He noticed the boy was filling a pipe. Manning got up and walked over to him.

"You need a light, boy?"

Peeter flinched when addressed. He nodded warily. Manning took the fuse from his musket and offered it to Peeter.

"You're the wolf-hunter," Peeter said, sucking on his pipe and generating cloud of smoke. He looked at the fuse and then at the musket with admiration.

Manning nodded, "Yes. And I brought the priest in."

Peeter returned the fuse and started taking great gulping draws on the pipe.

"Tell me, what will become of him?" Manning asked casually.

Peeter looked up and answered curtly, "can't talk to you."

Manning was getting used to being excluded from army business but a child's rebuff was too much, "I'm on a commission from Lord Ireton, boy. Take a different tone with me."

Peeter tried to explain, "Sorry, sir. I can't talk to anyone tonight."

This caught Manning's attention, "Tonight? What's happening tonight?"

Peeter realised his mistake and started to fidget. He started to leave, "I have to go."

"Wait," Manning reached into his satchel and produced his tobacco pouch. He stopped Peeter with a gentle hand on the shoulder, "would you like some more?"

Peeter nodded.

"Tell me, what's happening tonight? Is Mary involved?"

Peeter looked blankly into the distance, "I wouldn't hurt Mary, sir."

"No, of course not," Manning answered.

Peeter warmed to his subject, "She's like... an angel."

Manning smiled, "yes, she is."

Peeter didn't like Manning's tone. His face hardened, "She shouldn't be here, I told her, not tonight... with that creature."

Manning felt his heart thumping. He grabbed the boy's sleeve, "Creature? What creature?"

Peeter pushed Manning's hand away. He snatched at the tobacco in Manning's other hand, "Give it here. I told you enough."

"Here, take it! And mind my dog." Manning pushed the tobacco and the dog's leash into the boy's hands. Peeter and Samson watched dumbly as he ran over to the door of the prison and hesitated outside. Mary was in danger. He was sure of it. He had no business entering the prison under arms at night. But he couldn't stop himself. He looked back at the bailey. The soldiers were all busy celebrating. No one was paying him any attention. He tried the door. As he did, he felt someone else resisting on the other side. He shoved the door hard. Skerret was pushed backwards into the tower, a key in his hand, his mouth open in shock.

Manning raised his musket and hit the priest hard on the nose, "Jailbreak!" he screamed.

⁂

Upstairs, Mary heard the alarm being raised. Valentine was free, he had his arm over her shoulder and they were standing on the turret stairs. He was managing to support most of his own weight but he was groaning and mumbling incoherently.

"Change of plan," she said. She turned him around and they started to climb.

At the top, Worsley stumbled into their way waving his hands, "Stop, what are you doing? You can't do this!"

Mary felt a surge of strength course through Valentine and he practically carried her to the top of the stairs. There, he lifted the alchemist by the collar and threw him down the steps behind them.

"Come on," Mary said, "this way." She was heading for the battlement. They exited the tower and stepped onto the ledge. As soon as they were in the moonlight, Valentine doubled over in pain. He let out a roar that drew the attention of the soldiers down below in the bailey.

Downstairs, Manning heard the roar and left the priest unconscious on the floor. When he got to the first floor he found Worsley injured on the steps. The alchemist was delirious but alive.

Mary tried to lift Valentine upright but he was too heavy. Explosions were ringing out – whether from fireworks or gunshots – she could not tell. She looked down the battlement. There was a second mural tower halfway between them and the keep. It was manned by sentries but the stairs led to a postern gate onto the river. She had no idea how they'd get past the sentries or how they'd survive the fast-flowing river but they had to get out.

"Please Valentine, get up!" she shouted at him. His skin had turned red as though sunburned except at the joints which were strained white. His eyes were impossibly dilated. He looked back at her, tried to speak but couldn't. He nodded. His mouth was fixed open, as though to retch, the skin seemingly stretching from within. She jerked his arm and he reacted, rising enough to limp down the battlement. As they proceeded, Mary looked right and saw the seething river reflected in the moonlight. She could see the postern gate, the little jetty poking out and... a boat.

Inside the prison, Manning helped Worsley into a sitting position on the turret stairs.

The alchemist was dazed, "He'll kill us all. That Catholic whore freed him. I'll string her up for this."

Manning's sympathy shifted to Mary and he left the old man cursing in the darkness. He raced up the next flight of stairs. He could hear a bell ringing. The castle had responded to his alarm call.

Outside, Mary saw the soldiers down in the bailey loading muskets and firing in their direction. Their shots were missing wildly in the dark but with so many firing, one might get lucky. When they were halfway across the battlement, a young sentry emerged from the second tower ahead and charged down the battlement towards them, sword in hand. He came level and swung but Valentine pulled Mary back in time and the sword clanged against the stonework. Valentine grabbed the boy by the face and knocked his head against the inner wall. He fell limp.

The violence seemed to give Valentine life and he raced ahead of Mary as far as the door to the second tower. He turned and faced her. She read the look in his eyes. He was going to leave her there. She cried out, "No, Valentine!"

He hesitated but then his shoulder exploded with a spray of blood. Mary turned around. The shot had come from Manning. He was standing at the other end of the battlement just outside the prison tower. Mary turned back to Valentine. He had disappeared inside the second tower. She tried to follow but couldn't open the door.

Manning looked into the bailey. A column of soldiers was streaming into the second tower through the internal ground-floor door. Valentine would meet them on the stairs – he was trapped. Manning lowered his musket. In the distance, he saw Mary collapse in resignation outside the locked door. He took a step towards her but had second thoughts. She was staring at him. Even in the dark, he could see the anger in her eyes.

They were both distracted by an unearthly scream from the tower. The first scream was followed by another and then another. Manning raised his musket. The door crashed open. A figure appeared. He looked down at Mary and sniffed like a dog. He wore Valentine's clothes but he was monstrously deformed. His bare head and extremities were a painful marriage of man and wolf.

He howled. His teeth were like knives. He looked at Manning and crouched decisively. Manning understood. He spread his feet, grabbed an envelope of gunpowder, bit the paper and spat. The creature dropped to all fours and thundered towards him. Halfway between them, the sentry was waking up and scurried for his sword. Manning filled the pan with powder, filled the barrel, added a musket ball and paper stopper. He looked up at the charging beast and took a measured breath. The creature swung a paw at the sentry's feeble stand. The sword went flying the sentry fell back with a shrill scream. The monster raced on across the battlement. Manning took his scouring stick, compacted the mixture in the barrel, aimed and exhaled. The creature took a last gallop and leapt. The pair fell back in an explosion of blood, smoke and noise.

15

Lady Ranelagh wiped her nose and sniffed. She was upset but she was not about to cry. It was getting cold. No doubt the chill made her nose run. She strolled down to the river bank to be alone. She didn't want the servants in the house gossiping about her. Indeed, she didn't want her brother asking questions. He was kind and would say the right things but she valued her privacy and, though he was twenty-five and she a decade older, she tended to shield him from the world now, as she had in childhood.

It was another clear, dry November morning. The trees were still heavy with foliage though their colours had turned and the clover lawn was becoming littered with crispy yellow leaves. The sunshine belied the winter temperature. With a shiver, she pulled her fur stole close around her bare shoulders. Her clothes were only as practical as a lady's allowed. Beneath the fur, she was wearing a brown satin bodice and skirt which she liked for its ability to disguise the mud stains of Irish country life. She wore her long brown hair tied up in a simpler style than was fashionable. In London, as Lady Ranelagh, she'd take the time to style her hair in ringlets but here, she was plain Katherine Jones, and the practicalities of working in the laboratory demanded a simpler style.

The river bank at the end of the garden was her haven. Nevertheless, she was slightly wary as she approached the water's edge. The house was downstream from Limerick, so, much of what went into the river there, washed up at the foot of their garden. Colman, the gardener, had had to bury the remains of more than one victim of the recent siege.

In truth, she liked checking to see if anything had washed up. She wasn't insensitive to the human tragedy playing out in the city but she saw no contradiction in feeling a flurry of excitement when that tragedy made landfall in her father's garden. It was a welcome distraction from her own troubles. She walked the length of the bank checking the reeds for gas-filled corpses, bobbing heads or even a random foot. Nothing. There was a pier at the eastern end of the property. She'd finish her walk there, she thought.

She retrieved the troubling letter from her sleeve and re-read it. Her husband had shamed her with another woman again, it said. It wasn't news. This was the story of their marriage. It wasn't heartbreak which saddened her either. There was no love between them. It was the damage done to her children's reputation that made her upset. The three girls were old enough to understand the nature of their father's indiscretions and even if her son, Richard, was not, he would hear his father's name ridiculed in public. As she thought of the children, tears threatened to well up. Richard was in Cork and the girls were in London but, while the war raged, they were a world away. The letter itself was a month old. She had only received it because her friend, Hartlib, had thought to include it in a consignment of scientific apparatus which her brother had ordered from London. That delivery had only been completed thanks to the hazard premium he'd paid on top of the standard fee. Robert had been in his laboratory since its arrival, happy as a child at Christmas.

As she approached the wooden pier, she lowered the letter. Something had caught her eye. There was a man lying there. She looked back at the house. There was no one in sight. She ought to go back and fetch Colman or her brother. But she was within sight of the house and the man appeared unarmed, indeed incapacitated. She decided to investigate. He couldn't have washed up. He had either climbed onto the pier or had been deposited there. But he was still, like a corpse. Her footsteps on the boards sent a couple of ducks splashing into the reeds. The man did not stir. She approached slowly. He was a young man around her brother's age, though much larger. His clothes were expensive but ruined. His hair was fair and his skin was as white as marble. He was lying on his back which allowed her to see the terrible wounds on his torso. There was a hole in his shoulder and one in his chest. The latter wound must be fatal. Concluding this, she drew closer and knelt at his side. She was interested in the chest wound. There was a bloody, burnt hole in his doublet where a musket ball had penetrated. She decided to see where in the chest it had entered so she gently pulled open the doublet and pushed aside the silk shirt beneath. A glint of metal caught her eye. He wore a necklace. From it hung a peculiar ring. It was silver and elaborate. At first, she thought it represented a skull till she realised it was upside down. She turned it around. It was a heart held by two hands with a crown on top. It was pretty. The chain was slim so she decided to pull it free. She tugged. His eyes opened wide suddenly. He grabbed her wrist and squeezed hard. His mouth opened in pain but made no sound. He convulsed, rolled onto his side and started to vomit.

16.

"Is he dead?" Colonel Hewson asked.

"Merely drugged. I gave him a tincture of opium when he came in. He'll sleep for the day." Worsley answered.

They were in the alchemist's solar – the little wood-panelled bedroom at the top of the prison tower. The two men had squeezed around the ornate four-poster bed to get a closer look at their specimen.

"He'd be as comfortable in the empty cell downstairs – and more secure," Worsley added.

"You deserve to lose your bed after last night. Let him stay here. I want him to make the speediest possible recovery."

Worsley decided not to press the issue. Hewson had been furious to discover the alchemist in a drugged stupor the night before. He had reasonably inferred that Worsley's condition had helped the werewolf's escape. The colonel's wrath was tempered by the prize that lay before them now. William Manning was not dead. He had been bitten by the werewolf and had survived. This was what they were waiting for; 'the youth whom the wolf had bled'. He wasn't the night's only victim: Five soldiers lay dead in the southern tower. All were slashed or bitten by the monster. But only Manning lived.

"How do we know," Hewson waved his finger in a circle, trying to find a delicate phrase, "the boy is... suitable?"

"Why, that he lives, there's the proof. There's no magic in the virgin's blood per se. It's that they have a tendency not to die. The wolf has no taste for them."

Good. Once he was strong enough they could bleed him and create the potion which would bring the war to an end.

"Tendency... eh?" Hewson was thinking out loud. He pulled back the blanket and looked at the bandaged wound on Manning's arm. He could see bloody teeth marks beneath the linen. He poked the arm. Manning groaned in pain. Worsley squirmed at this rough treatment.

"Make sure he does survive, Worsley. You have ground to make up with me." The soldier left the bedside and headed for the door.

"Yes sir, Colonel." Worsley bowed and looked down at the patient who was starting to wake. More opium, he thought.

Before the colonel left, Worsley remembered a question, "Sir, the priest in the cell downstairs. What should we do with him?"

Hewson was blunt, "String him up, of course," then his imagination sparked and he added, "bring him out to the Cathedral and hang him beside his Bishop. Let him be exalted!"

In his drowsy state, Manning remembered the image that had greeted him on arrival in limerick. The bishop, his face as purple as his robes, swinging from the door of his own cathedral. The colonel's words demanded a reaction. There was something that Mary said. What did he have to do? He couldn't think. As his visitors departed, the room became quiet once more and Manning gave up the fight with his troubling thoughts. He drifted back into a stupefied sleep.

17.

"He's not breathing."

Robert Boyle was kneeling beside the body on the pier. He held his cheek close to the unconscious man's mouth to feel for breath and placed his fingers on the side of his neck to look for a pulse. Finally, he opened a little pewter flask he'd been holding and poured a few crystal granules into his hand.

"Salt of harts horn," he explained, "Should wake an elephant."

He held the crystals under the man's nose and waited.

"Nothing."

The young scientist looked up at his sister. He was silently hoping she'd revise her story. She stared back stonily. Then he looked to Colman, the grounds keeper, who stood behind her, a shovel in hand, prepared to either fight or bury the intruder. He remained dumb – knowing better than to take sides with either sibling.

Ordinarily, Katherine would point out the comedy in a scene like this. Her brother was not an outdoors type. She had run back to the house and shouted for him and Colman: A man had washed up on their property and needed help. Boyle had been in his laboratory. He'd thrown a long coat over his billowing shirt and raced down the garden to investigate. Now, the simple act of bending down to examine the derelict was proving a challenge. His breeches ballooned around his skinny legs as he knelt and soaked up the morning dew on the wooden pier. He had to tuck his long white cravat into his coat just to see what he was doing. He wore a periwig in the morning because his laboratory was cold. Now, as he leaned over, he needed to hold it in place with one hand.

It was comical but Katherine was not laughing, "I tell you he grabbed me, rolled over and emptied his belly."

"A convulsion perhaps? The dead sometimes jump and jerk as the spirit leaves... Harvey described such behaviour in frogs as he was dissecting."

"He wasn't dead. He looked at me." She was shivering. She'd pulled her stole tightly around her and her knuckles were white. Her right hand was closed in a fist, the necklace she'd taken from the body digging into her palm.

Robert saw the fierce look in her eyes. If she was certain then he believed her, "So he died in the interval. You saw him alive but the unfortunate man died before we returned?"

"I suppose. Yet he also seemed dead when I found him. We should make sure."

Colman stepped forward lifting his shovel, misunderstanding her words.

"No," she put a hand out to stop the grounds keeper, "I mean, we must watch him for a spell. See if his condition changes."

Robert looked sceptical but nodded, "as you wish, sister. Colman, take two men and carry him up to the woodshed. Lay him there and we'll watch him for the day. I'm afraid we won't see any change though."

Katherine left her brother with a sharp look and started back towards the house. Colman followed. Robert looked down and sighed as he noticed his cuffs were now stained with blood and his breeches wet through. He'd have to change. For the first time, he considered the dead man's appearance. His clothes had once been good. Not as expensive as his own, but he was no peasant. In life, he would have worn them well. He was a strong, soldierly type – a fellow to turn his sister's eye... once upon a time.

But not now, for surely he was dead. And even if he had only just died, how had he come to be here? He wasn't fit to swim and there was no sign of any boat. It looked like he'd been left here but if so, by whom?

18.

Peeter had seen everything the night before. When Manning had raised the alarm and roused the castle, Peeter stuffed his pipe and tobacco into his shirt and ran. He entered the prison tower and found Skerret unconscious on the floor. He could hear Manning and Worsley at the top of the Southern turret stairs. He didn't want to cross paths with them. If a prisoner was loose, Peeter would be blamed. He took the Northern turret stairs and passed the cells, passed Worsley's room and entered the solar from where he climbed onto the roof. There he crouched by the parapet and looked out onto the battlement. He saw Manning shoot Valentine in the shoulder. He saw Mary in the distance at the door of the second tower. He heard the beast transform and saw him emerge back onto the battlement. He trembled when the beast turned and sniffed at Mary. His heart pounded for his own safety when the beast charged towards the prison tower.

The wolf-hunter had shown real courage. He'd only had seconds to load and shoot as the beast charged towards him... and his aim was true. It did little good. The beast collided with him and sank his teeth into the soldier's arm. Before the creature could do more damage, he was assaulted by a barrage of gunfire from behind. The surviving soldiers from the second tower emerged onto the battlement and took up a position just past Mary. The werewolf turned and dropped Manning. The creature decided on flight. He looked into bailey where a hostile crowd of soldiers were taking pot-shots. He looked up and briefly locked eyes with Peeter. He looked left into the river and made his choice. He leapt over the parapet and plunged into the fast-flowing river. Peeter exhaled with relief. The soldiers on the battlement ran to the ledge and looked into the water. Some of them started shooting wildly into the river. Behind them, Peeter noticed, Mary took her chance. She got up and entered the second tower. Peeter looked and saw the figure of the werewolf floating with the current away from the city. He looked back to the second tower. At river level, outside the castle walls, he saw Mary emerge from the postern gate. She had found a lamp and a musket. She stood on the jetty and searched the river. She was going to follow the beast. She climbed into the little boat that was tied up there and cast off.

Peeter decided to follow. He raced through the prison tower and exited the castle by the drawbridge over the moat. The sentries who should have been slowing his progress were nowhere to be seen. They must have joined the shooting party in the bailey.

On the street, Peeter had to make a decision: He had often fished the river and knew the currents well. He decided that if the werewolf made shore he would do so on the Northern bank. He crossed the Thomond bridge and stayed close to the river. He'd lost sight of the beast and Mary's little boat but he carried on. He couldn't understand what she was doing. She had been lucky the werewolf had ignored her on the battlement but now she was chasing him. She was putting herself in danger. Peeter didn't know what he could do to help her. He had his little knife tucked into his belt but he wasn't sure he had the courage to use it. Let me find them first, he thought.

After twenty minutes, Peeter caught sight of Mary's boat. She'd beached on a little shingle strand close to the thick forest that skirted the northern edge of the city. A light rain had started to fall. The sky had darkened and the moon had disappeared. There was a faint orange glow from the dozens of bonfires in Limerick but only one other light: Mary's lamp was sitting on the ground beside her. It illuminated her own kneeling figure and the body she tended to. It was Valentine. Peeter recognised the yellow doublet which had belonged to the prisoner. He seemed to have transformed back into his human shape though he showed no signs of life. He got as close as he could without being seen. Mary had lost her cap and her long brown hair had fallen loose around her shoulders. Peeter crouched behind a tree trunk at the forest's edge, hoping to observe unnoticed but as he stabilised his body, his weight pressed a dry twig which snapped and startled her. She turned and her look of alarm turned to one of relief as she recognised Peeter.

"Peeter, thank God," she called him loudly, "come here. I need your help."

This woman was afraid of nothing, he thought. He stood up but came no closer.

"Come quick, Peeter. Please!"

He tentatively stepped onto the beach and started towards her. It was the wolf-man alright. There was a gaping hole in his chest and another visible in his shoulder. His eyes were closed. There was a muddy trail behind him where he'd dragged himself out of the water before passing out on the spot.

"Is he dead?" Peeter asked.

"He looks dead but no, I believe he yet lives."

Peeter crossed himself and spat for luck.

Mary looked up at the boy, "Yes, there's evil afoot, Peeter. But I believe he can be saved. There is a woman in Clare can cure him but he needs more immediate attention. Will you help me?"

Peeter stood at a distance and thumbed the hilt of his knife.

"He should be brought to Mr Worsley," he said. He looked up at the cloudy sky, "Might be safe now. Moon's gone away."

"Yes. The moon seems gone. I think he'll stay this way tonight," Mary stood up as she spoke. He noticed she still carried a musket. She made no threat with it but he felt sure she'd wanted him to see it. "I'm not bringing him back to the castle, Peeter."

He nodded. He wasn't going to fight her.

"I need your help."

"I have to go," he answered, "They'll beat me if I'm missed."

"Mr Worsley will beat you?"

He nodded again but kept his eyes fixed on the body of the prisoner.

"You said you were with Ormonde at Rathmines, didn't you?"

He nodded slowly, unsure where this was going.

She put a hand on her hip. "Where does your allegiance lie, Peeter?"

"I dunno," he answered, looking uncomfortable.

"No. Of course not." This was the wrong tack. Mary reached into her bodice which he'd already noticed was loose at the top. She withdrew a silver coin and held it out to him, "Take it. This will shorten your indenture. Help me and I'll pay more."

He stepped forward, took the coin and examined it. It was warm in his hand. He'd never been so rich. He put the coin into his shirt and answered, "Yes, miss."

She smiled at his wonderment then spoke seriously, "There's more where that came from, Peeter. Help me and you'll be rewarded." She looked down at Valentine and got back to the business at hand, "He needs a doctor but we can't return him to limerick. Do you know of any doctor west of the city?"

He shook his head, "doctors is scarce these days. The Irish are all dead or gone. The English all to the east."

"Is there no one?"

He looked to the river to jog his memory, "There's a man like Worsley, not a doctor, a philosophe I suppose. Worsley wrote him when we besieged the city. He has a house four miles up on the southern bank. I had to carry the correspondence. The letters stopped pretty quick, though. Suppose he could help?"

"And you could find the house again?"

Peeter nodded.

"I want you to take Valentine there. You can use the boat. Will you do that for me?"

It sounded like she had other plans. Peeter was disappointed, "where will you be?" he asked.

"I'm going to Galway. That's the source of this infernal plague. Perhaps I can learn more from this man's family."

He nodded slowly. He was relieved to hear she wasn't returning to Limerick where she'd surely be hanged. And Galway was an obvious refuge. But why she was bothering herself with this stranger's problems, he couldn't fathom.

"Let's get him into the boat," she said. She lay the musket on the ground and crouched by Valentine's shoulders. She looked up, asking Peeter to join her. She was strong, as was Peeter for his youth, but the wolf-man must have weighed two hundredweight. They struggled but eventually managed to drag him down to the boat and lift him over the gunwale.

"You won't manage to unload him by yourself," Mary said, out of breath, once he was in.

Peeter shook his head.

"I'll come with you, then," she said, somewhat unhappily. She had made herself an outlaw and needed to quit Limerick county as soon as possible. This was time she couldn't afford.

Peeter couldn't hide his pleasure though and Mary took comfort in that. They pushed off and Mary hooked the lamp onto the boat's little mast. Their progress was effortless as they followed the current. They had to cross the rougher centre of the river to get to the southern bank but once there, the water was calm. It remained cloudy and dark. Their lamp was the only source of light apart from the very occasional sighting of a bonfire or light from a dwelling on the land. A thin fog swirled around them causing them to veer into the reedy banks more than once. An hour and a half later, Peeter started to see landmarks telling him they were close. A small wooden jetty appeared out of the fog. A crane for unloading cargo loomed over it like a gallows.

"This is it," Peeter said quietly. They had no plans to rouse the household. They would leave Valentine and go. With the help of the crane, they were able to transfer him in fifteen minutes. A couple of dogs barked at one point and they held their breaths but there was no response from the house. Once their task was done, they paused over the body, as though respecting the dead, then Mary remembered herself, bent down by his side, fixed his clothes and tried his temperature by pressing her hand to his forehead. Then she held her cheek above his mouth to check his breathing. But the ordinary measures of health and signs of life did not apply to this poor wretch. She hoped the occupants of this house could do more for him than she could. She stood up, looked at Peeter and the two of them climbed back into their boat.

"He's at the mercy of these strangers now," Mary said as they pushed off from the pier, "let's hope they do right by him."

19

"Where's my dog?" Manning croaked. He had recognised his visitor. He was anxious to interrogate him.

Peeter the servant boy was standing at the door of the solar carrying a tray of food. He seemed reluctant to approach. "He's in the cellar. I'm taking good care of him," the boy edged further into the room, "he's as fine a hunting dog as I've seen."

Manning cleared his throat, "He should be, for the price."

Peeter started to warm to the subject, "I'll have one myself someday and an arquebus or a flintlock."

The wolf-hunter slowly lifted himself into a sitting position, squinting with pain as he did so, "Flintlock's no good. Flintlock's for artillerymen who couldn't shoot their..." then he remembered the boy was a little young for the image he had in mind. He skipped ahead, "Matchlock's what you need, for hunting."

Peeter overcame his fear. He brought the food over to the bed.

They looked at each other silently for a moment. Then Manning remembered their last conversation, "Where's Mary?"

"Gone, sir."

Manning looked confused. Last he remembered she was being blamed for freeing the werewolf. Like him, she was on the castle battlement surrounded by soldiers. Had she somehow escaped without consequences?

Peeter read his mind, "she took the postern exit and stole a boat. The sentries had all been slaughtered by the creature. There was nothing to stop her." He would say no more.

"God keep her safe." It was a treasonous statement but he didn't care who knew how he felt.

"Yes sir," Peeter answered, for once happy to share in their mutual affection for the maid.

Manning looked down at the food. There was meat, potatoes, bread and even wine. He lifted the tray onto his lap and started eating. His arm was sore but not as sore as it looked – indeed, less sore than he would have expected. Then he realised, his head was light, his senses dulled; the alchemist must have drugged him. Even so, he congratulated himself; he was recovering quickly. He looked around the room. It was a fine chamber, better than any he'd slept in before.

"Where am I?"

"Mr Worsley's solar," Peeter answered.

"It's very generous of him to loan it. And the food is better than I'm used to. I suppose this is thanks for dispatching that creature?"

Peeter looked embarrassed, "I'm afraid not, sir."

He left it at that.

Manning pressed him, "what is it? What's the news?"

"Only, the creature never died, he escaped also."

Manning was shocked. He knew his aim had been true. He had shot the werewolf in the heart at close range. What sort of devil walks away from that? He thought again about the fine accommodation and food. What sort of game was he part of? "You were instructed to take good care of me?"

"Yes sir."

The hunter grew suspicious, "tell me boy, who put me here?"

Peeter was growing nervous but he answered, "Colonel Hewson sir... together with Mr Worsley."

The wolf-hunter looked at the bite marks under the bandages and thought of the priest. Skerret had told him that what Hewson and Worsley desired was a victim to survive the bite of a werewolf. He blushed as he realised it was not toughness that kept him alive but innocence. He was the virgin they were waiting for. He pushed his food away. He'd lost his appetite. What else had the priest told him? It had all seemed fanciful at the time but that was before he'd seen the monster with his own eyes. He'd have to ask the priest again.

He looked up at Peeter and braced himself for another disappointment, "The priest – Skerret – where is he? Did he also escape?"

"Oh no sir," Peeter smiled, glad to deliver good news, "they brought him out to be hanged this morning."

20.

Katherine sat on a milking stool eating an apple. She had skipped lunch to keep watch over the body in the woodshed. She had provisioned her vigil with books and a small picnic but as the afternoon turned to evening, she was growing hungry and the proscription on candles among stacks of firewood meant she could no longer read. Colman had laid the man out on a bed of dry logs and he had remained as still as a statue all day.

He showed every sign of death but one: He didn't seem dead. He was still, he didn't breathe, there was no pulse, and he didn't respond to stimulus. But Katherine had seen many dead bodies and they all shared the same quality – they all seemed empty. This body did not. He had the quiet animation of a great statue – still, but poised to move. Was she being objective? She feared she was not. Like the statues of her imagination, this man was beautiful, impossibly white and outsize. She was fascinated by him and this clouded her judgement.

At six o'clock, Robert visited her and broke the news that Colman had a grave ready for the stranger. She rose without answering, lingered over the body one last time then left her brother and the gardener to consign him to the earth. Robert would say a prayer – he liked funerals and ceremony – and she could trust him to grant the man a dignified burial. She didn't feel able to partake.

She ate alone in the dining room and rather than retiring to the drawing room, she took a seat by one of the windows there and waited for her brother to return. From the window, she could see the river. The house, which her father had named Manwood, had a long, shallow plan. The downstairs rooms were all on the North side of the building facing the river. The South side of the ground floor consisted of a long gallery opening onto these rooms. The dining room was next to the entrance hall so she'd hear Robert when he returned. At nine o'clock, the dogs started barking and she heard the front door open. Mrs Kinnerk, the cook, shouted them down and gave her master ten minutes to prepare for dinner.

Robert entered the dining room and looked up, surprised, when he saw his sister, "How now, sis?"

"Brother," she answered.

Robert shed some of his outdoor clothes and made his way to the big fireplace. His sister wasn't going to talk so he started, "The deed is done. He's with the other derelicts at the end of the orchard. I'm sorry we could do no more for the poor wretch." He had a prayer book in his hand which he leafed through, straining to read by the firelight. It was a dark room. The walls were either painted red or panelled in dark wood. At night a dozen candles fought the gloom but the preponderance of light – and noise – came from the hissing and crackling wood fire. His sister was uncharacteristically silent. He gave up reading and spoke, "He made an impression on you?"

She looked over briefly and nodded.

Whenever he felt uncomfortable, he tended to babble about work, "it really is an interesting case. You were right to be intrigued. There was no question over the mortal signs. I mean, he didn't breathe, there was no heartbeat. Yet you saw movement and there was a vitality I've not seen before. And yet, those wounds...

they must be fatal. I'll write an account to Tom Willis and Susan Wren... If I can get a letter out."

He realised he was becoming too enthused. He spotted some bread left over from Katherine's dinner, crossed to the table and started eating it to give his sister a chance to reply. When none came he changed tack, "he was a Limerick merchant I suppose? Fine clothes. Fine looking fellow." Robert wandered to the door, opened it just enough to listen for activity perhaps sniff for his dinner, "We've taken Limerick now... the army I mean, so perhaps this will be last we see of death round here for a while. But perhaps you should stay away from the river bank?"

She turned and gave him a look which reminded him which sibling was truly the grown-up and he added, "well, as you please."

The hall erupted with noise as Mrs Kinnerk emerged from the kitchen with Robert's dinner and beat her way through the dogs to the dining room. She deposited the food, looked curiously at the silent siblings and left to take up her argument with the dogs once more.

Robert's attention shifted to the rabbit stew steaming in front of him and he sat down, left the book open on the table beside him and poured a glass of wine.

Once he was quietly eating, Katherine turned from the window and spoke to him, "you are sure, brother?"

He looked up confused.

"That the man is dead?"

Robert picked some gristle from his mouth and gave held his sister's gaze, "I make it a priority when I bury someone."

She frowned and stood up. She was about to speak but thought better and started for the door.

"Sis, please."

She stopped and faced him.

He continued, "We can do no more. Without the heart, the body cannot live. Without breath, there is no life. What other measures can we take?"

Her shoulders sank and she answered, "You're right, of course. I'm not being... scientific."

***

Katherine left the room and stood in the hall. One of the dogs came over and licked her. She pulled her hand away, then held it open and looked into her palm. The necklace she'd taken from the body was still there. The hall was cold and dark. She looked at the ring. Again, it looked like a skull and she felt herself shiver. It's not mine, she thought. If there's to be any rest tonight, I must return it. She hurried to her room and found her heavy winter cloak. She was chilled and could not get warm all day. She threw it on and grabbed an oil lamp from the upstairs corridor. The rain was beating against the glass. There'd be no moonlight to show her the way to the orchard.

She took the stairs leading directly to the laboratory to avoid meeting anyone. The usual smell of sulphur was cut with a less familiar scent of straw. The floor was still littered with the packing from Hartlib's delivery which Robert had opened but not yet cleared. The room was chaotic. It was no bigger than the dining room and might have served as an adequate library but, for the Boyles, it housed both books and an array of scientific apparatus. Glassware, bellows, stoves and reams of paper filled a long central table and the walls, where not glazed, were lined with over-stuffed shelves. Katherine moved carefully to avoid collisions. She exited silently through the heavy wooden side door and felt her face whipped by a squally shower of rain. She pulled her hood up over her head. November was finally living down to expectations. She raised one side of her cloak to shelter the lamp and proceeded towards the farmyard. There was little noise apart from the bleating of lambs in the barn and the rain hissing through the treetops. Once she reached the walls of the orchard and entered through the narrow stone archway, she found some shelter. She was able to hear her footsteps once again as they squelched along the central path towards a fallow patch of ground inside the back wall. There, half a dozen unknown souls had been buried without names, if not ceremony, since the war had come to Limerick.

The darkness under the trees was total and her lamplight counted for little. She slipped and wobbled a few times as her shoes hit some putrefied piece of fruit but at least in the relative silence, she could rely on her hearing. There was the drip drip of rainwater on leaves and an occasional thump when some sluggish apples gave up the fight with winter and fell to the ground. She was quick to rationalise the noises but they perturbed her nonetheless. Despite the lack of moonlight, there was still a contrast between the inky black cover of the apple trees and the dim light from the open sky. She was glad when she reached the clearing by the back wall. At the end of the orchard, she could make out the mounds of earth where the bodies plucked from the river bank had found rest. She knew where to look for the newest one. She expected to see a fresh mound of earth. Instead, she found an empty hole. Her heart pounded. Another thump. She whipped around. She could see nothing in the darkness of the trees. She looked at the grave again, this time holding her lamp close to the hole. It was a mess. Soil had been pushed out from the grave. A deep furrow emerged from one end where some great weight had dragged or been dragged out.

Far off a wooden door smacked in the wind.

Her nerve failed and she ran. As she raced down the orchard path, her hood blew down. She reached up and, distracted, stepped with her whole weight on some slimy fruit residue. She tumbled onto the muddy path and grazed her hands. Her lamp went flying and fizzled out. She looked up. All was black, save for the narrow exit in the distance. She rose and continued running. Once through the arch, she'd see the lights of the house. Near the tree line, the roar of the wind and rain filled her ears. The grey shape of the arch grew brighter, then suddenly dimmed as a huge silhouette blocked her way. She plunged into the shape and felt strong arms save her from falling. She looked up. It was the dead man.

21.

As Skerret was raised up, he was surprised to see what a lovely view he had. He was facing west, looking into a perfect early November morning over the Shannon Estuary. The sky was a tumult of crashing and tearing clouds blowing from the south set against a perfect background of intense blue. From up here he could see a pin cushion of masts bobbing gently beyond the city walls. One of those ships might have taken me to France, he thought. No, let's not end with regret. Yet, regret was all he felt. The rope around his neck was tightening slowly. He had expected to be choking as soon as the noose took his weight but it was a slower process. He was instead feeling agonising pain. Why did I become a priest, he wondered. To spite my mother, I suppose. "I told you so," she'd say if she could see him now. His airway was closing and he found his body jerking reflexively against the night. Thank God she's not here.

There was a commotion down below. That is to say, someone started shouting more loudly than the cheering soldiers who'd already gathered for the entertainment. Of course, Skerret couldn't turn his head but he attempted to look down. He found he had a rather good field of vision and wondered if the eyes popping out of his head had given him owl-like perception. He could see a man, his shirt trailing outside his breeches, waving a piece of paper at the captain of the guard. They were arguing. Then he passed out.

***

Skerret woke to feel the wet steps of the cathedral porch against his cheek. He was lying in a heap, his hands still bound, the noose still around his neck. I'm alive, he thought. Someone kicked him, and then another man intervened and fought off the attacker. This is far from over, he realised.

"This man is my property," his rescuer said.

That can't be good, Skerret thought, then he recognised the voice — the wolf-hunter, Manning.

Skerret opened his eyes and surveyed the scene. Manning was standing between him and a mob of hungover parliamentarian soldiers. They were thirsty for blood. Manning was half-dressed, wearing no boots. He had a sword in his right hand. He had passed the letter to the captain who'd organised the hanging and he was making his case to the assembled crowd, "...this letter sealed by Colonel Hewson makes it clear that until five pounds is paid to me, that this priest remains in my possession. I hereby claim the right to take my property now." Manning looked down at Skerret and tried to give him a reassuring nod.

Denied even the dignity of a routine hanging, the priest thought.

The captain of the guards responded, "this letter is authentic. I'm afraid that this bounty hunter must be given the prisoner in lieu of five pounds."

There was a disappointed murmuring from the mob. Then the murmur became thoughtful and purposeful. Skerret heard coins being collected. A spokesman for the mob, a short, mop-haired man with a bushy moustache, piped up, "captain sir, you'll not deny us the pleasure of seeing this Popish agitator strung up if we can raise the requisite five pounds?"

Skerret could hear that the collection was proceeding healthily. The captain was pleasantly surprised. He turned to Manning who was finally tucking his shirt into his breeches and spoke, "Can you beat five pounds for this papist?"

Roundheads were sticklers for respecting each other's property, Skerret remembered.

Manning was speechless and shook his head. Trust this idiot to get me hanged twice, Skerret thought. Finally, a cheer went up. The mob were fully funded and presented a hat full of coins to their captain.

The captain counted the money and handed the hat to Manning, saying, "It seems you left your bed for nothing."

An older, bald soldier pressed in close to remind Manning that his hat was not part of the ransom.

Two soldiers stepped past the wolf-hunter and pulled Skerret into an upright position. Another found the end of the rope and rubbed his hands together as a prelude to the pleasant effort of lifting the priest.

"Wait!" Manning shouted. He approached the prisoner, getting close enough to speak in private. Skerret looked at him stonily. He wasn't going to gift this Sasanach forgiveness just so he could sleep better at night. The wolf-hunter whispered, "Priest, tell me, where is your mother? I need her help."

That was all. Skerret held his gaze, opened his mouth and spat. But the noose and the fear of dying had conspired to rob him of saliva. What came out was more like a cat's sneeze. Manning just looked confused. But it was clear the prisoner was not going to talk so he stepped back, disappointed. The noose tightened around Skerret's neck once more.

Suddenly, there was a clatter of hooves as a small party of soldiers on horseback raced around the corner and pulled up at the cathedral door.

"All men back to camp!" a senior-looking officer shouted from the leading horse.

The captain on the scene stepped forward and demanded an explanation.

"Colonel Hewson's orders. We're to march out and pay our respects to our commander: Lord Ireton is dead!"

"Ireton's dead," and variations thereof echoed through the crowd. The soldiers removed their hats. The man beside Manning remembered he had none and the implications of this, "but we've paid good money for a hanging!" he shouted, "you'll not deny us?"

Manning took a chance. He threw the hat into the air and sent the money flying, "Here's your money! Now, go and show some respect for our glorious leader."

He'd struck the right note with the mounted officer who nodded his approval. The hanging party released Skerret and joined their comrades as they scrambled on the ground to recoup their investment. Manning turned to the priest, sliced the rope with his sword and led him over to the captain.

"We'll take our leave, as you must take yours," he said.

The captain looked annoyed. He tore the letter from Hewson in two but said nothing.

Manning led Skerret back towards the castle before the issue was pressed any further. It was getting cold. The wolf-hunter became conscious of his bare feet and partial state of dress. The priest was still bound at the wrist and the noose trailed along the ground after him. Before they went far, they'd have to tidy up their appearance. It was past time they left Limerick.

22.

Colonel Hewson looked down at the pox-ridden corpse and allowed himself a little smile. Henry Ireton, son-in-law of Oliver Cromwell, was dead. There were only two other souls in the bedroom and they were presently busy attending to the body. They wore the uniform of plague doctors; long black coats, broad-brimmed hats and long beak-shaped masks with glass eyes. There was little chance they'd notice Hewson's levity while their faces were so covered. It was a wonder they could see anything.

Ireton had been succumbing slowly in this farmer's bedroom for nearly a month. The general had taken possession of the large farmhouse close to the city when the siege had commenced. Unfortunately for him, the inventory included the plague. Now God had taken him and the house was buzzing with the business of death.

Hewson was indifferent to the fate of his former commander. If he felt pity, it was that disease and not the sword that had killed the soldier. There were better ways to die. No, Hewson was happy; he was in charge now. Ireton had been a capable enough fellow but his illness had put the brakes on the Irish campaign. Now they were free to finish the war. Ten years of fighting were nearly at an end. England, Scotland and most of Ireland were brought to heel. There was just one city left to conquer: Galway. Thousands might die in that attempt. Yet, the war was won. Why should even one more good Protestant soldier die for a cause already won?

Fortunately, there was an alternative.

There was a knock on the door and Hewson raised his kerchief to his face and called "enter!"

The two bird-beaks looked up briefly at the young soldier who entered. He stole a glance at the dead General before delivering his message, "Sir, there's a man from Galway to see you. Says you're expecting him. His name's Flaherty."

Hewson kept his eyes on Ireton's corpse and nodded, then noticed the messenger was lingering, "what else, boy?"

"Sir, he looks like a pirate, sir."

Hewson lowered the kerchief, looked at the young soldier patiently and said, "Clearly, you've never met a Galway man before."

Next door, Flaherty had made himself comfortable by the fire. He had the appearance of a man who'd dressed in the dark on three different continents. As he turned to greet Hewson, the tiny bells atop his Arabian slippers jingled. Hewson sighed.

"I hear you've lost a werewolf?" Flaherty said.

The bald reference to Valentine's escape silenced the room. The combined draw of a large fire and a Cromwell family funeral meant the space was full of servants, soldiers and doctors. The air was thick with smoke and every man seemed to have a drink in his hand. The silence was broken by one of the servants whispering a Gaelic imprecation against evil. The Popish-sounding oath caught Hewson's attention. He looked around at the assembled crowd and bellowed, "Out!"

The colonel and his visitor were quickly left alone. The soldier sat down. Flaherty carried a skin of wine and offered a drink to Hewson. The colonel ignored the offer so the Galway man continued speaking, "...only, the boss wants to know, where that leaves our plans?"

It pained the colonel to be seen with this rogue. His beard was braided with ribbons and gold rings. His teeth were rum-rotten. His shirt was silk beneath his leather doublet yet he tied his woollen breeches with a piece of rope. Would that I could hang him with his belt, Hewson thought.

Of course, he was a pirate – half Galway was – but Hewson preferred his men to believe their enemies uniformly bad and alien. And the people of Galway were all now the enemies of the New Model Army.

"You tell your boss, we proceed as planned. The werewolf has served his purpose. I'll have a consignment ready for delivery to Galway imminently."

"Just as well," Flaherty answered, holding up the wineskin, "as we're near running out of wine."

Hewson leaned in and said quietly, "this is wine you won't want to drink."

"Aye, so I've heard," Flaherty took another drink and smiled, "there's talk says Ormonde is on to you. He has spies after your wolf-hunters. If he finds out what you're up to and tells Sir William Blake then no one in Galway will want to touch your wine."

"He won't find out in time. Ormonde is in France. The Confederates don't listen to him anymore. Why he still takes an interest is beyond me. I have a boat ready. Go back to Galway. Tell your boss to expect a shipment this week. We'll stay one step ahead of them."

Flaherty was in no hurry to leave. He took another drink, "Now, as for your missing werewolf. The boss is worried."

"Your boss is sixty miles away. I'm sure he's in no danger of being bitten."

"It's not the wolfish aspect of the man that scares him. There's a family connection..."

"I had your boy in a cell for a month. He made no claims on behalf of his lineage. Wherever he is, he either wants to spare his family shame or, perhaps he believes them worse than he." Hewson stood up to finish the interview, "I could believe either."

Flaherty nodded quietly. The arrogance of these English. Every Irishman was a beast to them. The pirate stood up and looked down on the little colonel. "Well, then. I'll report the loss and my boss can take whatever action he sees fit. Let us know when to expect your boat."

23

Robert Boyle was more shocked than anyone. It was a disturbing image; his sister standing at the front door, arm in arm with the man he'd buried hours earlier. Katherine, by contrast, was all business; keep the dogs away from him, bring towels and bandages, fetch hot water to wash the soil from his body. The servants each repressed their horror in their own way and followed Katherine's orders. The cook turned purple and her husband, Mr Kinnerk, worked his jaw silently, trying to comment on the situation but never quite getting the words out. The dead man himself was dumb and pliant. Perhaps he too was deeply shocked but it wasn't he who fainted.

It was Robert who collapsed in the hallway. Katherine left Mr Kinnerk to revive him and steered the walking cadaver into the kitchen. A chair was placed by the fire and Katherine set to work cleaning the man. Soon, Mrs Kinnerk spotted Katherine's grazed hands and interrupted her mistress to care for them. As Katherine allowed herself to be nursed she had time to think. The man never took his eyes from her.

"What's your name?" she asked.

He opened his lips but said nothing. They removed his shirt to wash him. She had a good look at his two wounds. The hole in his chest was crusted over and the shoulder wound looked weeks older.

As the cook cleaned her hands, Katherine winced with pain. The dead man looked down and said something incoherent. Katherine looked down in response. The necklace was still in her hand. She flushed with embarrassment and handed the jewellery to him. He examined it and looked at her, "Thank you," he said quietly.

"You can speak," she said.

"And he has manners," the cook added.

Katherine pulled her hands away as a signal that Mrs Kinnerk should find something else to do.

"Do you know your name," Katherine asked again.

He nodded, cleared his throat and spoke, "Valentine."

"Valentine," she tried the name for size, "my name is Katherine. Do you know where you are?"

He shook his head. He looked at his own body and picked up some dirt from his lap and looked at it.

"You've been badly hurt," she said, "we thought you were dead." She didn't want to get into the details. "But you're getting better. Do you think you can eat?"

He nodded. Mrs Kinnerk, who had been hovering in the background, took her cue and brought over a hot bowl of rabbit stew and dragged a corner of the table closer to him so he could eat. As he ate, Katherine sat watching, till the cook became conscious of his bare torso and found a blanket to wrap around his shoulders.

Katherine stood up, "I suppose I'd better check on Robert," she said.

In the hallway, her brother was sitting on a wooden chest drinking a large glass of brandy as Mr Kinnerk stood over him.

"Sorry, sis. You gave me a fright," then he added, "not you, I suppose. Is he... ?"

"He's eating," Katherine said, figuring this answered a wealth of questions. Her brother looked as pale as their guest.

"And you?" he looked at her hands.

"I'm fine. I just had a fall in the orchard."

"No wonder."

She smiled thinly, then looked at the butler, "Mr Kinnerk, could you find some clean clothes for the derelict. He looks about your size."

"Aye," he said and walked away happy that his voice seemed to be working again.

Robert had another sip and looked at his sister, "I think I know what happened."

She sat down beside him. Nothing fazed her brother for long. He wasn't strong, he was frequently ill and he was often wrong but he had great confidence. It was just like him to get right back up and try again.

"I was wrong," he continued.

"Obviously," she teased.

"I mean, about the heart. There was no heartbeat, I thought," he nodded, demanding that she follow. She nodded back and he continued, "but what were the intervals? I was looking for the normal range, say sixty to a hundred beats per minute. Of course, I heard nothing. Maybe I listened for twenty seconds, maybe, at most a minute. I heard nothing. Does it follow he's dead?"

"Clearly, he's not."

"Clearly," Robert looked sheepish. He stood up and paced the dark hallway. The dogs looked up from their wicker beds and listened in. "So what does the heart do? Harvey is clear on this, it pumps the blood around the body."

Katherine found her thoughts wandering back to Valentine. She didn't need a lecture on Harvey at this hour.

"Sorry sis, I'm getting to my conclusion," he put his drink down beside her and added gesticulations to his lecture, "What is the first prerequisite of a working pump?"

She shrugged. He was just exercising his theories aloud now and didn't need her input. She was tired.

"A medium!" he announced, "something to pump. It's what our patient lacks – he needs blood."

He had her attention again. He was making some sense but the direction concerned her.

"He lost so much blood through the wounds that the heart had very little to do, a beat here, a beat there. Sufficient to sustain life in his case – thanks to his obvious strength. So, the treatment is obvious – we give him blood!"

"We?" she stood up.

"Well, me, I suppose."

"We spoon it to him like soup, I suppose?"

He looked confused – his sister was making an elementary mistake, "no, of course, not – that's the digestive system – there's really no connect..."

"Robert!" she shushed him, "we're in the middle of a war, in the West of Ireland. You're the one who says you don't have the tools to experiment here. Yet, you wish to try your untried theories on a living man?"

"To save his life," her brother responded.

She fell silent.

"Sister, dear. He is alive tonight but do you really believe stew and a warm bed will fix him? It's just a matter of time before he dies from those wounds."

He hadn't seen Valentine's progress, she remembered, "the wounds, they... there's been a strange improvement."

They were interrupted by a loud crash. They rushed to the kitchen. When they got there, they found Valentine lying on the flagstone floor. He was unconscious again. Mrs Kinnerk hurried in carrying blankets a moment later. She opened her mouth to apologise for her absence but Katherine cut across her and spoke first, "Mrs Kinnerk, call your husband and tell him we'll need a few men to carry our patient to bed."

"I have a room ready," she answered.

Robert knelt beside him and checked that he hadn't cut himself. It seemed pointless to check any other signs.

Katherine knelt beside her brother and directed his gaze to the pre-existing wounds.

"You're right, it looks like weeks, not hours have passed since we last saw them." He looked at her seriously, "yet he has collapsed back into the state in which I buried him. I still say he'll die unless we replace the lost blood."

She nodded. He may be right, she thought. For tonight, she'd prescribe a warm bed and rest.

***

Including servants' quarters, there were eight bedrooms in Manwood. It was the smallest of the Boyle's properties and least loved but Robert and Katherine's father, the Earl of Cork, felt it had potential. He was pushing west. Ireland was ripe for exploitation. The Earl, Richard Boyle, was neither a political nor a military mover but he'd successfully rode the coattails of the English annexation of Ireland. Now, he was one of the richest men in the country. Manwood was a further step west. But it flooded. It was Robert's job to drain the estate so it could live up to its potential. Richard set his son this task and Robert enlisted Katherine. Unfortunately, they were out of the gate too quickly. Military conquest followed rather than preceded them so they'd been trapped in the house since Spring.

It was the Earl of Cork who looked down on Valentine in the small guest room on the eastern corner of the house. There were other paintings in the richly decorated guest room but the Earl took pride of place above the fireplace opposite the bed. The gaze was not returned. Valentine's eyes remained closed. Despite the warm golden sunrise and the rich red tones of the bedroom's decor, he appeared as pale as he had when lying by the river the previous morning. Presently, this lifeless tableau was enlivened by the arrival of Robert and Katherine. They had dressed and said their prayers but had not yet eaten.

Robert skipped through a quick check-up of the patient. He anticipated – and found – no signs of life. He then stepped back to let his sister examine him. Katherine followed up by feeling his forehead and cheek then brushing away some dirt which still clung to his hair.

"If I didn't know better, I'd bury him again," Robert said.

Katherine just nodded in reply.

They watched their patient in silence for a minute then Robert announced, "Well I, for one, intend to have a rather large breakfast."

Katherine was briefly confused by her brother's sudden interest in his appetite till she understood the subtext.

She stared at Valentine's as she answered, "You're going through with it? The blood exchange?"

"I believe it will work."

"And if it fails?"

"Frankly, the risk is all on his side. I'll give him a pint of my blood. I can spare that. It'll be a simple incision in my radial artery. The blood will be drawn by gravity so it can be controlled and stopped at any time. I'm a good clotter so I face no risk."

"But we've no flexible pipe. Nothing suitable, I mean."

"Ah, but we do, just arrived from Hartlib yesterday."

Katherine turned around, looking angry.

Her brother was startled, "what?"

She took a deep breath before answering him, "this is your scientific method, is it?"

He still looked confused.

"As soon as you get a new toy, you must play with it. If you'd received a microscope I suppose you'd be examining his saliva for animalcules?"

She had a point. He had no answer. Seizing the upper hand, she continued, "and what of the risk to him?"

"I cannot say. Willis did some work like this, as did Harvey, of course, with mixed results. I heard Louis Quatorze received blood successfully and Pope Innocent allegedly received the blood of three young boys. The Pope survived... though the boys died," he gave his sister a mischievous look, "perhaps it works best on papists?"

She smiled despite herself.

"I'll need your help, sis."

***

By mid-afternoon, they were ready to go. Rather than shift the big man to the laboratory, Robert moved his equipment up to the guest room. They did however move him to the floor. He need-ed to be lower than his donor. Valentine remained unconscious throughout. He was now wearing clean woollen breeches and a linen shirt belonging to the butler and looked reasonably comfortable on a Turkish rug with a pillow under his head. Mr Kinnerk made sure a hot fire was blazing in the hearth and lit a dozen candles in anticipation of a long night. Robert spent much of the morning stretched out on the bed, grazing on cheese and cold meats while re-reading Harvey and Vesalius. Katherine swapped texts with her brother every so often and took charge of the logistics. The piping that Hartlib had sent was relatively short so the patients had to be positioned close together but with a sufficient drop to stimulate the blood flow from Robert's artery to Valentine's vein. To this end, she'd instructed her brother to stay on the bed while she set up the equipment. The two men finished in a 'v' shape, head to head, allowing Katherine access to the precarious arrangement of pipes which would unite their blood flow.

While Katherine worked on the necessary tools, Robert scribbled calculations into a notebook. He figured on no more than fifteen minutes for the transfer of a pint of blood but they planned to second-guess this by watching Valentine's vital signs. On the mantelpiece, Robert set up a candle clock – a fast-burning candle delineated with five-minute markings – to time the procedure. Of course, one pint was not what the man needed, rather it's all Robert felt he could donate in a sitting. If they saw benefits, they could always try again the next day. Katherine was impressed by her brother's resolve but she was worried. He was determined to play donor even though he was not physically suited to the role.

As the candles took over from the daylight, Katherine took a small sharp blade and made a neat slice into the Basilic vein close to Valentine's elbow. There was a dribble of blood before she inserted the tube at the lower end of her apparatus. She tied this in place with a clean linen bandage and then turned to her brother. Robert had stripped to the waist. There was no periwig and, like Katherine, he'd tied his hair back in a ponytail. He looked twelve again, she thought.

She cleaned the knife she'd used on Valentine and knelt close to her brother. He offered his arm to her. They'd traced the right spot in ink so she didn't need to search. Before she made the incision, she looked at her brother and tried to give him a reassuring smile. Then she made the cut. The blood flowed liberally. She worked quickly to open the hole and insert the tube. As she did, he stifled a groan but nodded that she continue. She quickly set about wrapping the wrist tightly with a bandage. The bandage quickly turned red but she added another tighter layer till she was happy that the blood was entirely flowing down the tube. Robert leaned over the edge of the bed and imagined he could trace the flow of blood down to the man below. Katherine turned and noted the height of the candle clock. They timed the start of the operation to coincide with the first of five marks. They planned to go no further than three. The first positive sign was a faint blotting around Valentine's bandaged arm. The blood was travelling down the tube, at least.

They waited in silence. A shower of rain started tapping on the glass and the fire hissed as stray droplets found their way down the chimney. They heard footsteps in the gallery and the clinking of china as Mrs Kinnerk approached with an evening snack. The household staff had been working in silent disapproval all day. They were used to their masters' eccentricities but there was something transgressive even diabolical about this adventure. Nevertheless, Mrs Kinnerk found comfort in meeting every problem with a meal so she made sure the siblings were well-fed all day. Katherine rose to intercept her, took the tray and sent her away with thanks. She returned to the bed, handed her brother a slice of bread and knelt down again. She looked at Valentine. Of course, in the candlelight, his skin looked warmer but she maintained discipline and made no attempt to check for signs of life. This was a long game.

When the candle passed the first mark, Katherine first checked her brother. His pulse was strong, his temperature fine and he was no paler than before. Only then did she check the patient. He was cold, there was still no evidence of either breath or heartbeat. She made a report to Robert. They had no reason to expect anything different but privately they had hoped for a radical outcome from a radical treatment.

As Robert finished his crust of bread he suddenly turned to his sister and said, "would you call this a resurrection, sis?"

She looked up wearily and then back at Valentine in the hope the unconscious man would save her from her brother's conversation. Finally, she answered, "Blasphemy perhaps. But not resurrection. The man's not dead. That was your mistake remember? He's not Lazarus... and you're not Jesus."

Robert smiled at the comparison and replied, "Yes, I always pictured Lazarus as a smaller fellow."

She tried to draw a line under the conversation by adding, "besides, you haven't resurrected anyone yet."

He was staring across at the portrait of their father, happily developing a new theory, "I mean, when we talk of miracles, why should they be incompatible with nature, why not just... nature operating beyond the cusp of our understanding and therefore, ultimately... knowable." He looked at his sister for validation.

"I have a theory for you," she said, "blood loss causes lunacy."

"No, that's the moon..." he trailed off.

Katherine glanced at the candle and noticed the second mark had passed. She checked the bandages to confirm that the blood flow was contained then stood up and checked her brother. He was colder. She pulled a blanket over him, leaving his right arm free. He continued daydreaming. Then she checked Valentine. Nothing. Yet the blood was going somewhere. Patience, she told herself.

She was getting cramped. She rose to stretch her legs and walked over to the window. The rain had stopped and the clouds were breaking up. The sun had fully set and the landscape had turned uniformly blue. She could make out the pier where she'd found Valentine and she considered for the first time how he must have climbed onto that pier before collapsing. He hadn't just floated down the river, he'd swam. There was strength in that man, though it waxed and waned. She turned around and looked at him. The warm light of the room gave him a healthy complexion now. Was it just an illusion? She crossed and knelt beside him. Even his expression seemed different. The neutral, statuesque set of his features which she'd studied in detail yesterday now had a warmer look of contentment. Again, it must be the light, she told herself. The silence was affecting her imagination. Silence. Robert was quiet. She looked over. His eyes were closed. She called quietly but sharply, "Robert."

He remained unconscious. Again, louder, "Robert!"

Despite the warm light, he looked pale. She stood, leaned over him and gave him a gentle shake – again calling his name.

He was out cold. We're done here, she thought. She pulled the tube from her brother's arm. Blood sprayed onto the bedsheets. She worked quickly to bandage the wound looking up at her brother's face and calling his name occasionally to check for consciousness. His eyes remained shut.

Had she let the time slip? She glanced at the mantelpiece. The candle was only just reaching the third mark. Beside the candle, a little pewter flask she recognised. "The harts horn!" She grabbed the flask, opened it and poured a generous handful of salt crystals into her hand. She shoved them under her brother's nose. His whole body spasmed as he inhaled the astringent substance. He rolled away from her and started coughing.

"Robert?" she cried, hoping she hadn't made him sick.

"Is he alright?"

She turned and looked down. Valentine was looking up at her.

24.

As they walked away from the cathedral, Skerret turned to Manning and said, "Why did you rescue me?" There was no hint of gratitude. Any chance he might have warmed to the wolf-hunter was dashed by Manning's insistence on leading him down the street by the noose still dangling from his neck.

"I need you to lead me to your mother," Manning replied.

"Ah... you heard about her?" Skerret was curious.

"Yes, from Mary," he said by way of explanation.

"She said your mother cures werewolves. Do you think she can help me?"

Skerret had no clue but, if his freedom depended on it, "Yes, I suppose."

"So where is she?"

Skerret hesitated. He'd have to lead this Sasanach in the right direction but there was no need to completely reveal his hand, "North of Ennis. We could be there by tomorrow afternoon."

That was contested country, Manning remembered, "Into the fire, then."

"That's where you'll find the Catholics," Skerret replied.

They returned briefly to King John's Castle to collect Manning's things. Peeter was still minding his clothes, boots and equipment as well as Samson. The castle was largely deserted as most of the soldiers had been instructed to march out to attend Ireton's funeral. Manning was glad to find that the prison tower was similarly empty. He sensed that he was as much a prisoner as Skerret had been and that it was best to keep a low profile. Fortunately, there was no sign of either Worsley or Peeter. Finally, a servant girl they met in the bailey suggested they try the beach west of Thomond Bridge where Peeter liked to fish. A few minutes later they were at the little strand and Samson came bounding over to greet Manning. He tipped the boy with the last pennies in his possession and turned his thoughts to financing the journey into County Clare. He considered selling Samson but settled on selling the arquebus. He could replace the weapon, he figured, but never the dog. His eagerness cost him. A soldier he met on the road walked away smiling with the weapon while Manning pocketed a measly fifteen shillings in return. It would have to do.

Once they'd stopped at the bakery and stocked up on biscuits for the road, they set out. Getting across the Thomond Bridge and onto the Galway road was Manning's first concern. But there was such an exodus of Catholic refugees heading for Galway that the sentries didn't question the appearance of a Parliamentarian soldier with an Irish prisoner. It was clear which side he was on.

They walked silently for the rest of the morning. Once out of Limerick, they made good time. The road followed a flat plain with the Shannon to the left and steeper bog-land and forest to the right. They found themselves continuously overtaking refugees burdened with their worldly belongings, their health broken by the siege. At Coonagh they briefly joined a group struggling to ford one of the Shannon's many tributaries. The catholic refugees looked askance at Manning and his captive but said nothing and happily accepted his assistance as they crossed the stream. It wasn't clear which army ruled this land so nobody wanted a fight. At Cratloe, the road busied again as they climbed a steep hill. Here the forest sheltered both sides of the road and there was an ominous silence as everyone recognised what an ideal ambush spot they were in. But they passed without incident.

There was no conversation but captor and captive were taking a more pragmatic attitude than they had previously. When Skerret requested food, Manning obliged. The wolf-hunter had left the noose hanging around the priest's neck but he took hold of it only when they met English soldiers. As they approached Bunratty, which was firmly in Parliament's hands, many of the refugees left the road rather than face the scrutiny of the garrison. Manning pressed on, taking up Skerret's noose so that, as he crossed the bridge, both Samson and Skerret were on a leash. The pull of the dog on his right arm was causing his injury to burn with pain. He had taken its healing for granted, he realised. But the castle was quiet and the road clear. As they passed, they could see bodies hanging from the castle walls. They weren't soldiers. Stealing livestock was the preferred tactic of warfare out here. In this country, allegiances were tribal rather than political or religious. But as the winds of war now blew decisively for Parliament, old feuds were being settled with ruthless finality.

By the time they approached Latoon, the evening was settling in. Skerret indicated that they were little more than halfway so they started looking for shelter for the night. There was a small force of Parliamentarians controlling nearby Dromoland Castle so Manning felt it was a good place to stop. He was more tired than he'd like to admit. He spied a large farmhouse beside a ford over yet another stream and decided to inquire after accommodation. The owner was a committed Parliamentarian by the name of Coppinger. He was barrel-chested with oversized horsey teeth which he was failing to hide under an unkempt moustache. He wore a sword in his belt. He welcomed Manning's money if not his company. His farm had been attacked and he was anxious to find a way to pay for repairs.

He was a blacksmith as well as a farmer and the collection of buildings by the river's edge suggested he had once enjoyed a healthy income. They were now in a poor state. As they walked around, they could see a young red-haired man fixing the fire-damaged roof of the farmhouse but the barn and the woodshed were in bits. A few children watched them from inside the shell of the burned-out barn. He led them to the last intact building – his forge.

"Where are you headed?" he asked as he ushered them into the small dark space. They looked around. The forge was almost devoid of blacksmith's tools. He'd been robbed as well as burned out. The fire was burning, however, and there were a couple of straw beds close by. The smith must have been regularly renting the space as accommodation now that he'd lost the tools of his trade.

"A few miles north of Ennis," Manning answered.

Skerret surprised them both by adding, "Inchicronan."

It was the first time Manning had heard the name of their final destination.

Coppinger spat, "Delahoyde country! The filth who stole my cattle and burned my property." He glared at Manning, "I hope you're not in league with this papist."

Manning had to work fast to reassure the smith, "No! This rogue is my prisoner," he smacked Skerret on the back of the head and added, "He'll be leading me to a nest of papists once I meet my reinforcements in Ennis."

"They're a treacherous breed alright," Coppinger nodded, digesting the story but still unconvinced. "Aye, well, you can stay the night but be off tomorrow. I have more to do than keep an eye on you." He returned to his house to organise food and drink for them.

Manning sat down on the raised stone edge around the warm hearth and scolded Skerret, "why did you tell this blacksmith we're going to Inchicronan when you wouldn't tell me?" He was aching all over and hoped the priest was as just as sore.

Skerret remained standing and rubbed his head. He studied the wolf-hunter with curiosity, then answered, "I just wanted to know what way the wind was blowing around here. The last letter I had from my mother said she was under the protection of an Oliver Delahoyde in Inchicronan. Sounds like they're still in charge. You'll need to change your tactics once we get there."

Manning started sweating but he found it easier to stay put than get up. He looked up and nodded. The priest's thinking was sound but his advice was a little too good. Skerret had brought him this far because he had to. They were fast reaching the point where it was in the priest's best interests to betray his captor. Best to do that in Confederate territory. Manning would need to be careful tomorrow.

Tonight he could not think beyond food and rest.

The smith returned with two generous portions of a pottage rich in barley, fresh brown bread, a large jug of ale and a collection of bones for Samson. Manning had remained rooted to the fireplace but had worked up the energy to remove his coat.

The smith noticed his bandaged arm and commented, "you saw action in Limerick?"

"After a fashion," Manning replied.

"Can you manage this one?" he cocked his head towards Skerret.

"I'll tie him up. He'll be fine," Manning said.

"You look weak," the smith added.

"I'm strong enough," he pointed at the priest, "you can see what happened the last time he tried to escape."

The smith studied Skerret's bruised face for the first time. He was met with an icy stare. He broke off with a forced laugh, "Cheer up, priest. You had no looks to lose!"

When the smith left, the travellers ate and drank their fill and prepared for bed in silence. The only sound apart from the fire was the gurgling of the shallow river beside them. The little forge was draughty and not suited to sleep but the fire was warm and their bodies primed for rest. Rather than tie Skerret to anything, Manning decided to tie the end of the noose around his own wrist. This saved him from having to talk to Skerret and he fancied it a more foolproof security measure. When he was done, he lay back and fell asleep in seconds.

But his sleep was restless. In his dreams that night, he was being chased in the darkness. He was running uphill. A snarling beast drew closer and closer. He shed his clothes to ease his struggle but the savage growling grew nearer. He raced through long grass which became more and more water-logged till he was struggling even to lift his feet. Finally, he crested the hill and saw a ruined abbey framed by a full moon. He looked back. Red eyes followed close behind. He stumbled into the grounds of the broken church. The growling had quietened to that low throaty rumble before the strike. Where was it coming from? The sound echoed around the stones. A giant shadow crossed the moonlit wall. Perhaps he could sneak away. He climbed through a hole into the graveyard. It was thick with ancient headstones. He struggled to find his footing. Limestone slabs shifted like crockery under his boots. From the cavernous church, the beast responded with a growl. He sped up but the stones were too thick. The edge of a broken monument slashed his leg. He spied a grassy gap, stepped heavily onto it but the ground gave way. Wood splintered, he fell forward into a grave. Earth piled in behind him. He flapped his arms in the darkness, wiping straw from his face. Straw. Suddenly, he was wide awake. The room glowed red from the fire. Manning felt a sting of embarrassment. He looked across expecting to see Skerret's mocking grin. But his prisoner was gone.

He tried to get up but a stabbing pain caused his right arm to collapse beneath him. He groaned as he fell back. Sweat broke on his forehead. Samson looked over and whimpered in sympathy. The dog had just been eating from Skerret's bowl of pottage. The priest must have saved his dinner to distract the dog. Manning remembered the rope. He lifted his wrist. The rope was still there. He gathered it up. The end had been methodically untangled. The priest had undone the hangman's knot.

There were footsteps outside. Might Skerret still be close by? Manning carefully raised himself up and reached for his sword. Before he got there, the door opened and the room lit up.

Coppinger entered, carrying an oil lamp. He looked at Manning with mock disapproval, "You need to be more careful with your belongings," he said. He stepped further into the forge. Skerret followed, looking depressed. Even in the dark, Manning could see fresh injuries to his face. His neck was purple from where the noose had been. The young, red-haired man Manning had seen on the roof earlier followed. He held a sword and looked out of breath but delighted with himself.

Coppinger crouched down to Manning's level. He picked up the wolf-hunter's coat and started going through the pockets, "now, as a favour, we caught this fellow for you. But we both know a priest is worth a lot of money. So let's say, you offer us some compensation." He found Manning's money. The wolf-hunter cursed silently. Why hadn't he hidden the silver in Samson's collar?

He showed the coins to Manning and said, "I'll take this. You'll be well recompensed in Ennis. At least now I'm sure you're not in league with the Delahoydes," he laughed and the redhead followed suit. He lifted the end of the rope. "I'll even tie him up properly for you this time."

25.

"How do you feel?" Katherine knelt down beside Valentine and felt his forehead.

"Weak."

"But you're awake."

"Thanks to you," he smiled warmly at her.

"And me." Robert popped his head over the edge of the bed and crowded the space.

"Thank you... also," Valentine said to Robert, his tone slightly more formal.

Katherine and Valentine smiled patiently at Robert till he grew uncomfortable. The young scientist was pale and seemed visibly thinner as though he'd lost enough blood to shrink.

"Well, I suppose I should have some soup or something," he said and rolled away so he could dress. Considering that he was the one who had just expended his own blood, he felt slightly excluded. I know where I'm not wanted, he thought, as he dressed. Once he had his shirt and shoes on he returned to the side of the bed and looked disapprovingly at the situation, "I'll get Colman and a few of the hands to lift you back into bed. And you'll want something to eat, too."

Valentine thanked him. Katherine waited till her brother had left the room before she continued talking, "Do you know where you are?"

He shook his head but then offered, "I know you're Katherine."

She was pleased he remembered, "Yes. And that was my brother Robert. You're in our house, Manwood. Four miles from Limerick."

"Limerick..." he whispered.

"Is that your home?"

"No."

Katherine was determined to find out more. "You told me your name is Valentine. You didn't say your last name?"

He hesitated, realised he owed her the courtesy, then answered, "Valentine D'Arcy. I'm from Galway."

"Welcome to our home, Valentine."

He tried to move and managed to lift his head a little. He looked to the window. Katherine noticed his face darken.

"Can you close the curtains?" he asked.

She went to the window. The night had dried up nicely. The clouds had cleared and a crescent moon lit up the garden. It seemed a shame to block it out but her patient must be feeling cold. She closed the curtains and turned around.

"There, better?"

He nodded. There was a slightly awkward silence because the room suddenly seemed very dark. Valentine realised his request had been odd and Katherine grew conscious that she had pressed him for his surname without offering hers.

She skirted the issue, "I'll light some more candles." She picked up the clock candle on the mantelpiece and held it beside the portrait of her father, "that's my father, Richard Boyle. Robert and I are working on improving the estate for him." She circled the room adding a few more flames to the candelabras.

"We've been stuck here... with the war..." She glanced back as she realised how insignificant their suffering had been. How much had this man lost thanks to the war, she wondered. "I'm sorry. It's not much of a complaint."

"What work do you do for your father?" Valentine had become aware of the elaborate mechanism of pipes and stands between him and the bed.

Katherine returned to his side, "drainage," she said.

He smiled, slightly perplexed, "you didn't drain me, I hope?"

She laughed, "oh no, the opposite! we gave you Robert's blood."

His face fell. He was horrified but he said nothing. Katherine saw his expression but misunderstood. She was used to the horror that their science experiments provoked. It made sense that such a violation should upset him. Still, they had brought him back from the brink of death. She felt no need to apologise. Deep down though, his reaction disappointed her. She was growing to like this mysterious stranger. She liked the way he enquired after her work. He seemed to take it in his stride that she was educated and employable. That was uncommon. She liked him for other reasons too. So, she told herself, if he didn't want to exchange his blood with a stranger, that didn't make him a reactionary.

He was still hooked up to the apparatus, she remembered, "Let me free you from this," she said. She carefully removed the tube at his elbow and bandaged his arm. "I'm sure this all seems very unorthodox but, if you were going to experience side effects, it would have happened by now. There's no need to worry." There was little scientific basis for this but she was experienced enough to understand the value of a good bedside manner.

Valentine had regained his composure but his tone was still foreboding when he answered, "It wasn't my own welfare that concerned me, but your brother's."

Katherine stopped what she was doing and looked at him. He was going to have to explain himself. But she wasn't going to rush him. He was as weak and, no doubt, his mind was as broken as his body. Once he'd recovered, she'd interrogate him properly. She stood up and brushed down her skirt. She hovered for a moment. There was one thing she wanted to ask now, "Do you have family you'd like me to write to? I can't make any promises... the post's not the best. But I could try."

"No, thank you."

She was disappointed. Perhaps he already felt too indebted to ask further favours. But she was too curious to leave it there. Who might he contact, she wondered? She prompted him again, "It's no trouble. Perhaps there's someone in Limerick? We found you on the river bank. We guessed you came downstream."

This reminder of his arrival made him think quietly for a minute. Eventually, he answered, "No, there's no one."

There was a knock at the door. Colman stood there, accompanied by two young farm hands. Their faces were hungry with curiosity.

***

Katherine found her brother in the laboratory. The room was still a mess of open boxes and packing straw. The fireplace was dark. Blue moonlight outlined the dark recesses of the room while Robert worked in the small yellow glow from the solitary candle on his desk. He was writing a letter. Beside him were the remains of his supper. Katherine was anxious to thank him for reviving Valentine. He'd been clever and brave and she was proud of him.

She was still his sister though, so she wasn't going to swamp him with praise, "Let me guess, you're already writing a triumphant account of your achievements to Tom Willis?" she said mockingly.

When he looked up, his expression was more serious than she'd expected, "not at all. I'm writing to the army in Limerick."

Katherine was taken aback. "The army, why?"

"It's time we found out who our guest is. He floated down from Limerick. He looks like a Confederate. He might be dangerous."

"I know who he is," she protested, "his name's Valentine D'Arcy. He's from Galway. And he's not dangerous. He's ill."

Robert put down his quill, folded his arms and attempted to look patriarchal. "Still, he's getting better. I expect he's just weak. We can't harbour tories, fix them up and send them on their way with a pat on the back."

Katherine looked at her brother. He was doing the 'man of the house' quite well. His self-confidence existed in a flux as changeable as the Irish weather. Right now, he was on a high and seemed every inch the son of an Earl. He never wore it thin, though, and for that she loved him.

"You're concerned about his welfare," he said, "I understand. I wouldn't want to do anything to put him in danger... I'm simply making an enquiry." He let out a short laugh, "I really don't know how to ask them, 'have you recently shot a man who refused to die? I think we might have him'."

She failed to smile.

He softened, "Very well. I'll say, on the night of November fifth, a man washed up – I won't say we still have him – I'll just ask if they've lost anybody... significant."

"And if they come for him?"

"If they come for him, I suppose they'll have good reason to."

"Because this war has been fought on such honest terms to date?"

She had a point. He conceded further, "if they come for him, we'll use our discretion – though by then, I'm afraid, it might be too late to resist."

Katherine wasn't satisfied but she decided not to press the issue. Robert was being reasonable. If Valentine was a combatant, he was a Confederate. Like her brother, Katherine liked to deal straight with people. She hated intrigue. It wasn't just pragmatic to inform on Valentine – it was the law. So, let Robert write his letter. The post was slow. Valentine had plenty of time to recover and Katherine herself would judge how quickly they could expect a response from Limerick and how early she would need to warn Valentine to run.

26.

After a dinner of game pie and a very large goblet of wine, Katherine prepared for bed. The house seemed very quiet. She'd eaten in the dining room alone – save for a book – and had heard no other sound apart from Mrs Kinnerk's routine passage through the hall and the dogs' inevitable barking. But she had no intention of sleeping. She'd briefed the servants to check in on Valentine regularly until it was only fair to release them to bed. She planned to take the night shift. She didn't want him slipping back into the deathly state from which he'd just emerged. She went to her room for an hour and rested but took care to stay awake.

She knew Robert wouldn't stay in the laboratory for long without a fire. As she lay reading, she heard him pass by her room. When he didn't call in to say goodnight, she remembered she'd failed to thank him for what he'd done for Valentine. She'd been distracted by his letter to Limerick and had forgotten. And now, she feared, there was tension between them.

At around eleven, she got up, tied her hair back up, tucked it under a cap and wrapped herself well in a dressing gown. She checked her appearance carefully, telling herself that she was attending to a strange man alone at night and that modesty demanded care. Still, the lace cap was her finest and the dressing gown was silk.

Satisfied, she relieved the servant on duty and made her way to Valentine's room.

Entering from the dark, moonlit gallery, Katherine noticed the room seemed brighter than before and she was conscious, for the first time, how luxurious it was. She wondered if Valentine was used to such surroundings. She found him sitting up, wide awake, looking bored. His face lit up when he saw her.

"I thought you were asleep," he said.

"No. I've let the staff go to bed. I thought I'd watch over you. Are you not tired?"

"No. I slept long enough."

There was a book open on the bed in front of him. His body was tightly tucked under the bedclothes but his arms were free.

"You're well enough to read?" Katherine asked.

He lifted a hand from the wrist up, "a little. Kinnerk was good enough to leave me a book but I don't really feel like it..."

Katherine was impressed, "But you're getting better."

"Yes, I am."

She crossed the room to a sideboard and opened the top drawer. From it, she retrieved a pack of playing cards and a cribbage board.

"I was planning to read while you slept but if you're awake, perhaps we could keep each other company?"

"I'd like that."

She pulled a seat close to his bedside and sat down. She invited him to cut the cards, then she cut and, revealing the lowest card, she started to deal. He watched her expertly set up the hand and realised this was a favourite pastime of hers. "You should know I've no money to wager if I lose," he said.

"You don't suppose we gamble in this house?" she answered with mock indignation.

"You don't play for any stakes?"

"Well, when I was young, I used to play with my sister, Mary. We'd play for secrets and dares..."

"...and with Robert?"

"No. That's not really a game to play with brothers."

"...maybe with your husband?"

The question took her by surprise. She hadn't talked about her family. Someone had, she supposed. She tried to take it in her stride. "No. We don't play cards," she said simply.

Valentine sensed he'd unsettled her so he offered a story of his own, "I played a lot in Spain. Not cribbage, something similar. There was little else to do."

She was glad of the shift in conversation, "you lived in Spain? Tell me about that," she said.

He was happy to talk about it. His time in Spain was a distant memory and safely removed from the evil turn his life had taken since his return to Ireland.

"I was a soldier for a while in the army of King Philip. My father arranged it. My family imports wine from Santander so we have many connections there. I travelled all over. I never saw action, as such. The war with the French had run its course by the time I arrived. My duties were not glorious. We spent three months in Galicia just closing brothels! Not really what my father had in mind. I was happy though... for a while. I ate well, drank too much and I enjoyed the sunshine. But the army lost its charm eventually. I needed something more meaningful. When the army released me, I followed the pilgrim's trail to Santiago De Compostela. That was something! I saw eight thousand pilgrims line the street there on Saint James' Feast Day, everyone holding a candle. The sound of such a choir..." he paused and seemed to remember something, "you probably don't approve. I'm having a moment of Popish ecstasy."

"Please... continue. True faith, in any creed, is beautiful."

"I make no pretence to piety but that night, I was moved."

"Go!"

Valentine was confused till he realised Katherine was advancing the card game. It was his turn to play. He turned a card and continued talking, "After that, I vowed to use my time more wisely. I travelled to Salamanca and studied law for a time. This might have been my calling. But, the war came to Ireland and I was needed. My brother had died."

"I'm sorry."

A faraway look appeared in Valentine's eyes.

"You were close to your brother?"

"Donal? Not especially. He was older, the favourite. The business should have been his but he joined the Confederates. He died in Clonmel."

"So... recently."

"Yes," Valentine grew nervous. He was happy to keep the reminiscing in Spain. He did not wish to talk of Ireland.

"What brought you to Limerick?"

"I think that's thirty-one," he said. He showed his last card. He'd won his first hand. Katherine counted carefully and conceded defeat. As she moved pegs on the board to keep score, Valentine attempted to change the conversation, "I've won a hand; you owe me a secret."

She gave him a stern look, "too bold, Mister D'Arcy. Perhaps when you're straight with me, I'll play your game. You deal."

That silenced him. He slowly lifted the cards and started to deal a new hand. His face showed some discomfort but she was happy to see him exercise. As he worked, she decided to question him with a little more subtlety, "so you're a wine merchant? Perhaps we can do business. Our cellar here had become very depleted. You were in Limerick on business?"

He glanced up, then back at the cards, "I no longer work for my father."

She dropped the line of questions and they played quietly for a while. "One point for the last card," Katherine said, when he made a mistake with the scoring.

"You play often?"

"I do, when I can get Robert to oblige. There's not much to do in this house. We hadn't planned to stay here so long."

"Where is home for you?"

"London, I suppose. Now."

"Your children are there?"

"Yes, the girls."

"And your son is in Cork?"

Curse the Kinnerks for their loose tongues, she thought. Can I have no privacy? "Yes. Your turn," she answered coolly.

It was his turn to count the crib but she might equally have been prompting him to divulge some personal information of his own. He could take her meaning either way. He failed to take the hint. He added his score from the crib and found he'd just lost the hand. "Your deal," he said.

She dealt and they played in silence. A politely competitive hush descended and the hand progressed quickly as one attempted to rush the other into forgetting to add a pair or a run to the pegging play. They were both quite alert however and neither missed a trick. When Katherine added her crib count to the final scores, they found Valentine had won by two points.

"You liar," she said.

He looked up, slightly worried, then smiled, "I didn't say I was a novice. I simply admired your skill at the deal. Anyway, I wouldn't give up hope just yet."

"That's what the card sharp always tells his victim," she answered. Valentine picked up the cards and she noticed he dealt much faster this time. She wondered whether his recovery was progressing that quickly or had he just played the invalid the first time around.

"Who taught you to play?" she asked.

He knew what she was doing. She was trying to get to know him. He felt torn. He wanted to open his heart to her. He wanted to get closer. Yes, he'd found out that she was married. Kinnerk had spat out the name of some husband in England. Four living children were also mentioned. She must be ten years older than me, he thought. But right now, sitting by his bed, she looked small and pale like a child and Valentine felt ancient beside her. Perhaps he should care that she was married, that he was being watched by her father's portrait, that her brother lay next door with a dozen servants on call. No, none of those things mattered. But something did – the curse.

A log split in the fire and collapsed with a wheeze and crackle of sparks.

"Well?" Katherine wore a curious smile.

"I'm sorry. Please cut."

So, I'm not going to get any answers, she thought. She cut the deck and quietly decided, I'll beat him, at least.

She won the next three hands. They spoke little. The night from there on was punctuated by the sounds of wind against the glass, wood crackling in the fireplace and cards slipping deftly in and out of practised hands. Valentine won the sixth hand. It was a fluke – by this time he was missing tricks and he was relying on her to keep score. She was pleased to see him return to a natural state of tiredness but she was also sorry their conversation had fizzled. There was something holding him back. He knew she was married; was it scruples kept him at a distance? She should admire him for it. But she needed no more cause to admire the man. She believed there was something else keeping his passion bottled up. Perhaps it's me, she thought. Well, if he wanted to know her secrets, she'd tell him. Then she'd know what he thought of her.

"You've won the hand," she announced, "perhaps now you've earned a secret." She instantly regretted speaking. She couldn't look at him so she picked up the cards and started to shuffle. But she persevered, "Someone told you about my family. Don't worry, I'm not angry about that. I suppose it isn't much of a secret, after all," she smiled at the irony, "Perhaps, they also told you...", she dealt a new hand to distract herself, "...my youngest child turned ten last winter... so it's been years since their father, Arthur, has been in my life. Do you understand?" She felt the heat bloom in her cheeks as she waited for an answer. She had exposed herself too much. Was it embarrassment that stopped his tongue? She looked up, steeling herself for disappointment.

But the man was simply asleep. She smiled and stood up. His nose made a faint whistle. She had no excuse to check his breathing yet she leaned in and held her cheek above his mouth till his warm breath told her she could go to bed.

27.

Skerret and Manning left early the next morning. The prisoner had spent the rest of the night on his side, arms tied behind his back, legs bound at the ankles. Manning took his dagger to the two knots and left the pieces of rope where they fell. They were heading into Confederate country so he could no longer act like Skerret's master.

Most of the blacksmith's household was still asleep as they left. The young man who'd caught Skerret was still on sentry duty outside the farmhouse door. He saluted Manning but the wolf-hunter ignored him. Though they'd done him a favour by preventing the priest's escape, the smith had also robbed him. He had no money to pay for breakfast and certainly didn't relish the company. He imagined Skerret felt the same way. He searched his bag and found they still had a few biscuits from the bakery in Limerick. Before they left, they climbed down to the river to fill up with water. Skerret and Samson hopped down easily but Manning struggled with the climb. He was aching all over. He realised he was getting sicker.

Skerret seemed to notice as well. How long before he runs off, Manning wondered. And then, what chance I'll find his mother in Inchicronan? These thoughts preoccupied the wolf-hunter as they walked north. Almost without him noticing, they passed Clare

Castle, the last Parliamentarian stronghold they were certain of. They were in Confederate territory now and Manning became more alert. His Roundhead uniform was a liability from here on. Soon after, they saw Ennis in the distance. They kept the town on their left and kept walking. The direct path to Inchicronan was along the Galway road but Skerret said his mother was further west and if they followed a certain stream, it would lead straight to her. Manning was happy, reasoning that they'd also be less conspicuous. North of Ennis, they left the road and quickly found the little stream. The flat plain they'd started out on had become pockmarked with hills and rocky outcrops. They were on the outskirts of the Burren now – the great rocky desert which covered half the county. The forest, which had been on their right-hand side all the way from Limerick, had disappeared and, to their left, there was nothing taller than an occasional windswept blackthorn tree. The going was tougher and less direct but Manning sensed they must be close and his spirits rallied.

Samson was in his element. The great hound took to chasing butterflies through the yellow gorse that lined the stream. He leapt and barked in delight and Manning felt glad he had sold his musket instead of the dog.

The stream they'd been following opened into a small lake which Skerret recognised. "We're here," he said.

The lake was surrounded on three sides by high stony ground and sheltered enough to support a small dense wood. Skerret walked ahead of Manning and started circling the lake. The dog was well ahead of them, engaged in another pursuit when they heard him yelp with pain. They hurried towards the sound and met Samson retreating with his tail between his legs. Something behind the trees had hurt him. The wolf-hunter put him on the leash and drew his sword. They retraced the dog's steps. Safely under the protection of his master, Samson started to bark at his attacker.

"Cé tá ann?" a female voice.

"Mise," said Skerret, stepping out in front, "a mhamaí."

A figure appeared from behind a tree, a stone at the ready in her hand.

She wasn't what Manning had expected.

He had never thought about Skerret's background but, seeing his mother, and the contrast, he realised that the priest had always struck him as a member of the merchant class or the son of a wealthy artisan. The woman standing before them looked like a peasant. She had a thick head of grey hair which she wore loose and uncovered. She wore what looked like a man's shirt and doublet which, though well-fitting and clean, were old and bore the signs of many repairs. Her skirt went just beyond her knees revealing strong tanned calves and leathery bare feet. She was short like her son but her head was rounder with a wide mouth. But the pale grey eyes were a clear match for Skerret's. She was older than Manning had expected too.

"Cé hé sin?" she continued.

"Saighdiúir Sasanach, tá tinneas aisteach aige."

The language was unintelligible to Manning. Skerret's use of Gaelic surprised him, though everyone spoke it outside the cities. Dearbhla dropped the stone and walked towards them. Samson growled. She continued talking in Irish, gesturing at the dog and then behind her to a small brood of chickens emerging from the tree cover. She reached her son and Manning noticed a look of horror as she saw his injuries. She quickly composed herself and, though he couldn't understand the conversation, there was little warmth on display. She touched her son's face, but with the manner of a doctor, and then she squeezed his arm but even this gesture accompanied a criticism of either his weight or the state of his clothes.

She turned her attention to Manning. Skerret looked back and started a long explanation to his mother. She stared at the wolf-hunter till he grew uncomfortable. Then she approached. Samson growled. She reached into a pocket of her doublet and made a peace offering of some kind of snack to the dog. He ate greedily from her hand. He was so easily bought off, Manning thought.

Dearbhla switched to English, "The unlucky Roundhead."

***

Once she'd started speaking in English, she stuck to that language and spoke with a refinement and intelligence which belied her circumstances. She was a charming host and seemed to hold no prejudice against the English soldier. He was relieved on that account. She brought them to the far side of the lake where she made her home. It was a cave. Two great slabs of limestone met to form a hole in the side of the hill. She slept within but had constructed an awning at the entrance, under which there was a fire burning and two logs for seating. She was thoroughly unselfconscious as she showed them where she slept, stored food, used the privy and corralled the chickens and a couple of goats. She told her son where she sourced firewood and bid him gather an armful. He left, sulky as every child returned to the parental domain.

Dearbhla told Manning to sit in front of the fire while she prepared food. She started him with soup and followed up with the same fermented milk drink he'd been served in Tarbert. Manning was hungry and licked his bowl clean but he hoped she had stronger medicine than that. Once he was warm and his belly full, she asked him to remove his coat. She examined his arm and decided to replace the bandages. This she did with a practised technique which restored his confidence. She spoke throughout but not about his injuries or her treatment. She talked about flowers and cheese-making, the poetry of John Donne and the expertise of Venetian glass-makers. Indeed, her conversation was so indifferent to her own extraordinary situation, her son's adventures, the war or Manning's encounter with a werewolf that he felt obliged to direct the subject matter to the here and now.

"You must be proud of your son?" he ventured.

She was sitting beside him grinding herbs and seeds with a mortar and pestle. She looked sceptically at him, "don't be plamásing me with your high regard for Ambrose. I know you had him locked up."

Manning did his best to sound offended, "I saved him from the hangman's noose. I paid for his freedom!"

"Yes, you gave up your bounty on him and that's why he brought you here. And I suppose, if it hadn't been you, it would've been someone else. He put the price on his head when he took holy orders."

"You don't approve? Surely, he didn't have many choices... he can't have started out with much?" Manning found himself looking around at the Dearbhla's primitive homestead.

"We didn't always live like this. We had a nice house in Galway. Ambrose was raised in comfort. Our current circumstance..." she gestured at their surroundings, betraying a hint of dissatisfaction for the first time, "... was caused by the English invasion."

This silenced Manning. Dearbhla returned to grinding the mixture with renewed vigour. When she was happy she'd achieved the desired consistency, she transferred the paste to a small pot, added a spoonful of oil and started cooking the mixture over the fire.

He decided the change the subject, "What are you making?"

She stirred the contents of the pot as she answered, "You're sore and tired because of the dirt that got into your wound. This will solve that problem. Also, I'll give you a draught that'll numb the pain and help you sleep."

The wolf-hunter nodded. She seemed to know what she was doing, he thought. But doesn't every village have some old woman posing as a doctor? Was she more than that? She hadn't yet told him how she planned to lift the werewolf curse. He began to question why he'd come here. It had suited Skerret to exaggerate his mother's skills. Then he remembered; it was Mary who told him that she could cure werewolves. The priest had no reason to lie to her.

He decided to find out more, "Where did you learn your craft?"

She looked at him, "You doubt my ability?" She didn't wait for him to answer, "I suppose you're not alone. It was the scepticism of men drove me out of Galway and into the wilderness."

She seemed keen to tell that story so he took the bait, "you said the war cost you your home?"

"I did," she said. Her long grey hair had started getting in her way so she took a moment to tie it back with a hairpin. "The war kept every doctor in Galway busy. I was no different. Though, for many, I was the last resort. That's not an ideal situation for practising medicine. Well, I lost one patient whose family you don't cross." She took up the pot and poured the steaming mixture into a wooden cup. "I suppose, had I been a regular doctor and, of course, a man, there might have been no repercussions, but no, a woman had failed; she must be punished. They said I must be a witch."

Behind them, a twig snapped. Skerret had returned with an armful of firewood. He'd been listening, "you're not doing much to correct that impression, Mam."

"Seafóid," she answered. She handed the cup to Manning, "Drink that and you'll feel better."

Skerret's return brought an end to the fireside conversation. He sat down on the log opposite the wolf-hunter and quietly helped himself to the remaining food. There were unspoken issues between the two men. Silence seemed the best way to avoid stumbling into them.

Skerret felt his debt was paid. He had brought the wolf hunter to see his mother. He should be free to go. But he was penniless and he was unwilling to make plans for any journey till he felt sure Manning was heading in the opposite direction. Galway had been his destination. There he'd find a boat to France – if he could somehow pay for it. But he feared Manning was headed there too. The fool nursed an obsession for that servant girl, Mary. And she was in Galway.

Manning was also brooding. He drank his medicine slowly. It tasted vile. Perhaps Dearbhla was poisoning him? She had every reason to. He didn't believe this though. She obviously took pride in her hospitality and in her medical skills. Skerret, he was less sure of. Admittedly, the priest had fulfilled his promise. This gave him mixed feelings: It was helpful to know he could be trusted to keep a promise; on the other hand, what was the price of the bounty he had foregone? Was it enough that Skerret had brought him here? No, he decided. He had promised a cure. I'll hold him to that or I'll have my bounty yet, he thought.

They were happy to sit silently while Dearbhla pottered around them doing her chores. But, perhaps irritated by her guest's sulkiness, she found an excuse to leave them alone for an hour. It was the first time they'd found themselves alone in the role of equals rather than captor and captive. Conversation was needed to break the tension. Manning fished for topics that wouldn't offend. The weather was cold, he started. No bite from Skerret. The chicken soup was good. Silence from the priest. Skerret evidently had no time for small talk.

"Your mother is a strong woman. You never thought to become a doctor, like her?"

"A doctor, maybe. But not one like her."

"Yet, you believe her medicine works? You led me to believe it."

"Hush, soldier. It does. But at such a cost to her. My childhood was spent in a shadow of fear and uncertainty. She faced accusations of witchcraft many times. She always struggled. It took the madness of war to finally defeat her. When the axe fell, she lost everything. I was never going to choose that life."

"Then why not obtain a licence and become a respectable doctor?"

"The doctors in Galway obtained their licence from the Bishop. He did not look kindly on my mother's practice so he would not indulge her family, though he sponsored my training as a priest. He had little choice. I had the education... and there's a shortage." He smiled wryly at Manning.

The wolf-hunter went quiet. After a minute, he managed, "The war won't last forever."

"No. But there's no place for me in Ireland anymore. I'll make my way to France if I can."

He looked pointedly at Manning.

The wolf-hunter stared back, "and I'll resume my wolf hunting and steer clear of priests in future... once I'm cured."

28.

When Dearbhla returned, it was dark. She looked tired and Manning noticed she'd slipped back into speaking Irish as she explained the sleeping arrangements. Skerret provided a running translation. It would be a cold night. The fire was critical, she said. It was the only source of heat and it required constant tending. There was only room for one in Dearbhla's little cave so the two men would have to sleep in the open. They agreed to divvy the night into two watches. Manning would go first, and then Skerret would take over. They'd need to keep the fire hot so they didn't freeze and also to ward off predators.

Dearbhla brought out blankets and divided them between the men. Smiling, she unfolded one of the blankets and showed it to her son. It was a relic from his childhood. It was small and red with simple but charming images of waves, sea creatures and sailing ships. Skerret looked embarrassed but accepted it with a muted thanks. Manning looked away and busied himself in preparing a warm and comfortable station for the first watch.

After a while, he was the only one left awake. Dearbhla disappeared into the cave and Skerret's snores were soon audible under a mound of blankets beside the fire. There was no other light. The night was dry but cloudy so there was no moon or stars visible. There was a light wind which rustled the remaining leaves in the trees and caused a continuous lapping of water on the lake. Now and then there was a splash as a trout leapt for food. The livestock was mostly asleep and corralled in the paddock but the plaintive bleat of a kid broke the silence occasionally. Samson had been tied up at Dearbhla's insistence but he still growled at every animal noise. Manning felt better. Dearbhla's medicine was working. He no longer ached and his energy levels were high.

There'd been no talk of werewolves or blood curses from Dearbhla but, right now, Manning was content. Enjoying a moment of solitude for the first time since he'd been bitten, he tried to disentangle what he knew and what he'd merely assumed. He'd been too quick to accept Peeter's story that Hewson and Worsley had identified him as a carrier of this alleged werewolf curse. Why had he believed the word of a child? Because he'd been ill and he'd been ashamed, he decided. It was true that he'd never known the touch of a woman. And he knew he compensated for this with bravado. Was it his fate, then, to become the English army's most famous virgin? To be so cursed felt like justice.

But that was not reasonable. Certainly, he had been bitten by some kind of monster – call it a werewolf. Did it follow that he was cursed? Who said so? Peeter, who was jealous of Manning's affection for Mary? Skerret, who needed rescue from the gallows? These were not people he could trust. Perhaps he wasn't cursed after all. He picked up a mossy log, threw it into the centre of the fire and smiled at that possibility. It was the illness that made me paranoid, he thought. The fire popped loudly as the flames licked the damp wood. A deep growl answered from the dark. He turned slowly. A huge wolf was watching him from ten feet away.

Manning looked at Samson. The dog was sleeping soundly. Skerret was equally still. The wolf came closer. It was a bitch, Manning guessed. He slowly reached for his sword and scanned the fire for a flaming torch. But the wolf's demeanour was not threatening. She had the look of an animal transfixed by curiosity rather than set to attack. She rolled her head back and forth and started whimpering. Samson didn't wake. His silence surprised Manning. It was usually impossible to sneak up on that dog. There were other aberrations; the livestock was silent; and there was no sign of any other wolf.

At least I can deal with a lone wolf by myself, he thought. He grasped the handle of his sword and turned his body towards the predator. The wolf came closer. Her head was enormous. Her eyes flashed yellow in the firelight. The wolf-hunter remained still. It was time to challenge the approach but Manning felt unable to move. He wasn't afraid though; he was entranced. The creature came level and stopped. The animal's breath was warm on his face. She started to lick Manning's bandaged arm. The wolf-hunter raised his free hand and stroked her fur. It was warm and deep. She smelled of wet earth. The is unreal, he thought. He turned his head back towards the fire and his sleeping companions. Samson was snoring. There was no movement from Skerret but then he noticed that the priest's grey eyes were open. He was staring back at Manning.

***

The wolf-hunter woke up slowly. His eyes were closed but he sensed daylight. He could smell eggs cooking. He was confused. Was it morning already? What had happened to the wolf? And what about Skerret's second watch? Skerret! He sprung up and looked around. Samson lifted his head and yawned at him. A heavy fog hung over the encampment but it was indeed morning. A mound of blankets marked the spot where Skerret had slept. He had to poke it to be sure the skinny priest was not inside. Dearbhla emerged from her cave, a pan of eggs in one hand, a plate in the other. She looked ready for a fight. Manning understood; Skerret was gone.

"Don't overreact," she said.

He stood up, indignant, "you drugged me."

"That's my job," she answered, slipping the eggs onto the plate and offering it to him.

He hesitated but then realised he was hungry. He took it without thanks.

"Sit down and eat. Stop looking so wounded."

He sat and stared into the eggs, "where did he go?"

"He's gone. That's enough for you to know." She sat down opposite him and tended the fire. She had built it up hotter than the mild morning demanded. "he did his bit, brought you to me. He earned his freedom."

"That was my decision to make," Manning answered sulkily, "and he promised me a cure. I've yet to see that." He continued eating.

"You feel better don't you?"

"You're saying I'm cured?"

"No." She continued stoking the fire. She said no more.

Manning needed answers. He was less concerned now by Skerret's absence than by Dearbhla's silence. "You can cure me, can't you?"

Dearbhla stood up and brushed the ashes from her hands, "oh, there's a cure alright."

Her evasion worried him, "But it's beyond your skills?"

He tried to think straight. The wolf's visit, last night, was that a dream? The visit had left him with an uncanny feeling. There was something that he had to do. But what?

"It's not about my skills. The cure is in your own hands," she said. She bent down and started to tidy up the blankets at her feet. Then she sat down and faced him. "Time is against you, soldier.

You have a week or two at most till the werewolf curse consumes you. Once that happens. there's no going back. You're lucky to have that, I suppose. The creature who bit you had no such stay of execution."

"You knew him?"

She broke eye contact and answered quietly, "I did. It was me that cursed him."

His stomach sank as he considered this. He put the eggs aside. Samson got up and sniffed at the plate till the smoke made him sneeze.

"Last night..." he began but he decided to say no more.

"Hush now, William," her voice was quiet and serious.

He looked up. Had Skerret told her his name? He couldn't remember sharing it with the priest.

"There is only one chance you can be cured but it won't be easy."

He nodded. He was ready to hear the truth.

"It will require silver."

So that was her game, he thought. No cure till I pay my bill. She read his expression and laughed, "no, it's not what you think. I don't want the silver for myself. You'll need it to make a musket ball."

"From silver?" he exclaimed.

"It's the only thing that will do the job."

"What job?"

"You'll have to kill the beast that bit you."

29.

In Manwood, the morning was alive with sound as only a clear winter's day can be. Cattle bellowed in the fields, blackbirds sang sweetly and the staccato of chopping wood echoed from the farmyard. Even the river's gurgling reached Katherine's ears as she walked in the garden. She had collected a basket of herbs and was heading back to the house. There was sage, thyme and rosemary for the kitchen as well as a few more obscure species for the laboratory. The garden was meaner than ever but, with a little imagination, they could continue to eat well and fresh for a little while longer. There was still fruit to be found in the orchard, she remembered, so she headed that way to finish her errand.

She could still make the medicine she needed. Valentine was on the mend but his injuries were making him weak and she knew how to treat them. She had collected what fresh herbs she needed which she would combine with various dried ingredients from the lab. There was a certain orchid which she had dried and stockpiled in early summer. This would speed his recovery. Robert may have won the battle with his blood transfusion but Katherine would win the war with her knowledge of medicines. If she felt an urgent need to heal their guest, then healthy competition with her brother was at least one of her motivations.

As she entered the farmyard, she was surprised to discover just how much Valentine had recovered. There he was – splitting logs for the fire with apparent ease. He was down to his breeches and shirt and, though still pale, he was a picture of strength. She called out to avoid being brained but also to express some disapproval. He stopped and turned.

"Ho there," he said – slightly out of breath, after all, she noticed.

"You're not fit for this!" she said. "You should be resting."

"I was bored and I have a debt to repay."

"If you want to work, there's plenty in the house. You could polish the family silver – from your bed. That would keep you busy."

"That's not..." he trailed off.

"Not manly enough?"

"Anything else?"

She smiled at his discomfort, "You could take my basket. We'll collect some apples. I'll make you feel useful."

He put down the axe and took the basket. She walked ahead but veered towards a shed by the arch.

"Wait, I've collected too much for the kitchen." She reached into the basket and grabbed a fist full of herbs. Young lambs were bleating in the shed. She paused by the half door, the lambs ran over and she shared the herbs between them. "It's good for them," she said.

"Good for flavour too," Valentine added.

She glanced at him to reply and seemed to catch a steely, faraway look in his eyes. He must be hungry, she thought. "Come on."

They stopped briefly at the entrance to the orchard and allowed their eyes to meet: here they'd had a very strange meeting, two nights ago, in a gale. Valentine broke eye contact first and ushered Katherine ahead. They passed through the little arch but didn't venture far. Neither wanted to be close to the graves at the far end. Katherine took her time. They were alone and it was nice to loiter in each other's company. She collected enough fruit to convince Valentine his strength had been valued and then bid him follow her to the kitchen.

The apples would make their way into a pie, Mrs Kinnerk promised – a nice follow-up to the lamb she was already cooking. Katherine took leave of Valentine but invited him to join her and her brother for dinner at three o'clock. She spent the rest of the morning working side by side with Robert in the laboratory, she preparing Valentine's medicine, Robert documenting his blood transfusion experiment. Valentine used the time to make repairs to his clothes. At three, he appeared in the dining room looking handsome and restored.

Robert stood up and greeted Valentine effusively. They hadn't really talked since the blood transfusion and though Robert had concerns about Valentine's politics, hospitality came first and he made his guest feel welcome. The three worked hard to keep their conversation safe and light for most of the meal. Valentine discovered Robert's ability to speak endlessly about science so long as the questions kept coming and showed interest. Robert was too polite a host not to listen as much as he talked so, on Katherine's prompting, he let Valentine recount his adventures in Spain.

But the frivolous conversation ebbed with the daylight and, as they each nursed a glass of port, Robert took on the mantle of patriarch. He cleared his throat and turned serious, "Valentine, I must tell you that I have written to the commander of Parliament forces in Limerick to tell him of your presence here."

Valentine lowered his drink in response, glancing quickly at Katherine to see if she already knew. Her calmness reassured him. This was no ambush, more like a tip-off. He answered calmly, "Of course. I understand. That is your prerogative."

"You must understand, as Parliamentary supporters..."

"There's no need to explain."

"We are curious, of course?"

"How I came to be here?"

Robert nodded. Katherine was uncomfortable but hopeful that her brother's directness would answer her questions too.

Valentine had prepared a story, "Well, you see I escaped from prison..." he started. The siblings looked at each other. With such an opening line, he was hardly planning to lie. And yet it was the last true thing he said. Yes, he stole details from the facts – the prison break, the leap from the battlements, the musket wounds. He told them that he'd escaped the noose in Galway with the help of a notorious pirate, Tadhg Flaherty; that he'd been innocent of the charge but had been left no choice but to run. But the pirate had betrayed him in Limerick and sold him to the Roundheads. It was a well-judged fantasy – juicy enough to seem true but flattering enough to maintain their sympathy. He was never going to reveal the true horror of his situation.

His condition had been dormant for two days but he could feel it being nurtured by the food and rest which had also restored his Christian self to health. He was losing a battle which was no longer just for his own soul – he feared this was already forsaken – the lives of others were now in peril. But not yet, he thought. Give me this evening and the last tendrils of human kindness. He knew not who he beseeched – God or Satan.

He finished his story and slowly looked up to read his audience. He had characterised himself as an unlucky, reluctant combatant on the wrong side of history. The Boyles had bought it. Robert's face had softened to the natural openness that marked him while Katherine's had stiffened into a mask of self-control which confirmed rather than concealed the empathy beneath.

He felt ashamed – to win two honest friends like these under such false pretences. And one... he looked at Katherine, then spoke, "Forgive me. I owe this family so much. I'm unworthy." He stood up.

The siblings rose as one and protested. Katherine reached out and took his hand, "you owe us nothing."

Robert skewered his arguments, "Nonsense, man! I'm still trying to make amends for burying you, then experimenting on you like a rabbit."

Valentine laughed politely.

"Please, sit down," Katherine said softly. He did and the siblings followed suit.

"How about a nice game of cribbage?" Robert suggested and he stood up again to check the sideboard for playing cards. Katherine and Valentine shared a private smile then she told her brother to sit and wait while she ran upstairs to get the necessary equipment. Robert refilled his guest's glass and sat down. The two men became awkward in each other's company and waited in silence. Valentine thought about Katherine taking his hand. It was an intimate gesture but her brother had not protested. It seems we have his blessing.

For Valentine, the evening progressed with the warm glow that such a thought brings. He played silently and contentedly, winning often, losing only to Katherine. Robert was a terrible cribbage player. He cursed the rules and bemoaned his hands but his yapping never upset the silent connection deepening between his sister and their guest. Indeed, the one-sided conversation allowed the couple to commune in private with looks and smiles, small kindnesses and chivalries. Their silence eventually penetrated Robert's ramblings and he became quiet and self-conscious. When he yawned, Katherine was quick to observe it and prescribe bed. He sulked that his glass was not empty and Katherine backtracked – not wishing to appear too hasty. They played another hand which they all understood would be their last.

Throwing down yet another losing hand, Robert called time, "Right, I'm off to bed." He rose, looked vaguely at his sister then at Valentine, muttered farewell and with a last, uncertain look back, he left the room.

The couple dropped the smile they'd been wearing for Robert and locked eyes. Katherine had rehearsed versions of this scene but none had played so smoothly. Valentine drained his glass and waited for Katherine's cue. Once Robert's footsteps had faded, she rose and he followed. She took his hand, gestured for silence, and led him out the door, up the stairs and into her bedroom.

***

She woke some hours later feeling cold. Her bare back was exposed and where she'd expected to feel Valentine's warmth, she felt empty sheets. The room was dark save for red embers glowing in the hearth and a frame of blue light around the curtains. She could hear nothing apart from the usual strains of wood and glass defying the winter's night. The wind was howling in the chimney and dead leaves whipped the window. She got up, pulled a nightdress over her naked body and tightly wrapped her dressing gown over that. The room was freezing. Who wants to leave a warm bed on such a night? Perhaps he'd returned to his own room to use a chamber pot? Does a man pee in a woman's presence in such a context? This was beyond her education. Her husband did, of course. But they were married. The comparison amused her and she thought again of the pleasure she had just experienced. Perhaps I'll catch him in his own room and we'll make sport in two beds in one night. She smiled at the thought. She stepped across the upstairs gallery and tip-toed to his room. But he wasn't there. The kitchen, maybe?

She was hungry herself but there was no appetite great enough to drag her from such a cosy bed. Still, if he was eating she'd join him even at the risk of waking the Kinnerks.

She quietly descended the stairs and shushed the dogs who were already awake and pacing the hall. So, he has passed through here, she thought. The dogs were whining to go outside. Surely, he wasn't outside.

But the kitchen too was empty, as was the dining room. Her good cheer died. A mild panic rose in her heart. Every other room was occupied apart from the laboratory. He had no business there so she checked it last. Also, a sixth sense told her she was destined for the farmyard, that she'd find him there. Later, she realised it wasn't a sixth sense at all, she could hear it calling. It was low but it was there and it sounded like screaming.

Now her heart was pounding. But she had to be practical. She took a light from the fire and lit a lamp. Her brother kept a coat in the always cold laboratory and she threw it on before opening the heavy oak door to the yard. She could hear it better now, screaming, crying, she wasn't sure, like children in terror, coming from the direction of the orchard. Whatever it was, Valentine was there, she knew it. She walked on, alert to every sound. A whirlwind of leaves hissed in the middle of the yard, the trees in the orchard creaked, the low plaintive screams continued and a half door flapped in the wind. The door of one of the sheds was open. The lambs. She raced over. The entrance was black but at least now she could identify the sound of bleating lambs. A lamb ran out looking confused and helpless. She picked it up. Its crying was wild and desperate. She stood at the open door of the shed. The light from the lamp swung wildly in the wind. Her eyes were drawn to the choir of screaming lambs in one corner, their backs pressed against the wall. She followed their gaze to the other wall.

Here was the cause of their distress: One of their brothers had been torn in two. His entrails stained the yellow straw.

Behind him, naked and on his knees was Valentine. His face, chest and arms were covered in blood. He looked into Katherine's eyes but didn't seem to know her.

30.

The sun was shining when Mary reached Galway. The unpaved road leading into the city was dry for once, and there was no wind. Thin columns of smoke rose from within and divided the blue sky like lines on a ledger. It looked like business as usual.

The city was smaller than Mary had expected but the number of towers and private castles peeping over the walls told a tale of independent wealth which Limerick couldn't match. It was past its peak perhaps but the smell of wine and the memory of Spanish silver had endured and the city retained a cosmopolitan brio which its burghers still leveraged at the bank. The narrow streets were dotted with showy town-houses – a testament to both the rivalry of the rich as well as to their almost republican sense of independence.

The besieging army was less threatening than the force that had just conquered Limerick. They were taking no immediate action against the city so their forces were organised into tidy rectangles of tents and equipment which belied their murderous intent. A small checkpoint controlled access to the eastern approach to the city to ensure new arrivals only brought further hardship rather than relief to the city.

Mary was part of a refugee train from the south. These banished Catholics of Munster were nearing their journey's end in Galway city. The Parliamentarians were happy to let them in. The citizens of Galway could decide who to feed and who to eject through the West Gate and into the wilds of Connemara. If they survived their stay in the besieged city, they could begin new lives as an exiled underclass in Connacht. Mary's destiny was different. She had some hope.

Her secret – and she had many secrets – was the little leather purse she wore around her neck. It was heavy with silver. Together with a sharp mind and an even sharper knife beneath her apron, she was adept at surviving the worst calamities men could engineer. Nevertheless, Limerick had been a real test. She'd been lucky to get out alive. She'd come face to face with a monster and she'd survived. The image of the beast meeting her gaze on the battlement continued to haunt her. She had expected to die. But it didn't attack. Why? Sure, she wasn't actively attacking it, like the soldiers and that fool, William Manning, but the idea that this beast could use discretion rocked her world. She had told Valentine that she didn't believe in monsters but she had believed that a beast was a beast – mindless, not conflicted and certainly not possessing a soul. So what had she witnessed?

She pondered this as her convoy approached the Great Gate. Then she was distracted by the city gallows. Built to hang a single condemned man, it was leaning precariously under the weight of half a dozen. The bodies had been used for target practice and bristled with crossbow bolts. The smell was appalling. The convoy steered well clear, raising a flock of carrion birds as it passed. Fortunately, there was ample room; the road had widened to a flat plain where the townspeople would ordinarily gather to witness executions. These days the citizens stayed inside the walls and the besieging army stayed well out of musket and crossbow range. This was no man's land. To the left, there was a jousting ground empty and overgrown. Beyond that, an abbey surrounded by recent fortifications but apparently deserted. The convoy had veered to the right into a man-made moat which led to the first of six gates which secured the eastern approach to the city. The first gate was up and they entered in hushed anticipation.

Once they were inside, unseen hands lowered the gate behind them. They shuffled like livestock between the inner and outer wall as far as the next closed gate. Inside, beyond a long dark arch, they could see the main street. The citizens of Galway were going about their business indifferent to the plight of the arriving refugees. The sight was oddly reassuring until Mary noticed the gang of hustlers waiting just inside the gate. They were grinning malevolently at the new arrivals. Mary grasped the hilt of her dagger and made sure her shift was fully buttoned. These vultures would attempt to rob and con the vulnerable refugees out of every valuable. She'd seen their like in Limerick.

As the gate went up, the refugees poured in. Thieves surrounded them. They identified a family pulling a cart full of furniture as the most attractive target. Sure enough, the father, an elderly Limerick lawyer by appearance, was quickly surrounded by three young men offering to help carry his possessions. He tried to shoo them away but they took his rejection as an invitation to haggle loudly. His young wife, distracted by the noise, went to his aid. This was their partners' cue to raid the cart. They took everything but the children. The woman realised it too late and raised the alarm. Her husband beat back the remaining thieves but the damage was done. Two armed militia men watched but took no action. Mary walked straight ahead, burning with shame but relieved not to be targeted.

Once she was at a safe distance she looked back and felt another pang of guilt when she saw the children sitting in the cart crying with confusion. She felt her hand cramp. The dagger was still tight in her grip. She released the hilt and spread her fingers till the tingle eased. Evil is like the plague, she thought; you can either suffer from it or profit by it but you can't escape it untouched. She had been in Galway no more than a minute and already viewed the city with contempt.

Suddenly, there was a strange clicking sound followed by a musical chime. She looked up. There was a mechanical clock above the arch facing the main street. It was one o'clock. "Once I've eaten and freshened up, I'll look for a job," she decided. She knew exactly where to go for that.

**

The D'Arcy's house was on Pludd Street on the western side of the city. It was a large four-story building dating back to the city's heyday. The first floor featured an overhanging bay of three leaded windows while the street level was dominated by a gated arch leading into a courtyard. The heavy wooden gates were wide enough to receive the cartloads of wine that had established the family's fortune and heavy enough to protect that investment from the rougher elements of the city. At the back of the house, an ancestor had built a tower to overlook Galway bay. From here the D'Arcy paterfamilias could literally watch his ships come in. Behind the tower, the real attraction of the site was the extensive garden and outbuildings which were keeping the household fed, if not fat, during the siege.

Mary arrived shortly after lunch figuring that was a good time to make demands on anyone. She was greeted impatiently by a servant girl too used to deflecting beggars to remember the manners due to strangers. She had all but shut the door on Mary's polite enquiry when the name, 'Valentine D'Arcy' caused her to freeze. She asked her to wait and left in a flutter. A minute later she returned and asked Mary in, with an expression of fear mixed with curiosity.

She led her up the stairs into the first-floor reception and asked her to wait. The room was large with a low, heavy-beamed ceiling. The bay windows allowed in as much light as the narrow street offered. The furniture was expensive but the overall character was somehow different from a typical merchant's house. It took Mary a moment to pinpoint the difference; it was the smell; the large stone fireplace in the far wall was burning turf. To Mary, this was the fuel of the poor. Was this a Galway custom, was it the siege effect or were the D'Arcys short of cash? There was more to learn here.

She looked around. The walls were covered in pictures. She started a slow circle of the room to examine them. There was little furniture to impede her – just a heavy desk and chair close to the fire, a cabinet for papers and several sets of keys hanging on a hook.

The pictures were mostly business related – studio commissions of ships and vineyards to court investors. There were just two small portraits on the wall. Neither represented Valentine but both featured a family resemblance. One was of a young man dressed as a soldier but this man's hair was dark and his face different enough to rule out Valentine. This was the dead brother, Donal, she guessed. The second portrait must be the boys' mother. Mary was hovering over the likeness when she heard a man clear his throat at the door. He stepped into the room and spoke, "That's my wife, Elizabeth, God rest her soul... I'm Richard D'Arcy." He extended a gloved hand. She took it, curtsied and introduced herself.

He was tall like Valentine with broad shoulders. His face was a tale from Valentine's future – the same bones but dressed in sagging clothes, still handsome if sadder for the thirty years between them.

He was richly dressed, all in black, with a finesse which reminded her of his son. A silver breastplate and a purple sash marked him as a commander of the city militia. He saw it catch her attention, "We're drilling in the market square this afternoon. I was just about to leave. But you have word of my son?"

She did, but she was here for a job, so she framed her answer around that, "He told me you could offer domestic work; I cared for him in Limerick."

The alderman walked to his desk and took a seat. "Limerick?" he said, "and he's there now?"

"As far as I know." Her story was straight in her head: She'd cared for him in jail and had left him there a week ago. She wasn't going to acknowledge the events of Guy Fawkes Night in case they were already known in Galway.

The alderman, for his part, seemed ignorant, "he's well, I take it?"

"No, your honour, not really. He's in jail... in King John's Castle but he's well enough for all that, I suppose."

"In jail?" his eyes darted towards the door, "and he sent you to solicit help?" He was less surprised than a father should have been. Was Valentine's reputation so bad, she wondered?

"He didn't send me at all, your grace. I was bid leave Limerick like every free Catholic. He was good enough to give me a rec-ommendation and your address."

The alderman smiled, "Yes, that sounds like Valentine."

She said nothing.

"And he wasn't sick at all or in any other way unwell?" he asked. "Jail can be a harsh environment," he added with a raised eyebrow.

"He wasn't thriving, sir; but I had no immediate concern for his health on Monday." The equivocation shamed her but the alderman clearly wasn't playing straight either. He must have reasons to think his son unwell.

"So you saw him on Monday?" he counted the intervening days on his fingers and reached for his quill and a clean sheet of paper. "And you came in with today's refugees?"

"Yes, sir."

"Then you'll be tired and hungry. I'll not shame my son by turning you out. It's a little presumptuous, landing you on us but the boy has other things on his mind, I suppose. I'll write to Limerick and see what I can do for him. I still have friends there. Our city leaders may be enemies right now but surely a father's entreaties count for something?" He flashed a smile to finish the interview. As he did, a tumult of male voices drifted up from the street.

She curtsied again and the servant who'd shown her in appeared at the door carrying a coat, sword and belt, "Sir William is outside, sir."

He dropped the quill and stood up, "My commander awaits. Grace here will set you up. You can cook, clean, and work the garden?"

"Yes, sir."

He looked Mary up and down, "yes, you look strong. I can see why my son liked you. We can't offer charity, you understand." He donned the coat and started to tie the belt around his waist. "This is a town in crisis. You'll work hard but you'll be fed and you'll have a bed. I'll make enquiries after Valentine when I return."

She understood. She had a job – until he checked her story.

31.

Samson jumped up and rested his huge flat paws on Dearbhla's shoulders. He tried to lick her face but this was too much for the doctor and she pushed him away. "Síos, amadán!" she exclaimed. She was happy to say goodbye to the creature but she didn't want a kiss. Manning was packing his bag. He had a few days' supplies of biscuits, a flask full of beer and a week's supply of medicine and bandages to tend to his wound. The dog's affection and Dearbhla's apparent lack of sentiment allowed Manning to bid her a cooler farewell but he was sorry to leave her. "Thank you for your kindness," he said.

She smiled, touched his arm and said, "I'm sorry I could do no more for you. Apply that medicine every night and change those bandages as often. The rest is up to you. It takes a lot of strength to kill a werewolf and I don't just mean here," she touched his arm again, "You'll need courage. You saw the devil in Limerick. Look for him there. It's a long walk so you'd better get started."

"It was easier when I had company," he said, lifting his bag over his shoulder.

She bent down, gave the dog a last pet and answered, "We only miss things when they're gone, eh? At least you have this dog to talk to." She wiped the dog hairs from her hands and straightened up, "I think you and Ambrose might have been friends under different circumstances."

He smiled, "I'm beginning to realise that," Then he turned serious. "But I'm afraid he'll just remember that I beat him, chained him and tried to sell him."

"I don't think so." She laughed quietly to herself then added, "Ambrose doesn't bring every boy he meets home to meet his mother."

Manning didn't know how to respond. Dearbhla smiled and gave him leave with a pat on the shoulder. He started off. It was mid-afternoon. He couldn't expect to finish the journey before nightfall so, like before, he planned to find a halfway point at dusk.

As he followed the stream south towards Ennis, he found himself thinking about Skerret. Probably the priest had taken the road north and was well on his way to Galway. Had Dearbhla sent him off with money for a passage to France, he wondered? He hoped so. Manning would have been happier heading to Galway – on a new road, into a new life, not burdened with a seemingly impossible quest: Find a werewolf and kill it or fail and become a monster.

Samson seemed disappointed to be covering old ground too. The exuberance he'd shown on the way from Limerick was gone. He trotted close to the wolf-hunter and answered the occasional sounds of wildlife with a terse growl rather than a playful chase.

It was getting dark by the time they rejoined the Limerick road. Manning didn't want to board at the smith's house where he'd been strong-armed out of his savings two nights ago. The absence of Skerret – and the mirth this would provoke – was a humiliation he couldn't face. Fortunately, Dearbhla had recommended a different route via the old abbey in Quin. Here he'd also find shelter for the night. He took the road she'd described and walked on into the evening.

After sunset, he began to listen for the gurgling of a river as a sign that he was close. He could see nothing below the horizon but the darkness was alive with sound. Eventually, he heard the river and he was surprised to catch sight of the abbey at the same time. The ruined walls of the old church were lit up by a fire. Someone had already found shelter there. He stopped at the river bank and considered what to do. The abbey was to the left of the ford, sheltered by a low, dry-stone wall. He could spy on the travellers from behind it. There was no way of telling whether these were friends or foes but he didn't need to get too close to learn more. Loud voices echoed against the church walls – English voices. Manning was relieved until their drunken tone made his heart sink. He peered through a gap in the wall. He could see two men, both English soldiers. They wore the Parliamentarian uniform but, like Manning, theirs were embellished with signs of plunder. They were both big men, both in their mid-thirties. One wore the bowl-cut hairstyle beloved by the New Model Army. The other was bald on top and close-cropped where nature still allowed some growth. They had built their fire in the middle of the graveyard. It was a strange place to camp. The one with the mop-top was sitting on a headstone, the bald one was warming himself over the fire, swinging a large flagon as he talked. Around them were muskets, bandoleers and leather satchels. They had enough bags for three or four men. They looked dangerous.

Manning decided to find shelter elsewhere. As he turned to leave he suddenly realised they were barking orders at some unseen third party. They had a prisoner. Looking closer, he realised they were forcing a man, just out of sight beyond them, to dig a grave. Samson began to pine and Manning had to shush him. But the dog had sensed something. The prisoner straightened up. It was Skerret.

The dog pulled forward when he recognised his old friend. Manning held him back. What to do? They're not forcing him to dig his own grave, he told himself. They're deserters – or like himself – bounty hunters. Admittedly, they've stooped to grave robbing but their motive is greed, not cruelty. Probably they grabbed Skerret on the Galway road and they're working him all the way to Limerick where they'll claim his bounty. But they're not going to kill him. Whereas they might kill me, he thought. As Manning worked on this sophistry, Samson looked at him and pined again. Damn sentimental dog, he thought.

He stood up and made his movements as loud as possible. There was a gap in the wall which he made for, "Ho, there!" he shouted a loud greeting.

As he entered the abbey grounds, the men looked his way. Manning pretended not to recognise Skerret. He read confusion in the priest's eyes. The sitting soldier reached for a musket.

"Peace, brothers," Manning said, holding his hands up in a show of goodwill. "I'm a fellow Englishman seeking shelter. Can I share your fire?"

The other soldier waved his flagon at Samson. He looked at the dog. "Wolf-hunter, eh?" The bounty hunters glanced at each other and then back to Manning.

"Aye."

"You're in the right place, then." He looked around into the dark. "This country's crawling with the beasts."

His comrade was sharp, "You won't shoot any without a musket, though."

Manning looked embarrassed, "no indeed. I had to sell my matchlock."

"Perhaps you'd sell the dog too?"

Manning was delighted by the suggestion; this was his plan. "Yes, I'd consider that. That's a priest you've got there," he pointed at Skerret, "I'd trade the dog for him."

The two soldiers looked at each other again and laughed. The bald one scoffed, "what's the matter boy? Are you so cold at night?"

The other took up the joke, "has your dog grown tired of your affection?" Their laughter was loud and forced and seemed to slight the silence of the night. Somewhere in the distance, a wolf howled. This stopped the laughter. Manning came no closer. They're baiting me, he thought. They want Samson and any excuse to start a fight for him, "Forgive me," he said, "I've disturbed your revels. I'll leave you in peace." He took a step backwards.

But the soldiers had grown serious. Mop-top stood up and raised his musket. Baldy put down his drink and when he straightened up he had a sword in his hand, "You're not going anywhere, soldier."

Mop-top turned to Skerret, "Was that your jailer? The wolf-hunter, Manning? Speak the truth, boy."

Skerret looked from one to the other and then at Manning, "No." he said.

But it was too late. Manning had flinched at the mention of his name.

The big bald soldier spoke next, "There's a bounty on your head, wolf-hunter. Colonel Hewson will pay fifty pounds for your capture. Come quiet, and we'll go easy on you."

Samson growled.

Of course, he should have run. It would have been easy to disappear into the darkness and outpace these two drunks. He could have no reasonable expectation to rescue Skerret now that the priest's captors had proven so irascible. And yet, he drew his sword.

The bald one smiled and stepped forward. "As you wish, soldier. Hewson doesn't need you alive. He just wants your blood."

His comrade chuckled evilly and waved his musket at Skerret, prompting the prisoner to climb out of the grave he had been digging. Manning issued an order to Samson to stay and the dog crouched, though he continued to growl.

Manning was having second thoughts. Swordplay was not his forte and, though he had the advantage of sobriety, size was always the arbiter hand-to-hand. And this man was big. He stepped down from the hillock of the graveyard and swished his sword theatrically.

"We need not fight…" Manning said with no particular argument in mind.

"I want to fight," came the soldier's answer. He started a slow circle around Manning who mirrored his moves – from good form if nothing else.

Wolves started to howl all around them. Samson whined and the deadly foreplay paused a moment while the men stopped to listen. But the blood was up in Manning's opponent and he formed an aphorism that pleased him, "they'll feast on your bones tonight, wolf-hunter."

"Please…" was all Manning could manage. With his eyes fixed on the bald man's sword, he failed to notice a rock hidden in the grass. He tripped and fell backwards. His opponent showed no mercy. He raced forward to plunge his sword into Manning. Samson wasn't having this. The dog jumped up and clamped his teeth into the soldier's free arm. The man howled in pain and tumbled into the grass, breaking the dog's hold on his arm as he did. The dog regained his footing and turned to attack once more. Manning was back on his feet and he called off the dog. Too late. A shot rang out. Samson was thrown back by the impact. Manning dropped his sword. His dog lay dead. The second soldier lowered his smoking musket and smiled with satisfaction. He didn't see Skerret. The priest had found a suitable weapon. He smashed a paving stone over the man's head.

The other soldier saw his colleague fall and started to charge at Manning. Terror suddenly stopped him in his tracks. It took Manning a moment to understand. He looked back into the darkness. Yellow eyes – maybe twenty of them – were watching.

"God protect me," the soldier said. He looked at Manning, then at Skerret and decided he was friendless. He turned and ran away in the opposite direction. The wolves came forward and sniffed with curiosity. Manning ignored them. He knelt beside Samson and cradled the dog in his arms. The animals gathered around him. Skerret watched from the hillock, frozen in fear. He looked down. Blood oozed from the head of the second soldier. "I've killed him," he thought. He didn't dare move.

Manning came to his senses. He stood up. A wolf approached and licked his hand. Unthinking, he stroked its head. One of the wolves had a sniff at Samson's body. This, Manning would not abide. He kicked out and yelled, "Away!" The pack recoiled. Manning crossed to where Skerret stood, climbed onto the hillock and stood beside him. He looked down at the dead soldier then he reached out and laid his hand on the priest's shoulder. "They want food," he said simply. He bent down and started to undress the soldier. "Sit down over there. You won't want to see this," he added. Skerret obeyed. He looked around. He found the flagon of wine, picked it up and retreated to a seat by the walls of the church.

Manning started to undress the dead soldier. Framed by the firelight, the hunched silhouette plundering the dead man's belongings looked truly devilish. The priest decided to lose his mind in wine. When he was done, Manning rolled the body over the hillock and into the hungry mouths below. The wolves yelped with delight. Manning crossed to Skerret and sat beside him. The priest passed the flagon of wine to him. The sound of the wolves feasting was too much for him. He started to sing to cover the noise,

"Tráthnóinín déanach i gcéin cois leasa dom,
Táimse im' chodhladh is ná dúistear mé,
Sea dhearcas lem' thaobh an spéirbhean mhaisiúil,
Táimse im' chodhladh is ná dúistear mé,
Ba bhachallach péarlach dréimreach barrachas,
A carnfholt craobhach ag titim léi ar bhaillechrith,
'S í ag caitheamh na saighead trím thaobh do chealg mé,
Táimse im' chodhladh is ná dúistear mé,"

Manning had been drinking deeply. He lowered the flagon and looked curiously at the priest. Skerret answered his look by repeating the verse in English,

"As I was walking late one evening,
I am asleep, don't waken me,
I saw a beautiful apparition,
I am asleep, don't waken me,
Her long and curly, surplus tresses fell over her shaking, trembling limbs,
As she launched the arrows that pierced the side of me,
I am sleep, don't waken me."

As the verse ended, they heard the sound of a bone snapping from below the hill. The men winced. Manning decided to try his hand at the song,

"As I was walking late one evening,
I am asleep, don't waken me,"

Skerret joined in,

"I saw a beautiful apparition,
I am asleep, don't waken me,
Her long and curly, surplus tresses fell over her shaking, trembling limbs,

As she launched the arrows that pierced the side of me,
I am asleep, don't waken me."

32.

It took Katherine twenty minutes to coax Valentine out of the shed and back into the house. He remained in a trance but at least he was docile. She brought him to the kitchen and sat him by the fire so she could wash the blood from his body and try to bring him to his senses. She went to get water and lit a few candles. When she returned she looked at him and despaired. We're back where we started, she thought.

He didn't seem human. His eyes were hollow black circles and his movements were more animal than man. She tried to work silently but it wasn't long before Mr Kinnerk poked his head into the kitchen and called out in alarm. He was followed by his wife who he promptly shielded from Valentine's nakedness. This seemed to remind them to worry about their mistresses' morals too. Another servant was sent for Robert while the Kinnerks implored Katherine to leave the kitchen. She ignored their pleas and set them practical tasks which they ignored back. Katherine was left to do all the work till Robert burst in on the scene.

"What has happened?" he cried as he ran to his sister's side.

She quickly explained where she found him and reluctantly repeated the orders she'd given the Kinnerks; to secure the lambs in the shed, to fetch blankets, more hot water and Valentine's clothes.

Those last words were out of her mouth before she remembered where those clothes lay.

Not wishing to repeat his sister's commands, Robert merely nodded at the Kinnerks who composed themselves and set to work. Robert was not insensitive to appearances however and he pulled the linen from the table and draped it around Valentine's shoulders.

He tried to excuse the Kinnerks to his sister, "They've just had a shock."

Katherine looked at her brother incredulously and then returned to washing Valentine but Robert could see her hand was limp. She too was in shock. He took the cloth from her hand. Hot tears fell down her cheek. Valentine looked on dumbly. Robert gently lifted his sister. "Come on. I'll take care of him. You lie down."

Upstairs Robert helped his sister to her bed. Before he left, he looked around, spotted Valentine's clothes and gathered them up. He said nothing but, as he worked, a look passed between the siblings.

✳✳✳

When Katherine woke, it was bright. Blue light coloured the room and further chilled the icy air. She was still wrapped in her dressing gown. She found her slippers and hurried out into the upstairs gallery. She went to Valentine's room. It was empty. Where had he passed the night? She ran down the stairs, passing one of the younger servants in the hall. She thought she caught a look, judgemental? Insolent? Damage has been done, she thought. She made for the dining room. Robert was there finishing his breakfast and reading a book. The keys to the house gathered on a great iron hoop, sat on the table beside him. There was a hard set to his face. Uncharacteristic.

"Brother?"

"Sister. Sit down. Have some food."

"Where is he?" She was sorry to find herself slightly breathless.

She could see Robert considering how to play her. There was only one way, of course – straight. "He's locked the larder." He stood up and walked to the window.

She'd had time to expect the worst so she kept her cool, "so this is how we treat our guests?"

"I didn't want to take any chances. It's the most secure room in the house."

"What were you expecting?"

"I don't know?" he turned to her, genuinely at a loss, "...more violence? An attack on one of us?"

Katherine walked over to him. He looked out the window. She spoke softly, "he wouldn't... Robert. You can't think..."

"I don't know what to think. I thought we had cured him. Now, I doubt our medicine had any effect at all. This is... outside my experience. I'm just glad I never published an account..." he trailed off.

"Oh for God's sake, Robert, do you have to see everything in terms of your scientific reputation? He's ill. He needs help... and you lock him up like an animal. We may not understand what ails him but we can do no good unless we treat him like a man."

He turned and faced her. He looked hurt. But he wasn't going to take any criticism from her this morning, "Is that what you were doing last night? Treating him like a man?"

Her mouth fell open in shock. She kicked him in the shin and stormed out, scooping the ring of keys from the table as she passed.

***

In the kitchen, she found the Kinnerks in a huddle – their faces frozen with the guilt of interrupted gossip. Katherine crossed to the heavy pantry door and unlocked it. Mrs Kinnerk looked ready to make some remark but she had second thoughts. Katherine left the key on the outside and said, "you can lock me in with him if it makes you feel safer." Then she disappeared inside.

The larder was lit by a little window high in the wall opposite the door. It took her a while to adjust to the gloom. Valentine was sitting under the window, dressed and cleaner than she'd left him but dishevelled and flecked with blood.

He looked up and recognised her and Katherine was immediately reassured. He's back, she thought. But he didn't return her smile. He found he couldn't look her in the eyes. "I lied to you... and to your brother," his voice was hoarse.

She knelt beside him and lifted his chin. She ignored the admission. "What happened?" she asked.

"I am cursed. I told you I was a prisoner in Limerick. And yes, I was shot. You saw my wounds. But the ordinary musket ball cannot kill me. I never said why. It was because of this curse."

"Cursed? How?"

"Cursed by a witch..." He looked up into her eyes. He seemed to have second thoughts. "No. Not a witch. I... my own fault, I think."

"What curse?"

"The curse of the werewolf."

She didn't understand.

"Last night, you were lucky... and your household. I should never have stayed here. It was lucky I just had strength to whet my appetite, not gorge it. Had I been strong, I would have killed everybody."

"How?"

"With the moon, I change. I become a wolf, or like a wolf."

Katherine was quiet for a minute, "I have heard stories... of men becoming wolves under the power of the moon. But surely these are just stories?"

"Alas, no. I must bear this curse forever. The werewolf cannot die – at least not by mortal means."

"How can I help?"

"There's nothing you can do."

"Then tell me, who can help? Your family?"

He turned away, "No. I've brought shame enough on them."

"I don't believe it," she answered, then, fearing he'd be insulted, she added, "There must be someone who can help?"

He turned and faced her. His mind was emerging from a fog and dimly lit memories were taking shape. "Maybe..."

"Who?"

He answered, talking as much to himself now, as to Katherine. "The priest... in Limerick. He said his mother could help. It was she who cursed me."

"So, there was a witch?"

"No. I don't think she meant to hurt me. And she might yet have a cure."

"Perhaps I could bring her to you... if you stay here."

"Here?" he looked around the little larder.

"No, I'll return you to your room. I'll make things right with Robert." She smiled. She seemed to think the solution was very straightforward.

Valentine's heart sank. He suddenly understood; she didn't believe him. Not a word. Of course, she'd seen no evidence – no real evidence. She'd found him naked, bloody and out of his mind. That was it – she thought him mad. And now she was planning to let him roam her house again. She had no idea what danger she was in. There was only one thing he could do. He nodded and answered with an empty smile.

When Katherine left him alone, he raided the larder, hiding as much food as he could carry inside his clothes. No harm if she catches me, he thought ruefully, she'll discount it as another sign of madness. An hour later, she returned. She made a show of opening the larder door wide and inviting him to exit. In the kitchen, he noticed the servants' looks; they clearly thought him mad though they looked less sympathetic than their mistress.

Katherine led him back to his bedroom. He saw no sign of Robert. Once inside, she fussed over him and encouraged him to rest. He played along. Katherine was as kind as ever but there was wariness in her eyes. He knew he could break that spell if he tried but he chose not to. Let her think me mad. If she believed me, she'd follow me into danger.

33.

The house on Pludd Street was secured like a bank. No door was left unlocked, and no window was unbarred. The better part of Mary's orientation involved memorising what rooms were off-limits. She was not allowed in the shop; the stables; the master's office – unless the master called; the family rooms on the second floor – except at noon to clean; the tower; the wine store and the sheds. The restrictions were not a hardship to Mary – the fewer rooms she could enter, the fewer she need clean. But the security piqued her interest. And it was not just etiquette that so many rooms remained off-limits to her. As she passed them, she noticed most were locked – even the sheds at the end of the garden.

The tour was short – by necessity – and given grudgingly by Grace. As she led Mary through the dark, creaking corridors of the house, she'd sulkily lift a finger as they passed another closed door and mumble, "stay out of here... here... here..." After a few minutes in the girl's company, it became apparent that Grace's doorstep rudeness was not a pose reserved for strangers. The girl was miserable and inclined to share her misery with an even hand. Mary was patient with her. She looked about fourteen and Mary remembered that age. There's no cure for this malaise but time, she thought. The pair were set to share a bed in the servants' quarters in the attic. This imposition would do little to improve Grace's attitude. Mary was a foot taller than her and likely to monopolise the bedclothes. For Mary's part, Grace made an unappealing bedfellow. Watching the back of her head on the tour, she'd noticed the girl's hair was alive with parasites.

She found the rest of the house no happier. There was an elderly cook, Mrs Taafe; a rather dour shopkeeper, Garavan; and about half a dozen other staff too charmless to consider nodding a greeting to Mary as they went about their business.

The day after she arrived, Mary experienced a welcome break from the gloom of the D'Arcy household. While Grace was at the market, Mary was instructed to answer the door. The alderman indicated that he was expecting another call from his militia commander, Sir William Blake. At about half three – a little earlier than expected – Mary heard the door knock. She ran downstairs, keen to meet Galway's chief defender – a man who was reputedly friends with the exiled Confederate leader, the Marquess of Ormonde.

She opened the door and smiled. But the smile that answered her was yellow and rotting. "How do, pretty lady? You're new," the man said.

Unless Sir William had joined a troupe of players or a pirate ship, this was someone else. His dress was eccentric – a mad mix of the palace and the gutter. His shirt was silk but his belt was just a rope. He wore the shoes of a Turk, with turned-up toes topped with little bells. Mary tried not to prejudge. She remembered Grace's poor form at the door. "How can I help you, sir?" she said.

"Well now, let me count the ways," his smile twisted into a leer and he leaned against the doorpost.

She ignored the attitude, "is the Alderman expecting you – or perhaps you have business in the wine shop?"

His smile died as he digested the riposte and he remembered his business. "Oh, he'll want to see me alright. Tell him Flaherty's here with news. I'll wait."

"I'll tell Mr D'Arcy," she answered and closed the door on him.

The alderman was surprised by the visitor but keenly interested. Mary showed the man upstairs. On the way up, his footsteps were accompanied by the jangling of bells. "This one needs watching," she thought. She closed the door to give them privacy but lingered outside. She could only make out snatches of conversation. The tone was business-like but easy. Clearly, the two men knew each other well. Flaherty said something about a shipment... in two nights... give succour? salad? Hewson! Yes, she was certain he'd mentioned the English commander. The alderman's voice was lower but he seemed pleased. They continued in this vein for a while. "Have men ready," D'Arcy said at one point. Then she identified a shift to a new subject. Flaherty spoke at length while D'Arcy listened. Then the alderman's tone changed. He became angry and Flaherty became defensive. At last, as the voices rose, she heard the word she'd been listening for, "Valentine". It was the first time she'd heard the son's name uttered since she'd arrived.

She sensed Flaherty had delivered all his messages. She prepared to creep away but then the alderman started talking again. He was calm and his voice was low so she could make out nothing till Flaherty responded, a little louder, "the new girl?" Mary held her breath. They were talking about her. D'Arcy continued speaking but she understood none of what he had to say. At last, Flaherty answered. His words – and the evil laugh that followed – suggested they were finished, "that'll be a pleasure!"

A loud knocking made her heart leap. There was someone at the front door. She tip-toed back down the stairs and answered. This time, there was no surprise. An elderly man in an elaborate grey periwig stood before her. He was finely dressed, all in black, apart from a long white collar and the purple sash of the Galway militia.

"Sir William?" Mary asked as a formality.

"Yes, mademoiselle. Tell the alderman I'm here, please."

When Mary went back upstairs to deliver the news, she felt Flaherty's eyes examining her shamelessly. D'Arcy instructed her to show Sir William to the wine shop and indicated that he would follow.

About half an hour later a jangle of bells in the kitchen told Mary that service was required in the wine shop. She entered and found a smiling Sir William cradling a bottle of wine and chatting cheerfully to the alderman. The shelves, like every other shop in Galway, were conspicuously bare.

"Is Grace back yet?" D'Arcy asked.

"No sir," she answered.

"Perhaps this young lady might help me?" the old peer was smiling warmly at Mary.

D'Arcy looked slightly put out but not enough to argue with his commander. He turned to Mary, "Can you accompany Sir William home? His grace insists on making a payment for this humble gift. They've had some good hunting on the Corrib and he wants to send you back with some wild duck. He'll also need help with the wine on the way over and I have pressing business in the Tholsel House."

"It's only fair, Alderman. Why this must be some of the last wine in Galway!"

"For the time being, my Lord. I'm expecting a shipment next week."

Sir William looked slightly embarrassed. He turned to Mary. "Mademoiselle, I'd be obliged. It's always a pleasure to meet new people and a rare one in this closed city." Mary looked down and saw the opened crate of wine at his feet. She hurried over and picked it up. She was glad of the chance to get out.

"Don't delay, Mary!" Alderman D'Arcy added.

"No, sir," she answered. She did a little curtsy for the alderman and stepped into the street.

The fresh air did wonders for her spirits. The crate of wine was heavy in her arms but the streets were paved and their route followed a gentle hill down to the port. As they walked down Pludd Street towards Blake's castle, Mary smiled and took in the sights. Sir William saw her pleasure and cheerfully acted as the tour guide, naming every notable building and point of interest along the way. Pludd Street gave way to Earl Street where the peer took a moment to show Mary the Red Earl's House, a once fine building, now fallen into ruin. "The DeBurgos once ruled this city from this house... till we pushed them out, the Blakes, the Lynchs and the other tribes. How long before our own houses lie in ruin, I wonder?" He turned to look at Mary who understood no answer was required. Then he asked, "Where are your people from, Mary?"

The question surprised her. "Dublin, sir," she blurted out.

"Dublin?" He seemed lost in thought for a moment.

"Yes, sir," she answered. She didn't like sharing personal information but she decided to go out on a limb for Sir William.

"Well then, let's continue, shall we?"

She nodded and they walked on. The city smells had all but vanished by now. The sea was near. Up ahead, Mary saw a great stone gate which she guessed must open onto the quays. Gulls screeched overhead and the sky darkened briefly as a cloud passed by. The streets betrayed few signs of the siege which had choked the city for months. People went about their business as usual though, as Sir William observed, these days they had no concern for traffic.

There were no carts clogging up the streets since no goods were coming or going and, anyway, every cart-horse had long since been eaten. All this, Sir William explained with a heavy heart. "Our days are numbered, Mary," he picked up his earlier theme as he neared his home, "a new order is upon us. I grieve for your generation. When we lost the King, we lost all hope."

"What about the Marquess?" Mary ventured.

Sir William stopped and stared, "Ormonde? What do you know of his grace?"

Mary answered the peer's unbending gaze, "that he lies in France, that he would yet be an ally to those in Ireland who support the cause of the King."

"My dear," Sir William took Mary by the arm and ushered her out of the way of passers-by with eager ears. "You interest me. Tell me, how did you come to be in Richard D'Arcy's service?"

It was time to be frank. Mary opened her mouth to answer but the sound of tiny ringing bells stopped her tongue. Flaherty, the rogue, was following, some thirty feet away. He smiled at her when she caught sight of him. He didn't mind her knowing he was watching her. Sir William turned to see what had distracted her. "Good Lord protect us," he said. "Flaherty. Do you know this man?"

"Yes sir. That is, I've met him. He had business with the alderman."

Sir William was surprised. He thought out loud, "what can Richard D'Arcy want with a rogue like that?"

Mary kept quiet. She needed to get away from Sir William. She didn't want Flaherty reporting on a long conversation between them. "Please sir, might we move along? The alderman told me not to delay."

The old peer studied her with curiosity. She was hiding something but she wasn't ready to talk. "Very well, my dear. My house is just around the corner." As they walked on, Mary took one look back at Flaherty. He was still watching. He wiped his mouth with the back of his hand and winked. He looks thirsty, Mary thought.

Sir William's house was one of the largest buildings in Galway. The original building was a Norman keep but the castle now made up just one corner of a complex of buildings which dominated the gates onto the quays. Sir William was clearly one of Galway's richest citizens. At the door, they were greeted by a strong-looking porter who took the wine as well as instructions to return with a brace of ducks.

"I'm in your debt, mademoiselle," Sir William said. "Won't you step in while you wait?"

"No thank sir, if you please. I'd rather not be seen going inside. And I'd best be back before the curfew."

"Hmm..." the peer looked over her shoulders. Flaherty was hovering around the open area by the gates. Traders were selling from stalls but the rogue was uninterested in their wares. He seemed to be waiting for Mary.

"You don't like that fellow do you, Mary?"

She looked back. "No sir."

"Let me at least offer you safe passage home."

"Please no sir, I don't want the alderman to know..."

"Don't worry, Mary. There's more than one way to skin a cat."

When the porter returned, Sir William turned to him and said, "Seamus, young Flaherty there needs company. Go buy him a drink. Tell him you insist." He passed a coin to the porter who smiled. The big man looked into the street, found his mark and loped over to him. In a moment, Flaherty was caught in the porter's friendly arm-hold and the deal was secure.

"There," Sir William turned back to Mary, "you have at least an hour to make your way home."

"Thank you, sir."

"A pleasure, my dear. I'll keep my offer of hospitality open for whenever you're free to oblige me."

She bowed and left. I have an hour, she thought. She wasted no time. It took five minutes at a quick pace to return to Pludd Street. She knew the alderman was out. She hoped the other staff would be too busy to mind her. Once inside, she entered the kitchen. Mrs Taafe was nowhere to be seen. Mary left the ducks hanging in the pantry and then quietly climbed the stairs to D'Arcy's office. It was empty. She crossed the room to where several sets of keys hung on hooks. One set was bigger than the rest. "This must be the one," she thought, and lifted the great iron hoop off its perch. She buried it under a fold in her apron and hurried back downstairs. Passing through the kitchen, she peeked into the yard to make sure it too was empty. There was no one to be seen.

The kitchen was on the right-hand side of the building. In the middle was the arch and on the left was the shop. The wine store was behind the shop and behind that was the tower. This had been built to store grain when a D'Arcy ancestor had once fancied himself a brewer. It was now little more than a storehouse. Then there were eighty feet of garden and at the back, against the city's west wall, a long row of sheds stretching the width of the property. She went to the tower first. It took a while to find the right key but soon she was inside. The space smelt sweet like wine. That was all she found there. She climbed the sixty steps to the top but there was nothing other than crates of wine – mostly on the ground floor as the timbers upstairs were too weak to hold too much weight.

Up top, she paused a moment to enjoy the spectacular view over the city walls onto Galway Bay. She could see half a dozen vessels on the water. Close to shore there were a couple of small fishing boats. In the distance, there were two huge English carracks. These heavily armed boats were enforcing the blockade. Nothing could get past their guns by day and few risked the sea by night. Mary didn't linger. She hurried down the tower steps and locked the door behind her. The yard was still quiet. I have time to check the sheds, she thought. She admired the well-tended garden. There was little growing there right now but the D'Arcys were still doing better than average.

One shed was home to half a dozen pigs, she knew this because she'd heard Grace complain about the chore of feeding them. But the other was much bigger with bars over the windows. She found the key and entered. The smell was quite different. At first, it was tricky to isolate from the stink of the pig-sty next door but she recognised it eventually – gunpowder.

The shed was divided into two rooms. Each was lit by a small window. The first room was full of crates and barrels. This was nothing unusual for a wine merchant but the smell had been a give-away. Mary opened the crate nearest her. It was full of muskets and pistols. She put her nose to one of the barrels. The smell of gunpowder was unmistakable. She checked the rest of the room and concluded that there was an arsenal there well-suited to defending a city. Had the Galway Militia entrusted the alderman with their store of weapons? If they had, they were fools. Mary knew such a concentration of powder needed to be a thousand feet from houses, or in a compact city like Galway, spread across multiple locations. And this was just the first room. A half-open door led to the second room. She pushed it open with a creak. She was relieved to see no more barrels. Then her relief turned to horror. At the back of the room, almost lost in the gloom, were shackles fixed to the wall. Underneath, there was a mess of dried blood and bones.

Valentine had been chained up here. That much was obvious. Then what? He'd escaped? He'd been sent to Limerick to wreak havoc? He'd told Mary there was no connection between Hewson's plan for Galway and his own family's background. Had he lied? No, she still believed he was a pawn in this evil business. His father, on the other hand, was up to his neck. Galway was under an imminent and deadly threat. And it seemed the threat came from the inside.

34.

Manning's head was sore the next morning. His limbs were stiff and cold and he was parched with thirst. He had fallen asleep where the wine had left him, tucked up by the ruins of the monastery walls, close enough to the sleeping priest to share bodily warmth. He smiled at the strange turn of events. Then he remembered Samson and the pain of his hangover and his physical discomforts were joined by the grief for his dog. Had the wolves turned on Samson's corpse once they'd stripped the poor soldier of meat? He sat up slowly. A thin layer of frost glistened on the grass and on his clothes. The fire still smouldered though it had been too far away to do any good. He could see nothing beneath the hillock so he stood up. As he did, a weight rolled in his head like a cannonball. He steadied himself against the church wall and shielded his eyes from the glaring morning sun.

He smelt blood. He advanced slowly towards the edge of the hillock and saw Samson's body, unmolested, on the grass below. The wolves had obeyed him and left the dog alone. What am I become, he wondered, that wild animals obey me? He heard stirring behind him and looked around. Skerret was awake.

"Did they leave the dog alone," he asked.

"Yes."

"You have some power."

"I didn't ask for it."

"No." Skerret stood up slowly and joined Manning by the smouldering fire. "What did my mother say? Can you be cured?"

Manning turned and looked at Skerret. With his face crumpled from a night's drinking, he looked older and resembled Dearbhla more than ever. "She said, I must kill the werewolf that bit me."

"Lord protect us." Skerret made the sign of the cross and shook his head.

"I would have preferred a good leeching," Manning said.

Skerret laughed, "hard luck, she doesn't go in for that." He crouched down and started to examine the contents of the dead soldier's bag. "What will you do?"

Manning started to wipe the glistening frost from his doublet and looked around the old monastery, "Return to Limerick – that's where I last saw him. I suppose he still lives, as I am still cursed. So I'll search for him there."

Skerret stood up. "What you did last night. You had no cause... but you saved my life. And at the cost of your dog."

Manning faced him. He was embarrassed. "Your mother treated me like I was a friend of yours. It was time I acted as such."

He reached out his hand. Skerret shook it and smiled. "Will you have my company on the road to Limerick?"

"Are you not walking to Galway?" Manning asked.

"Not if I can take a boat," Skerret held up a bulging coin purse he'd found in the soldier's bag. He passed it to Manning. "We have the fare right here and much more besides."

Manning felt the weight of the purse and grinned. He looked around. There was indeed a wealth of plunder here. The soldiers had left their weapons, their money and – in the case of the dead man – their clothes. He picked up the dead man's musket and grew serious. "These rogues... one of them is still on the loose and, doubtless, finding reinforcements. If they catch us, we're dead."

"Then we should hurry."

They set about examining the deserter's kit and took everything of value. Within half an hour they were ready to go. There was plenty of food which they agreed they could eat on the road. An early start was safer and would ensure arrival in Limerick in daylight.

The morning never really warmed up but it remained dry and bright. The road was much worse than the main road via Bunratty and Dromoland. This was a rough, hilly landscape, peppered with small lakes and covered in long, dun-coloured grass. A great forest loomed on the horizon till midday when they finally reached the tree line. It offered little shelter and no cheer. It was grey and lifeless and silent apart from the clattering of bare branches and the squawking of crows. After a rest and a late breakfast of cheese and biscuits, the pair followed the rough track through the forest for a couple of hours. Occasionally they stepped off the road to hide from passers-by until the traffic became so constant that they had to take their chances and face down these strangers or they'd make no progress at all. They never saw the surviving deserter again. Everyone they met was an Irish refugee heading for Connacht and no one overtook them from behind. The eyes of the refugees were far more fearful than their own and for this they were glad.

It was mid-afternoon when they rejoined the main Galway road and found themselves within sight of the River Shannon. They were no more than an hour from Limerick. Skerret had spent much of the journey telling Manning everything he knew about the werewolf. He didn't hold a grudge against Valentine D'Arcy. That man who'd occupied a cell next to him had seemed more a victim than a villain. But he didn't trust those impressions. He knew Richard D'Arcy – the man who'd forced his mother out of Galway. If the son was anything like the father... Not that it mattered; the man was only half the story. It was the werewolf inside him that needed killing. In this, Skerret was happy to help.

A niggling worry had begun to itch the surface of his thoughts: Valentine D'Arcy had been in the next cell when Skerret had told Mary where his mother lived. He had not been worried about this till now. After all, he'd just seen his mother safe and well. The werewolf had been loose for days. And the man had been barely lucid when the information had been shared. If Valentine wished his mother harm then surely he'd have acted by now. Still, the knowledge worried him. He realised he shared an interest with Manning in seeing the werewolf dead. He explained his thinking to Manning and was glad to find the wolf-hunter agreeable.

"So what's the plan?" Skerret asked, satisfied that they were now working as a team.

"We should look for the servant boy, Peeter. He knows everything that happens in the castle and he's not above taking a bribe. The trick will be getting in to see him. From what I understand, Hewson and Worsley have unfinished business with me and I suspect there's still a place on the gallows for you. Are you sure you want to see this through?"

"Aye. Until the werewolf's dead, my mother's not safe. But perhaps we could avoid the castle altogether."

"How so?"

"The boy, Peeter. We last saw him fishing on the north shore of the river. I'll bet that's a regular haunt of his."

***

They found the little pier where they'd last seen Peeter and settled down to wait in the shelter of some trees. They ate a second meal and even felt well enough to wash it down with wine. They passed the time dividing up the money they had taken from the deserting soldiers. They were flush. They had twenty pounds between them. As the sun began to set, Skerret spotted a small boat approaching. Peeter was rowing it. They let him pull up to the pier before breaking cover and running down to meet him. Peeter had thrown his rope around the first cleat before he spied his visitors.

"Well met, Peeter," Manning said as he caught the boy's second rope and obliged him by tying it up.

Peeter was dumb-struck.

"Don't worry, boy," Skerret added, "we mean you no harm. He reached his hand out to help Peeter out of the little dinghy. "We just need information."

Peeter found his voice, "what are you doing here? They'll kill you if they catch you, you'll be hung." He looked all around him in panic. He wasn't looking for an escape route – he was more concerned about being seen with these outlaws.

Manning ignored the boy's concerns and spoke again, "come, we have food and drink. You must be hungry after your exercise."

Peeter nodded. He had little choice and he never refused a meal. The three walked up the pier and back to the little nest where Manning and Skerret had waited in the trees.

When they were seated, Manning got down to business. He showed Peeter a pound coin. The boy's eyes popped. "We need information and we're willing to pay for it," Manning said.

Skerret laid on the charm by cutting a length of salt meat and passing it to Peeter along with a flagon of wine. As the boy ate greedily, Skerret started asking questions, "what happened after we left, Peeter? Is there any word on the werewolf?"

Peeter lowered the food and looked warily at his interrogators. He chewed slowly, as though relishing what might be his last meal. "Why do you have to ask me that?"

Manning and Skerret looked at each other. Their instincts had been right. The boy knew plenty. Manning played his hand. He put the coin on the ground in front of Peeter and said, "a pound coin if you can tell us where he is."

But the boy made no move for the money. He took another bite of meat and a drink, wiped his mouth and said, with an air of finality, "I can't tell you that."

Skerret was annoyed, "you mean you won't tell us."

Peeter certainly wanted the money but Mary had sworn him to secrecy that night on the river. "I won't tell you."

Skerret showed his knife to the boy, "you'll lose that tongue if you don't use it, boy."

But Manning stayed his hand. He remembered Peeter's attachment to Mary and suspected she was behind the boy's late-blooming integrity. He hazarded a guess, "Mary told you not to talk?"

Peter nodded. There was no betrayal in admitting this.

"We're not her enemies. You know that." Manning spoke softly and held the boy's gaze, "We're worried about her. If she's in the company of that werewolf, she's in danger."

Peeter looked unmoved. He knew they weren't together. He had no reason to fear for her safety.

Skerret continued, "Even if he's no longer a werewolf. I know the D'Arcys. If Valentine is half as bad as his father..."

Peeter flinched. "What do you mean?"

"Richard D'Arcy is a villain. As bad as any werewolf. If Valentine..."

"But that's where she's gone," Peeter said.

"To the D'Arcys?"

He nodded furiously. The men looked at each other.

Manning spoke first, "So we're going to Galway after all. Thank you, Peeter. With luck, we'll find Mary safe and we can kill the beast in his lair."

But Peeter wasn't finished, "But they're not together. The werewolf never went to Galway." Peeter released himself from his promise to Mary. It was apparent she hadn't known the danger she was facing in Galway. The wolf-hunter and the priest – this unlikely alliance – seemed to have her best interests at heart. So he told them the whole story.

Manning was slow to take it all in. Mary had a taste for adventure that he found hard to believe and harder to reconcile with the woman he'd imagined her to be. Sure, he had witnessed her attempt to rescue Valentine but he had viewed this as a sentimental gesture, not as the calculated actions of a what... who was this woman he admired so much? He wasn't sure how he felt about this new aspect of her personality. "So, on Guy Fawkes Night – she stole the boat and followed the beast down the river."

"And found him not far from here." Peeter continued.

"And you helped her?"

"I helped her find a doctor," Peeter explained. He looked thoughtful for a moment. "God help that household. We left a monster on their doorstep."

"Where?"

"I can direct you. But you'll need a boat."

Skerret remained sceptical. "Surely there's no doctor left down there among the Irish."

"Okay, not a doctor, and not Irish. A lord of some sort... Boyle. He's a philosophe or an alchemist. It was all I could think of that night."

"Boyle?" Skerret thought for a minute then let out a low whistle, "the Earl of Cork's son! We'd better brush down our clothes, Manning. We have an appointment with a viscount…"

"If he's still alive," Manning added.

35

Robert stood watching from his bedroom window as his sister prepared to leave. The coach was being loaded with bags and Katherine was overseeing the organisation. Robert was scrutinising the arrangements too – from a distance. She still wasn't talking to him and wouldn't have his help but he wanted to make sure she was taking every precaution. It was a risky journey but she was preparing well. The coach was one of the finest in the country. Jet black, like the horses pulling it, there were few vehicles as large and imposing on the Irish roads. The Boyle family crest, painted on each door, was the only concession to colour but its imperial symbolism – the rampant lions, the crown and embattled shield – made the coach even more intimidating.

Today, they needed more than just the appearance of strength. Four servants armed with swords and muskets would make the journey with Katherine. The country was at war and Katherine might make a prize ransom for any outlaws they encountered.

The horses scraped their hooves impatiently on the gravel drive. They were already hitched to the long black coach and they looked as eager as Katherine to get started. She held the door open for one of the servants who was loading the interior. As she did, the painted arms on the door caught her brother's attention. Beneath the family crest, he could see their father's motto: 'God's providence is my inheritance'. At that moment, Katherine looked up at the window where Robert stood watching and met her brother's gaze. We have enjoyed good fortune till now, Robert thought. Please God, let it hold.

The past week had been a strain on the family's luck and this new adventure of Katherine's might prove the breaking point. The siblings looked at each other till Katherine's eyes broke away. How could a woman of her intelligence act so rashly, he wondered. She was going to Galway – a city under enemy control. She would enjoy no legal protection there. And why? So she could entreaty some merchant to care for his mad son.

Valentine D'Arcy wasn't the only lunatic in Manwood, Robert thought. No, he corrected himself, not anymore. He's gone.

***

Valentine had spent one more night in their guest bedroom. Katherine had talked Robert into allowing this. She was still angry with him. He knew he'd behaved badly. There was no one he loved more than his sister yet he'd slandered her viciously. But he couldn't bring himself to apologise. He was witnessing her self-destruct, he felt. An apology now would galvanise her madness. So, instead, he compromised. Let her return the madman to the guest bedroom. Robert had no strong objection as long as he could lock his own bedroom door. He advised the household – including Katherine – to do the same. And this morning Valentine was gone.

Of course, they could have locked him in his room. Even Katherine could have been persuaded of that but Robert had not even suggested it. Let him run, he'd thought.

The Kinnerks had warned Robert that Valentine had already raided the larder. It wasn't hard to guess what was coming. So Robert rose early the next day and checked his guest's bedroom.

The door was open, the bed was unused. Robert checked the house thoroughly and then searched the outbuildings. He was gone. It only remained to tell Katherine. She took the news calmly. Indeed, she proceeded with her breakfast. This reassured Robert. Immediately after, however, she began to make preparations for an outing. She's going to look for him, he thought. But the truth was worse. At about eleven, Katherine visited him in the laboratory and demanded his attention.

"I'm going to Galway," she said.

"That's not a good idea," he answered shaking his head.

"I'm not asking for permission."

"Of course not." He put down his quill. "You're going to see the D'Arcy family?"

"Yes."

"You'll need a guard."

"I've already asked Colman and his boys."

"Very well. They're strong fellows. Make sure they're armed."

"Of course."

They watched each other in silence for a moment, and then both spoke at once.

"Sister, I..."

Katherine spoke over him, "I also wanted to say goodbye."

"Naturally..."

"I mean, I'm not coming back."

His mouth fell open. He stood up and shuffled his papers.

She knew she was hurting him but she had to go. She'd already formed a plan. She'd meet with the D'Arcys and convince them, pay them, if necessary, to search for and care for Valentine. He needed help. He needed something other than what she had to give to him. She had been foolish. She had mistaken their rapport for a meeting of minds, not the chance encounter of two lost souls that it really was. If he was mad, what did that say of her? She'd made a mess of her life in this house. She understood the damage done by a scandal. Her husband had taught her that well. It can't be undone but maybe it can be outrun. So she'd go to London.

But before she left she still had hope that Robert – her rock – would show her some understanding. She was prepared to start afresh, alone but, if he just showed her a sign...

"You'll be missed," he said without looking at her. He sat down again, putting his great wooden desk between them. He picked up his quill. The interview was over. So it's like that, she thought. She turned and left quickly.

***

An hour later, as Robert stood watching from his bedroom, Katherine climbed into the coach and closed the door behind her. He looked at the book he'd been holding tight – his bedside copy of the King James Bible. He cast it aside. What use was all this science and religion and all the sacrifices he'd made to elevate his mind and soul, he wondered. He felt desolate. The only person he truly cared for was leaving. At twenty-five he had no wife to comfort him, no children to show for the passing years, not even a lover to shorten the winter nights.

"God help me," he whispered under his breath.

Truly, he'd leaned on Katherine for every happiness in his life. He'd lived in a world of theory but he'd been oblivious to the foundation that had allowed him to do so. And he had been happy with the choices he'd made. Indeed, it was the ability to choose which made him happy. Suddenly he understood that this was a freedom that Katherine had never enjoyed. Engaged while still a child, married to a blackguard while still in small shoes, and a mother at seventeen; she had never been free. So how could she be happy? She deserved any taste of freedom she could find, he decided.

The coach driver cried out and cracked his whip. The team of horses neighed and pulled off.

"Good luck, sis," Robert said quietly as the coach disappeared down the avenue. A clock on the mantelpiece chimed twelve. It was the hour for chemistry experiments. He looked at the clock, then at his bed. He chose the bed, pulled back the covers, and curled up under the cold, dark blankets.

36.

As the sun set in Inchicronan, Dearbhla prepared for Valentine's arrival. She knew something dangerous was approaching. She guessed it was the werewolf. There was no settling the livestock who sensed a presence beyond the tree line and it was too early for regular wolves to make a foray into her little valley. This was some other kind of threat. So she said her prayers, made sure the animals were secure and then made dinner for two. There was no point putting up a fight. Finally, she sat by the fireside and allowed the aroma from the stew-pot to distract her while she waited.

They had never met when she'd treated his brother and they only knew each other by reputation. But when he emerged from the gloom, she knew him; he was the cut of his father. She decided to play dumb – he was expecting a sorceress so it was best not to spook him with mysterious foreknowledge. Still, English was in order so she called out, "Good evening, sir. Have you come to see the doctor?"

"Is it Dearbhla Skerret? I've spent the day searching for you."

"It is," she answered, "and I hope I can reward your diligence."

When he reached the light of the fire they were able to read each other's eyes and dispense with the formalities.

"You know who I am," Valentine said.

"As you know me. Please sit down." She gestured to a stone seat close to the fire and the bubbling pot of food. Best to gain his trust before I offer him dinner, she thought, since he thinks me a poisoner as well as a witch.

But Valentine was hungry and not shy, "may I have some food?" he asked.

Dearbhla felt a great release of tension and smiled at her guest. "I waited for you. We'll eat together."

"You were expecting me?" A flash of suspicion crossed his face.

She had dropped her guard too quickly. "The animals wouldn't settle. I knew someone was out there."

"Someone," he said, "or something."

She decided not to answer that and instead scooped a ladle full of fish stew into a bowl. She passed it to Valentine along with half a loaf of bread. As he took it, she had a good look at him. From a distance, he had appeared handsome and strong. Up close she saw the wear and tear that had debased his looks. His once good clothes were torn, then mended, then torn again in new places. Dark circles haunted his eyes and he wore the grime of a long day or more on the road. And yet, this man has shaved within the last two days, she noted.

As she helped herself to food, Valentine assessed Dearbhla. He also took in her surroundings and concluded that her recent existence had been as tough as his own.

"You've lived here a while?" he asked. He knew it was a loaded question but he wanted to see if she'd dare take the high ground with him.

He found her too wise for that, "just over a year now," she said.

"It must be hard in winter?"

"It is."

"You're by yourself?"

The question unsettled her till she reasoned; it made no difference whether she was alone or not. He has the strength of ten men. Unless she had a private militia hiding in the cave, she was at his mercy. "I'm alone now but my son was here recently."

"The priest?"

"Ambrose, yes."

"I'm happy he got out of Limerick. He told you I met him?"

"He did."

"He's the reason I came."

She was blowing on her soup to cool it as he spoke. She paused. "Do I have any reason to fear for my son?" she asked.

"No, not from me. But he said something to me. Well, a few things. First, you should know, he never told me where you lived. I was lucky to overhear that. I don't think he'd give you up easily."

It was good of him to say it. She felt he was being overly generous to Ambrose but perhaps she was wrong. Either way, this D'Arcy has manners, she thought. Then she remembered her own and poured a drink for her guest.

Valentine continued, "Your son said something about my father. I need to know the truth. He blamed my father for your current circumstances." He looked up and Dearbhla nodded. So far there was no debate.

"I've always known my father was a hard man – harder still since my mother died. When I returned from Spain, Donal was dead. My father blamed you. He called you a witch. I know he had you kicked out of Galway. I didn't question it then or after... when I was cursed." He stopped eating and fixed her in his gaze. "But I need to know from you; was it you that cursed me?"

She swallowed hard and answered, "Yes."

He continued calmly, "I suppose you saw the pain he felt in losing one son so you decided to take away the other?"

"No," she was glad to have a chance to explain, "it wasn't supposed to be you. I sent him wine – a sample from a would-be supplier. Tainted, of course, with a potion so evil I wish I'd never known it. It was addressed to him. He was supposed to drink it. I never thought..."

Valentine let out an ironic snort, "if you'd known my reputation. I remember now. It was foul-tasting stuff. He couldn't leave anything around the house but I'd drink it. More so when Donal died. There was no cheer in that house except what could be found in a bottle."

"I'm so sorry, Valentine."

He waved his hand. There was no malice in his heart. "It's not important. I don't hold it against you. There was something else. Skerret said my father had 'Flaherty' drive you out."

"Yes. when the war started, Flaherty did all your father's dirty work. He and his gang knocked our door down, drove us into the street and set our house on fire."

He knew she was telling the truth but he had to be sure of the facts, "Tadhg Flaherty, the pirate?"

She nodded again.

Then it was true. He put his food to one side. His shoulders sank and he stared into the fire.

"What is it?" she asked.

"It was Tadhg Flaherty who handed me over to the English."

So, he was learning how bad his father really was. Even to Dearbhla, this was a new low. She found herself making excuses for her enemy, Richard D'Arcy. Perhaps Flaherty did it on his own initiative? Maybe he'd fallen out with D'Arcy? But she could see that Valentine needed no further proof. He must have other evidence against his father.

After a while, Valentine spoke again, "I should have guessed earlier. It was obvious in Limerick that the English had a well-connected agent in Galway. Their plans were so devious. Use me to take Limerick then use my blood to spread the plague through Galway. There's no faster way to spread poison than in a bottle of wine. My father must have concocted the whole scheme when a werewolf fell into his hands."

"But why?"

Valentine looked up, "The war is lost. The Tribes of Galway are finished. When the Roundheads take over, my father wants to profit. So he's helping them from the inside." He shook his head in disgust.

Dearbhla still had questions, "Your blood alone wouldn't do it unless..."

Valentine cut across her, "I know, I know. They need, 'Blood of the wolf, blood of the dead, blood of the youth whom the wolf hath bled.' I learnt that verse well in Limerick. That's why I must go far away before I bite someone who survives..."

Dearbhla interrupted him, "Oh no. But you did – William Manning."

"Who?"

"The English wolf-hunter. You did bite him. He survived. He was here with Ambrose."

"Why?"

"For a cure."

"And did you cure him?"

"I must confess, I gave him the secret." She looked uncomfortable, "I told him that he must kill you."

Valentine considered this in silence for a moment.

"I'm sorry Valentine."

"T'is no matter. It would be a release," he answered.

"Then you didn't come to me for treatment?" She felt some relief that she didn't need to disappoint him on this score too.

He looked up, "It occurred to me," he started, "someone gave me a glimmer of hope but..." he looked at Dearbhla and saw there was no encouragement in her eyes, "I suppose I've always known I was beyond a cure."

She put down her bowl of food. "I'm afraid so," she said simply. And Valentine understood. Like his brother, Donal, before him, he was past help. They both sat in silence for a moment while Valentine digested the truth. The curse was irreversible. It was what he always understood, of course, until he'd allowed Skerret's promise to open a chink of hope in his heart. It was perhaps the touch of love he'd felt around the same time – first Mary's selfless concern then the deep connection with Katherine that caused that hope to kindle.

"You see, Valentine, there is a window of hope after the first infection. But it only lasts a month. After that, the werewolf's nature is fixed forever." This is why I sent William Manning after you. There is hope for him – but only in your destruction."

"Then I should find him and face my destiny. I'll do my best to keep him safe from Hewson and my father. Without his blood, Galway might be spared..." Then he remembered something, "'Wait, you said 'blood alone was not enough unless...' Unless what?"

"Well, in combination with a strong impression. It's been known to happen... just as a shock to a pregnant woman can shape the baby. The werewolf's blood consumed by someone who has been strongly affected by a werewolf – a terrible apparition for instance – it might be enough to cause a transformation."

"A terrible apparition?" Valentine's thoughts turned to Katherine and her brother. Then he spoke urgently, "But only if they drink the blood?"

"But how else can blood be shared?" Dearbhla asked.

"Oh God," Valentine went pale. "I must warn them."

37.

Robert was still in bed that evening when Manning and Skerret came to see him. First, he heard a commotion in the garden. Then he heard Kinnerk shouting a warning. Then he heard voices, Irish or English, he could not tell, beg for an audience. He heard his name and sat up.

Strangers had landed at the pier and wanted to see him urgently. He looked out of the window. Kinnerk was armed with a musket and threatening the intruders. They were a curious pair. One looked like a Roundhead soldier, the other like a Catholic priest. They held their hands up in submission but continued towards the house. Kinnerk aimed his musket at the soldier. They continued pleading their case. He heard one of them say 'Valentine'. Robert opened his bedroom window and shouted at Kinnerk to let them approach. He threw on some slippers and a wig and ran downstairs.

At the front door, the visitors started babbling. They were looking for Valentine D'Arcy. Had he been there? Thank God the household was safe. Did they know he was a dangerous...? Here, the priest interrupted his English friend and offered the word 'fugitive' in place of whatever the soldier had in mind. What was he hiding, Robert wondered. He decided to dismiss Mr Kinnerk who had been hovering in the background and ushered his guests inside. He showed them to the dining room and had Mrs Kinnerk bring port.

Once they were settled, Robert interrogated his visitors, "You say this Valentine character is 'dangerous'. How? And be frank with me."

The pair looked at each other. "Tell him from the beginning," the priest advised his friend.

The soldier drained his glass for lubrication and started talking. His story started strangely and only grew more macabre as the last rays of sunlight crept up the walls of the dining room and finally gave way to flickering candlelight. It was dark when he finished with their journey from Limerick to Robert's doorstep.

"Werewolf!" It was all Robert could think to say.

"It is no lie," the priest said.

"No," Robert was almost whispering. "I think I believe you. I had some correspondence from this Worsley fellow you mentioned – several months ago. He fancied himself a like-mind... knew my work with the Invisible College. But he was more alchemist and wizard than man of science. And he had a peculiar fascination with experimenting on the living. I stopped answering his letters." He stood up, walked to the fireplace and looked into the flames. He started thinking about Valentine and his sister. "Thank God, she's rid of him."

"Sir?" Manning asked, confused.

Robert turned. He hadn't told them his side of the story. But he still had questions. He looked at Manning, "And you, William. You have this curse?"

Manning felt ashamed. "I still have hope of salvation," he said.

"In Valentine D'Arcy's destruction?"

Manning nodded.

"With a sword or musket ball? You tried before yet he lived. How does one beat the devil?"

"With silver, sir." Skerret offered.

Manning elaborated, "Sir, we were advised that he can be killed with a silver musket ball. Though we lack the skills to forge one."

This turned Robert's head. "Then you'll gain more than just a lead on your quarry by your trip to Manwood. Stand up, men. Let us adjourn to the laboratory."

***

The first thing Robert did was light the furnace. The laboratory was dark and cold. He'd been absent all day so the fire had never been lit. His visitors stood dumbly behind him, perhaps wondering what sort of viscount gives his time over to metalwork. Indeed the strange room teased other mysteries. While Robert hunched over the incipient fire with an oily taper, Skerret took the initiative and lit every candle he could find. The room appeared to be part forge, part kitchen and part library. The floor was lined with straw and the scent of harts horn recalled the privy but the large central table was covered with kitchenware and herbs. Meanwhile, the furnace Robert tended might have served as a blowing house. If anyone in the county could forge a silver musket ball at short notice, it was clear this man could. Robert had been explaining his plans since they'd left the dining room. He intended to make the required silver musket balls there and then. As they'd passed through the kitchen, he had grabbed a large meat pie, some plates and a handful of cutlery.

While the furnace warmed up, he encouraged his visitors to eat the pie quickly as he intended to melt the cutlery once the fire was hot. He stuffed a large slice into his own mouth and pumped the bellows vigorously. "It's not like casting lead," he said, "Silver needs much more heat but we'll get there within a few hours." He turned to Manning, "Do you know what a bullet mould looks like?"

Manning nodded.

"Good. There's one around here somewhere. I want you to look for it. I'll also need tongs and a large crucible."

Manning got to work. Then Robert turned to Skerret who was licking his fingers, "Looks like you're nearly finished eating, can you take over at the bellows?"

Skerret swapped places with Robert and started pumping. The room had taken on a rhythmic red glow as the bellows fed the flames. Manning quickly found the crucible and handed it to Robert. It had recently been used as a plant pot so Robert started cleaning it meticulously. The priest took in his surroundings as he worked. He quickly concluded that the room showed signs of two separate personalities. There were two handwriting styles in evidence on the carefully labelled bottles and jars that filled every surface. There seemed to be two distinct workspaces too. And he noticed Robert seemed to gravitate exclusively to just one of them. The other workspace was dominated by herbs and medical paraphernalia. It reminded him of his mother. As the initial flurry of activity gave way to tedium, Skerret's curiosity brimmed over into conversation.

"You share your workshop with a doctor?" he asked.

"A chymist – my sister, Katherine," Robert answered. He had finished cleaning the crucible and was using a vice to fold the cutlery into more manageable shapes for the furnace. He seemed reluctant to say more.

Skerret was undaunted. He had been given the most boring job so he wanted distraction. "She's not here?"

"No," Robert answered. Manning had found the tongs and delivered them to the scientist. Robert seemed glad of the interruption and turned to the wolf-hunter. "Thank you. Keep looking for that bullet mould. We'll get nowhere without it." Manning went back to his search.

"My mother was something of a... chymist," Skerret said. "Always grinding herbs and cooking some foul-smelling poultice..."

"Really." Robert had opened the furnace door and was using the tongs to lift the crucible and its silver contents inside. He could do without the conversation.

But Skerret continued, "did your sister attempt any treatment on Mr D'Arcy?"

Robert shut the furnace door and stared at Skerret. But there was no malice in the priest's face. The scientist dropped his voice low and answered, "Yes. But to no avail. The werewolf was beyond her help."

"I found it!" Manning's head popped up from a corner of the laboratory. He was carrying a two-handled device like a nutcracker.

Robert held Skerret's gaze for a moment then melted, "Excellent! Bring it here."

I've upset him, Skerret thought. And where is this sister? He was curious but he decided to drop the interrogation for the moment. Manning delivered the bullet mould to Robert who explained its workings to Skerret. Once the furnace was hot enough, the silver would become molten and they could start the moulding process. "We'll need a bucket of cold water to cool the metal," he remembered, "Would you mind, William?" Manning nodded and left.

Robert felt he needed to explain his attitude to Skerret, "My sister tried to help Mr D'Arcy and failed. She felt bad about this. She wanted to help somehow so she went to Galway to seek his family's help."

Skerret let go of the bellows, "Saints preserve us, she hasn't gone to Richard D'Arcy?"

Robert looked alarmed, "if that's the father's name, yes."

"Then she's in terrible danger," Skerret said.

A look of horror contorted Robert's face.

"First Mary, now this man's sister. We can delay no longer. We must go to Galway." Manning stood frozen in the doorway with the bucket sloshing in his hand. He had heard enough.

Robert looked at him. "But my sister has one of the fastest coaches in the country. We won't catch her by road."

"So, we sail." Skerret turned to Manning.

The wolf-hunter nodded, "I know a man."

38.

"Still no word?" Tadhg Flaherty was impatient for news. Richard D'Arcy lowered the letter he had been reading. He looked disappointed. He was standing by his office window. He removed the pince-nez that helped him read and scrunched up the letter.

"They've failed," he said. "First they lose Valentine; now they've lost the blood donor. Without him, there can be no shipment. God knows how these Roundheads ever took the country in the first place." He walked over to the fire and contemplated the painting above it. It was a ship in full sail on a stormy sea, working the very weather that threatened to sink it.

Flaherty continued, "There's still the arsenal. There's enough guns and powder there to take the city."

D'Arcy dropped the crumpled letter into the flames and watched it burn. "A softened, cowed and bloodied city maybe. We're not there yet. Blake's militia are far too sprightly yet to face in battle. Their spirit must be broken. They need terrorising; werewolves lose on the street, wives and children slaughtered. They must be abandoned by God before they surrender hope."

"If we still had Valentine..." Flaherty started.

D'Arcy exploded, "Valentine is dead! Do not..."

He stopped suddenly in response to a sound behind the closed door. D'Arcy raised his finger to his lips, walked to the door and opened it quickly. The landing was empty but a scent lingered. The alderman sniffed and turned to Flaherty. He lowered his voice, "Mary."

"I tell you, she's a spy," Flaherty said.

"Aye, she's spying alright," D'Arcy continued speaking quietly and only half closed the door, "and she'll meet a spy's end."

"She's mine then," Flaherty said.

"In good time. I want to know who she's talking to,"

"Blake! I told you."

"She talked to Blake but she's not working for him. She came from Limerick. She knows about Valentine. There's money behind her. She might be working for anyone. She might even be working for Hewson." D'Arcy returned to the window and looked down at the street.

"Let me find out," Flaherty's eyes widened.

The alderman was silent for a moment. "I was hoping to use her but she's become too dangerous," he looked at Flaherty and made a decision. "Very well, we'll do it your way. You can use the shed. Bring her there tonight. I'll make sure the house is empty in case she sings too loudly."

Flaherty smiled.

***

Mary hid under the arch and caught her breath. That had been too close. D'Arcy's shouting had made her flinch. She should know better. But she had escaped detection and she had learned a lot. She could relax a little longer. The werewolf invasion was not imminent. It seemed Hewson and Worsley had not yet managed to produce the potion with which they threatened Galway. And she had heard confirmation that D'Arcy was working for them. She needed to talk to Sir William Blake – only he had the power to dislodge D'Arcy from his position of power inside the Galway Militia. But she couldn't think how. She believed she could convince him of D'Arcy's treachery – she could be very persuasive – and Blake seemed friendly but she was never going to sell the werewolf story. It was too fantastic.

She felt her breathing return to normal and she looked around. A wash tub sat accusingly outside the kitchen door. This was the worst part of being a spy, she thought – working two jobs. She brushed down her apron and fixed her cloth cap before approaching the tub and resigning herself to hours of drudgery but she was interrupted before her hands got wet.

Grace called out from the kitchen door, "Mr D'Arcy says you're to go to the market."

Mary was surprised. "Not you?"

"No," she answered sulkily.

Getting out of the house was always a blessing – one which usually fell on Grace, who knew the city and the traders better. Mary tried not to look too pleased and returned to the kitchen where Mrs Taafe would tell her what was wanted.

The cook seemed as put out as Grace. Dinner was already arranged but the master had developed a sudden craving for parsnips. Didn't he realise, she complained, that there was laundry to do and Mary's time might be better spent than crossing the town for a few vegetables? "Hurry back," she said as Mary stepped out onto Pludd Street.

Outside, the shadows were lengthening. When Mary turned onto Glover's Street, she had to shield her eyes from the low sun in the distance. Traders were busy closing up and there was a liveliness in every step as the towns-people hurried home before curfew. These days, anyone caught on the street after dark faced arrest. Mary's long stride made short work of the journey. She was conscious of the curfew but also that the route was lined with tanneries that stank of piss and filled the air with stinging quicklime.

She was able to breathe freely by the time she crossed Great Gate Street at Lynch's Castle. She glanced up at the clock above the arch. It was already half-five. It would be dark soon. Beneath the clock, the gate was up and more refugees were pouring into the city. The new arrivals interested her but the traffic soon forced her to move along. Little Gate Street was quieter but gloomier. The shadows in doorways and courtyards had already darkened to black. She felt a little vulnerable and twice looked over her shoulder for signs of danger. She was looking for Tadhg Flaherty. But he didn't seem to be following her. She quickened her pace as she climbed the gentle hill up towards the market. There were a few stalls left open. Eventually, she found what she was looking for and made her purchase.

By the time she started home, the sun had dipped below the city walls and every window she passed was shuttered or boarded up. At Lynch's Castle, the crowds had thinned out but she still took care crossing the road. Looking south towards High Street she thought she saw Grace and Mrs Taafe in the distance. She stopped for a moment to make sure, but she was barked off the road by an impatient porter leading a sedan chair. When she looked again, they were gone. Could it have been them? It seemed unlikely; Mrs Taafe was never far from the kitchen at this hour. The apparition had made her anxious though and she quickened her steps back to Pludd Street.

She became more worried when Mr D'Arcy, not Grace, answered the door. Something was wrong. The alderman read her expression – or perhaps he had predicted her unease. He smiled paternally and said, "Come in, Mary. You're surprised to see me at the door. Come into the kitchen and we'll get those parsnips on.

I sent Grace out for something else." He stood aside so he could follow her into the kitchen. Her mind raced; so Grace and Taafe are gone. Is Garavan here, perhaps some of the stable boys? Or am I alone with Mr D'Arcy? She entered the kitchen and received an unwelcome answer. Flaherty was there, sitting by the back door. He was whittling a stick with one of Mrs Taafe's knives. I'm trapped, Mary thought. But the game's not up yet.

"Mr Flaherty," she curtsied at the pirate and brought the parsnips to the basin so they could be washed. D'Arcy stayed by the door to the hall, silent for the moment. He's not bothering to explain where Mrs Taafe has gone, Mary thought. She set about washing the vegetables. When that was done she glanced at the two men. Flaherty was focused on his whittling but D'Arcy was watching her. He threw her a smile when their eyes met. But he was tense and fidgeted with his lapels. Mary suddenly realised the natural thing for her to do was to turn the parsnips before they could be cooked. She needed a knife. It was a bold move but she turned to Flaherty and cleared her throat. He looked up.

"Please sir," she pointed at the knife, "it's the knife we use for turning vegetables."

He looked confused.

She persisted, "might I have it?"

The pirate smiled and reached out with the knife in his hand. When she tried to take it, he grabbed her with his other hand. He twisted her arm till she cried out. She looked at D'Arcy. Was he going to allow this? He made no move to stop Flaherty.

There was a loud knock on the front door. The alderman changed his mind and barked at the pirate, "Flaherty! Enough!" He turned and left to answer the door.

Mary pulled her hand free. The pirate stared at her but remained sitting. She backed away. At the fireplace, she reached for a poker. Flaherty smiled. A fight was on. But the conversation from the hallway changed their calculations. They broke eye contact to follow an unexpected development. A woman was talking to D'Arcy and she was talking about Valentine.

***

It took half an hour to manoeuvre the Boyle family coach through the archway into the D'Arcy's courtyard. During this time, the alderman had no choice but to leave the viscountess alone with Mary. Katherine, or Lady Ranelagh, as she'd introduced herself, had made a mess of his plans. He had quickly ushered her up two flights of stairs to the dining room and instructed Mary to bring her refreshments. Then he tended to the coach and servants. In an instant he dropped his plans regarding Mary – they could wait. Indeed, he didn't even have to dismiss Flaherty. The pirate understood his night's work was not going to happen and disappeared before the alderman could beg for any help from him. So D'Arcy was alone.

Mary, for her part, was first relieved, then baffled by the sight of a viscountess calling on a Galway wine merchant in the middle of a siege. That she wished to discuss Valentine seemed less surprising somehow but it explained nothing.

Katherine was too tired to be amused by the consternation she had caused. Her first reaction was quiet displeasure that this alderman, who seemed comfortable enough, ran a house with just one servant. The journey had been exhausting and though she had been anxious about her interview with D'Arcy, she had been relishing a comfortable rest and refreshments.

One thing they all took for granted was that an alderman was duty-bound to receive a viscountess with every courtesy. Besides, this woman knew things about Valentine. D'Arcy needed to find out just what, and with whom she'd shared her knowledge. For once, Mary's thoughts matched the alderman's.

So Katherine became a guest.

While he was overseeing the parking of the coach, D'Arcy borrowed one of his neighbour's servants and gave the lad a groat to look for Mrs Taafe and the rest of the household staff. Their impromptu night off would end as quickly as it had begun. In the meantime, Katherine was under Mary's care. She found the fish pie Mrs Taafe had originally intended for dinner still warm, if a little dry on the shelf behind the fireplace. She quickly warmed some wine, sliced some bread and brought the meal up on a tray for their guest. As she stoked the fire, she considered the new arrival from the corner of her eye. It didn't take Mary long to connect the lady in the parlour with the foggy wooden pier on the banks of the Shannon where she and Peeter had deposited Valentine the previous week. That was a fine house – worthy of a viscountess. Had this woman cared for Valentine? Perhaps she'd travelled this far to deliver, in person, the worst news a parent can hear.

Then Mary remembered the monster on the battlement in Limerick Castle. She remembered the gunshots that would have killed a mortal man. No, Valentine was not dead, she was sure of it. So why was this woman here?

"Is the house always so quiet?" Katherine had found a kind way to comment on their staff shortage.

"Oh no, my lady," Mary stood up and faced Katherine. "There was a... celebration. The staff had a night off but I do believe Mr D'Arcy has sent for them now that you've arrived."

Katherine was eating hungrily. "Oh good," she said. Mary must have reacted to this presumptuous attitude because the viscountess followed through with, "I'm sorry to be such trouble."

245

Mary poured some wine for Katherine. "You've travelled far, my lady?" Mary asked. There's a delicate etiquette to addressing a Lady, she remembered. A maid is allowed a question or two but only if she's providing some service to justify her presence.

"Limerick," Katherine answered. She did not elaborate. Mary adjusted the curtains and then fussed with the fire for a minute. When Katherine said no more, Mary understood and took her leave.

Outside, on the landing, she nearly collided with D'Arcy. They locked eyes briefly. Right now, it suited both to continue the pantomime that Mary hadn't just escaped some kind of violation right under D'Arcy's nose. Both had witnessed this and both knew D'Arcy had arranged it. There was only so long that such a charade could be maintained and only so long before one or the other would act in response.

"Mrs Taafe has returned," D'Arcy said quietly, "please return to the kitchen to help her."

"Yes sir," she answered. She hurried down the stairs.

Lady Ranelagh had been accompanied by four servants. Mary wanted to have a look at them. They wouldn't be armed, since the besieging army confiscated the weapons of anyone heading into the city, but they had looked like big, strong men. Their presence offered some reassurance. Mary was now seriously worried for the safety of everybody in the house. If D'Arcy was prepared to cross a line with her, she had to assume Lady Ranelagh was also at risk.

She met Grace carrying an armful of bed-clothes in the hallway. The girl looked disappointed by her cancelled night out.

"Grace, where are Lady Ranelagh's men going to sleep?" Mary asked, trying to sound casual.

"The barracks, with the militia," she answered sulkily and tried to continue on her way.

Mary held her arm, "But why? Surely there's room in the stables or the store?"

Grace looked disapprovingly at the hand on her arm, "'The master says they'd be more comfortable."

Mary thought fast. She retrieved a coin from her apron and gave it to Grace. "Here, her Ladyship told me to give you this. She's ever so generous. Give me those blankets and I'll make her bed."

Grace stared dumbly at the coin and let Mary take the bed-clothes.

"You go help Mrs Taafe," she added.

Grace returned to the kitchen, staring at the half-crown in her hand. Mary stood at the bottom of the stairs. This was bad. Did Lady Ranelagh know her servants had been sent down the street to bunk with the militia? Mary had witnessed D'Arcy's rage when Flaherty had simply mentioned Valentine. How would he react if the viscountess revealed that she knew his son's dark secret?

The guest bedroom was behind the dining room. Mary now had an excuse to go there. It was a good place to eavesdrop. She removed her shoes and climbed back up silently to listen. D'Arcy had left the door open. He had taken a seat opposite Katherine. He started with a preamble about what an honour it was to welcome her Ladyship to his house. She apologised for the imposition and the lack of notice. Then they got down to business.

"Mr D'Arcy, I'm not sure where to begin. As I explained at the door, your son, Valentine, was a guest in my father's house for several days." She started with Valentine's sudden appearance on the pier at Manwood. She left out some important details; the burial, her personal involvement with Valentine, of course, and she omitted the blood transfusion – only saying that she and her brother 'nursed him back to health'. At this point, the alderman interjected. He had already established that Katherine's husband was in England. This brother was news to him and D'Arcy made sure to check that he had stayed behind in Limerick. Katherine was slightly put out by D'Arcy's interest in her brother. She assumed he was clarifying who the male patriarch was in her house. He probably couldn't understand why she'd been allowed to travel to Galway alone.

When D'Arcy had finished clarifying her domestic arrangements, Katherine told the most difficult part of her story: She described how she'd found Valentine, one night, slaughtering a lamb and eating it raw. D'Arcy listened in silence. She repeated the story Valentine had told her about his werewolf curse and she concluded with his disappearance. "So, I thought it best to consult his family. It is clear to me now that he has lost his mind. He needs his family to care for him."

"Of course," he said quietly. Then he was silent for a minute. "I will do everything in my power to help the poor wretch. And I will forever be in debt to you, My Lady, for taking such good care of him."

Mary heard a chair squeak and understood the alderman was leaving. She tip-toed back to the guest bedroom and set to work making the bed. She was reassured. She had relaxed as soon as Katherine had mentioned her brother. If her brother knew where she was, she was certainly safer for that fact. And Katherine hadn't believed the werewolf story either. This offered some protection too. D'Arcy might not like people knowing his son was a lunatic but it was better than people believing him a werewolf.

So, he'd let Katherine stay a day or two, then send her on his way with assurances that he would seek out Valentine and care for him. That was the likeliest path. Indeed, while Lady Ranelagh was in the house, Mary was safer too.

39.

"The wolf-hunter returns!" Captain Salah bellowed from the deck of his ship when he saw Manning approaching.

It had taken several hours to row the little boat from Manwood to Tarbert. The three men – Manning, Skerret and the Viscount, Boyle were exhausted. They'd worked through the night, forging half a dozen silver musket balls before setting off at dawn for Tarbert. None were used to the water so the rowing and the fear of drowning and taken a further toll.

The Meshuda which had carried Manning north from Dingle only a week earlier was a welcome sight. Manning had recommended the pirate over Skerret's protests. This was the man who'd tricked the priest out of his fare to Galway and had nearly drowned him in the process. Trustworthy, he was not. But he couldn't argue with Manning's assertion that this boat was the fastest way to Galway – if he was going that way. The ship was a caravel – a small, shallow draught boat with two triangular sails. There were few boats as fast on the west coast and none as sure on the estuary. Boyle, for his part, reassured the pair that, if the boat was in Tarbert, then he would hire the whole ship to take them to Galway.

As they tied their little dinghy up at the pier, Salah disembarked his ship to greet them. The new arrivals were surprised to see how keen he was for business.

"He has seen Robert and smells the money," Skerret ventured.

"Whatever works for us," Manning answered quietly.

Salah studied the odd little group and recognised Skerret. He bowed and pressed his hands together, "I owe you my apologies. I failed to make you welcome last time we met."

"You owe me twelve shillings too," Skerret answered.

"And Mr Manning here owes me money," Salah turned to the wolf-hunter.

Manning reached into his purse and handed the pirate captain a handful of coins, "There, my debt is settled. Today we need you for another job."

Salah counted the coins and replied, "I have kept your cargo safe, wolf-hunter. It's stinking up my boat, in fact."

Manning had forgotten about the wolf's blood and had no desire to ever see it again. "You can throw it over-board. I'm finished with that business."

"Your soul will thank you for it," Salah answered. He turned to Robert Boyle and smiled as he assessed the viscount's wealth and status "Now, please introduce me to your illustrious friend."

"Viscount Robert Boyle, son of the Earl of Cork," Manning said.

Salah bowed and said, "My Lord, I would be honoured to welcome you onto my boat."

"Excellent," Robert answered. "We need your boat to get to Galway urgently."

Salah stroked his beard, "I can bring you to Galway, yes. They'll admit refugees – but only on pain of inspection." He looked at the three eager faces and flashed his gold teeth, "but something tells me you'd rather avoid official channels? That can be expensive."

The three men looked at each other. It was true that all priests were outlaws and Manning had a price on his head. Boyle spoke for the three of them, "Yes. I think we'll pay for a discreet passage."

He opened his purse and looked inside. "How would you like us to pay – gold or silver?"

***

An hour later they were beating into a fresh south-westerly wind towards the open sea. Salah had his cook prepare breakfast for his guests and invited them to use his small cabin for the duration of the journey. After a welcome feed, the three men tried to get some rest. Sleep proved impossible though. The ship was fast but she clambered over the waves rather than ploughing through them. The constant rise and fall hit Skerret and Boyle hardest and they had to go on deck to save their stomachs.

From there they watched the lush green shore-line diminish as the river opened into the sea. The weak November sun soon disappeared behind a wall of grey clouds. The air became suffused with a salty mist and the rolling became more pronounced. Skerret and Boyle held tight to the shrouds of the mainmast as the ship began to round Loop Head. They were coming to open water. Captain Salah stood on the quarterdeck keeping an eye on everything while his first mate, Ahmad, made micro-adjustments to the wheel. The small crew worked diligently under his watch and did not attempt to converse with the passengers. Skerret and Boyle were forced to make their own conversation.

"Let's hope we can trust him," Skerret said to the viscount when they felt the captain's gaze land on them.

"I suppose one can never fully trust a pirate," Boyle said. Then he added, "but he'd be a fool to turn on me. He may be an outlaw and a foreigner but he seems to understand rank and money. I'm sure my presence will keep us safe on this journey."

Skerret continued to look doubtfully at Salah, "Let's hope so," he said, "but there is a war on and that often makes a mockery of convention. You're trusting he'll show more respect to a viscount than your parliament lately showed a king."

Robert was about to argue the priest's logic but he was interrupted before he had a chance to reply. Salah had ordered his crew to run downwind and moments later half a dozen men were scrambling for the ropes to adjust the sails. A brief deceleration was followed by a lurch forward as the two sails billowed like wings over the sides of the boat. They started north along the coast of County Clare. Salah who had been watching his passengers from a distance shouted over the rising wind, "Now, sirs, we will make some time!"

The rolling they had experienced till then had been just a foretaste. In open waters and with a stiff wind behind them, the little caravel seemed to plunge into the waves with a violence that left the passengers reeling. Manning soon emerged from the cabin looking dazed and stumbled across the deck like a drunk to join Skerret and Boyle. As he reached them, a huge wave crested the starboard side and the three men were soaked from head to toe.

Manning read doubt in his friends' eyes, "It was the same coming up from Dingle," he reassured them. "Salah knows what he's doing. We'll not come to any harm."

"Well, perhaps not from the weather," Skerret answered but his warning was lost to the crash of another wave.

There was little opportunity for conversation from there on. The thunder of waves breaking over the gunwale followed by the hiss of water draining from the deck drowned out all talk.

But there was much to see.

By noon, they'd passed Spanish Point and Skerret pointed to the rocks where the Armada had lost half a dozen ships seventy years before. By three o'clock they were at Hag's Head, a sharp promontory that marked the start of the Cliffs of Moher. Those cliffs started high and continued climbing for an hour till their peaks disappeared above the clouds. The shoreline, which had seemed a refuge from the waves, from then on became a focus of fear. Here, the sea and sky were joined in the middle by an endless wall of jagged limestone. It was a colourless vista but it was far from lifeless. Birds filled the air. All around the boat, gannets and guillemots pierced the sea like arrows. Higher up, gulls floated on stiff wings, powered purely by the churning air. Boyle craned his neck and stared in wonder. It was something to behold. He was distracted by a message from the captain; dinner was ready. As the three passengers stumbled back to the cabin, Boyle spotted the Aran Islands on the port side. These barren rocks would hem them in all the way to Galway Bay.

In the sky above the islands, a small spot of light made him squint, then fizzled in the dark as he entered the cabin. The pale winter sun which they hadn't seen since morning was beginning to set. They were halfway there.

***

They struggled with dinner but eventually ate their fill. It took such an effort to keep the wine upright, the drink was finished quickly. An hour later, the ship's rolling subsided as they entered Galway Bay. The three men found themselves able to relax for the first time on the voyage. Sleep followed soon after. The sea air, the lost night and the fear which gnawed at their hearts all combined to ratchet their exhaustion to the limit.

But Salah was not relying on nature. He had drugged their wine to make them sleep. The poison sneaked up like a thuggee and smothered them in a blissful coma. As they approached Galway, the first mate, Ahmad, looked in and was pleased by what he saw. All three were unconscious. Boyle occupied the captain's bunk, Skerret was perched on a settle under the stern window and Manning had curled up on the floor with some blankets.

Ahmad spied the cache of weapons they'd brought on board and gestured to one of the crew-men. The sailor tip-toed in and removed the bag in silence. The timing was good. They would be at their destination soon. He closed the cabin door, locked it carefully and returned to his captain on the quarterdeck.

"Well?" Salah asked when he saw his mate return.

"Sleeping like babies," Ahmad said.

The two sailors looked out over the port bow and took in the view. Two English carracks sat guarding the entrance to Galway.

"There was no approaching the city unseen by them. Our English friends were fools to believe it."

"Yet their money was good," Ahmad said.

The first mate watched the compass for his captain and spoke his mind. Salah valued both services but, ultimately, he made his own decisions.

"Yes," agreed Salah, Then he smiled at his mate. "But, Hewson will pay more!"

Indeed, the two English ships looked intimidating but this was not a concern tonight. Salah's lights were out, he was keeping his distance and the prevailing wind was taking him past the city. He was heading for Oranmore where the English army had been camped since the summer. He wasn't expected but he would be welcome. There was a fifty-pound reward for William Manning and Salah intended to claim it. There was a few pounds to be made on the priest too and, with luck, the English would view Boyle as an enemy agent which would allow him to ransom the viscount. This could be a very profitable voyage.

40

It was late when Valentine reached Manwood. A light frost crunched under his feet as he made his way up the avenue but he heard no other sound. He had been walking all day and had not eaten since he'd left Dearbhla. He was determined to get to Manwood as quickly as possible. The house was dark and the grounds devoid of life. He knocked hard on the front door but received no answer. The first sound he heard was the barking of dogs in the hallway. But the door didn't open. He thought he heard two voices whispering.

"Katherine!" he shouted. "It's Valentine! I have to talk to you," The door remained shut.

"If there's anybody there, I need to talk to Katherine or Robert. It's urgent." he cried. His voice was hoarse and he stuttered with the cold.

A shadow darkened the dining room window. Someone was watching. Valentine searched his memory. Who were the house-keepers? Kavanaghs? Kieltys? He remembered; "Mr Kinnerk, Mrs Kinnerk? Please open the door. I have an important message for your masters." He turned to the dining room window. "Their lives are at stake."

The shadow in the window disappeared. He saw a flame flicker in the window light then heard the lock turn. Mr Kinnerk opened the door a crack. He looked old and frightened and Valentine stood back to appear less threatening. He tried to sound calmer, "Mr Kinnerk, thank you. Please, where are Katherine and Robert? I must talk to them."

Kinnerk winced at Valentine's disregard for his masters' rank. "The master and mistress are not here. They have gone away. If you have a message, you can tell me and I'll tell them when they return."

Valentine half-absorbed the answer. He was not expecting this. "Gone? Where have they gone?"

Kinnerk pulled the door a little tighter. This man was incorrigible, he thought. "Their business is their own, sir. Now, if you have a message, please convey it and be off." A female voice whispered in support from behind the door. Mrs Kinnerk was just as keen to be rid of Valentine.

Valentine gave up wondering about the Boyles and focused on Kinnerk. "Please, I didn't mean disrespect. I swear their lives depend on hearing what I have to say it. But if I don't know where they've gone, I cannot guess when they'll return. My message is time sensitive. Now, please, if you could only tell me when they'll be back?"

Kinnerk thought for a moment. His wife jabbed him for continuing to listen but this just made him contrary and he opened the door wider. He was holding one of the great dogs by the collar but the beast remembered Valentine and whimpered instead of growling. This display of affection seemed to soften Kinnerk further. "I'd help you if I could Mr D'Arcy. The mistress held you in high regard," he said, "but I don't know the answer to your question." He looked Valentine up and down and realised the man had been in the elements all day. "Why you're freezing!"

"Aye, I've been walking all day," Valentine answered weakly.

He opened the door fully. The other dogs came bounding out and Valentine hunkered down to greet them. Mrs Kinnerk stepped into the light and looked at Valentine and her husband with a mix of disapproval and resignation. "I suppose he'll want feeding," she said and headed for the kitchen.

***

Mr Kinnerk led Valentine inside and sat him by the fire in the kitchen. His wife warmed some soup over the fire and served it to him with some bread. Valentine watched them both and felt a pang of guilt for the ongoing trouble he brought to this house. The Kinnerks sat together at the table and returned his gaze in silence. They seemed to be the only souls in the house. As his senses returned he noticed he'd be given a wooden ladle to eat his soup. It seemed petty to refuse him the household silver but he certainly wasn't going to complain.

But Mrs Kinnerk saw him study implement and offered an explanation, "It's all we have left. The master had all the silver melted shortly before he left."

Valentine was taken aback. He'd seen no sign of financial trouble during his stay. "He's not in debt, I hope?"

The Kinnerks gave each other a look which suggested debt would be a preferable condition. The husband spoke. "The master melted the silver for one of his... experiments... the night he left."

A dread thought struck Valentine. He slurped down the remains of his soup. "Might I look?"

Mr Kinnerk shrugged his shoulders. He had let Valentine into the house; the young man could do pretty much what he wanted now. Valentine thanked his hosts for the food and asked to borrow a candle. He made his way into the Boyle's laboratory.

The cold air and the return of some circulation to his body made him shiver. The room was even more chaotic than before. Tools, papers and ashes littered the floor. The large furnace to his right was evidently the scene of the most intense work. There were indeed still a few knives and forks strewn at the base of the furnace alongside the object Valentine had feared – a musket-ball mould. He picked it up. It was frozen shut. Robert hadn't had the strength to open it. But he had made others. How many? He needed to see the evidence with his own eyes. He pulled the handles of the mould apart. The effort took all his strength. Finally, he heard a crack. The handles parted and a perfect, gleaming silver ball sat within. It could only have one purpose – to kill him.

He popped it into the palm of his hand and sat down to rest. The heavy metal ball shimmered yellow in the solitary candle's light. So this is my destiny, he thought. Let it be a friend, then, who guides me out of this world. He felt no animosity towards Robert. He was impressed. He was clever enough to discover my weakness. Then a thought struck Valentine and he sat upright. If Robert knows I'm a werewolf, Katherine must too. He had to be certain. He raced back to the kitchen and burst in on Mr Kinnerk alone.

"Robert and Katherine – your master and mistress," he corrected himself, "they are together?"

Kinnerk was taken aback by his energy, "yes... I suppose..."

He had no time for this, "you suppose? What do you mean? They are or they are not?"

Kinnerk had no energy left to be offended, "well, they must be by now. Lady Ranelagh left first and the viscount followed her."

"Followed her? Followed her where?"

But Kinnerk had composed himself. He hadn't shared this knowledge before. He wouldn't share it now. He didn't answer.

Valentine grabbed the servant's shoulders and shook him, "Dammit man, I must know. Their lives depend on it."

Mrs Kinnerk's voice answered from the door to the hallway, "They're both gone to find your father and have him lock you up."

Valentine's stomach sank. He looked up. Mrs Kinnerk was pointing a musket at him.

"My father?" he said weakly – oblivious to the threat of the musket.

"Leave this house," the housekeeper said, stepping slowly towards him keeping the musket high, "or I'll shoot you like a dog."

Valentine released Kinnerk and fell back against the wall. The strength had left him as quickly as it had returned. Katherine was going to his father. She was in terrible danger. How had it come to this?

He was bitterly amused by Mrs Kinnerk's analogy, "Madam, would that I were just a dog."

41

The three men in Salah's cabin woke up within minutes of each other. It took them a few seconds to realise something was wrong. The boat was apparently in port yet nobody had come to wake them. Skerret peered out of the stern window but could see nothing. Boyle fumbled for a light, found an oil lamp and lit it with one of his phosphorous matches. They looked at each other and realised that wine couldn't account for their weakened states. They began to suspect foul play. Then Manning noticed their weapons were missing. He stood up, took a moment to steady himself, and stumbled to the door. Even then, he was surprised when he found it locked. So, the pirates have betrayed us, he concluded. He turned to tell his friends but they had already understood.

"He'll be sorry," Boyle said. "If he hands us over to Englishmen, I'll have him strung up like a topsail. Don't worry, friends, Charles Coote is the Parliament's man in Galway – he won't harm a son of the Earl of Cork." His confederates listened but their faces remained wary. They needed further reassurance, "...and you can count on my protection, of course," he added.

"And what if he sells us to the Irish?" Manning wondered.

Skerret answered that. "What can he profit? There's no trade in priests amongst the Irish. And they have no bounty on you. Even

Robert here would be treated as a non-combatant. No, it must be the English. We can only hope Robert's nobility protects us all."

They both looked at Boyle, whose face now showed a little less confidence than they would have liked.

They were distracted by noises from the deck. Someone was boarding the ship – a large party of men by the sounds of it. There was some shouting then they recognised Salah's voice. He was explaining something quickly. His visitors became more reasonable. A few minutes of negotiations followed. They couldn't hear what was being said but Salah was obviously making his bargain with whoever had come aboard. A moment of silence was followed by footsteps and the turning of a key in the lock. The three men stood up to face their captors. The door opened and Ahmad, the first mate, stepped in. His eyes searched those of his prisoners. He was gauging their mood before he spoke. He was relieved to find them awake and apparently appraised of their situation.

"Gentlemen, the captain has made a better deal with the English. I'm sorry it must be this way." He broke eye contact and added, "please come out on deck."

There was nothing else to be done. They followed the pirate outside to meet their fate. A hundred eyes greeted them. The pirate crew and dozens of Roundheads stood watching. Skerret looked around to find his bearings. He knew Galway and its surroundings. The boat had sailed up a narrow inlet where some daylight still lingered in the west and was tied up at an old stone pier. The deck was lit up by a bonfire at the water's edge. Salah was watching the proceedings in isolation on the quarterdeck. Dozens of smaller fires dotted the fields to the east suggesting the presence of a large encampment. A dim blue twilight framed the flat horizon all around them but gave few other clues. Then Skerret noticed the silhouette of an old Norman castle. This, he recognised. We must be in Oranmore, he thought.

"We're in the English siege camp," he whispered to Manning.

"And that's the colonel from Limerick," Manning whispered back.

In front of him, stood Colonel Hewson. He was in full uniform wearing his helmet, breastplate and a sword on his belt. He recognised Manning and smiled with satisfaction. Boyle identified him as the most senior officer present and walked straight over. The scientist was the only be-wigged man in sight and the Roundhead soldiers parted in deference to his apparent rank and obvious self-confidence.

He had no idea who Hewson was so he took a wild stab at his rank, "Captain, I am Viscount Robert Boyle, son of the Earl of Cork. This man..." he pointed at Salah, "is guilty of an act of piracy. I commend him to your custody."

Boyle's tack surprised everyone. A moment of silence seemed to hold infinite promise till Hewson answered in a loud voice – "Your father is a good Parliamentarian, sir. How ashamed he will be to learn of your treason."

Shock held Boyle's tongue for a moment. He had been expecting a debate, bureaucracy, at worst stubborn indifference. This was the English army; he was not expecting belligerence. He raised his voice. "Where is Charles Coote? Where is the Earl of Mountrath, I demand an audience. I am a loyal Parliamentarian".

At the mention of Coote's name, Hewson judged it prudent to remove Boyle from the earshot of his regular soldiers. Charles Coote was indeed the commanding officer of the English troops in Galway but, Hewson reflected, he was like Ireton – a slow, idle fool, content to watch his men fall to dysentery while the Irish sat inside their cosy city walls. Hewson had no such patience but he'd rather keep his little operation quiet for the moment. Boyle could upset that goal. The Earl of Cork had a dozen sons, he mused; he was unlikely to miss just one.

First, though, he'd remind his men of the privilege Boyle represented. "You'll have a fair trial, sir – the entitlement of all Englishmen."

There was a murmur of approval from his men.

"Tie these three up. The rest of you men, return to camp," he said.

Boyle, Manning and Skerret each protested but their cries were drowned out by the easy chatter of soldiers freed from duty and by the anti-Irish and anti-royalist epithets of the dozen men who set about tying them up.

"Prisoners secured," one of the soldiers reported.

"Take them below," Hewson answered.

Now, it was Salah's turn to be affronted. He ran down from the quarterdeck and confronted the colonel. This is my ship; I decide who gets tied up on it."

Hewson looked at the pirate with disdain, "Your boat, heathen, is ours till I'm done with it. I'll use it as I please." He hated dealing with these God-forsaken mercenaries but the look of defiance in Salah's eyes and in those of his crew gave him pause. He softened. "Don't worry, captain. You'll be paid for your time. You are still the master of your ship. I would be obliged if we could hire you for another job. Perhaps you'd do me the honour of securing these men in your hold?"

That was all Salah needed to hear. His face remained hard but he answered, "At your service, Colonel."

Hewson waved the prisoners out of his sight but had second thoughts about Boyle. As Manning and Skerret were dragged away, the Colonel held Boyle's arm and spoke to him again, "I would speak with you further, sir." He indicated to the soldiers holding Boyle that they wait. "How did you come to be entangled with these tories?" Hewson asked the scientist.

As they were shoved down the stairs, Manning and Skerret took no comfort from the fact that Boyle was having a second – this time private – interview with Hewson.

But Boyle was relieved to have a second chance. He refrained from pushing his noble connections – this colonel was something of a Leveller, he decided – instead, he spun a tale of family ruin that any father or brother could buy. Ten minutes later, he rejoined his friends in the hold of the pirate ship. Manning and Skerret looked up at him expectantly. They had been chained together and sat shoulder to shoulder in one of the sailor's cots.

The scientist wasn't too sure what had just happened. He looked back at the soldiers who had dumped him in the dark and waited for them to leave.

"Well?" the priest broke the silence.

"Well, he said he'd talk to Coote," Boyle answered.

"And that's it?" Skerret asked.

"He was more reasonable than before," Boyle replied.

"He has dumped you in the hold," Manning said.

"He asked me to wait here."

Manning feared the worst. "What did you tell him?"

"Don't worry, I didn't tell him any tales about werewolves or magic potions. I told him we were on a private rescue mission. That my sister was in danger of ruining herself with a wine dealer in Galway and that we were on our way to rescue her."

"Did he ask the name of this wine dealer?" Manning demanded.

Boyle began to doubt his strategy, "yes?"

"And you told him?"

"Yes," he answered meekly, "I saw no disadvantage in it."

Manning and Skerret looked at each other. Manning spoke slowly, "Colonel Hewson is the man behind the werewolf plot. He's in league with D'Arcy."

***

The rest of the night crawled by. There was no light in the hold save what seeped through the two latticed openings in the deck. One was a sort of chimney; towards the bow, there was a fireplace for cooking surrounded by a stone-tiled floor. Further aft, there was another opening, large enough for cargo. Beneath this was the long table where the crew ate. The walls of the ship were covered by a three-foot-deep wooden framework of cots and shelving. But tonight there were no sailors asleep there. While they were in port, there was only a skeleton crew on board and they had left the prisoners alone in the hold.

The tedium of captivity was a familiar experience for Skerret and Manning. They soon found comfortable spaces to sleep and resigned themselves to finishing yet another day in gaol. But Boyle could neither sleep nor clear his mind. He had endangered his sister by telling Hewson that she was with D'Arcy. And he had discovered something unthinkable – that an English soldier was willing to murder an English nobleman. He was coming very late to the Civil War. Manning and Skerret had made it very clear to him that Hewson was a killer and that he could count his life cheap in the colonel's hands. If that applied to him, he had to assume it applied to his sister. He didn't believe Hewson's bluster about a trial. The colonel was clearly a maverick. Boyle and Katherine were therefore an embarrassment to his plans. In retrospect, he concluded, it would have been better if he'd never left Manwood.

After wrangling with his situation, Boyle began to consider the bigger picture. From what he understood, Salah had sold them out because there was a price on Manning's head. They needed Manning's blood to create this potion which would infect the people of Galway and turn them – at least enough of them – into werewolves. But to do this, Hewson would need to transport the deadly cargo to Galway. Was that why they had been sequestered on the boat? Were Hewson's plans going to move so quickly? And what could he do to stop this devilry? Boyle wrestled with the problem for hours but he could see no solution. Eventually, exhaustion and the cold winter night forced him to give up and rest. He found an empty cot, pulled a flea-bitten blanket around himself and drifted off into an uneasy sleep.

--*

The next morning brought new light but no solace. The sound of activity on deck stirred the prisoners. Manning, Skerret and Boyle looked at each other then looked to the openings in the ceiling where voices gathered and made plans. Something was happening. The ship was being loaded with cargo. The prisoners could hear the clink-clink of bottles being transported. This went on for some twenty minutes. Then a shadow crossed the grating. A man who hadn't been present last night took a long look into the hold. He could see little in the darkness but Manning recognised him. "Worsley," he said under his breath. This confirmed the prisoners' worst fears. Now that he had captured Manning, Hewson had summoned the alchemist, Worsley, to perform the blood-letting.

On deck, Worsley removed his eyeglasses and wiped them with a kerchief. He was wearing a heavy coat, fur hat and gloves. A coach waited on the pier, its team of horses spent and shining with sweat. The alchemist had arrived in a hurry. The colonel was standing in the middle of the deck surrounded by half a dozen soldiers, none of them officers, all of them strong. The pirate crew were keeping their distance but looked on warily. Salah was practising nonchalance from a seat on the quarterdeck but he never took his eyes off the visitors.

Worsley addressed Hewson, "who else is down there? I saw more than one man move."

"The priest – Skerret. The one we'd originally chained to the younger D'Arcy in Limerick."

"They're in league?"

Hewson scoffed, "It's as well for them. They'll be going to hell together."

"And the third man?" Worsley's eyesight was better than it seemed.

Hewson's face darkened, "he is of no concern to you."

The alchemist knew when to change the subject. He paused, then spoke, "I can begin right away. I'll need help." he cocked his head at the gang of strong men around Hewson.

"They're at your disposal," Hewson said. "Start your work, doctor. When I return, we sail." He started to leave.

Worsley fidgeted. "I will need a lot of blood, you understand?"

Hewson answered without breaking his stride. "Take it all, Doctor. Take it all."

42.

Richard D'Arcy had drawn the same conclusions as Mary. As long as Lady Ranelagh's brother knew where she was, the viscountess was untouchable. This made disposing of Mary almost impossible. And the servant girl was more of a liability than ever. But there was nothing he could do. So he had decided to bide his time. Lady Ranelagh had delivered her message – it had tested him to keep his counsel when he'd heard it. What presumption! What entitled gall! The Lady seemed to think every father had pockets as deep as her own. Had Valentine been only mad, D'Arcy would have cast him out, not incubated the wretch in his own home. But it was better to lie. Presumably, she would go home in a day or two. He could bear that. Hewson's shipment did not seem to be arriving anytime soon so he would wait.

Those were the calculations he had made at his morning toilet. Isn't it marvellous how quickly things can change, he thought?

As he put down the letter newly arrived from Oranmore, his mind raced with fresh possibilities: The shipment was arriving tonight. Hewson had found his man and his alchemist was making substance of their plans. D'Arcy was not a religious man but he felt divinely favoured by the postscript in Hewson's letter; Robert Boyle, Lady Ranelagh's brother – fly in the alderman's ointment

– was captive, under a sentence of death. Hewson indicated that a similar fate should befall the sister.

So, I have two birds to kill, he mused. He sent for Flaherty. Half an hour later, Grace led the pirate up the stairs into D'Arcy's office.

He read the alderman's face quickly. "Tell me it's on!" he said.

"Tonight!" D'Arcy answered.

Flaherty flashed his rotten teeth. "What about your visitor, and your house spy?"

D'Arcy sat back in his chair. They had a lot of business to attend to. "That's why I called you."

Divide and conquer was the best policy, he had decided. He gave Flaherty his instructions. First, he was to send word to his loyal militiamen in the Tholsel House. Lady Ranelagh's four servants were to be detained. Accuse them of spying or smuggling or anything to hold them in a jail cell. Next, he needed Flaherty to deal with Mary. This pleased the pirate no end. But there would be no interrogation. The pirate's smile dropped. There was too much to do. Mary was a spy, and they might never know for whom, but she wouldn't die in Pludd Street. She was to be the victim of the street. He cheered again at that thought. There was no reason a murderer shouldn't play with his victim down the alley, he thought.

"And the viscountess?" his eyes widened at the prospect of another victim.

"I'll handle that," D'Arcy said. "But first, I'd better have breakfast with the Lady."

***

Mary was on her knees scrubbing the floor of the wine shop when Flaherty left. There was no escaping the chore while the shopkeeper, Garavan, looked on. Her back was sore and her fingers raw but she had already pushed her luck; eavesdropping on D'Arcy's conversations. She was sharp enough to draw some conclusions from the pirate's visit; D'Arcy had an aristocratic guest staying with him yet he was willing to host the rogue, Flaherty, under the same roof. Something important must be happening. And the only kind of business she knew Flaherty to have with D'Arcy was evil. Did she need to worry for her own safety and for that of Lady Ranelagh? Perhaps. Mary still felt the Lady's presence made the house safer for her than it had been the previous night. As she scrubbed, another nail broke on the rough wooden timbers of the shop floor. This maid routine was wearing thin. She had to face facts. If D'Arcy believed her a spy, he'd harm her at the first opportunity. She couldn't afford to wait. She wasn't planning to break cover but she needed to take action. And she knew who to call. As soon as this damn floor was done, she decided.

The opportunity presented itself just before noon. Mary, Grace and Mrs Taafe were in the kitchen dealing with the detritus of D'Arcy and Lady Ranelagh's breakfast when the alderman entered. He apologised for the cancelled night off the previous evening and announced a half day for the household staff. While Grace and Mrs Taafe shared their delight with each other, Mary boldly met D'Arcy's eyes to read his motives. He stared her down, "You'll enjoy some time off too, won't you, Mary? After all, you didn't even get to start your evening off yesterday."

What could she do? "Yes sir," she answered. She was torn. She feared for Lady Ranelagh. But her reasoning had been sound. He can't harm her while her brother knows she's here, she thought. So she must be safe. And Mary needed this opportunity. She had plans – and her own safety depended on her taking action. D'Arcy indicated that all the staff would be free for the afternoon but asked that they return by six o'clock. It sounded reasonable. So Mary put on her coat and stepped out onto Pludd Street. She started in the direction of Sir William Blake's castle. Seconds later, a pair of bare feet stepped out from a dark arch across the street. They set off in pursuit.

**

Lady Ranelagh was growing impatient. Where were Colman and her other servants? She hadn't liked the idea of them staying in an army barracks but, in the chaos of her arrival, she had accepted it. She was the one imposing after all – the least she could do was make her presence convenient to her host. But she needed them now. She had decided to stay in Galway one more night to refresh the horses but she wasn't going to pass the day cooped up in the D'Arcy household. She wanted to explore. For that, she needed an escort. The alderman had promised to send for them at breakfast. He had apologised for failing to accommodate them in his own house and had welcomed her plan to stay a second night. In this and everything else, he had been a gracious host. But he could not mask the discomfort he felt or the obvious strain her presence had placed on his house.

Breakfast had been late. He had apologised, citing pressing business. They dined alone. Again, he apologised; he had no female relatives to keep her company. She told him she enjoyed a man's conversation as much as a woman's. But it turned out he had no conversation to share with a woman. She had tried small talk but their shared connection with Valentine, the funk of war and the household's general gloominess, had exhausted her store of cheer after only a few minutes. They passed much of the meal in silence, turning with exaggerated enthusiasm to engage with the servants' comings and goings. The sulky teenager attending them did not help the mood. Katherine wondered where the woman who had attended her the previous evening might be. She had shown spirit.

D'Arcy tried to counter his shortcomings as a host with adjectival excess: He was 'extraordinarily' honoured by her company. She was 'eminently' welcome to stay another night. He would 'immediately' summon her servants from the barracks.

An hour after breakfast and she was wondering how honoured or welcomed she really was. There was no sign of Colman.

When D'Arcy had left her to attend his business, she had started a watch at the window. There was no shortage of traffic. She witnessed half a dozen household staff leave the premises. She spotted Mary, the servant from last night. Then she'd seen Grace, the sulky teenager, and an older woman she guessed to be the cook leaving the house. Who remained, she wondered? She began to feel uneasy.

A light rain began to trickle down the window panes. She pulled her shawl tight around her shoulders. The fire behind her was smoky and mean with the heat. It was a turf fire – the only fuel in the west where trees were as scarce as money. She wouldn't miss these cold houses when she left Ireland, she thought. But she'd miss the smell.

She thought about travelling and the journey that lay ahead. There'd be talk when she reached London. They'd say her brother was a fool to expect a woman to take a job seriously. Look how she'd quit before the winter, they'd say. Perhaps he was a fool. Perhaps they both were. They were both needy. Maybe a lonely farm in this war-torn country was not the best place for them. There were no safety valves there. She began to think of Valentine.

Downstairs, Richard D'Arcy was alone. He prowled the ground floor. He made sure the doors were locked and headed for the wine shop. All was quiet. There was nobody left in the house except him and the viscountess. He needed a stout length of rope. He remembered seeing barrels of wine coming in from the boats with rope for handles. He found what he was looking for and headed for the stairs. He snapped it in his hands to test its strength and ascended into the dark.

Katherine stood up to get a clearer view of the street. Galway would get nothing done if it stopped for rain so the street was busy as usual. Katherine heard steps on the stairs and glanced at the door. The alderman must be coming with news of Colman. She turned her attention back to the window. She hadn't seen any sign of her servant. A floorboard creaked behind her.

"Has Colman arrived, Mr D'Arcy?" She spoke without turning.

D'Arcy stood at the door, watching her back. Something on the street held her attention. Good. He held the short length of rope tight in his hands. He paused. He could cross the room in a second. But something stopped him. What was she doing?

"Who are you waving at?" he asked breathlessly.

"I don't know," Katherine answered. "This man started waving at me when I stood up. Do you know him?"

D'Arcy crossed to the window and looked down at the street. Katherine noticed him stuff something into his pocket. It was Sir William Blake looking up at them. His waving intensified and he smiled when he spotted D'Arcy.

"Sir William," D'Arcy spat out the name.

Katherine looked at the alderman. He looked pale.

***

Mary left Sir William's house disappointed. The militia leader wasn't home. As the door closed on her, a shower of rain started to fall. She looked around the little square outside Blake's Castle. Pedestrians were quickening their steps and traders were covering their market stalls. Mary wondered what to do.

She had been planning to tell Blake about the cache of weapons in D'Arcy's outhouse but she had planned to do it face to face. She had no idea whether he'd believe her but she felt she had to take some action. She didn't know how imminent the threat to Galway was but both she and Lady Ranelagh were in danger. Exposing D'Arcy would hopefully protect them. And she couldn't afford to wait. As she walked away, she decided; he must know today. She needed to write a note.

She intercepted a local boy and asked where she might buy stationery. He recommended a haberdasher on Market Street not too far away. She had time. She started northeast up Quay Street. This was the main thoroughfare that led through Market Street up to Great Gate Street where she'd first entered Galway. It was crowded with pedestrians and sedan chairs. There were quite a few shops here engaged in a similar business – trading mainly in textiles but also groceries and with luck, paper. She quickly found what she was looking for. The friendly shopkeeper, perhaps curious about her level of education, provided pen and ink and invited her to write her note there and then.

She closed the note, borrowed a wax stick and candle from the shopkeeper and, when he wasn't watching, she took a ring from her purse and used its face to seal the letter. This ring was more precious than the considerable amount of silver in her purse. Now was the time to use it. She set out once more into the busy street. The rain was easing as she knocked once more on Sir William's door. She left the note in a servant's hand and departed. Where now, she wondered? She was at a loose end for the first time in a while. She decided to treat herself to lunch. There wasn't much choice or quality on offer. She found a stall selling something that may have been chicken pie and settled for that. The rain had stopped so she was content to eat outside but she wanted a seat and some peace. She remembered the Red Earl's House that Sir William had pointed out to her. That would do nicely.

Five minutes later she was crossing the ruined threshold of the old DeBurgos Castle. The roof was missing but the interior was still dark and relatively dry thanks to the trees which had sprouted inside. Mary's arrival disturbed some birds but otherwise, she found the building empty. The ruin was one of the largest empty spaces inside the city walls. The DeBurgos had clearly been wealthy and their legacy cast a long shadow. Mary found a ledge that had been spared the rain and sat down to enjoy her lunch. The space was quiet like a church. The floor was strewn with the sodden leaves of more than one autumn and in the corners, she noticed broken jugs and sooty stains where the city's youths must have gathered at night to spite their elders. As she ate, she listened to the raindrops which had only now trickled through the thin canopy of leaves above. From behind her, she could hear gulls and the chatter of traders down by the port. To the east, she heard the bells of Saint Nicholas' Cathedral ring out for noon. In the distance, she heard the booming of artillery. This was the English army. They were not yet fighting but they were not idle. Every day, they trained and reminded the townspeople that their fate hung in the balance. Then she heard another sound – closer. Footsteps, behind her. She was no longer alone.

She listened for the tinkling bells on Flaherty's ridiculous shoes but they were absent. She reached into her apron. Best to be prepared, she thought. She heard breathing and smelled a familiar odour. Now! She turned and stood her ground. Flaherty stood there, ten feet away. He was leering. He held a long knife in his hand. He showed it to her. She looked at his feet. They were bare. He followed her gaze.

"I don't like to make any noise when I'm out hunting," he said.

"You might try having a wash, next time," she answered.

He flinched. This one is too bold, he thought. "You need schooling, girl." He kept his eyes on her but fumbled with his belt. "I'll teach you." He took a step forward.

So that's how it's going to be, Mary thought. She took her hand from her apron. She was holding a flintlock pistol. Flaherty froze. Mary pointed the weapon at him and pulled back the hammer. She was in control.

There was a moment's silence and then a wild yell. Valentine D'Arcy stormed through the doorway behind Flaherty and pulled the pirate to the ground. Mary was as surprised as the pirate. Valentine pinned Flaherty down and took a second to look up.

"Hello Mary," he said.

But he was over-confident. The pirate still had the knife. He slashed blindly and struck Valentine's hand. Mary saw blood. Valentine cried out and rolled off. Flaherty didn't hesitate. He threw himself on top of Valentine and brought the knife down hard. But a musket ball sent him flying. The flash blinded momentarily but the explosion seemed to echo for seconds. Finally, silence descended and nothing moved but the smoke rising from the pistol barrel.

Mary lowered the weapon and spoke, "Your hand! You're bleeding."

Valentine was in shock. He looked at his bloody hand, then he looked at Flaherty. The pirate lay dead. His face was destroyed. From the street, they heard shouting. Someone was coming to investigate the gunshot. "We have to get out of here," he said.

Mary nodded and hid the pistol under her apron. She started heading for the eastern door. "No," Valentine said, "this way." He led her west towards the city wall. He knew where to hide.

***

Teach an Eirí – the Rising House – lay just outside the city walls on the edge of a shallow inlet between the old Augustine Abbey and the city's Eastern wall. It was a great place to watch the sun-rise as Valentine knew too well. In times past, when he didn't sleep in Pludd Street, he slept here. Like all brothels, it was tolerated but only outside the city walls. This was where he was bringing Mary. It was hemmed in by the walled Abbey and the sea so neither the English nor the city's defenders had garrisoned it. It was hard to get to. Typically its patrons rowed up the inlet in from the quays. Valentine led Mary through a well-hidden postern gate close to the middle tower. They stopped in the dark passage under the city wall just long enough for Mary to bind Valentine's hand and stop the bleeding. On the battlement up above they could hear troops marching. Flaherty's body had been found and the militia was responding.

As they hid in the dark, Mary took the opportunity to ask questions, "What happened, Valentine? What are you doing in Galway?"

"I might ask you the same," he answered but her silence demanded a proper answer. "I was watching the house in Pludd Street. I saw you leave and I followed." He lowered his voice, "I came to help Katherine," he said.

Mary read his expression and understood, "You're a fool, Valentine D'Arcy. You have no idea what's at stake."

"I know enough," he answered.

"Do you know the man I just killed?" she asked.

"Flaherty, and it was a fate he deserved. He was my father's agent."

Mary studied Valentine, "So, you've learned more about your father since we last spoke?"

"That he's the very devil," Valentine said quietly.

"Yes," Mary answered. "He's a devil who wants werewolves loose in Galway. And now here you are." He squirmed as she tightened the makeshift bandage. This statement of truth shocked Valentine. Even now, he seemed to be doing his father's bidding. He had no answer.

Outside, the shouting intensified. They were still quite close to the Red Earl's House. They could hide for only so long. They needed to move.

Mary spoke, "We need to get out of here."

Valentine led Mary through a dark tunnel to the other side of the wall. The postern gate opened onto the sea. An inlet of water fifty feet across lapped the length of the city's western wall. They could see Teach an Eirí on the other side. But there was no bridge and no boat waiting.

"What now?" Mary asked.

"The water's shallow. We wade across. We can hide in the Eirí till tomorrow."

"I can't," Mary answered. Valentine studied her for a moment. Did she disapprove of his choice of hideout?

"I have to return to Pludd Street," she continued. "It's okay, as long as I can avoid the soldiers, all I have to worry about is your father."

"That's enough for anyone," he said.

"I have to be in Pludd Street tonight. Your father's hoarding weapons. I've alerted the militia leader but I'll need to show him."

Valentine began to understand. "My father won't go quietly... and he has loyal men. Katherine will be in danger."

"I'll try to get her out of there. Though, why she'd listen to a servant... ?" Mary realised she had her work cut out for her.

"Send her to me," Valentine suggested. He started to fiddle with his injured hand. Mary looked on, confused. Then he showed her the ring he'd just removed. Two hands holding a crowned heart – it was flecked with blood. "Give her this."

"Valentine, I haven't time to carry love tokens across town. Don't you understand how serious this is?"

He looked at her patiently. "I think I do," he said, "I have something for you, too." He reached into his pocket and showed her the silver musket ball. "You know what this is for?"

She looked at it and began to understand. She nodded.

"Good. I'm giving it to you. I know you know how to use it. When the time comes..." They said nothing for a moment. Mary studied his face and pieced together the journey that had brought Valentine to this point.

He broke the silence. "Now, I can get you closer to Pludd Street, past the soldiers. You'll still have to get your feet wet though."

Mary had seen enough to trust Valentine. He stepped into the freezing water and she followed. Together they walked knee-deep alongside the city wall till they came to the next opening.

"We're under Steire NaGunaigh. You can re-enter the city from here. We're the far side of Pludd Street so you won't be connected with Flaherty or The Red Earl's House."

Mary climbed onto the ledge and looked into the dark arch that led back to Pludd Street.

Valentine continued, "Send Katherine to me. I'll wait in Teach an Eirí."

Mary made an effort to wring the seawater from the hems of her skirts. "You're sure she'll come? I'm not sure I can convince a Lady to wade into the sea, let alone to a bawdy house."

Valentine smiled, "I believe she'll come."

43.

As they sailed from Oranmore, Captain Salah stood at the wheel, deep in thought. He had agreed to carry Hewson and his soldiers to Galway. He had agreed on a price and had been paid half in advance. Hewson warned him that he planned to torture one of the prisoners on the way. Did Salah have a problem with that? No, he'd answered. Being a party to torture was not a transgression for the pirate. Yet he was deeply troubled.

To reach Galway, he'd need permission to pass the two English carracks in the bay. That would not be a problem with Hewson on board. But what then? He also couldn't leave without their permission. He was afraid Hewson might deny him passage. The colonel's treatment of Viscount Boyle worried him. It looked like Hewson was going to execute the son of an Earl. If a viscount wasn't safe from Hewson, who was? This question made Salah very uncomfortable. But what could he do?

He stood behind the wheel and surveyed his ship. His crew were also unhappy. But they were outnumbered and out-armed by the thirty soldiers who had joined them. They sulked around their new passengers and spoke little and only in their native Berber.

The English soldiers, who paid their wages, were lounging on the deck, playing cards, cleaning their muskets and sharpening their blades. They too were silent, their tongues held in check by the screams that rose from below.

***

William Manning cried out as another blow landed on his face. Worsley the alchemist was a clumsy physician and his attempts at drawing blood from the wolf-hunter had been cruel. Robert Boyle looked on, horrified. He knew how to bleed a man and would have advised but he was gagged and chained. Hewson, who watched impassively, had seen fit to silence the viscount – the fewer witnesses to his identity the better.

The procedure had commenced hours before they'd sailed and Manning had lost enough blood to kill a weaker man. Worsley was unskilled but he understood that he needed to keep Manning alive and awake to pump his blood. The wolf-hunter kept threatening to pass out so Worsley had him beaten.

One of the English soldiers stood by, shirtless. His knuckles were red with Manning's blood and his sweat glistened under a patchwork of sunlight from above. The thin ribbons of light also picked out the glassware that now filled the hold. Hundreds of bottles of wine had been loaded in Oranmore. Added to these were a small number of jars and amphorae which Worsley himself had carried downstairs. These were mostly filled with dark, gelatinous and evil-smelling liquids. But some had started empty. One sat on the floor and was slowly filling with blood. Above it, Manning was lying on the long dining table. Skerret was still chained to him. Boyle had been chained to one of the thick beams that supported the deck and looked on helplessly from the dark. Hewson watched from the bottom of the stairs. Worsley picked up the bottle of blood that had been collecting beneath Manning. He felt its weight then he turned to his boss and smiled.

"I believe we have enough," he said.

Hewson stepped out of the gloom and studied the blood for himself.

"There's more in him," he said. He looked at Manning. The wolf-hunter was still conscious and twisting against his restraints. "Don't be niggardly."

"With respect, Colonel, I have no need at present and, if the subject can be kept alive, he'll continue to supply what we need... indefinitely."

This was a new idea to Hewson. His eyes brightened at the thought. Perhaps Galway would not be the last time he'd need this weapon. He nodded slowly as he considered the implications. "Yes, indeed... of course. Get to work with what you have. We'll be in Galway in a few hours. I want that potion ready."

Worsley removed the needle from Manning's arm and bandaged it quickly. He would do the rest of his work in the comfort of Captain Salah's cabin. Hewson dismissed the soldier who had delivered the beatings then he turned to leave. The wolf-hunter groaned in pain. As the colonel climbed the first step, he noticed Boyle was squirming and attempting to talk through his gag. Hewson was now alone with the prisoners so he removed the gag.

Boyle got straight to the point, "Colonel, I think I can be of assistance! If you don't want your man to die, I can help you. Unchain me and I'll attend him."

Hewson looked back at Manning. The wolf-hunter was deathly pale. The alchemist's words had piqued the colonel's interest. Indeed, he did not want Manning to die. He studied Boyle for a moment. "Very well," he said, "Consider your lives intertwined now. If he dies; so do you."

If Boyle wasn't quite resigned to death, he was certainly resigned to Hewson's inevitable treachery. The hope implicit in this bargain counted for nothing. He nodded his agreement.

"I'll send the captain down to unchain you," Hewson said as he disappeared up the stairs.

When they were left alone, Skerret spoke to Boyle, "Can you save him?"

"I don't know," he answered. He looked at Worsley's untidy bandage. It was already turning red. "If he doesn't clot soon, he'll die," Boyle said.

Manning began to mumble in response to his friend's voices. Skerret tried to calm him but the wolf-hunter seemed determined to speak. His words were incoherent till one phrase, repeated several times, became clear, "Change me."

"He must know his wound needs dressing," Boyle ventured.

But Skerret shook his head. Manning was too delirious for such practical sentiments. His friends were at a loss. Manning rallied his strength. He took hold of Skerret's shirt and pulled him close. His face glistened with sweat as he used his remaining energy. "One way to stop... you must change me. Use the blood."

Skerret looked at Boyle. A glimmer of comprehension flashed between them but they couldn't acknowledge the idea. But Manning knew he was getting through. He knew his friends understood him. He grew impatient with their reticence. He pulled Skerret closer, almost nose to nose. "You know what to do! Change me. Mix the wolf's blood with mine. Change me and I can stop this..." His strength failed and he fell back unconscious.

Skerret's face was pale when he looked at Boyle again, "Did you understand that?"

Boyle nodded. Manning wanted them to turn him into a were-wolf. He'd destroy the boat, and stop the cargo from ever reaching Galway. And they would all drown.

Boyle's face hardened, "Don't think me a coward, Ambrose, but I won't do it." He looked for a reaction from the priest but Skerret gave nothing away. He continued, "It's madness. Even if we were agreeable. We don't have the ingredients or the tools... and it's wrong. We'd be damning him to hell. You're chained to him. I wouldn't do that to you."

Skerret mopped the sweat from Manning's brow and answered, "I don't think he'd hurt me even in that state."

Boyle shook his head with exasperation. The priest was just being sentimental now. But he didn't argue. He'd already made enough arguments to rule out the plan.

But Skerret wasn't finished, "And, as for tools, we have everything here," he gestured at Worsley's equipment.

"And the wolf's blood?"

"...is in the hold somewhere, that's what Salah said."

Boyle returned to one of his previous arguments, "And his soul? You should be most concerned with that."

Skerret exhaled, "I have no answer there, except that it is his wish."

"He doesn't know what he's saying."

"Perhaps," Skerret answered. "But if we do nothing? What happens to Galway?" He looked to the stairs. They didn't have long to talk. "And your sister?"

Boyle couldn't argue with that. They had to act. If Manning was willing to sacrifice his soul, could he really be damned for eternity? And if he was willing to take that chance, then Boyle could certainly face death. His mind began to race as he considered the equipment he'd need and the steps involved. Almost as an afterthought, he answered Skerret, "Very well. I'll do it."

44.

D'Arcy was speechless when he opened the door to Mary.

She tried to sound natural, "I'm sorry to be a bother, sir." She gestured at her wet clothes, "I'm afraid I had an accident. I thought I might return early and change." She was cold and her skirts were still dripping with seawater but it was helpful to have an excuse to return to the house.

She heard laughter echo from the wine shop. Lady Ranelagh, she supposed, and some man's voice. The sound woke the alderman from his reverie. "Come in, Mary. Change your clothes and attend us. I'm alone with guests. Lady Ranelagh is here and we've had a visit from Sir William." He did not sound happy.

Mary studied his face before she allowed herself to step past him into the house. She saw no hint that the alderman had heard of Flaherty's death. This bought her some time. And Sir William was here. These were both strokes of luck. And yet, she was sure D'Arcy had sent the pirate to kill her. She was playing with fire by returning here. The sound of the door locking behind her reminded Mary of the danger she was in. She shivered as she climbed the stairs to her room. She was one step ahead of D'Arcy for now.

***

As soon as she was changed, she went to the wine shop to wait on the alderman and his guests. The three of them sat at a little table at the back of the wine shop where favoured customers tried samples for the price of a sales pitch. A dusty half bottle of claret sat before them. Sir William greeted Mary warmly but with a searching look that made her wonder, had he already received the note she'd left for him? She got the impression he'd like to speak to her alone. He spoke kindly of her to Lady Ranelagh who also complimented her, noting that Mary had attended her the previous evening. At this, D'Arcy himself observed that Mary seemed to be the only member of staff who could be reliably found at home. The self-deprecation amused Sir William but not Lady Ranelagh who was reminded to enquire after her own servants.

D'Arcy picked up the bottle and made a move to top up the drinks before he answered, "I cannot account for it, My Lady. I sent for them hours ago."

Katherine was not satisfied. She raised a hand to refuse the drink and said, "Then it seems I must search for them myself."

But D'Arcy wouldn't hear of it. He made every excuse: Lady Ranelagh couldn't walk the streets alone; Galway was unknown to her; and it was his responsibility, so he'd personally look for them. His arguments were reasonable enough for Sir William to nod in agreement but Katherine's patience was at an end. "Wait!" she said.

D'Arcy stopped pouring his drink.

"I'm sorry, sir. Please don't think me rude. It's this siege. It has me worried. I'd be obliged… would you search for them now?"

The alderman's charm slipped a moment and his eyes narrowed. But he recovered and gently replaced the bottle. "Of course, My Lady." He looked at his guests and then at Mary. He was making the same calculations as her – who to leave alone with whom? For Mary, it was a win, win situation.

In the end, he feared leaving Mary in Blake's company the most. Better to leave Mary alone with Lady Ranelagh and return and deal with them both, he figured.

***

Five minutes later, Mary closed the front door on D'Arcy and Sir William. I don't have much time, she thought. The alderman will be on the street for minutes at most before he hears about Flaherty. Then, he'll come for me himself. She looked up the stairs. Lady Ranelagh had retired to the dining room as soon as her host had left. She was apparently returning to her vigil at the window. I need to talk to her now, Mary decided.

Upstairs, Katherine had barely sat down when she heard a knock on the door frame. She turned and saw Mary. For a moment, she felt irritation. She wanted no servant right now unless it be her own. Then she made eye contact. Mary's expression was different. The averted gaze of a servant was gone. A knot of discomfort twisted in her stomach before Mary started speaking.

"My Lady," she crossed the room and stood in front of her, "we haven't much time." She reached out her closed fist and offered something to Katherine. The viscountess instinctively opened the palm of her hand. Valentine's silver ring dropped into it. She gasped. Then started, "Where did you..."

But Mary was in a hurry, "Your life is in danger. Please, come with me, now. I'll bring you to Valentine."

Katherine didn't move, she continued staring at the ring but she raised her head at Valentine's name.

"He's in Galway?"

"He's in a place called Teach an Eirí just outside the walls. I'll bring you there." Mary was just about to doubt Valentine's hold on Katherine when the Lady started to stand up. She looked around, in a dreamlike daze, found her cap and tied her hair under it. Mary waited and tried to be patient. She kept an eye on the window and her ears open for any sign of D'Arcy's return.

"Is he well?" Katherine next asked as Mary led her downstairs. "Yes, My Lady, and he's anxious to see you."

Before joining the street, she looked left and right for D'Arcy. There was no sign. He would likely approach from the left, whether he was returning from the Tholsel House, Blake's Castle or the Red Earl's House. Unfortunately, this was where Mary had to lead Katherine. It was in that direction, under the Middle Tower, that Valentine had shown her the shallowest crossing to the Eirí House. If she had to convince Katherine to wade into the sea, she would do her best not to drown her.

She walked at such a pace that the much shorter viscountess was forced into a trot behind her. Katherine's heels slipped on the still-wet cobbles and she found herself scanning the streets for an empty sedan chair. But the city was quiet and prematurely dark under a ceiling of wintry clouds. It wasn't long before Katherine tugged at Mary's sleeve and begged a rest. "Please, why is there such a hurry and such mystery? You said I'm in danger?"

Mary didn't like to stop but she turned and answered, "I'm sorry, My Lady. Valentine bid me hurry. It's a long story..." She noticed Katherine's eyes drift away from hers and over her shoulder.

"Why, here's Mr D'Arcy now..." Katherine said.

Mary misunderstood. She turned and realised her mistake – it was the alderman, not Valentine who approached. He was upon them in a moment, flanked by six militiamen.

He looked first at Mary but then addressed Katherine. He was short of breath. "My Lady, I have grave news," he looked again at Mary, "This girl is to be arrested, charged with murder."

Katherine took a step in front of Mary, "Murder? But there must be some mistake. She's just brought the most wonderful news; Valentine, your son, is here in Galway."

D'Arcy was caught off-guard. But his shock was followed by a sly re-calculation. He looked at Mary. His voice was heavy with sarcasm, "Our murderess won't thank you for sharing that information, My Lady."

Katherine looked at Mary. The servant's eyes were downcast. She looked back at D'Arcy and raised her chin and her voice. "Nevertheless, your son's welfare takes precedence. We can attend to this accusation afterwards. I'll vouch for Mary. I'm sure you'll take the word of a viscountess?"

"I'm afraid that won't do, My Lady," he answered.

Katherine's jaw tightened. She needed backup. She suddenly realised D'Arcy had failed to return her servants. "Where's Colman? Where are my servants?" she demanded.

D'Arcy began to relax. The die was cast now. "Also under arrest, My Ladyship." He shared a joke with his men, "smuggling? wasn't it, men?" The soldiers laughed grimly.

Mary felt the alderman had forgotten something, "you understand that the Lady's brother, Viscount Boyle, is aware that she is under your protection?"

D'Arcy began to enjoy himself, "Ah, yes, Robert, isn't it?"

Katherine gasped. Real fear gripped her heart.

D'Arcy continued, "Also under arrest... on a boat to Galway, as we speak."

"But why?" Katherine was incredulous.

D'Arcy began to look bored. Mary played for time. Perhaps his soldiers weren't aware of his schemes, she thought. "Because the alderman is in league with a Roundhead named Hewson. That boat, I imagine, is carrying the plague that they plan to unleash on Galway, the plague that started with Valentine's werewolf curse."

But the soldiers were unmoved, they already knew as much and cared as little.

Only Katherine was shocked, "werewolf?" was all she could say.

The small group stood in silence for a moment. Then D'Arcy tired of the game. "Arrest them both. For murder and treason!"

"Stop!" Mary shouted. Before the soldiers took a step, Mary's hand was up and D'Arcy found a pistol pointing at his head. Mary spoke firmly to Katherine, "Go, My Lady. You know where. I'll follow."

Katherine's head swam. She took in the scene with a look of disbelief and then made her decision. She ran. She had no idea where she was going. Galway was unknown to her. She took the first turn she came to, just to be out of sight of D'Arcy and his gang. She collided with a militia man who fell back and cursed her. He considered making chase but she was already gone. What was she running from, he wondered. He decided to investigate.

Around the corner, fourteen eyes watched Mary for any sign of weakness. D'Arcy had a thought, "Is that the same gun you used on Flaherty?"

She tried to give nothing away.

"Have you had a chance to reload it since?" he asked. He edged forward. His men followed his lead.

"Why don't you find out?" Mary answered, she waved the barrel about in a move which stalled their advance.

But D'Arcy felt no hurry. He had seen the other militia man come around the corner and appraise the scene. All he had to do was distract Mary. "I'll miss young Flaherty," he said. "He was a talent. He could squeeze a Hail Mary from a Quaker. I'll have my work cut out with you when I get you home."

Mary started, "Well, you won't be..." but then the butt of a gun smacked the back of her head. She crumpled on the damp cobbles. The newly arrived militia man beamed at his good work.

But D'Arcy cut him short, "Well, don't just stand there! Get after the other one!" The soldiers started off in the direction Katherine had gone. D'Arcy held one of them back, "Get reinforcements – loyal men only. Find that woman." He looked down at Mary. "And get a cart. Bring this one back to Pludd Street. Valentine's old quarters."

The soldier smiled at the euphemism and nodded.

45.

There was little Boyle could do to help Manning or to carry out his wishes while he was still in chains. Fortunately, he did not have to wait long before Salah arrived to free him. The pirate paused on the bottom step and adjusted to the gloom of the hold. Skerret glared at him but he ignored the priest. He didn't want a fight; he wanted information.

"Colonel Hewson has asked me to unchain you." he said, "You are to nurse the wolf-hunter's wounds."

"I understand," Boyle answered.

Salah stood behind the scientist and unlocked the first of his chains. As he worked he noticed the fine silk fabric of his outer coat. He tried to sound casual as he asked, "Why does this English colonel imprison you – the son of an Earl?"

Boyle sensed an opportunity. Salah was beginning to doubt Hewson's authority. "Hewson can't let me live," he said, "because I know too much. I know that he acts against Parliament."

Boyle sensed the pirate captain freeze in response to this news. A pirate was, by definition, outside the law but a pirate had to know who was in authority and who not to offend. Salah was listening. Boyle's arms were still bound so he nodded towards Manning. "Hewson plans to use this man's blood to unleash a plague of monsters on Galway. If Coote knew about it, Hewson would be finished. The colonel has his company of soldiers and some allies in Galway but otherwise, he acts alone." Boyle sensed that Salah was taking his time undoing the chains. He was interested in what the scientist had to say. He finished with the chain that bound Boyle's torso and circled around to unlock his hands. They came face to face.

Boyle continued, "He also has my sister captive in Galway. He plans to kill her too." His voice faltered with these words but he recovered, "You see how he hides my identity from Worsley but not from you?" Salah answered with a silent look. The last chain fell loose and Boyle rubbed the stiffness from his arms, "Now, do you think he'll let you live?"

Salah did not answer. He turned and looked at the wolf-hunter and at the bloody paraphernalia around him. He said nothing for a minute. "This is the devil's work."

"Yes," Boyle answered. He seized the moment, "Fight them before we reach Galway. You have the men." He took hold of the pirate's arm. "You know I can pay. And you'll have Parliament's gratitude."

Salah was not shocked by the suggestion but he found it impractical. "I'm sorry. It's not possible. Hewson has too many soldiers."

But Boyle wasn't finished, "You understand, once we pass the blockade, you'll be trapped."

"Yes," Salah answered, stroking his beard. He seemed to be looking for options. He started to walk around to help himself think. "The English have two carracks." he said, "We have to send a boat over to show our credentials. That's the only opportunity."

Boyle followed him across the floor, excited by the pirate's train of thought.

Salah continued, "I could take one ship, board it, capture the crew..." But his face darkened as the scheme failed in his head, "...but not two."

Boyle deflated as Salah expanded on the problems, "The second carrack would blow us out of the water and the English would take this boat. No, I cannot fight two ships with one. It's hopeless."

"Then you can do nothing for us," the scientist concluded.

Salah was equally pessimistic, "...or for myself."

Skerret cleared his throat, "I think I know a way," he said.

The other two looked at him.

"But you won't like it," he added.

46.

Katherine stopped to catch her breath. After colliding with the militia man, she'd taken the next right and quickly found herself at a t-junction. She could go left or right. She looked behind her. She cursed her corset and stupid boots but she would have fared little better without them. There was no rehearsing running for your life. As she inhaled great gulps of air, she realised she was in some kind of tanner's quarter. The stink of waste and lime added to her discomfort as did the stares of strangers. She straightened up and took a left turn so she wouldn't double back on D'Arcy too quickly. But she couldn't wander aimlessly, she'd have to find this Teach an Eirí. She started walking and tried to look less conspicuous but she found every eye watched her. Naturally, her clothes were the finest on the street and she was unaccompanied. She'd lost her cap so her hair fell loose and this marked her as some kind of trouble. The staring died down a little when she reached Lynch's Castle. She turned left onto High Middle Street, one of the busiest streets in the city.

The respectable citizens of Galway stole glances at her, children of every rank stared openly and the lower kind of men, common to every gutter, winked and invited her to read their thoughts. But it wasn't long before these strangers looked elsewhere. A ripple of shouting was spreading through the town. These must be the sounds of soldiers looking for me, she thought. She needed shelter. She spied a church at the end of the street and headed straight to it. It was a fine building, a cathedral, surrounded by railings and set at a jaunty angle off the main thoroughfare. The nearest entrance was the side door. Katherine studied the handbills on the door before she entered. It was her habit in a new town, in these days of religious upheaval. She saw a timetable for confessions. So, this one was Catholic – for the moment. She entered, unabashed. God was God.

The interior was dark, even for a church. There wasn't a single candle burning. It seemed the church had no immunity to the siege. But the stained glass windows brought colour and at least a feeling of warmth. She stopped in the porch for a moment, remembering her uncovered hair. But then she noticed the church was empty so she found a bench close to the door and took a seat. The aisle was wide, as wide as the knave, and she felt exposed. She lowered her head and started to pray.

Her prayers were quickly followed by tears. What had happened to Mary? Had she escaped? And Robert, dear Robert? How had he found himself in chains on his way to Galway? These thoughts pierced her heart and she welcomed the pain; it was penance for the guilt. She had proved such a failure. She had led Robert into danger – she was certain of this. She had trusted D'Arcy – against her instincts, she now realised. And she had betrayed Valentine. She had failed to listen to him or to believe him.

What would be the cost of her failures? Her tears turned into a series of staggered sobs that echoed through the church. Each one brought a tiny release and, after a few minutes, she calmed and began to think clearly. But she knew she'd lost her privacy. When she looked up, an elderly woman was standing patiently close by.

She was displaying a black woollen shawl between her two hands. She was wearing a similar one on her own head.

"Le do ceann," she said, pointing at her head.

Katherine understood and nodded. She took the shawl, wrapped it around her hair and fished in her purse for some money. She found a suitable coin but had second thoughts. She doubled the amount and passed it to the woman, saying, "Cathaoir iompair, le do thoil."

The woman nodded and left by the side door. Katherine had asked her to find a sedan chair. She spent another minute fixing the shawl till she felt she blended in. Then she stood, wiped her eyes and blew her nose with a kerchief. A sliver of light cut through the gloom when the elderly woman half opened the side door and called to her, "Gabh i leith!" The chair was here. Outside, two porters stood at either end of a handsome-looking chair. The old woman stood by, seeing the job through. "Cá bhfuil tú ag dul?" she asked as though an interpreter was needed.

"Teach an Eirí," Katherine answered. The old woman's face twisted in horror. She spat at Katherine's feet and walked away. The two porters grinned at each other before opening the door. Katherine sat in and blushed. What was so disgraceful about her destination, she wondered? She closed the curtain and felt the chair lift. The journey was short and downhill, to judge by the porters' pace. The scream of seagulls grew loud and the air temperature dropped. Just before they stopped, the interior grew dark as it passed beneath an arch. Then the chair was lowered and Katherine heard a knock on the door frame. She pulled back the curtain. They were by the quays. Dozens of masts bobbed up and down but there was little activity. These boats were trapped by the siege. Sailors came and went but only because they lodged on their ships. There were no traders present. The quays were busy nonetheless – soldiers marched by with purpose while others kept a lookout from the city walls.

The lead porter addressed Katherine in English, "You'll have to get a boat from here."

She looked searchingly at him, "A boat? Is there no other way?"

He studied her, then looked around at the soldiers. He was no fool. She was hiding from them.

"Not if you want to keep your feet dry," he said.

"I can pay," she said. She knew she was inviting trouble. I have money and I'm desperate, she was telling two strange men. The porters shared a look and the first man nodded at Katherine. The chair lifted and she was on the move once more. The path they followed this time was quieter and two minutes later she felt the chair lower and heard a rap on the frame. She looked out. They were down a quiet lane alone. At one end, she could see a wide street, at the other end a dark arch at the bottom of some stone steps. She stepped out and reached for her purse. She would play straight with the porters and hope for the best.

"What now?" she said.

The lead man pointed to the arch, "Down those steps, through the tunnel. You'll come to an inlet. The Rising House is on the far side. It's not too deep."

Katherine nodded. He set a fair price and she paid him. Then she descended the steps. She waited a moment in the dark till she heard the sedan chair and the porters leave. Then she followed the tunnel through the city wall. There, an arch opened onto the sea. Katherine stood on the precipice and hesitated. She could see Teach an Eirí on the far side, to the left of some surprisingly ornate gardens. She could hear music and she noticed half a dozen row boats were tied up at a pier outside. Fifty feet of water stood in between. It was impossible to gauge the depth of the soupy green sea. But she felt oddly fearless. She removed her boots, tied them together and looped them around her neck. Then she lowered one foot into the water. It was bitterly cold but it rose no higher than her ankle. But the seabed was soft and sucked her foot several inches deeper. She corrected her balance and took another step in. This wasn't too bad, she thought. But the depth increased quickly. Ten feet in and she gulped for air as the water pooled around her waist. She felt the current for the first time. This inlet must be fed by a river. There was a pull out to sea. Her skirts rose in a tear-drop around her and she found she had to gather them to minimise the drag. The smell of seaweed filled her nostrils, then something brushed against her bare leg. She quickly lost control of her breathing. Short, panicky breaths took over. I can't do this, she thought. She looked around for help, or ashamed that someone might be watching – she wasn't sure – but the look behind her helped. She was making progress and the water was getting no deeper. About halfway, the seabed plunged unexpectedly and she found herself thrown forward up to her chest. She experienced another moment of doubt but then she felt an incline she knew this ordeal was nearly over.

She clambered out of the water on her hands and knees. She was shaking and her clothes were filthy. She stood up and wrung as much water from her skirts as possible. She heard someone close by but couldn't see where. Someone was working in the garden in front of her. But the shore was ringed with a thick growth of hedges. After all her hard work, she now found herself trapped between this hedgerow and the water. She cried out, "hello?" The sound of labouring ceased.

A female voice, heavily accented, answered, "Walk towards the house. There's a gap. You're wasting your time though."

Katherine took the advice and followed the muddy shoreline towards the house. She found a gap in the hedge and passed through. She entered a well-tended garden and was met by a woman of about her own age, carrying a pruning shears. She held the shears high with a certain menace but when she saw Katherine, she started to laugh, "Madre dios! I hope you're not looking for a job!"

Katherine followed her gaze over her ruined clothes but she was too cold to see the joke. "Please, I'm looking for Valentine D'Arcy."

The woman stopped laughing. She dropped the shears and stepped quickly to Katherine's side. She took her arm gently and began to lead her to the house. "Vale! Come with me. He is here." Katherine sighed with relief that she was on the right track and began to take in her surroundings. The woman holding her arm was evidently a friend of Valentine's. She was finely dressed, for gardening or any activity, in black and red silk with loose hair and the décolletage of a bawd or a madam.

"My name is Rosa. Welcome to my home."

They passed under an ornate arch from one walled enclosure to another passing herb gardens, vegetable patches and flower beds all lovingly tended, though mostly dormant for winter. Even in her traumatised state, Katherine couldn't help but admire the work.

The house was a long, low building, about the size of an inn and Rosa led Katherine through a back door into the kitchen. There, she sat her by the turf fire and left with a reassurance and a cup of red wine which she seemed to produce out of nowhere. "I'll get him."

Of course, she heard him first. She recognised his heavy steps on the stairs and, when Rosa told him what had happened, she heard his hoarse voice called out in anguish.

Katherine felt her chest tighten in anticipation. She stood up before he entered. He threw open the door and stood looking at her. There were no words. They ran to each other and locked into a silent, soggy embrace. After a minute, Katherine pushed his shoulders back so she could see his face and speak. "They have Robert... and Mary, the servant."

"This is my fault." He looked around the room as though the solution would present itself. "I'll have to help them."

"There's nothing you can do for Robert, yet. He's on a boat bound for Galway. And Mary..." Katherine stroked his face, "It was your father who took her. He has soldiers all over town looking for me. I'm afraid I told him about you."

Valentine deflated. "That's bad. But I have no choice. They're both in danger because of me. I must help."

"Wait then, till dark. Till Robert arrives. You have some friends here?"

He nodded. "Rosa is a good friend, and she has men." He let her go and realised for the first time that she was soaking wet. "Come upstairs and change. I'll find some dry clothes for you."

***

Minutes later, Katherine was alone in Valentine's room, removing her wet clothes. He left her there and went downstairs to make plans for an assault on Pludd Street after dark. Katherine's head was reeling. She was undressing like a distracted child, one item, then a daydream, till the cold prompted her and another item was removed before her thoughts would drift again. The relative comfort of this well-appointed bedroom jarred with her state of mind. Her world was upside down. She tried to imagine Robert's situation. He would be rising to the occasion, she knew that. He was not a strong man but he thrived in adversity. Then she thought about Mary. She had never met such a brave woman. She had given Katherine the head-start she needed to escape. But she had not followed. D'Arcy must have overpowered her. Katherine had never seen such evil. How could that blood run through Valentine's veins? It was a casual thought, a simple turn of phrase, but it made her freeze. She suddenly remembered Valentine's condition. There was a knock on the door. Outside, Valentine spoke, "Are you dressed?"

She was not. "Come in," she said.

He opened the door but jerked it closed again, feeling he'd made a mistake. But she reassured him. "Please come in."

She stood naked, looking at him. He entered carrying a tray with soup, bread and wine. He found a table and put the food aside. Then he sat on the bed and looked into the fire. Katherine sat beside him and took his hand. Both were about to speak. She took the lead.

"I wronged you," she said. He listened silently. "I didn't believe what you told me. I thought you were mad. So I went to your father. I thought I could convince him to help. I understand now, you were trying to protect me... by leaving." She paused. He looked into her eyes. "But I want you to know, I'm not afraid of you."

She released his hand, turned her shoulders to him and leaned close.

But Valentine turned away. "I'm sorry," he said. "...why I came looking for you, I haven't told you yet." He looked at her again but kept his distance. "I came to warn you, and Robert."

Katherine listened, her eyes still locked on his.

Valentine continued, "The shared blood, there's a danger. I might have passed on my condition, to Robert, and to you too, I suppose."

Her heart beat faster. The news should have horrified her. But it felt like a release. There was no barrier between them anymore.

"Then what's done is done," she said.

She touched his chin and guided his mouth to hers.

47.

It would be quiet in Pludd Street for a few more hours. D'Arcy had let the staff off till six. Plenty of time, he thought. He was standing in the shed where he'd once kept Valentine. One of his soldiers was fixing the shackles to Mary's arms. She was still unconscious.

"She'll talk. I'll find out who she's working for after all and she'll wish it was Flaherty, not me, asking the questions."

The soldier finished and stood up. He looked at his boss, unsure what answer, if any, was expected.

The alderman made it easier for him, "Well, don't just stand there. Get a bucket of water and wake her up."

He was about to leave when another soldier appeared at the shed door, "Sir, there's a woman here to see you."

D'Arcy looked spooked. "A woman? Who?"

The soldier shrugged, "An old trader. She says she has information."

D'Arcy relaxed. Part of him feared Lady Ranelagh's money and power and imagined her descending on his house with an army. The sooner she was eliminated, the better. He strutted out of the shed and headed for the front door.

There he sized up his visitor. She was a poor trader, alright, a small, old woman dressed in black – complete with the black woollen shawl of her class.

She spoke no English and D'Arcy's Irish was poor. One of his soldiers translated.

"She says she saw a woman here, a rich woman. She thought you might want to know where she's gone."

The alderman smiled broadly and the elderly trader smiled back. D'Arcy paid for the information and sent her off. But he stayed at the front door, deep in thought. His priorities had changed. So, Ranelagh, and Valentine too, no doubt, were in the Rising House. He'd need to deal with them. Mary could wait. He gave instructions to have her gagged so she wouldn't be heard by the staff when they returned, and then he called off the search for Lady Ranelagh.

He gave new orders for his men to gather by the quays with arms and torches. Before Hewson arrived, he would tie up the loose ends that threatened their plans.

48.

The sun was setting by the time Salah reached Galway. A cold blue twilight coloured the bay. The walls of the city drew a blunt silhouette on the western sky. No life, nor lights were visible within. Only the yellow lanterns on the English carracks stood out and marked the entrance to the port. Come this far and no farther, the lights said. That suited Salah just fine. He instructed his men to lower the oars to manoeuvre the caravel more precisely. They were aiming for a point halfway between the English ships. A hundred feet out, he gave orders to drop the first anchor. The boat would drift till the line was taut then he'd drop a second anchor and fine-tune their position. It was a mooring manoeuvre more typical of a long stay rather than a quick stop but, if it was suspicious, the English could reassure themselves that it was not conducive to a quick getaway.

In the captain's cabin, Colonel Hewson heard the anchor drop. "We're here at last," he said.

"And I am also finished," Worsley answered. He poured a glass from the large brown jug in the centre of the captain's table. Then he warmed the bottom of the glass over a candle and showed it to the colonel.

"It's ready?"

"The blueish tinge at the edge, see, and that floral aroma. Those are the signs I was waiting for. The potion is ready. A drop of this will turn a man into a beast."

Hewson took the glass, held it to the light then sniffed it. "How much do we have?"

"There's a quart here to start with. It would only take a teaspoon to poison a bottle of wine. There's enough then for sixteen cases of wine."

"Good, we can finish the job in D'Arcy's house once we get ashore. D'Arcy will have them sold within a day or two. Once the chaos begins, the people of Galway will throw open their gates to Parliament."

There was a knock on the cabin door. Hewson put the poison down and bid the visitor enter. It was Salah. He opened the door and glanced at the apparatus that had taken over his quarters but he passed no comment. He gestured with a letter in his hand, "Colonel, the boat is ready. I just need your seal on this letter of transit for the blockade captain."

Hewson took the letter and read it while Salah searched in one of the drawers. He found a quill, an ink-pot and a stick of wax. The three men stood in silence while Hewson finished the letter. Finally, he signed it, heated the wax and sealed the letter with the stamp from his ring.

"How many men are you taking?" he asked Salah.

"Half a dozen oarsmen and the same number of porters," the pirate answered.

"Porters?"

"These English captains expect a tribute. I'll need some men to carry a gift."

Hewson studied the pirate, "A gift, eh? Well, don't delay. I want to land in Galway in an hour."

Salah nodded, "Yes, colonel." He turned to leave.

Hewson remembered something, "A word please... outside." Worsley started shuffling papers in an effort to look busy. The less he knew of Hewson's secrets the better, though he suspected the colonel wanted to discuss the wealthy prisoner whose identity remained a mystery to him.

Hewson and Salah exited the cabin. On deck, the colonel continued speaking to Salah, "How does the wolf-hunter? Has Boyle been able to save him?"

The deck was dark save for a faint moonlight behind the clouds and two lanterns on the port side where Salah's men were lowering the longboat the pirates used as a tender. The only other light came from the cabin and it allowed Hewson to examine Salah as he spoke to him.

"I cannot say," Salah answered. The pirate was anxious to go but even keener not to arouse Hewson's suspicions. His mind worked fast. "Shall I send Boyle up to you to make a report? I'll need to hurry if you want to land in Galway in an hour."

The longboat made a splash as it hit the water. The noise reminded Hewson where his priorities lay. "No, take the letter over to the blockade captain and get back here quick. I'll go down and see for myself."

As though in answer, a cry erupted from below. "Englishmen! Loyal Englishmen! Come close and listen to my words!" It was Viscount Boyle shouting at the top of his voice.

Salah looked at Hewson and hovered for a moment but the colonel dismissed him with a wave, "Go! I'll deal with this." Hewson clicked his fingers and a great brute of a soldier appeared at his side. Salah stood watching as Hewson took a lamp and started his descent into the hold. Hewson waved the pirate away, "Go! This is not your problem. I need you back here as quickly as possible."

Salah nodded. He looked over the deck. Some of the English soldiers had heard Boyle's cries and were wandering over to the latticed hatch that served as a window into the hold.

"Englishmen, a terrible injustice is being done!" Boyle continued shouting. As Hewson entered the hold, the lamplight made it easier for the soldiers on deck to follow the action. What they saw caused them to mass around the opening and press their faces close. Boyle was standing just beneath the hatch. He held the half-conscious wolf-hunter in his arms. But there was no affection in the embrace. The lamplight flashed against the sharp blade he pressed into Manning's neck. The wolf hunter was upright but unconscious. Behind these two men, the priest, Skerret stood in league with Boyle.

When Hewson drew near, Boyle raised Manning's chin so the colonel could clearly see the blade pressed against it. "Come no closer, Colonel, or I'll kill this Golden Goose and all your work will be for nothing."

Hewson relaxed but he came no further. If this was the best Boyle could do, he had nothing to fear. "Go ahead, my Lord, I've got what I came for. His life means nothing to me."

Boyle seemed unfazed by the colonel's reaction but content enough that the colonel had stopped approaching. He raised his voice and returned to addressing the rest of the soldiers, "Englishmen, before me stands a traitor to Parliament and to God..."

On deck, Salah made eye contact with his crew and nodded. His men began to move towards the port side and the ladder down to the longboat. Suddenly, Worsley emerged from the cabin. Salah intercepted him and grabbed his sleeve, "Doctor, the colonel needs you in the hold. Please hurry!" Worsley looked confused but followed the captain's orders and went below.

Below deck, Boyle saw the faces pressed into the openings in the hatch and played up to his audience, "Your colonel is engaging in witchcraft. He is against your commander, Lord Coote, against Parliament, and against God. Join me, loyal Englishmen, and help me take this ship for Parliament!"

Hewson put the lamp down and applauded. The soldiers looking on began to laugh. "Well men, you heard the young upstart. I'm a witch! Put me in chains and drag me back to Oranmore." The soldiers laughed louder. Boyle's resolve faltered and, as he loosened his grip, Manning rolled his head and a flicker of consciousness, then a grimace of pain, crossed his face.

Worsley appeared by Hewson's side and took in the scene. Boyle had been busy; the table had much the same appearance as his makeshift laboratory upstairs. He looked at Boyle and tried to divine his purpose.

Boyle caught the look and thought of a different strategy. He addressed Worsley directly, "Doctor, you must know my name, for the colonel here would hide it. I am Viscount Robert Boyle, son of the Earl of Cork. You know me by correspondence."

Hewson looked annoyed to find the alchemist at his side but he ignored him and spoke to Boyle, "Put down the knife, viscount. You haven't the heart to kill a mouse any more than a man."

But Boyle disagreed. His voice quivered as he answered, "Oh, but I've done worse than kill..."

Worsley looked at the apparatus on the table and understood. He tugged Hewson's sleeve. "Colonel..." he said. The colonel shrugged him off. So what if the alchemist knew Boyle's identity? There were bigger affairs at play. But Worsley wouldn't be ignored. "Colonel, he has done it."

Hewson turned and read the horror on Worsley's face. Boyle lowered the knife and let Manning lie back. The wolf hunter groaned as he slumped onto the table.

"He has made the potion," Worsley said. They both looked at Manning. The wolf hunter's eyes opened. They were black. His face was turning red.

"My God. He's transforming," Hewson said. He shouted at his bodyguard. "Get him off the ship quick." Then Manning spasmed and the clink of iron reminded Hewson: "He's still in chains. Get the keys."

His bodyguard raced upstairs but shouted from the deck. "The pirates! They're all gone."

Hewson looked at Boyle and Skerret. The prisoners had conspired with the pirates – that much was obvious. But how did they expect to win? "But you'll die too," he said.

***

Salah sat on the stern of the longboat and looked back at his ship. He tried to imagine the scene below deck. The Meshuda was doomed. According to Boyle, they would have about half an hour until the transformation. Then, all hell would break loose. He studied her lines for the last time. He loved that ship. She was small but she was fast. Even in port, her swept-back mast and shallow draught promised speed. The pirate was taking a huge gamble. But he believed he had no choice. He faced forward and was reminded how precarious his position was. The longboat was only built for ten but he'd managed to squeeze fifteen on board. The rest of his crew – some six other men – had drawn the short straws, and clung to the boat's side in the freezing water. His first mate, Ahmad, was first into the water. He clung to the longboat on Salah's left with a knife clenched between his teeth. Even he, the biggest man in

Salah's crew, was shivering in the cruel Irish water. Fortunately, it was a short journey across to the English ship. No one on board the English vessel could hope to see these events in the dark so the pirate was able to circle the carrack and offload his excess crewmen onto her mooring ropes. As they rowed under the bow, they read her name in the moonlight – the Bagenal. The other ship they had earlier identified as the Bristol. Neither was known to Salah. Above the name, they saw the sequence of flags that had identified her as the senior ship in the blockade. Hopefully, this meant she was better armed. Once he'd off-loaded his men, he rowed out and approached the carrack a second time and hailed her crew in a loud voice. His shouting brought an officer and a lantern to the port side and once his business was deemed satisfactory, a ladder was lowered and he was invited aboard along with half a dozen men laden with gifts.

The Bagenal was clean and well-ordered but her crew appeared sleepy and off-guard. Months of inaction blocking the entrance to Galway had dulled any instinct they might have had for trouble. Salah was pleased.

He showed Hewson's letter of passage to the senior officer on deck and asked to see the captain. The first mate sniffed and studied the letter slowly. Salah drew his attention to the chest full of gifts. This and Hewson's endorsement was finally enough. He was led into a tidy, sparse cabin. Captain Bing was the man in charge. He was a short, curly-haired man of about thirty. He was naturally friendlier than his subordinate. He grew positively sociable once Salah opened a bottle of Madeira and invited the captain to test its quality.

49.

Mary woke up with a thundering headache. She was confused. Wherever she was, it was dark. It took a moment to feel the shackles on her wrists and the gag in her mouth. When she did notice them, she almost felt relief – at least they helped remind her what had happened. The events of the afternoon fell into place. Someone had hit her hard on the back of her head and she was waking from a long stupor. She seemed to be chained up in an outhouse. D'Arcy had taken her, she remembered. She sniffed the air – pig shit, straw and gunpowder. So, she must be at the back of Pludd Street. Her situation was not good but she was glad to know where she was.

She could see nothing inside the shed. Four blue squares above and to her left suggested a window and gave her an idea of the time. The sun had set but it was not yet fully dark. She wondered whether Sir William Blake would pay heed to her note and come to Pludd Street. She couldn't rely on it, nor could she afford to wait. She struggled against the shackles and chewed on the gag. They were quite secure.

She cried out as loud as could but the gag was effective. Her voice wouldn't be carried beyond the shed and certainly not as far as the house. She studied her chains. One long iron braid led to a pair of cuffs which bound her hands tightly behind her back. But the chain was long, perhaps three feet long. It was attached to a flat iron plate bolted to the wall. She felt her way along the chains looking for any weakness. Where the chain met the wall, she recoiled as a sharp edge pricked her finger. She cursed and then thought better of the discovery. A sharp edge has its uses. She knelt and turned and began the delicate process of finding the same sharp edge with the touch of her cheek. It was the hook which held the chain in place. It had been twisted close enough to the metal plate holding the chain but the sharp edge remained. With great care, she pushed the folds of her gag around the hook and pulled them till the cloth began to fray. After ten minutes she had torn enough of the cloth to free her mouth. She allowed herself a minute to catch her breath and let her still sore head recover from the effort.

Now she could shout. But was it wise to do so, she wondered? She had no idea where D'Arcy was. Perhaps it would be better if she didn't draw attention to herself.

She decided she had no choice. She wasn't going to escape unaided so she needed to attract attention. She started to shout as loud as she could, "Help!", "Help me!", "In here!" and variations thereof. She established a rhythm of one minute's shouting followed by a rest and a chance to listen for activity in the garden.

She counted an hour this way and felt her voice growing hoarse when she finally heard sounds outside. The pigs were squealing. They were anticipating their dinner. Mary listened close. She heard the back door swing closed, then footsteps on the path. Shards of orange light caught the edge of the window frame. A lantern was approaching. Mary started shouting for help. She stopped to listen. Silence. She yelled again, louder than ever. A shadow crossed the window. A hand tried the shed door and found it locked. The shadow returned to the window and raised a lantern to see inside. A voice called tentatively, "Who's there?"

It was Grace. She pressed her face to the window and took in the scene. She looked shocked.

Mary shouted through the window, "Grace, please help me. I need you to go to the master's room and retrieve the great iron hoop of keys he keeps on a hook behind his desk."

Grace didn't move. She looked puzzled. Mary turned and showed her the chains. "He plans to kill me, Grace."

The girl stepped back. She shook her head. "He'd never."

"Please Grace, you have to help me."

"I expect you were stealing. I shouldn't have..." her voice faded as she started to leave.

Mary raised her voice, "Grace, please!"

She returned to the window, not quite decided. Mary changed her tactics. "I have money."

"How much?" Grace asked.

"Three crowns for the keys."

Even if it cost her a job, it was worth it.

Mary added, "And Grace, when you return, leave the lantern outside – the shed is full of gunpowder." Grace looked incredulous but she nodded and left.

She was gone for fifteen minutes. Mary feared she'd changed her mind or had been caught by D'Arcy but then she heard the kitchen door open and footsteps on the path. She heard multiple keys being tried in the lock till the door eventually creaked open. Grace had left the lantern outside so she had to feel her way through the first room and then on to Mary. They both struggled with the keys in the dark till at last the shackles on Mary's wrists opened. They hurried outside and Grace picked up the lantern once more and looked into the interior of the shed.

"Hold, the light up for me Grace but keep your distance," Mary stepped back into the shed and opened several barrels. "One spark would blow up the whole street," she said. She found pistols, gunpowder, ammunition and cartridge paper. She helped herself to a pistol and the means to fire it.

Grace looked at Mary and said, "What about my money?"

Mary reached into her shift and found her purse. Grace watched open-mouthed as Mary counted out three crowns from a still-fat purse of silver.

"Why, you are a thief," she said, snatching the money.

Mary tucked the pistol into the belt of her apron and answered, "Not a thief, Grace – a spy."

50.

Katherine woke to find Valentine lying beside her. It was dark outside. They had fallen asleep in a tight embrace that shouldn't have felt so comfortable. Her cheek was warmed by his bare back, her arm wrapped tightly around his waist. He snored happily like a dog.

She inhaled deeply. He needs a wash, she thought, and smiled to herself. The little room in the Eirí House was hot. The fire cracked loudly. Downstairs she could hear shouting. This is a brothel, she thought; there's bound to be a rough element. She pulled herself even closer to Valentine and tried to enjoy a moment's peace. But she was conscious now and unhappy thoughts forced their way forward for her consideration – Robert, in chains somewhere on the sea, Mary, the servant, also likely in captivity. She had to help them. And Valentine, what could she do for him, cursed by the devil, cursing those who touch him? 'What have I done,' she suddenly asked herself. The question slipped out before she could choke it. Her heart answered, 'whatever happens, I have no regrets'.

She heard glass break. That seemed like too much, even for a bawdy house. She squeezed Valentine to wake him up. He snorted in response. Outside, a gunshot rang out. This got his attention. He bolted up suddenly, looked at Katherine and then at the window.

They both leapt out of bed and looked out. In the moonlight, they could see men carrying torches scurrying about. More gunshots rang out.

"We're under attack!" Valentine grabbed his breeches and pulled them on.

Katherine grabbed her clothes from in front of the fire. As she pulled on her still-damp dress she realised that the heat and the sound of flames had not come from their little fireplace.

"They're burning us out," she said.

"Then they'll have a fight!" answered Valentine running for the door.

In the corridor, men and women in various stages of undress looked fearfully from doorways as Katherine and Valentine hurried past. Downstairs, they heard Rosa shouting orders, slipping from English to Spanish as her panic rose. They found her in the hallway hammering on a locked door. Inside they heard screams and the devastation wrought by flames.

"The door's locked. I don't think they can reach it," she said. Valentine sized up the door, stepped back and rushed it. His first attempt failed but his second broke through. A ball of fire pushed him back and knocked him to the ground. The open doorway revealed a further corridor in a halo of flames. The screams came from a room at the far end. Valentine looked up at Katherine, then he raced into the inferno. She tried to peer into the flames after him but the heat seemed to sear her eyes. She felt a hand grab her wrist.

Rosa was pulling her away. "The roof will fall. Come, we'll escape out the back," she said. Katherine was looking back to where they'd left Valentine. "Don't worry, he'll follow." But there was no sign of him returning. "The gardens may be no safer than the house," she added before she again took Katherine's hand and led her outside.

The first garden was empty but all around the sounds of soldiers shouting, gunfire, and timbers snapped by flames filled the air. They crouched by the hedge that bordered the second garden and took stock. They were not safe here and they would not be alone for long. A portion of the first storey collapsed with a crash. At the same time, three figures emerged through the back door. Two women in night clothes supported Valentine between them. His clothes were smoking. Once outside, their strength failed and they dropped him on the grass. Katherine and Rosa rushed over.

"He broke down the door that trapped us," one of the women started explaining to Rosa, "but the flames must have been too much. He was senseless... we had to help him out."

Valentine's skin was red and seemed stretched to bursting over his joints. His eyes were closed tight in anguish. Smoke seemed to seep from his bones.

"He's badly burned," Rosa said.

Katherine collapsed on her knees and supported his head. She said nothing. This is not the work of the fire, she thought. He's transforming. The attacking soldiers had found their way around to the back of the house and were getting close. She looked at Rosa, "Go!" she said. "I'll stay with him."

Rosa looked at the two young women that Valentine had tried to rescue. They must escape the soldiers. "Very well," she said, "If you can follow, go the way you came – through the garden and across the water. Good luck." She turned, nodded to her companions, and the three women disappeared into the dark of the garden.

Valentine's eyes opened but they no longer resembled his. Two black circles – alive but alien looked back at her. "Get away," he said, his voice twisted and stretched in pain. She shook her head and felt tears well up. But she resolved to be strong. She would not leave him alone. "Go!" he gurgled. Spit foamed in his mouth. His back arched suddenly as the two opposing spirits fought for his body. He screamed. It was a chilling, unearthly sound. It was also loud. Katherine knew it would draw the soldiers. She reached her arms under Valentine and tried to move him. She could barely lift his shoulders off the ground.

She tried to rouse him, "Get up, Valentine, the soldiers are coming! They will kill you."

He regained some composure and looked at her. His eyes were strange but she glimpsed a smile she recognised when he spoke, "Not me – no man can kill me. But you, you must escape." He let his head flop back onto the grass. He was not going anywhere. "Please... go," he said.

Their time was up. There was rustling in the trees to her left. She bent and kissed him on the lips then stood up. She saw flames reflect against steel in the dark. "God help you," she said, to whom she was unsure. She turned and ran through the arch that led into the depths of the garden.

As she ran, she heard the soldiers identify Valentine and celebrate. Just before she passed into the third garden, she heard one of the soldiers comment on his strange condition. That was the last conversation she could hope to hear. But that didn't stop her from following what happened next. As she skirted the hedge looking for an exit onto the shoreline, she heard shouting. This was followed by several gunshots. Her chest tightened and she looked back. She could see flames leaping into the night sky but nothing else. She felt sure the commotion was coming from the back of the house where she had left Valentine. Had she left him to his death? She made a move to retrace her steps. Then she heard the screaming: A man screamed in pain – not Valentine, she was sure of that. Then another man screamed. She stopped in her tracks. She wasn't afraid for her safety but she was afraid of what she might see.

She stopped looking for the break in the hedge that might lead her to the water. Her eyes fixed on the arch that led to the middle garden. A crescent of light separated it from the gloom. She thought she could hear someone running and out of breath. A figure ran through the arch, his helmeted silhouette marked him as a soldier. Katherine instinctively pressed her body against the hedge to hide. But the man saw her and veered in her direction. "Help!" he cried, his voice high as a boy's. Before he could say more, a shadow passed through the arch and pulled him to the ground. The dark was too absolute for Katherine to see what was happening but the sounds left little to her imagination. The soldier screamed before a grisly tearing and snapping noise silenced him forever.

A moment's silence was followed by a howl that weakened Katherine's stomach. The shadow rose and turned towards her. She had to run. She plunged one arm deep into the hedge and followed it till she found the break. She felt her face being scratched as she pushed too fast through the little gap. But she broke through. The city wall loomed large across the inlet and the tide was much lower than before. She raced into the water, scratching a foot on a sharp stone, suddenly aware that she wore no shoes. She kept her eye on the middle tower which she could just make out against the moonlight. The water was blessedly low and halfway across she was only up to her knees. But the mud sucked her feet down and slowed her progress unbearably. Behind her, she heard the branches snap as her pursuer took the shortest route through. Finally, her hand touched the greasy steps that led through the city wall. She looked back. In the moonlight, she could see the hole in the hedge on the far bank where her pursuer had broken through. She could clearly see his silhouette. He advanced into the water on four legs. His form was black against the silver surface of the water and few details escaped the dark. But even from the other side she saw the glint of enormous teeth and she fancied she could see them drip red with blood. This was once Valentine, she thought. And now he's after me.

***

At the front door of D'Arcy's house on Pludd Street, Mary pressed another coin into Grace's hand.

"Grace, I'm expecting Sir William to call. He'll ask for me. Tell him to bring his men to the quays. Tell him... he'll need plenty of men."

The young servant was proving to be an eager accomplice and had followed Mary to the door like a puppy. She looked in awe at the self-confessed spy and made a silent prayer that this new adventure wouldn't end. Mary checked to make sure the street was clear. It was after curfew now. Every door on this street was locked and every window shuttered. Mary had to venture out but she didn't want to be slowed down by some random militia patrol. She had too much to do.

"Go in, now, Grace. Lock the door. Wait for Sir William."

The girl stood frozen in the doorway. She found herself unwilling to reply so Mary pulled the door closed herself.

She hoped she could trust the servant to deliver the message. Hewson had said there was a shipment arriving tonight. This was the poisonous cargo she was expecting. She'd be there to meet it – hopefully with Sir William. But first, she had to keep a promise. She had to get to the Eirí House. She jogged quietly along the silvery strip of wet cobblestones that led towards the quays. A full moon and a clear sky suited her well. The streets were bright enough to navigate but the shadows were dark enough to hide in, if necessary. The city obviously took its curfew very seriously. She had expected to see some signs of non-conformity – drunks spilling from taverns or lovers fumbling in corners but there was no one around but her. It was all the more chilling then to hear the voice of a woman screaming in the distance.

***

Katherine banged on the door with both hands.

"Help!" she cried. She stepped back to look for a response. She had seen a candle move through an upstairs window. There was someone inside. Why wouldn't they help? She looked back. The black arch from whence she'd come seemed to return her gaze. It was the same lane where the sedan chair had left her six hours earlier. The arch led to the sea. It now hid the monster that had followed her from the Eirí House. A low growl echoed about the stones. Katherine felt her heart pound. She gave up on the first door. She zig-zagged her way up the lane hitting every door hard once while shouting. "Help! Please, someone, open up." There were some sounds; dogs barked inside, owners shouted at them to be quiet, babies started crying. But no latches lifted. No keys turned. She looked down the lane again. She could see the top of the creature's head caught in the moonlight. It was just inside the arch. It could reach her in seconds. She looked in the opposite direction. The lane ended at a t-junction where it met the much wider Earl Street. The houses there were dark and featureless and offered no refuge. Then she noticed, they were turning red. The pounding in her veins was so intense she fancied the blood was filling her eyes but no, the red light was moving and getting brighter – someone carrying a lamp was approaching. This was her salvation. She ran towards the light. As she reached the junction she collided with a pair of soldiers. One carried a lantern and a pistol at the ready. The other took the brunt of the collision and fell with her to the ground.

"Jesus, Mary and Joseph," said the soldier with the lamp as he tried to make sense of the tangled limbs on the ground.

"Get off me, ye stupid bitch," the other soldier said. He had lost his halberd and his helmet had fallen over his face. He kicked Katherine away without mercy and climbed back onto his feet. Katherine groaned from a kick in the stomach and lay still, clutching her sides.

"Stupid whore," the dishevelled soldier said as he brushed down his clothes, "...not supposed to be on the streets at night."

As the pain subsided, Katherine tried to get up. She was dazed but her heart was still gripped by the urge to run. Then she felt the sharp point of the halberd press against her neck. She froze.

"Not so fast, sweetheart. You've got some explaining to do."

The cold steel to her throat brought her to her senses. She looked back down the lane. Something was moving fast. It was too late to escape.

The second collision was nothing like the first.

A great shadow enveloped them. A crunch, a scream, Katherine was thrown backwards. Warm liquid splashed her face. Her head hit the cobblestones. Blood filled her mouth. A ball, a bag or a heavy parcel landed on her stomach and winded her. She cradled it instinctively. Every sound diminished to a muffle. She reeled for a moment wishing to vomit but unable. The sound of the second soldier begging for his life brought her to her senses. She sat up just in time to see the creature pull the soldier to the ground and tear him asunder. She felt the weight in her hands and looked down. She was holding the severed head of the first soldier. She recoiled and sent it rolling.

The werewolf turned and looked at her. His form was black against the night sky. He took a moment to recover from his evil work. His great chest heaved and his breath formed clouds in the Winter moonlight.

Shouts echoed from the river. The soldiers at the Eirí House must have regrouped and started a pursuit. Thank God, Katherine thought. The werewolf glanced in the direction he had come. Katherine began to push herself away. But this caught his attention. The creature looked at her again.

"Valentine," she said, her voice barely a whisper.

The werewolf turned his head a fraction as a dog might. Then he growled – a long, low sound like a saw blade on stone. Her stomach turned. She heard more shouting and footsteps running, this time from several directions. The werewolf crouched as though to pounce. There was nothing Katherine could do. But something behind her caught his attention. She dared to look back. A figure had quietly approached from the shadows – it was Mary. She came closer. Both arms were extended before her with a pistol aimed squarely at the beast. Her face was white and her body was shaking. With difficulty, she pulled back the flint.

Katherine found her voice. "No," she cried.

The werewolf pounced as Mary fired. A howl of pain loosed – a pure animal noise. The creature fell to the ground beside Katherine. Smoke rose from a bloodless wound in its head. It was dead.

Mary lowered the pistol and looked behind her. A troop of soldiers were running towards them. To her left, another group had passed through the arch and was running up the lane. There was no escape. She looked at Katherine. The lady sat in a daze by the body of the beast, by Valentine. There would be no persuading her to run. Mary had one hope – that these soldiers were sent by Blake. She turned to face them. Behind the eager vanguard, she could see an officer strutting towards her. Her heart sank. It was D'Arcy. The first soldiers surrounded them and stood in silence around the carnage.

D'Arcy came level and studied the scene. He looked at Katherine and the dead werewolf. Then he looked at Mary.

She dropped the pistol at his feet. "Your son is dead," she said.

The soldiers watched their commander for a response but D'Arcy didn't answer. He chewed his tongue and studied the scene in silence. Then he spoke to his soldiers. He demanded a report from the men who had come from the Eirí House and instructed some others to remove the bodies.

"The rest of you men, down to the quays with me. We have a ship to meet."

He turned to Mary. His face had coloured, she thought. But only God knows the working of the man's heart.

D'Arcy flinched under her scrutiny. He spoke with false bravado. "Come, spy. I'll show you what you've been waiting for."

***

A few minutes later they were climbing the steps to the south pier above the Spanish Arch. From there, they could see the whole bay. The two English carracks that watched the port were lit up. Halfway between them, somewhat fainter on the dark sea, stood a smaller caravel. This was the ship that D'Arcy was waiting for.

They were a small company – D'Arcy, Mary, a dozen of D'Arcy's most loyal men, and Katherine. The viscountess was still in shock and had been half carried, half dragged behind them. Her face was still covered in blood. On the pier, Mary turned to help her. She used her sleeve to wipe away some of the blood. The viscountess stared back, her expression unreadable. Mary opened her mouth to speak but she was interrupted by D'Arcy.

"Pay attention, spy, our ship is here! I expect she's parleying with the Parliamentarian boats right now."

"It's your ship, not mine," Mary answered. She looked over the bay. There was indeed a little caravel at anchor. She looked around. No sign of Blake, no movement whatsoever on the quays, nor any sound further off. The curfew gave the alderman the perfect cover. The city slept, oblivious to the danger.

"No, not my ship either," D'Arcy said, "this is not my doing. History is at work here. Galway must fall, as Ireland has. This cargo will simply speed things up." He turned to Mary. In the lamp light, his features were sharp. His grey curls brushed his cheeks in the wind. He has aged tonight, Mary thought.

D'Arcy continued, "Aye, blood will spill but fewer will die than otherwise might..."

"You're doing this for your own profit, not for Galway," Mary said.

But the insult failed to land. He shrugged. He was tapping a hand on his hip and had begun to pace. The man is giddy, Mary realised. He's like a boy at Christmas.

He was watching the boats in the harbour when he finally answered, "There's no sin in being right and being profitable. Old Galway's dead. The old English... the Blakes, Lynches, Brownes... are finished. England has renewed itself. So must we."

Mary had nothing more to say. She was suddenly exhausted. She hung her head. There was no winning this fight.

D'Arcy took his eyes off the ship at anchor and studied her. "Come now, spy. Have you nothing more to say?"

She held her tongue.

"Not even to deny that you are a spy. I've called you one twice. You don't deny it?"

"You're beyond reason. Why should I argue?" she said.

The alderman came close. They were the same height and met eye to eye. She could smell his breath – the odour of wine, of course. She stayed quiet.

He raised a gloved hand to her hair and caressed it.

"Who are you spying for?" he said quietly.

She held his gaze but said nothing. He pulled a lock of her hair with force. She cried out.

"Savage!" Katherine shouted. D'Arcy released Mary, turned and looked at Katherine. The alderman's brutality had jolted her to her senses. "You're a savage and a bully. You're unworthy of your son," she added.

His face grew red. He pulled a dagger from his belt. "I still have business with this spy, My Lady. But you've just reminded me, I have no further use for you.

Katherine's eyes widened. He was going to kill her here in front of his men. She stepped back but strong hands grabbed her arms. Mary found herself quickly subdued too. These soldiers were practised in murder.

D'Arcy stepped forward but one of his men suddenly cried out, "Sir, the ship!"

They all looked. A thunderous crack of timber echoed from the little caravel. The mainmast collapsed onto its deck. Splashes of white pocked the sea all around her. Men were jumping into the water from her deck. A light flared and a fire quickly took hold.

"What in hell... ?" D'Arcy started.

Hell answered. A howl – diabolical, animal – filled the bay.

"Another werewolf!" Mary spoke from experience. She looked at Katherine. The viscountess struggled against her captor.

"No! Robert!" she cried.

51.

The collapse of the mast on the Meshuda startled everyone on the Bagenal. Captain Bing had been raising a second glass of Madeira to his lips when the noise shattered the peace of his cabin. Something was up. Salah did his best to look innocent but Bing was no fool. The crash of timber was followed by an unearthly howl. He had a sword within reach. He grabbed it and raised the point towards his guest.

"Outside, pirate." He stood up and gestured at the door. Salah raised his hands. He said nothing as he opened the door and stepped onto the deck. The first thing he saw as he stepped outside was the Meshuda sinking. The mast was down, a fire had taken hold on the middle of the deck and she was listing. Only the sea could quench those flames, he thought.

Captain Bing was also distracted by the sinking pirate ship. He watched the conflagration and called for his first mate. But there was no answer. Salah smiled and turned around. Captain Bing kept his sword high and directed at Salah but, with a quick glance around the deck, he discovered the pirate had outmanoeuvred him. Armed pirates surrounded his men from bow to stern.

His first mate stepped forward with his hands raised. "I'm sorry, sir. They have the ship."

A stocky pirate, wet from head to toe, stood behind the first mate, poking him with the end of a blade. Captain Bing dropped his sword and the pirates cheered.

Salah spoke, "Now, Captain, what ransom do you think will Parliament pay for you?"

"You'll hang for this," Bing answered.

"For this or something else, no doubt."

Another crash of timber from the Meshuda reminded him to get a move on. He addressed his own first mate, "Take the captain below."

Ahmad knew what to do. He turned to face the deck and started issuing orders, "You heard the captain. Take the prisoners below. Douse the lights, and lower the oars. The Meshuda will do us one more favour. She'll give us cover while we break anchor but those flames won't last all night."

Salah's smile faded. He turned to watch the last moments of his old ship. She was sinking fast. Men were jumping into the water to escape the flames. Their screams mingled with the howling of a beast. So, it wasn't just the flames they fled.

Ahmad joined him at the gunwale. "The Englishman spoke the truth," he said. "...truly a beast from hell."

"Yes," Salah answered, deep in thought.

"And the priest was wise."

"Yes," Salah looked into the embers of his burning ship. He was trying to ignore Ahmad.

"He steered us well. This is a fine ship, better than the Meshuda."

"Yes."

"It's a shame..." the first mate started.

Salah just looked at him. "A fine cut-throat, you make," he said, "what do you want? Out with it."

Ahmad bowed, "The longboat, two strong men and half an hour."

Salah stroked his beard, "You'd risk your life?"

"It's less than they did for us," Ahmad answered.

Salah sighed and slowly turned and faced his first mate. "You're right, my friend." He put his hand on Ahmad's shoulder, "but this is my debt to pay. Take charge of this ship and wait for me. I'll try to help our English friends."

52.

It took D'Arcy a few seconds to understand his plans had come to nothing. The cargo on which he'd staked everything would soon be at the bottom of Galway Bay. He watched helplessly as the flames consumed the Meshuda. Even from shore, they could hear the cries of the drowning and the howls of this other werewolf. It was a chaotic scene he could not account for. When the lights went out on the Bagenal, he learned a little more. So, he thought, the pirates have jumped ship. He didn't know how this had come to pass but he suspected either Mary or Katherine was involved.

Their guilt mattered little. What mattered now was their silence. D'Arcy pulled his eyes away from the sea and looked at Katherine. He still held his dagger.

"Hold her tight," he told the soldier restraining her. The man obeyed and the whole company focused again on the knife. Katherine watched in horror.

Mary cried out, "Stop! Help, someone!"

D'Arcy looked angrily at the man holding Mary, "Silence her!"

Too late. A pistol shot rang out behind them. D'Arcy stopped in his tracks and looked around.

A company of men had passed through the arch onto the quays. At their head stood Sir William Blake. A wisp of smoke rose from the pistol he pointed into the air. D'Arcy's men raised their weapons and prepared to fight but D'Arcy stopped them with a gesture. They were outnumbered five to one. He walked down the steps to meet Blake.

"Richard..." Blake started when they came face to face. He looked upset and exhausted, "I've come from Pludd Street. I received a message..." – even in the moonlight D'Arcy saw the glance at Mary – "the powder, the weapons, you've been hiding..." His voice had started hoarse but he straightened up and raised his voice as he realised how weak he sounded. "I'm afraid you're under arrest, Richard, on charges of treason."

D'Arcy didn't answer. He was calculating. The gunpowder, the muskets, this is why he's here. He really has no idea what has been going on. He'd find it hard to explain away his treatment of the viscountess – but not impossible. "My Lord, it's not treason. It's true, I've been acting on my own initiative. I should have told you. I have discovered a conspiracy against this city. Lady Ranelagh has been plotting against the city with her brother. The ship you see sinking, they were bringing Parliament agents into the city. As you see, the danger is passed."

Blake looked at the ship which was almost completely submerged. It was barely visible in the moonlight but a few flames still licked what was left afloat and some isolated splashing and screaming still reached the shore. Then he looked at Katherine and Mary who were still being restrained by D'Arcy's men. He seemed to think about his response carefully. "And Mary?"

D'Arcy was confused by Blake's concern for the servant. He took a moment to answer. "A spy for Parliament and a murderess." Here he felt the truth would do no harm. "She's wanted for the killing of Tadgh Flaherty in the Red Earl's House this afternoon."

Blake seemed satisfied. But he didn't command his troops to stand down. They remained alert with weapons at the ready. "Wait here," he said to D'Arcy. He climbed the steps and stood in front of the two women. He first addressed the alderman's soldiers, "Release them and join your commander." They glanced at D'Arcy for confirmation and, on his nod, they released Katherine and Mary and marched down the steps to join their leader.

Up close he realised Katherine was covered in blood. She was watching the sinking ship and barely registered his presence.

"My Lady, forgive me a moment. I need to speak to Mary."

Katherine just nodded and returned to watching the wreck.

Blake spoke to Mary. "Is it true you killed Flaherty?"

"Yes, my Lord."

"You admit it freely? It's a hanging offence."

"I'd have no one else hang for it, my Lord."

He seemed impressed by her candour and nodded to himself thoughtfully. Then he pointed at the scene in the bay where the last flames had died and the Meshuda had disappeared beneath the waves. "What do you know of this?"

"Everything," Mary answered but said no more.

"And can you explain the ring you used to seal the letter you wrote to me?"

"Given to me by my Lord, the Marquess of Ormonde. I am in his service."

"Yes, I guessed as much..." he bowed at the mention of the Confederate leader, "as we all should be."

Mary breathed a sigh of relief. So, Blake was indeed an ally. She dared to take control of the conversation. "Sir William, Lady Ranelagh has suffered two grievous losses this evening. And, as I believe her host is about to become indisposed, perhaps you might accommodate her in your house?"

Blake nodded. He looked at Katherine. She had stopped watching the sea and stood on the edge of the pier, her head held low.

"I can see that she has suffered. I will take care of her." Then he looked back at D'Arcy. The alderman was becoming restive. He understood the tide was turning though he hardly knew how. This servant had some pull with Blake he couldn't understand. He shouted up, "My Lord, delay no more, Arrest these scoundrels!"

Blake shouted down to his second in command, "Captain, place Alderman D'Arcy and his companions under arrest. Bring them to the Tholsel House and hold them there."

D'Arcy's men jeered and raised their weapons in defiance. For a moment, it looked like a fight might break out. But their commander ordered them to surrender. Loyal to the end, and sensing the futility of it, they did so, and soon a clatter of swords echoed on the cobbles. D'Arcy made no further protest. He took one long last look at Blake and then allowed himself to be led away.

Katherine had stirred at the mention of the Tholsel House. She wiped a tear from her eye and straightened up. "Sir William, my servants – a Mr Colman and his sons – are being held under false charges, in the Tholsel House, I believe. I would appreciate it if you could secure their release."

The peer bowed again. "As you wish, My Lady. I will have them join you at my house. If you are ready I'll bring you there now."

"Thank you. Please, just give me a moment."

"Of course," Blake offered his arm to Mary who took it and they both descended the steps to give Lady Ranelagh some privacy. Out of earshot, Blake spoke to Mary quietly, "The Lady seems devastated. What happened here?"

"Her brother was on that ship," Mary answered.

"Good Lord! And the other loss? I thought she was a stranger in Galway."

"Valentine D'Arcy. He died here in Galway tonight."

Blake was confused, "She knew the boy?"

"It seems she knew him from Limerick. They were together tonight in the Eirí House."

"Ah, I see."

Mary looked back at Katherine, hoping the Lady had heard nothing. She regretted her words. She had caricatured the relationship for Sir William. "I really know little about it. I spoke out of turn."

"Never fear. It will go no further."

They both watched Katherine from the bottom of the steps. Her form was in silhouette against the moonlit sky. They watched her fix her hair and clothes and wipe her face. She noticed them looking and indicated that she was coming. Then, with a last glance to the sea, she turned and descended the stone stairs. The sea was silent now. The Meshuda was gone and the Bagenal had slipped away quietly in the confusion caused by her destruction.

53.

Katherine pinched her cheeks hard to raise some colour. This was not her habit but the pallor that had haunted her for the past two days was beginning to wear thin. Today was the funeral. She would be in company. She didn't want to look like a ghost.

She put the looking glass on the dressing table by the window and looked outside. The sky was grey but the cobbles were dry. The market square outside Sir William Blake's house was still quiet though it was well past eleven. With the city still under siege, there was less to trade today than there had been the day before. She saw one of Colman's sons chatting to a pretty girl selling fish. At least his ordeal is over, she thought. She looked at the bed. Her clothes were all laid out. They weren't ideal mourning clothes but they would have to do. Sir William had all her things carried over from D'Arcy's house and he had taken pains to keep her in style. But she was done with Galway. She was hungry to get home and this brought on a strange realisation. She ached for Limerick, for Manwood.

It was all the stranger for the knowledge that the journey home would be a lonely one, and that Robert wouldn't be there to greet her. There was no way she could resume her old life without him. She realised now that she'd been happier there than she'd been for many years. She'd had a job, she'd had the respect and the friendship of her brother. She'd had a degree of freedom that she'd never known in the house of her father or in that of her husband. That was over. The urgency that gnawed at her heart was the desire to see for herself that Robert was truly gone. After all, there was no proof that he had drowned. There was no body.

Of course, she was fooling herself. Sir William had searched D'Arcy's house for evidence against him. He had found plenty. Amongst his private correspondence, he had found the letter from Colonel Hewson that told him Robert was indeed on board the Meshuda. There was no reason to doubt that.

And there had been bodies. Ten so far – or thereabouts – it was hard to tell. Bodies mauled beyond recognition and severed limbs had washed ashore the next day. What clues had remained before they hit the beach were lost to the scavengers who took every scrap of cloth and metal before any official record might be kept. Their identities were a mystery so no funeral had been arranged for them yet.

The funeral was for Valentine. His naked body, intact but defiled by a massive head wound, was found half submerged in the water under the Middle Tower. Word came to Sir William who told Katherine immediately. She sent a message to Richard D'Arcy – still locked up in the Tholsel House – begging permission to make arrangements for a funeral. When no response was forthcoming, she pressed ahead regardless.

It was not practical to wake Valentine in Pludd Street. The munitions in the sheds were being carefully removed and the surrounding houses had been evacuated. That suited Katherine. She did not believe Valentine would have wanted to spend his last night above ground in such an unhappy place. She spoke to the warden in Saint Nicholas' Cathedral and he agreed to hold a vigil there. Katherine did her best to stay by his side and passed much of that night by his coffin. The doors of the cathedral were open so Valentine's spirit might wander freely. A chill winter wind made the few candles they could spare flicker wildly in the dark. The cold kept her awake as did the wailing of the keeners. They were four elderly women in heavy black shawls pressed together for warmth on the other side of the coffin to Katherine. They maintained a steady half song, half moan for hours on end so that a moment's silence wouldn't shame the dead. She had hired them on the warden's advice to keep Valentine company in case she tired. But, it turned out, Valentine had plenty of willing company in death.

Rosa came and stayed a long time. Surely this woman had lost more than anyone the night before, Katherine thought, but she found her well of empathy dry and barely managed to thank her for coming.

Sir William was there and stayed till his complexion grew so pale she forced him home. There were many others she didn't know. Word was out who was dead and though the circumstances of his death were being suppressed, Valentine found he had many friends in the city he had long since left.

But not everybody came. Richard D'Arcy had been offered leave from jail but had declined. And Katherine was disappointed not to see Mary. The spy, for such she was, was staying with Sir William but Katherine had not seen her since the previous night. Perhaps she felt unwelcome. She had, after all, killed Valentine. But Katherine did not blame her. She had been working with Valentine – it was Mary who led her to the Eirí House and saved her from D'Arcy. Katherine suspected Valentine had been a party to his own death – or rather the death of the beast.

As she brushed her hair the next day, Katherine hoped she'd see Mary at the funeral. She would thank her, she decided, for everything. She picked up the looking glass again and was pleased to see a little more life and colour in her face. It was going to be another long day but she felt strong enough to meet it. She wasn't sure what to wear over her hair. She took another glance outside to keep up with the Galway weather. And her blood froze. Two men had wandered into the market square. One was a small man with a bandaged head – she didn't recognise him – but the other had the unmistakable walk of her brother. She dropped the mirror and screamed, "Robert!"

***

They held hands all through the funeral mass and stood shoulder to shoulder by the graveside. There had been little time for explanation. Robert had been rescued by pirates and dropped ten miles up the coast in Spiddal. The small man was a priest named Skerret and was now, obviously, a friend of Robert's. He'd been injured and Robert had nursed him there in that fishing village till he'd been well enough to travel. Indeed, by the look of the priest, they had travelled earlier than was wise. They had been worried for Katherine's safety and had pressed on regardless.

All this they shared in a breathless reunion outside Sir William's House. Later, once Boyle and Skerret had freshened up and eaten, Katherine had found a quiet room to speak privately to her brother.

The room was a little study just off the ancient banquet hall that dominated the house. It was dark but cosy, insulated with fading tapestries and floored with an impressive Turkish rug.

Robert had by then heard some version of the events that had occurred in Galway while he was at sea. "I'm sorry about Valentine," he said.

Katherine sat down at the window seat. "Yes, so am I," she answered. She bowed her head thoughtfully.

Robert sat at a reading desk opposite her and toyed with a paper globe. He studied the design as he spoke to her. "And I'm sorry I failed you."

Katherine looked up at him. She shook her head gently. "You nearly died," a lump rose in her throat, "I thought I'd lost you. What more could you do?"

He continued concentrating on the images of the seas and faraway lands, "I mean, before that, in Manwood. I slandered you. I failed to put myself in your shoes." He started to spin the globe, "I've always had it easy, I suppose – compared to you." He looked up to see if she was following. She nodded. "I pushed you away and I'm sorry."

It was true. She felt no need to reassure him. They sat for a moment in silence.

Robert continued, "and I failed Valentine. If I had just listened to either of you..."

"...Valentine would still be dead," she said, "maybe the circumstances would be different but his life was already over."

"But you'll miss him?"

"Of course, I'll miss him." She smiled. Sometimes her brother made everything so simple. "I'll say goodbye to him today but I'll always remember him."

"Then I shall too."

He had spoken with some finality but Katherine remembered there was something she needed to say, "Brother, the reason Valentine came to Galway..." she fidgeted with her hands as she spoke, "he received a warning from a woman, a doctor..."

"Skerret's mother?" he ventured.

"I don't know. She said there's a danger the curse might be passed on... through an exchange of blood."

Robert dropped his head in thought. He grew pale. Finally, he looked up and gave her a stoic smile. "Well then, I'll just have to face up to that," he said.

"We both will," she said.

He looked at her, puzzled.

She smiled.

"Sex, Robert."

He blushed and a curious spasm crossed his face. He let out a short laugh. He crossed the room and took her hand. "Well, I suppose we'll have to face the future together then."

***

The D'Arcy family plot was set at the back of the cathedral grounds in the shelter of an ancient oak tree. This was already the final resting place of Valentine's mother and brother. A large crowd gathered around to hear the priest make a final blessing. In the absence of Richard D'Arcy, Katherine and Robert stood in for family. Sir William had lost Katherine's company as soon as her brother had reappeared so the old man stood alone towards the back, glad that the morning was dry but still exhausted from the excitement of the last few days. As he shifted uncomfortably from one foot to the other, a strong hand slipped under his arm and offered him support. He was pleased to find Mary by his side. It was the first time she'd been out since the events of two nights ago. She was glad of his company too.

As they stood together, the English guns outside the city walls started booming. Sir William closed his eyes. The siege was taking its toll on him. Mary squeezed his cold hand.

He started speaking quietly, "Perhaps D'Arcy was right. I'm afraid we've just delayed the inevitable, Mary. The city can hold out for another week or two but that's all."

"Yes," she said.

He seemed surprised and looked at her, "then your work was for nothing?"

"I didn't come to stop Parliament taking Galway. I'm afraid you're right. That is inevitable. Cromwell has won. The war is nearly over."

"And the Marquess?"

"Ormonde is a patient man and a young one. Cromwell is neither. The King will return someday."

"Ireland will suffer regardless," he answered.

"I'm afraid so," Mary said.

"What really happened here, Mary? Why did Ormonde send you?"

She looked at him and waited till he returned her look, "You still don't believe me?"

"You're a fine woman, Mary, but you test my faith too dearly."

"You read Hewson's letters?"

"And I trust Hewson less than you. I'm sorry. I'm too old to change my ways. Perhaps if I saw the creature..."

"...You saw Valentine."

"I saw a man."

"And the creature from the boat, the bodies washed ashore?"

"Yes, and where is that creature now?"

Mary turned back to look at the grave. "I wish I knew."

She scanned the crowd. She could see Katherine and the man she supposed to be her brother, Robert – she'd heard the story of his escape from the Meshuda. She looked for the priest, Skerret. That part of the story intrigued her most. She had questions for him. When she found him, he was staring at her. Like her, he was keeping a low profile towards the back of the crowd. Their eyes locked for a few seconds before Skerret acknowledged her with a little nod.

After the burial, the priest read out Sir William's invitation to lunch in the Blake household. The crowd began to disperse. Mary encouraged Sir William to walk with the Boyles. She wanted to speak to Skerret. She caught up with him on Crosse Street. The funeral party were turning right onto Kea Street. Skerret was continuing straight.

She called out, "Ambrose!"

He turned. He didn't look keen to see her.

"You're not coming to lunch?"

"I have other plans."

She tried to imagine what plans might draw him away from a free lunch. "You're leaving, aren't you?"

"I promised the viscount I'd reach Galway for the sake of his sister. And we found her well. And you too. I'm finished here."

She smiled. It was touching that he'd been concerned for her well-being. "So where will you go?"

"There's a flotilla leaving Galway this afternoon," he answered. "There's just one English ship left guarding the bay. They reckon most boats will get through the blockade. I thought I'd seek a passage before the city falls."

"Sir William thinks that will happen in a week, or two at the most."

"And priests won't be safe when that happens."

She nodded in the direction he had been going, "I'll walk down with you."

He shrugged. They continued up Crosse Street. Up close, she noticed the bandage on his head.

"You were badly hurt," she said.

"A bad cut," he answered.

"From the werewolf?"

"No."

He said no more for a while but eventually, curiosity got the better of him, "Why did you go to Galway, Mary, to D'Arcy's father?"

"I thought I could help Valentine," she answered.

"It was a curious thought for a servant girl."

She laughed. "I've given up that pretence, Ambrose. I'm no servant girl."

"I wondered. I saw how Sir William spoke to you. You'd better make plans to leave, yourself."

"Don't worry about me," she said. "I've been wondering too," she added, "the werewolf on the ship, where did it come from?"

He stopped and looked at her. "You really don't know?"

She shook her head.

"It came for you, Mary," he said.

Her face darkened. "What do you mean?"

"That werewolf was once William Manning."

Her face remained blank and at that moment Skerret understood what a cruel and wanton God ruled the world.

"The English soldier," she said at last.

"So, you do remember him," he said.

"The one who beat you?" she said.

Skerret winced, not at the memory but at the imprecation. "He saved my life," he said at last.

"And you became friends?" she said. None of this was making sense to her. She had a feeling the priest was deliberately speaking in riddles.

"Good friends."

They continued walking and soon reached the junction at the Red Earl's House. A scrawny dog, begging for scraps, approached and sniffed at Mary's skirts. She stopped and gave him a pet. She remembered Samson.

"What happened to Manning's wolfhound?" she said.

"He lost it," Skerret said.

The night at Quin Abbey – and all its horror – came flooding back to him.

"He was such a fool!" Mary said.

Skerret turned and stared at her. "Is that what you think?" he spat out the words. "Then I'll take my leave. You're a fine spy, Mary, but you're not much of a woman."

He stormed off. She stood in the middle of the street watching him go. The blood rose in her cheeks. She was angry. She'd never cared for the good opinion of any man – especially a priest – but his words stung. Finally, she decided to run after him. She still had questions. "Wait Ambrose, wait, I'm sorry." She caught up with him and touched his shoulder to slow him down.

"I'm sorry. I didn't know him. I shouldn't pretend. Please, help me understand. You say he came for me?"

"William Manning crossed the country because he loved you... or he thought he did." Skerret still looked angry. He looked her up and down. "Maybe he was a fool."

"I see," she said. It had never occurred to her.

They were silent for a minute but Mary's mind quickly returned to business.

"What happened to him?"

"He went down with the ship," Skerret answered.

Mary knew this wasn't the end of it. Perhaps Skerret did too.

"He let you live?"

"I saw his eyes when he brought down the mast. He looked at me. He killed Hewson and Worsley with a stroke. We were next.

But he stopped and gave us time to escape the hold. That was William's doing."

Mary remembered how Valentine had spared her on the battlement in Limerick. "I understand," she said. Then she added, "You saw him drown?"

"I saw him sink with the ship."

So, Skerret understood the difference too.

They had arrived at the quays. There was more activity there today than Mary had ever seen. People were flooding in from every direction. Many pushed cartloads of belongings. All carried bags. Some were citizens but most were already refugees who had found no refuge in this city. Gangways, stashed for many months, crashed onto the quays with the urgency of wartime. Capstans clicked and ropes purred through pulleys. The ground fell under a shadow as the fleet raised a canopy of sails like a forest after winter. Up above, seagulls screamed in concert with the cries of desperate refugees. Mary heard a small boy coughing and recognised the family who'd been robbed when she'd first arrived in Galway. They too were leaving. They looked haunted and she wondered had she counted one more child when last she'd seen them.

A big man pushed past her roughly. He held his money high in the air and shouted for a place on one of the boats. Others followed suit. The air was soon filled with numbers as deals were done for passage. The price would quickly prove too high for Skerret. It was time to act.

"I have to go," he said.

"Where to?"

"Anywhere but Ireland," he said. Then he smiled and added, "or y'know, England."

She held out her hand for him to shake.

"I had no idea how he felt, you know," Mary said, "I only knew him for an hour. Sometimes, it's all on one side. He was lucky to have you as a friend."

Skerret failed to take her hand. "Well, we can't help who we love," he said. Then he turned and joined the throng of refugees and disappeared into the crowd.

Also by Eoin Stephens
*coming soon *

The Jesus Machine

When time travel is invented, a sociopathic billionaire leads an invasion of the Roman Empire pledging to locate Jesus Christ before his crucifixion. His sinister hidden agenda is uncovered by a famous ex-gladiator, two determined journalists and three bickering friends.

The Golden Legend

When the Archangel Michael hears that Joan of Arc will be his downfall he plots her destruction. Fighting him, Raguel, the Angel of Justice, and the saints he trusts, must save her and themselves by crossing a secret bridge to the next world. But when Joan starts to care for one of history's greatest villains, that plan is jeopardised.

About the Author

My name is Eoin Stephens. I'm a native of Galway in the west of Ireland but I've lived in Dublin for the past thirty years. I'm married with two children, and I earn a living as a freelance graphic designer. I've been writing fiction for the past seven years. Thanks to my self-employed status and the support of my wife, I'm able to write every day. This is my third book and have plans for many more. As well as writing novels, I write and draw comic books.

Thank you for reading this book. I guess it took a few hours. It feels like a great privilege to take up that much of your time so I'm very grateful. Eoin Stephens, May, 2023

Who published this?

Well, I did. Amazon require an ISBN for print books. They'll supply their own but who wants to be beholden to the behemoth? I set up Brown Bull to independently own the ISBN. My interest in comics has introduced me to a world where self-publishing – sometimes hand-making – books and zines is the norm. Nobody calls it vanity publishing in comics, nor should they. Comic creators have to slowly claw their way towards recognition. There's no glamorous debut. So, I'll publish and be damned.

Nobody else would publish you then?

First, I pitched to literary agents and a couple of publishers directly. As of writing, I've sent out about thirty queries, most for Blood of the Wolf, and some for The Golden Legend. I've had a few replies but I'm still waiting for a breakthrough. I understand that this is not an exhaustive attempt by any means and so I'll continue pitching The Golden Legend to prospective agents. I'd love to see what a publisher could do with my books. I'd love to see them edited, packaged and marketed by professionals.

Why not wait till the industry thinks you've got something?

I'll be starting another book next year. Perhaps it will be an easier sell than my first three? In the meantime, I am not going to hide my light under a bushel. I've written three books. They are pretty good. I hope you enjoyed this one. Perhaps some industry professional will stumble across this and see potential that wasn't evident in the synopsis. A few indie sales might help convince them. If you enjoyed this book, please spread the word.

Mind the Bones

I created this short comic as a teaser to promote Blood of the Wolf. I'm excited to include it here. It starts where we left off: It's the night of Valentine's funeral. The Boyles are still in Galway. Sir William – perhaps at Lady Ranelagh's insistence – has posted a guard to watch over Valentine's grave...

I'LL TAKE MY PLEASURE WHERE I CAN, AND WHILE I'M STILL ALIVE. SO SHOULD YOU.

WANT SOME?

I WOULDN'T TOUCH IT! IT WAS TAINTED WINE THAT TURNED THE DEAD MAN INTO A WEREWOLF. IT WAS CURSED, I HEARD.

SUPERSTITIOUS NONSENSE. EVEN SIR WILLIAM DOESN'T BELIEVE THAT. HE'S DOING THIS FOR LADY RANELAGH. SHE'S THE ONE AGITATING... SAYS HE MIGHT RISE FROM HIS GRAVE.

I'VE HEARD HER FATHER OWNS HALF OF CORK. I SUPPOSE SIR WILLIAM IS SUBJECT TO RANK AS WE ARE.

IT'S NOT RANK HE BOWS TO. HE'D BE AFRAID NOT TO DO AS SHE SAID, THE WAY SHE CAME TO HIM, HEAD TO TOE COVERED IN BLOOD.

THAT WOMAN WAS TOUCHED BY THE DEVIL.

SHE SHOULD HAVE STAYED AWAY FROM THE EIRI HOUSE. D'ARCY LOST FIVE MEN THERE. THEY SAY TAYLOR WAS SPLIT IN TWO. TAAFE LOST HIS HEAD. YOU'D SWEAR AN ANIMAL...

I DON'T BELIEVE ANY OF IT.

PAT DIRRANE WAS THERE. HE WATCHED FROM THE BUSHES. HE SAW THAT MAN TRANSFORM; HIS BODY CONVULSING, HIS BONES TWISTING, HIS SKIN SPLITTING AND THOSE EYES – **RED EYES** – HE SAID, BURNING IN THE DARK.

SO WHERE'S THE CREATURE NOW? THEY SHOT HIM, DIDN'T THEY?

HE'S IN THAT GRAVE. DIRRANE SAID HE TRANSFORMED BACK WHEN HE DIED. ALL THEY FOUND WAS THIS DEAD MAN, HALF NAKED, WITH A A GREAT BIG HOLE IN HIS HEAD, PEACEFUL LIKE A BABE, DEAD AS THE O'NEILL.

DIRRANE WAS DRUNK. YOU'LL NEVER FIND AN HONEST MAN IN A BROTHEL.

WHAT WAS THE LADY DOING THERE? THAT'S WHAT I WANT TO KNOW. AND WAS HE THE LADY'S LOVER? I THOUGHT HE WAS HER BROTHER?

366

THIS BONE IS THE CULPRIT, SOLDIER. YOU'RE LUCKY I HAVE SOME MEDICAL KNOWLEDGE OR YOU WOULD HAVE CHOKED TO DEATH.

THANK YOU M'LADY.

YOU HAD BETTER GO FIND YOUR FRIEND.

YES MA'AM.

YOU'RE STILL IN YOUR GRAVE THEN? THANK GOD. I COULDN'T SLEEP. I KEPT THINKING OF YOU ...

I'M GLAD YOU'RE GETTING SOME REST.

I PRAY IT WILL BE ETERNAL.